# ONLY YOU

EVA JORDAN

First published in 2023 by Bloodhound Books.

www.bloodhoundbooks.com

Print ISBN: 978-1-5040-8889-3

*This book is dedicated to Jackie and Lisa, two of my closest friends, whose love and support is never hindered by time or distance.*

*"Love is composed of a single soul inhabiting two bodies."*
*–Aristotle*

# PROLOGUE

*C*onfused, she threw her hands to her head; pain searing her eyes, a frothing sound between her ears. She heard screaming too. But it was muffled. Impossible to tell who, or where it was coming from. Instinctively she stepped back, aware of a strange caustic smell, and stumbled. She lowered her hands to steady herself which only intensified the pain behind her eyes. Shaking, she tried to make sense of what was happening but her thoughts, like little incendiaries exploding at the back of her mind, only added to her confusion.

She heard a voice. Not one she recognised but surely one that belonged to the same individual that only seconds ago she'd answered the door to. The same individual whose face, shielded by a hoodie or a hat, or a scarf, she'd been unable to see. Their words though were muted by the gushing in her ears.

She blinked, once, twice, three times, frantic to see who it was, only to be met by a whirring insignia of strange shapes and shadows. She could smell them though, whoever it was. Fetid breath, stale sweat, strong whisky. It was nauseating... yet... familiar?

Alarmed, she tried to feel for the door to close it, but the abrupt movement only exacerbated the throbbing behind her eyes.

Heart thudding, her only instinct was to get away, and get away *fast*.

The faceless voice spoke again, low and looming, each word jumbled and nonsensical. She tried to reply, to plead with her tormentor to leave her alone, but the words wouldn't come, wouldn't leave the back of her throat.

Then she heard someone screaming again. Smelled the same wretched smell. Only... it was odd... like charred meat, maybe? But rancid, like the rank entrails of a dead animal on a disinfected barbeque. Head spinning, she trembled as a new wave of pain coursed through her body. The fight or flight reflex kicked in. She needed help and she needed it *now*.

*Joan*, she thought. *Joan will help me, or rather, Milo will.* Milo, a German shepherd, whose bark was much worse than his bite, was a big teddy bear at heart. A stranger wouldn't know that though.

Gripping the doorframe, she listened. Silence. Had her perpetrator gone? Or were they watching her, lying in wait, in the shadows, ready to pounce again, like some twisted version of cat and mouse. The sensible thing to do would be to wait a few minutes, be sure they had gone, but waiting wasn't an option. She was in too much pain. It was now or never, so, putting one foot in front of the other, she inched forwards, blindly grasping at thin air.

With each painful step she listened, but the voice of her attacker was quiet. The screaming, however, continued, puncturing holes in her sub-aqua hearing. Only, this time it was different. This time it was pitiful. Base and guttural. Alien, yet cognizant. Terrifying, in fact. But she couldn't, *wouldn't* let it slow her down.

Pushing on; arms thrashing this way and that, she intuitively made her way towards her neighbour's house, desperate for the refuge she urgently needed. It wasn't easy though, because her vision, like her hearing, was blurred, muddied. What the hell had happened to her? Terrified, she paused, tried again to listen, but except for the distant screaming raging like a bush fire, all was eerily quiet. Fear pushed her on but the closer she got to Joan's house the louder the screaming became, her confused mind conjuring a terrifying thought. What if the person screaming was Joan? What if, whoever had attacked her, had also attacked Joan? Then she heard him, the fierce staccato of a dog barking.

*Milo*, she thought. *Thank God.*

Her relief was palpable and gave her the courage to push on. She couldn't see Milo, couldn't see anything except a strange kaleidoscope of bizarre shapes and colours, but she could picture him, at the window; ears pricked upright, huge paws resting on the windowsill, head tilted; two piercing eyes absorbing her distress.

*Please come to the window, Joan. Please, please see me.*

Milo's barking, like an incessant siren, continued. She tried to call his name, but her throat – like her lips, her eyes, her hands – was an inferno of heat. She continued moving forward, one clumsy foot at a time.

Her attacker, she was convinced, was now well and truly gone. Whoever it was could come back though, so she placed her hands along the crumbling brick wall that divided her house from Joan's, feeling her way to safety. Then she heard it, a door opening. Joan calling her name, Milo, restrained on a lead, howling behind her. Relieved, she felt faint; the swirling mass of colour that had plagued her vision melting away as down, down, down she fell like Alice in Wonderland falling down the rabbit hole.

It was then she realised who was screaming.

It was her. She was the one screaming.

How though? How was that possible, given the burning ball of fire in her throat? Nevertheless, it was her. So surely, if she could scream, she could talk... couldn't she?

She wasn't sure, but she had to try.

'Help... me,' she whispered, before darkness devoured her.

# CHAPTER 1

*M*outh dry, Ben raised his hand to knock on the door of the hotel room. Well, it was *rooms* plural. The top-floor suite no less. Lifestyles of the rich and famous, he supposed. Not a way of life he was used to, and not one he craved either. Hand hovering, a wave of nausea rose from his stomach. He'd thought about this moment for the last couple of years. And now, here it was. His moment had arrived. He'd finally been granted an audience with the famous Leora Jackson. He should be pleased. So why then, did he have an overwhelming urge to turn on his heel and run.

He wouldn't, of course. It had taken months of persuasion to get an appointment with her. Besides, if nothing else, he owed it to her to say what he should have said… all those years ago. What though, if after seeing him today, she never wanted to see him again, *ever*? What then?

He sighed, lowered his hand, and stepped away from the door. Rocking back and forth on his heels, he looked down, momentarily fascinated as his feet disappeared then reappeared in a shallow pool of sumptuous red carpet. Bending down, he noticed a couple of scuffmarks on one of his brown leather brogues. How had he not noticed them earlier? He frowned, wondered again, not for the first time that morning, if, alongside his blue jeans, they were a mistake – too casual maybe?

Straightening up again, he thrust his hands deep into his pockets. *Too late now,* he thought, loose hair tickling his cheek. He tucked the lock of hair behind his ear, cursing himself for not getting it cut. He hadn't realised, until this morning, just how many flecks of grey were running through it, an indication that he was rapidly heading towards the winter years of his life. Still, with winter comes wisdom, right? He shook his head; laughed to himself. He may be older, but he was definitely none the wiser. Life was, and continued to be, a conundrum to Ben, full of riddles rather than answers.

Except *her*, of course. He knew how he felt about her, and that had never changed... even after all this time.

Tilting his head to one side he listened to the muffled sounds of the city drifting in through the large window at the end of the corridor, which, compared to the loud thudding of his heart, was quite soothing. Closing his eyes, he took a deep breath and tipped his head back. When he opened them again, the ceiling, like a desert of brilliant white, reminded him of the Bonneville Salt Flats of western Utah where sky and land collide, forming the perfect backdrop for something he once imagined heaven might look like, had he believed in such a place.

In keeping with the hotel's heritage, it was bordered by delicately moulded coving depicting Georgian swags and tails, as gold light emanating from antique chandeliers bounced off huge gilt mirrors hanging on both walls of the corridor.

He shook his head again.

He didn't belong in places like this.

*I should leave,* he thought.

Squaring his shoulders, he had a quiet word with himself and headed to the door again. This time he knocked, surprised how quickly it opened, and equally surprised to be met by a rather large, rather tall individual whose broad shoulders obscured any view behind him. Poker-faced, he stared at Ben, his square jaw complementing his thickset build. Ben was thrown. Who was he? Boyfriend? Husband? Then the penny dropped. Man mountain, he quickly realised, was security, Leora's bodyguard.

Lifestyles of the rich and famous.

Ben nodded, held out his hand and introduced himself but man mountain ignored his hand and said nothing. Instead, holding Ben's gaze with his own steely stare he gave him a curt nod, stepped aside, and let him in. Man mountain was trying to intimidate him. It probably worked on most people. But Ben wasn't most people. He'd had altercations with much bigger individuals than this burly bloke, plus appearances could be deceiving. Experience had taught Ben that mean and lean were capable of causing just as much damage as big and bulky. He had to give it to man mountain though, he looked the part, which, when it came to Leora, was comforting. It would take a brave man, or woman, to try and get past this bloke.

Confident, Ben marched in and immediately sensed a change in man mountain's demeanour, as if he had recognised something familiar about Ben. Maybe it was the way Ben carried himself, his precise military walk. All Ben knew was, when he looked at him again, there was a definite hint of wary respect in his eyes. Man mountain may have been watching him, but Ben had been watching him too, and everything about the guy, the way he moved, his quiet self-assurance, screamed ex-forces, which again, when it came to Leora, was comforting.

He nodded towards a seating area. Ben scanned the room, taking in the original parquet flooring, the walnut wall panelling, the huge ornate fireplace, and the beige and cream soft furnishings. He felt too agitated to sit so he went to the window, peered out; watched the sprawling city that was London flowing beneath it. It was a beautiful day and thanks to the enormity of the old sash windows, the room was bathed in a canary yellow light.

'Ben!' A familiar voice called behind him.

He turned to see Andrea who, dressed in a navy-blue trouser suit and crisp white shirt looked every bit as immaculate as he'd expected her to. Like her daughter, Andrea had always taken pride in her appearance.

'Ben,' she repeated, her tone warm and welcoming, hand outstretched, reaching for his. 'It's so lovely to see you. You're looking well.'

Ben smiled. 'So are you.'

She laughed, waved her hand dismissively. 'You think?'

Ben nodded. 'Not a day older than the first time we met.'

'Liar!' she scoffed. 'I've aged a hundred years since then.' Smiling, she gestured towards the sofas. 'But I do look a damn sight better than the last time we met; I'll give you that.'

'Don't we all.' Ben took a seat next to her.

Andrea reached out and patted his hand, her smile slipping. Ben studied her tired eyes and wondered if, like him, she ever found herself waking in the middle of the night thinking about the 'what ifs'.

He coughed. 'So... what's your secret?' he asked. His lame attempt to lighten the mood.

Andrea stared at him blankly. 'Secret?'

'To staying so slim... so youthful.'

'Still a charmer, I see.' She grinned. 'I suppose I should lie, say something inspiring like... good diet and exercise... but the truth is, most of the time, it's down to living on my nerves. And the odd large glass, or two, of Sauvignon Blanc of course.' She laughed and Ben followed suit. 'I'm glad you came, though,' she added. 'Really glad.'

Ben blushed, which surprised him. 'Thanks. I'm glad I came too.'

Andrea reached for a handbag on the floor beside the sofa and pulled out a pair of expensive sunglasses which she placed on top of her head. 'It's the eyes, you see,' she continued, slim fingers tapping her delicate cheekbone. 'They give so much away, don't you think? Windows to the soul, my mum used to say.' She placed the bag on the floor again, adjusted her jacket. 'I'm going out in a minute.'

Ben shifted in his seat. 'Oh… okay… but don't feel you have to leave on my account.'

Andrea nodded towards a closed door that Ben assumed must be concealing a bedroom. 'Don't look so worried. But I'm sure you don't want me hanging around any more than she does.'

Ben blinked, sat forward. 'I… well… erm–'

'Kind eyes,' Andrea interrupted him. 'I always thought you had such kind eyes.'

Ben looked surprised. 'Really? You wouldn't say that if you'd seen the stuff these *kind* eyes have seen over the years.'

'Of course.' Her smile faded. 'I can only imagine. But you don't need to be a soldier to witness human tragedy.'

Ben ran a hand through his hair, smiled in a way that conveyed an apology. 'No. That's true. Shit happens. To everyone… I guess.' He glanced again at the closed door. 'Sadly, to some more than others,' he added. 'And you know what, there's nearly always some arsehole behind it because… well, let's face it… there's no shortage of them in the world is there.'

Andrea's eyes softened. 'Do you regret joining the forces? Wish you hadn't?'

Ben placed his hands on his knees and took a deep breath. 'I used to. There was a time… for a while… that I blamed it for the break-up of my marriage, the loss of my kids. But it's easy to do that, isn't it. Blame *someone* or *something* for all the fuck ups in your life. Then one day I woke up. Realised I had no one else to blame but myself. I was struggling and I needed help. Professional help. And once I got it, I realised it hadn't all been bad. Yes, I saw some things I'd rather forget, but I did a lot of good too. Not to mention all the amazing people I met along the way. So, I learned to forgive myself... to a point... and focused on the good instead of just the bad. And besides, like my dad always says, regrets are a waste of time. In the end, all they do is hold you back.'

Andrea nodded, looked thoughtful. 'Easier said than done though... sometimes.'

Ben realised how fragile she suddenly seemed, how tired she looked. Which was hardly surprising, he supposed. But at least she didn't look as grief-stricken as she had when he'd last seen her... at the hospital... all those years ago. So much had happened since then, but still, he remembered it like it was yesterday. The squeak of linoleum as he hit the ground running. The familiar smell of disinfectant; of blood, sweat and tears. The cries of the sick, of the wounded, and the grieving. Safe in the knowledge that somewhere, on another floor, along another corridor and beyond another set of swing doors, professionals were doing their best to save a life... Leora's life.

She hadn't looked like Leora of course; bandaged, breathing tubes jutting from her mouth, drips connected to her arms, she could have been anyone. Outraged, Ben stood at the foot of the bed watching the rise and fall of her chest, listening to the mechanical clunk of the ventilator helping her breathe.

'You and me, were meant to be,' he had whispered, moving round the bed, holding her hand in his. 'I know you can hear me, Leora, and I know you have the strength to get through this... and I promise you... somehow or another... I'll help you.'

Not long after that, he left... and had never seen her again... until now.

# CHAPTER 2

*S*he checked her reflection in the mirror; in awe of the power it held, often when she least expected it. It took her breath away at times. So much so, in fact, she almost didn't recognise herself. Such was the miracle of cosmetic surgery, she supposed. She liked what she saw though, especially her lips. The Botox had worked wonders.

*What will Ben think?* she wondered. He'd never been impressed by those that sought the surgeon's knife. 'Why risk it' he'd once said. 'Besides, isn't it our little imperfections, our differences, that make us all who we are? What makes us human.'

Vanity, he'd called it. Is that what he thought she was then, vain? She shivered, the thought of seeing him again filling her with the same giddy schoolgirl excitement she remembered having all those years ago. But like then, her euphoria quickly dissipated, giving way to a familiar feeling of worthlessness, of fretfulness. What if he didn't like what he saw? Not that it mattered. She was long past caring what others thought. Hers was the only opinion that mattered, not Ben's, not her followers – *followers*, she hated that word, it made her sound like a religious cult leader – not anyone. Not really. And she certainly didn't need anyone's approval. Especially his.

Ben wasn't just anyone though. He was someone that had loved her... *really* loved her... once. A link to her past, to the old her. To the girl she once was instead of the woman she now was. *Oh God*, she thought, putting a hand to her head. *Why did I agree to meet him? It was a stupid idea.* She massaged her temple, the throbbing behind her eyes threatening another migraine. That was all she needed. It was probably just nerves. It was years since she'd seen him, so she was anxious. She just needed to... calm... down.

*Why though... after everything I've been through... do I feel so bloody nervous? What does it matter what Ben Thompson thinks of me? It won't change anything, not really. Even if I never see him again after today, which I probably won't, life will still go on. As it always has.*

Laughter interrupted her thoughts. Her mother was talking to Ben in the next room. *Does he still sound the same?* she wondered. Their voices were muffled so it was hard to tell. Smoothing down her dress, she took a final glance in the mirror. Her mother was right, as usual. The pale blue looked good; as did the killer navy-blue stilettos, and the simple silver bar drop earrings. She took a deep breath, smiled. She'd got this; of course she had. She'd given speeches all around the world, often to thousands of people at a time, and from all walks of life. Talking to Ben again was nothing.

Why then, didn't it feel like that?

She walked towards the door that separated them and stared at the handle. One twist of that large shiny doorknob and there'd be no going back. She put her hand out, realised it was shaking, and used her other one to steady it; gripping it so tight that her nails dug into her skin. She closed her eyes, listened. The loud beating of her heart hammered against her chest, while her tongue, like Velcro, gripped the roof of her mouth.

*For God's sake, stop it. It's only Ben Thompson,* she reminded herself, repeating it like a mantra.

She practised her breathing too, like she'd been taught, counting backwards from ten to one; a slow, deep breath in; holding it, before slowly releasing it again. It wasn't easy though because her nose was blocked *again*, which worried her a little. Nonetheless, she did her best, and slowly but surely her breathing settled and her shaking hand stilled.

This time, when she placed her hand on the doorknob, its metallic coldness strangely comforting, she was determined to open it.

*It's just Ben,* she reminded herself again. *Just Ben Thompson.* And with a swift flick of her wrist, she turned the handle and pushed open the door.

Shoulders back, she strode in.

'Hello, Ben,' she said.

# PART II
## 1985

# CHAPTER 3

## 13TH JULY

*L*eora stared at the back of her father's head as he carefully loaded the video recorder with a new tape. She glanced at her friend, Ali, sitting next to her on the sofa, and rolled her eyes.

'Quick, Dad.' Frustration lifted her voice. 'We'll miss the start.'

Martin Jackson glanced over his shoulder and smiled at his impatient daughter.

*It's 12 noon in London, 7am in Philadelphia...* the TV commentator announced.

Leora leapt from the sofa. 'Oh my God, Dad. It's starting! It's actually starting.'

'Lee-or-a,' she heard behind her. She looked round to see the bemused face of her mother, Andrea. 'Have some patience,' she warned.

Leora pointed towards the TV where her father was still faffing.

*...and around the world it's time for Live Aid...* the commentator continued.

'But, but... it's starting. I wanted to record the whole thing... from the beginning.'

Lips pursed, eyebrow arched, Andrea stared at her daughter then glanced at the TV. 'I'm sure your dad is going as quick as he can.'

Leora stared at the ocean of faces now filling the TV screen. Heard a clunking noise as the videocassette loaded, a whirring as her father pressed the record button. *Hoo-bloody-ray*, she thought.

Marty, her father, inched back on his knees and sat for a moment, staring at the screen, as did Leora, who watched how the sun, like a brilliant orange orb, filled the gap between the Wembley towers highlighting a sea of people; their heads, like an ocean of colour, bobbing up and down, filling every square inch of the famous football pitch. The terraces too were crammed with people waving homemade flags and banners, while the pop of flashbulbs intermittently bounced around the stadium like fireworks.

Leora sighed; slumped back onto the sofa next to Ali. 'Wish I was there,' she grumbled.

'You're too young,' came her mother's clipped reply.

'But I'm nearly sixteen.'

'Not until November. Which means you're fifteen. Which is far too young to be going to a concert on your own.'

Leora folded her arms. 'Is not...'

Her father turned round and looked at her – he could say a lot with his eyes. 'We've had this conversation before, young lady.' He placed a hand in the small of his back, the other on the armchair, hauling himself up. There was finality to his words and Leora knew the conversation was over. 'Cuppa?' he asked, exchanging glances with his wife.

'I'll make it. You fire up the barbeque. Girls – cup of tea?'

'Yes please,' they replied in unison.

Leora watched her parents exit the room just as the Queen's Guard finished playing the Royal Salute and the TV commentator introduced Status Quo.

'Who else is coming... to the barbecue?' Ali asked.

Leora shrugged. Her parents' idea of having a 'bit of a do' with friends and family while watching Live Aid had all been very last minute. 'No one special. Some of the neighbours. My nan and granddad... Jules and Eileen–'

'What about Angie?'

Leora grinned. 'Of course, Angie's coming.'

'Yay!' Ali clapped her hands like a performing seal.

Angie was her mother's best friend, which Leora struggled to get her head around. Like her mother, Angie was a Londoner, or 'Landaner' as she pronounced it, but whereas Andrea, who barely had any accent at all, came from North London, Angie, who sounded just like Pauline Fowler in *Eastenders*, came from the East End. She swore a lot too. Especially after a couple of glasses of wine, which always made Leora and Ali laugh, mainly because Andrea couldn't abide swearing. She'd once threatened to wash Leora's brother Lonny's mouth out with soap when he dared to say 'piss off' at the dinner table. However, whenever Angie swore, Andrea just laughed; shrugged it off. Leora thought Angie was one of the biggest, loudest, brashest people she had ever met. The opposite of her mother, in fact, and yet both women adored one another.

'She's pretty, isn't she?' Leora pointed to the TV where Princess Di was smiling and clapping along to Status Quo.

'Yeah – don't know why she married *him* though.' Ali nodded, as the camera zoomed in on Prince Charles, clapping awkwardly out of time. 'I wish my mum was pretty... like Princess Di.'

Leora glanced at her friend. 'Your mum is pretty,' she said quietly. It was much easier to lie if you spoke softly.

Ali threw her a sideways glance. *Liar,* her unspoken reply. 'Your mum's pretty... isn't she?' she said instead.

Leora smiled. Her mother was pretty, and unlike some of the pasty-faced, dowdily dressed mothers on the estate, took pride in her appearance. 'She's nice too.' Ali continued, concentrating on a strand of hair she'd wound around her finger. 'Kind... I wish my mum was like your mum.'

Leora looked at her hands, picked at the wick on one of her fingers. *Your mum is nice* is what she was supposed to say, which she was – once. Lately though, she had become neglectful, in her appearance, and as a mother. Her hair, like her clothes, was limp, and whenever she left the house, which wasn't very often, she always wore sunglasses – even in the middle of winter. Ali's dad – who always had a sickly-sweet smell about him – wasn't much better. He'd never been right since he'd been made redundant from his long-term job a couple of years back. He'd had other jobs since, but never seemed to hold on to them for very long, which made him angry, which in turn meant Leora no longer liked going to Ali's house just in case he was there.

Even when he wasn't home though, Leora still didn't like going because the house was a mess, a ramshackle of chaos and disorder. There was never any food in the house or money to buy any, which *always* made Ali angry. Sometimes she'd get so mad she'd shout at her mum, and sometimes her mum would cry. Which was embarrassing; made Leora feel uncomfortable. She'd tried talking to Ali about it, tried asking her what was wrong; if there was anything she could do to help, but she was always met by the same sour face, the same stony wall of silence.

'Do you think I look like her?' Ali continued.

*Oh God, here we go*, Leora thought. 'Like who?' she replied, feigning nonchalance.

'My mum. Do you think I look like my mum?'

Leora knew this was one of those questions where she was damned if she said yes and damned if she said no. She shrugged. 'I don't know... I guess you do... a bit.'

'You look like your mum... only...'

'Only... what?'

Ali smiled – or was she smirking? It was hard to tell the difference with Ali sometimes. 'Only... not as pretty.'

It was true, there were similarities between Leora and her mother. Like Lonny, she had her mother's cinnamon eyes, her wide nose, and plump lips, but unlike her mother she didn't have her mocha-coloured skin, her dark hair, or her curvaceous figure. Compared to her mother, Leora, who was flat-chested and embarrassingly tall, was more like a stick insect.

She reached for one of the scatter cushions on the sofa and playfully set about beating Ali about the head with it, if only to hide her shame. 'What. Do. You. Mean. Not. As. Pretty?' she said, delivering a separate blow for each word.

'Ouch!' Ali yelped, crossing her hands in front of her face before nabbing a cushion and joining in.

A few minutes later, breathless and giggling, the girls threw the cushions down and lay in a tangled sculpture of limbs.

'You do know I was giving you a compliment, right?'

Both girls laughed. Leora knew Ali meant it as a compliment – sort of – even if it was a backhanded one. Still, Leora wished she didn't look like she did. She wished she looked more like Lonny who, although like her, and their father, was also tall and skinny, in every other sense looked just like their mother. Leora, however, was a strange mix of both her parents. An odd in-between. She didn't want to be an in-between, she wanted to be 'normal'. Because if she was normal, then maybe, just maybe, Ben Thompson might fancy her.

A familiar frisson of guilt washed over her as she and Ali unravelled themselves and turned their attention back to the TV where Queen was now playing and front man, Freddy Mercury, was thrusting his signature 'stick' microphone in the air like a cheerleading baton. Outside, they could hear the shed door opening and closing just as her mother walked into the room carrying a tray of chinking mugs and a teapot, when, as she placed it on the coffee table, the doorbell rang.

'I'll get it,' Lonny called, galumphing down the stairs.

'Open a window, please, Leora,' her mother said, gesturing

behind her. 'It's a beautiful day; let's get some fresh air in here. Give your dad a call too, will you, love,' she added, as Leora dived under the net curtains. 'Tell him tea's up.'

'Da-ad... Mum said tea's ready,' Leora called, staring at the powder blue sky, the heat of the sun warming her face. She couldn't see her father, but she could hear him rummaging around in the shed. He shouted back; he'd be there in a minute. Leora turned round again; her face concealed by a veil of white lace. She giggled, drew her hands together in prayer, and slowly stepped forwards, one foot in front of the other; humming 'Here Comes the Bride'.

Ali, who was watching her, started laughing just as Lonny stepped into the room, closely followed by Jules and Eileen.

'Hello, you two,' Andrea said, smiling. 'You're just in time for tea.' She nodded at the plate of biscuits. 'Help yourself.'

Eyebrow arched; Lonny looked at his sister and grinned. 'What are *you* doing?'

Leora took her final step forward, her makeshift veil slipping from her head, her hair crackling with static.

'It looks like she's practising being a bride,' Andrea suggested, a hint of bemused disapproval in her voice.

'Really?' Lonny sounded surprised, but his voice was breaking, so maybe not. 'Who's the lucky man?'

Ali rolled her eyes. 'George Michael, probably.'

'Or Prince,' Jules added. 'Except he's too short.' His voice was also breaking but whereas Lonny's voice was soprano, Jules's was bass.

'Or Ben Thompson,' Eileen offered, eyes wide, her smile blissfully innocent.

The room went quiet.

Eileen's hands flew to her mouth, whereas Ali, who looked first at Eileen then to Leora, wore her 'what the hell' face.

Leora, in turn, looked away, wincing with embarrassment.

# CHAPTER 4

*T*he doorbell rang and Ben went to answer it. He knew who it was, even though the bevelled glass distorted his image. The agitated stance, the obvious tossing back and forth of a football between his hands, had all the trademarks of Dobs.

'Fancy a kick-about?' Dobs asked, striding straight past Ben and pulling off his trainers by the stairs. 'Anyone in?'

Ben shook his head. Ben's parents were never home. His mum, the manager of a shop, was working, his dad, Ben guessed, probably down the pub, or fishing maybe? It was the perfect day for a fair-weather fisherman like his dad. He hoped he hadn't gone fishing; liked to think his father would still ask him if he wanted to tag along.

He swallowed the bubble of self-pity welling in his chest. He couldn't remember the last time he and his dad had done anything together. Life was different lately. True, his house had never exactly been the hive of activity that Dobs's house was, but it had also never been the morgue it felt like of late.

His parents hadn't exactly abandoned him; the cupboards were always well stocked, the heating came on when it was cold, and other than a minor set of house rules they expected him to adhere to, including getting his homework done, Ben was pretty much left to his own devices. Why then, did he feel like a spare part in his own house? Dobs's house was never quiet. One of five children, including two brothers and two sisters, 'Our House' by Madness, always came to mind whenever Ben visited Dobs's house, mainly because, there was always something happening, and it was usually quite loud.

Dobs placed his football next to his trainers and strode into the living room. Although not fat by any stretch of the imagination, he was sturdy; thickset, which was probably because, like Ben, he played a lot of sport, especially football. So when he threw himself onto the sofa, Ben winced, remembering how his mother had reprimanded him for doing the same thing a couple of weeks ago.

'Whatcha watching?' Dobs nodded at the TV where Freddie Mercury was now striding across the stage, shaking a triumphant fist at the audience.

'Live Aid,' Ben replied.

'Live... what?'

'Live Aid... That music concert Bob Geldof put together?' Dobs frowned, cupped the back of his neck, flattening his hair. Why *did* he have a mullet? It didn't suit him, not really. Then again, did mullets suit anyone? 'You know... for the Africans,' Ben continued, as Freddie, now centre stage, microphone in one hand, fist bumped the air like a Roman Emperor with his other.

Dobs looked thoughtful. 'Oh yeah... right. I remember. The Africans.'

'Starving Africans,' Ben added.

'Yeah... the starving Africans. Which reminds me, I'm famished. Got any crisps?'

Ben rolled his eyes, got up, and grabbed a couple of bags of crisps from the kitchen.

'Cheese and onion, okay?' he asked, chucking Dobs a packet. Dobs caught it, prised it open and stuffed a handful of crisps in his mouth, all before Ben had sat down again. It was gross. Still, even though he was an annoying twat at times, Mark Dobson was also one of Ben's best friends. His *best* friend, probably, after first meeting four years ago at Abbey Road Comprehensive, even though they'd both been born in, and grew up in the same town.

Ben, however, had grown up on a private housing estate on one side of town, whereas Dobs had grown up on the local council estate on the other, which meant they'd attended different junior schools, which also meant that until starting Abbey Road, their paths had never crossed. Not that they didn't venture into each other's territory every now and again, but for the most part, younger kids generally kept to their own side of town.

As an only child, Ben's mother had been quite protective of him; said the council estate wasn't safe, that the kids who lived there were rough; different to them. However, on the rare occasion a younger Ben and his parents found themselves driving through the council estate, it hadn't looked much different to where they lived, at least, not in Ben's eyes.

Every so often there would be an odd dodgy house; front garden strewn with litter, feral cats, a tied-up mangy barking dog, discarded tyres, a rusting car on blocks on the drive. In those instances, Ben agreed with his mother; those houses did look more like dumping grounds than people's homes. However, there was a house near them, two streets away, that wasn't dissimilar. Okay, it didn't have the abandoned tyres, or the tied-up dogs or the jacked-up car, but the garden was overgrown, the paint on all the doors and window frames was peeling, and the net curtains, unlike the starched white ones that hung in the windows of the houses either side of it, were a dirty dishwater grey. An eyesore his mother called it, a disgrace to the rest of the street *and* the estate.

So, mostly thanks to his mother's neurosis about *that council estate* Ben had grown up slightly wary of the place, unsure what to expect on his first day at Abbey Road when the fourth-year students from all the junior schools in the area came together. The irony being, of course, one of the kids from 'that council estate' was now sitting on his mother's sofa, stuffing crisps into his fat gob.

Settling next to Dobs again, Ben yanked open his own packet of crisps; a pungent pong of cheese and onion wafting up his nose. Queen had finished performing and the face of Bob Geldof with his trademark scruffy hair now filled the screen. 'Give us yer money NOW!' he said, in his thick Irish accent. He sounded annoyed, pissed off, even.

They sat around for the next hour or so watching more performances before a short film was shown, explaining the plight of the starving Africans. Images of pot-bellied men and women with sunken eyes, protruding jawlines, and matchstick arms and legs filled the screen, the camera pausing at a group of women who were topless, their sagging breasts on display. Embarrassed, both boys glanced at one another and grinned.

Their childish smirks quickly faded though as they watched the half-naked women try and muster the energy to comfort their whimpering babies. Babies that, with equally twig-like arms and legs and distended bellies, stared from huge eyes set in gaunt faces attached to heads that looked too big, too heavy for their feeble little shoulders.

Most of them; men, women, and children alike, were wearing little to no clothes, trying their best to hide what little modesty they had under the same generic blankets. Not nice blankets though. They looked rough, itchy, more akin to hessian sacks. Mesmerised, Ben studied their sorry faces and couldn't spot a single smile among them; the horror of what their lives were firmly etched into their taut, miserable faces. It was even too much effort to raise a hand; swat the flies away that buzzed around them in the dusty, soaring heat of their makeshift salvation.

'Shit,' Ben mumbled.

'Why are their bellies so big?'

Ben sighed, put his head in his hands. 'Dobs... don't be a twat.'

'What!' he cried. 'I'm not taking the piss. I genuinely don't get it. If they're starving to death, which clearly they are, why are their bellies so big?'

Ben shrugged. 'I dunno. Something to do with malnutrition, I think. Lack of protein or something.'

'Bloody weird is what it is.'

Annoyed, Ben stood up. Dobs could be a real idiot. 'For fuck's sake, Dobs, why don't–'

'What! I don't mean nothing by it. I'm still gonna ask my mum to pay me pocket money into the bank for them on Monday.'

Ben smiled. Dobs really could be a twat, but he always redeemed himself. They both agreed to pledge a month's pocket money. It wasn't a lot, but they were pretty sure Mr Geldof would be pleased with their donation, no matter how small.

After another hour or so Dobs started getting restless. 'Are you gonna watch this *all* day?' he asked.

Ben shrugged. 'Dunno – I guess so.'

'Can't you record it? Then we can go for a kick-about down the reccy?'

Ben looked through the VCR tapes that sat in neat rows behind the doors of his parents' mahogany sideboard. He found a new one, still in its cellophane, which he tore off, and carefully inserted it into the video recorder. There was a loud clunk and Ben pressed record.

'Right.' Ben flicked his wrist to check his watch. 'This is a three-hour tape and I need to be back before it runs out. So, we've got–'

'Three hours,' Dobs interrupted.

'Just under,' Ben confirmed.

# CHAPTER 5

*L*onny folded his arms and looked at his sister. 'Ben
Thompson?' He grinned. 'Really?'

Leora glared at Eileen who in turn looked at her
feet. What the hell did she say that for? She promised not to tell…
anyone… ever. God knows there'd be hell to pay for this later,
with Ali, demanding to know why Eileen had been entrusted
with such important information and she hadn't. She could
already feel the heat of her questioning gaze boring into her
skull. Leora closed her eyes; sighed inwardly. She hadn't meant to
tell Eileen. She hadn't meant to tell anyone – full stop. It had
been a secret. *Her* secret. One she'd kept to herself for years.

She remembered the first time she spotted Ben. It was her
first day at secondary school. She'd been a keen pupil; polished
shoes, smart uniform, new folders, a slightly agitated feeling in
her tummy as she, along with the rest of the first-year students,
tried to familiarise themselves with their new surroundings. It
wasn't easy searching the maze of classrooms among the rabbit
warren of corridors marked on their timetables, and somehow,
amongst all the pushing and shoving, she became separated from
Ali and the others. Hearing her name called, she spun round,

hoping to see her friends, but instead found herself colliding with a stranger.

A very handsome stranger.

Like her he looked lost, and like her he was tall for his age. However, it was his eyes that stood out the most. They were deep blue, like the middle of the ocean. While his blond hair, short at the back and sides, was fashionably long and floppy on top. He smiled and suddenly the room swayed. She wondered if she was hungry. She'd been too nervous to eat breakfast that morning, so it was possible. She doubted it though. A lack of sugar didn't start at the pit of your stomach and work its way down, and it was all she could do to stop her knees buckling.

He was smiling, but surely it wasn't at her, was it? She glanced over her shoulder to check. Boys like him didn't smile at girls like her – did they? She couldn't see anyone behind her though, so glancing back, her heart thudding against her chest, she dared to smile back. She wanted to say something – anything – but the words wouldn't come, wouldn't form in her mouth.

Out of nowhere, a pretty girl, the one with the heart-shaped face and straight dark hair that she'd spotted earlier that morning, was standing behind him. She draped both her arms around the boy's shoulders and fixed Leora with a steely stare. Leora smiled, but the girl regarded her with the same chary contempt she had shown earlier.

Why were some girls like that? Leora wondered. Hated you on sight without ever really giving you a chance? Tipping her head to the side so that her long shiny hair fell across the boy's chest like a scarf, the girl threw her arms forward. 'Hey, Ben,' she said loudly. 'There's space on our table. Come and sit with us.'

The boy, who Leora now knew was Ben, glanced round at the girl; placed both his hands on hers. Embarrassed, Leora turned away, relieved when, from the corner of her eye she saw someone waving, calling her name. *Ali. Thank God*, she thought, scuttling away. She couldn't remember the last time she'd been so pleased to see her friend. What on earth was she thinking? Boys like Ben would never in a million years fancy a frizzy-haired weirdo like her.

Lonny's voice interrupted her thoughts, dragging her back to the present. 'So... do you like, fancy Ben Thompson then?' He grinned.

'Ben Thompson? Who's Ben Thompson?' her mother, pouring tea from the teapot with the chipped lid, asked.

Flushed, Leora glanced at the TV where the Boomtown Rats were now performing on the Live Aid stage. God how she wished she could climb inside the telly and hide.

'Sorry,' a rather sheepish, rather red-faced Eileen mouthed.

'He's a boy... in our year, at school.' Ali's face was thunderous.

Leora gulped, unsure who she was more afraid of – Lonny, in case he ratted her out to Ben, or Ali because she might never speak to her again. 'Don't be so daft. Course I don't fancy him. I just said he's quite nice-looking. Besides, even if I did fancy him – which I *don't* – he'd never look twice at someone like me.'

Andrea replaced the teapot on the coffee table and looked at her daughter. 'Someone like me?' she repeated. 'What's that supposed to mean?'

'Did someone say tea?' Leora's father asked, wandering in from the garden, rubbing his hands together, eyeing up the plate of biscuits.

Andrea looked at her husband and pointed to the steaming mugs of tea beside the teapot. 'Yours is on the right, Marty, in your Superman mug.'

'I'm going out,' Lonny said, heading for the door.

'Don't forget to come back for some food later,' Andrea called. 'When it's gone it's gone!'

Lonny put his hand up, waved. They all knew Lonny would come back when he was good and ready. And despite her threats, everyone also knew Andrea would set aside a plate of food for her son, regardless of what time he walked through the door.

Hotfooting it behind him, Leora followed her brother; keen to talk to him, keen to make sure he wasn't going to say anything to Ben Thompson, if he saw him.

'And none of that breakneck whatsit dancing,' their father added.

Lonny paused, sighed heavily. 'It's called *breakdancing*, Dad. Not breaknecking.'

'Yeah, well.' Martin sniffed, unfolding his newspaper, and reaching for another biscuit. 'Not if you keep spinning on your head like you do. Likely to break your blinkin' neck if you're not careful.'

Outside in the shed, Leora noticed Lonny eyeing up their older cousin Ash's new racing bike. He was away on holiday and had left it at their house for safekeeping for a couple of weeks until he got back, by which time Uncle Bill was going to clear some space in the garage for it. Ash had saved hard for that bike; it was his prized possession. Leora also knew her brother was thinking of nabbing it, and if he did, she also knew Ash would kill him.

'I wouldn't if I was you,' she warned. Lonny looked at her, his grin impish. 'Where are you going, anyway?'

Lonny grunted and groaned as he tried to move Ash's shiny new bike out of the way so he could get to his old, clapped-out rust bucket of a thing. 'Why?'

Leora shrugged, looked down at her feet. 'Well... it's just, you know... that thing Eileen said... about Ben Thompson.'

'Don't worry. Your secret's safe with me.'

Leora studied her brother's face. 'Really? So... you won't say anything then?'

'Nah.'

'Promise?'

'Course. Besides–'

'Besides what?'

'He ain't good enough for you.'

Relieved, Leora smiled. She knew her secret was safe for now. Lonny could be a real pain, but as brother and sister they were extremely close. She didn't know if it was a twin thing – even though they were fraternal twins – or just a sibling thing, but they often knew what the other was thinking, could sense when one of them was feeling down or upset. Ali may have been her best friend, but Lonny was Leora's other half. If he said he wouldn't rat her out to Ben Thompson, then he wouldn't.

Watching him, she wondered, not for the first time, how different her life might have been if she'd been the 'dark' skinned baby and he had been the 'light' one. Physically, they were both tall and skinny, and they both had similar shaped mouths, but other than that it was hard to believe they were brother and sister – never mind twins. Most people didn't believe it when they told them.

Apparently, they'd caused quite a commotion when they were born. They'd even been on the TV, on the regional news, and in some of the local and national newspapers. Their mother had kept all the cuttings in a scrapbook. 'Mother gives birth to miracle Ebony and Ivory twins', one read. Hence their names: Leora, which meant 'my light' or 'I have light' and Lonan which, among other things, meant 'blackbird', which was also their mother's favourite songbird.

Although, for as long as Leora could remember, Lonan was always referred to as Lonny. Except by Grandma Cedella, that is, their maternal grandmother who, with her soulful, soothing accent always referred to them as Lee-Ora, and Lo-Nan.

Leora adored her Grandma Cedella, but she both loved and loathed her visits from London in equal measure. Unlike Leora's mother, who was born in London, Grandma Cedella came from Jamaica, having sailed to England in 1948 on a banana boat five months after her husband, Joseph, arrived. In her childish imagination, Leora could never quite work out if the banana boat was banana shaped, or, if Grandma Cedella was a lone passenger aboard a huge boat filled with bananas.

Grandpa Joseph, however, had been rushed to England on the wind – at least, that had been her childish interpretation of her grandfather's arrival. Although, quite why she believed the wind, no matter how big and powerful, had transported her grandfather thousands of miles across the sea to London, was curious, nevertheless that's what she had believed. However, as she grew older and began to question her grandfather's ability to ride the wind, Andrea had explained how he had been a passenger aboard a ship called the *Empire Windrush* that had sailed into Tilbury in 1948.

Leora wondered why she had never heard of it before; it wasn't part of the history curriculum at school. Sadly, she hadn't known her grandfather; he had died of the 'C-word' not long after her second birthday. She had seen photographs of him though. Slim, wearing a smart suit and a trilby hat, he had the same dazzling smile as Lonny. Leora thought him a handsome man, and her mother said Grandma Cedella still missed Grandpa Joseph very much … even all these years later. Grandma Cedella though, had a strong Jamaican accent, which was partly why Leora dreaded her grandmother's visits, because people looked at her like she was odd.

'Well, kiss mi neck. Dat gel of yours get prettier by di day, Andrea,' she'd say after hugging Leora and examining her at arm's length. 'And such a handsome soldier,' she'd add, turning to Lonny. 'Yah, give your grandmotha a keese,' she'd insist, which they always did, albeit somewhat reluctantly on Lonny's part. All of which was fine when said in the confines of home. It was when they were out and about; popped to the local newsagents, say, or the corner shop, that Leora would worry.

Take for instance the time Grandma Cedella had a run-in with Mrs Digby, the local gossip: a plump lady with grey Brillo-pad hair, thin lips, and a sticky-out chin. You could spot her big white legs, criss-crossed with blue and green cable-like veins, a mile away. Shit stirrer, Ali, who, out of earshot of any adults present, had no qualms about swearing, called her. Leora once overheard her mother telling her father that she thought Mrs Digby one of the most intolerable, narrow-minded women she'd ever had the misfortune to meet.

To be fair to Grandma Cedella though, it was Mrs Digby that started it... sort of. The bell at the top of the door, as they stepped into the corner shop, announced their arrival and Mrs Digby, who was being served at the counter, immediately turned round to see who it was. Frowning, she glared at Grandma Cedella. That's when Grandma, arms crossed, a defiant look in her eyes, had nudged Leora and asked her, in a big loud voice, who the fatty boom-boom was looking at.

'Ere... what did she just call me?' Mrs Digby demanded.

'Nothing.' Leora steered her grandmother back towards the door. 'She just said she's got a bad tum-tum.'

'Orta piss off back to her own country, is what she orta do,' Mrs Digby shouted behind their retreating backs. 'An' that mother of yourn,' she added, for good measure.

Angry, Grandma Cedella was determined to go back and have it out with Mrs Digby. But, desperate with embarrassment, Leora pleaded with her not to, and thankfully, after a bit of coaxing, Grandma Cedella relented, choosing instead to walk away from such bigotry. Not all of Grandma's visits were like that though, and the best thing about them was her cooking, especially her famous fried fish with rice and peas, which everybody loved. Andrea had cooked a batch of rice and peas for the barbecue, and although not quite as good as Grandma's, the mere thought of it was making Leora's mouth salivate.

'Ah fuck it,' Lonny said, throwing his bike down into a clanging heap on the path.

Startled, Leora jumped, all thoughts of her grandmother now carried away on the temperate breeze. She watched her brother disappear into the shed again, re-emerging with Ash's gleaming new racer. 'Right, I'm off,' he said, cocking his leg over the cross bar. 'Do us a favour and put my bike back in the shed, will you? Oh… and by the way,' he winked, putting his finger to his lips, 'don't tell Mum and Dad I've taken Ash's bike, eh?'

Leora promised she wouldn't and watched her brother slip through the back gate, which she closed behind him, before wheeling his bike back into the shed.

She kept her word, of course; didn't say a word to her parents about Lonny 'borrowing' Ash's bike.

She only hoped he would do the same and keep his word… about Ben Thompson.

# CHAPTER 6

*P*anting, Ben grasped both knees with his hands. He was knackered, not to mention hot and hungry.

Dobs ran up behind him and wrestled him to the ground. 'Well done that man.' He ruffled Ben's hair. 'That last goal was spot on.'

The way Dobs carried on you'd think it was one of the school's major-league games, not a kick-about the park with a few mates. Still, if Dobs was happy, Ben was happy too. Laughing, Dobs rolled over and lay flat on his back, shielding his eyes from the glare of the sun, pointing at the cotton wool clouds set against a cobalt sky, each one morphing into faces and places pulled from his childish imagination.

Ben's tummy rumbled.

'Hungry?' Dobs asked.

'Starving.'

'C'mon then,' he said, rolling onto his side, resting on his elbow, 'let's go back to mine, get some grub.'

Heaving himself up, Ben brushed the blades of grass from his T-shirt that Dobs had thrown at him.

'Oi – Benny boy? Pull this.' Dobs waved his index finger at Ben.

Ben grinned, stepped back. 'Nuh-uh,' he said, shaking his head. 'I'm not falling for that again.'

Dobs smirked, stepped towards him. 'This is a different trick. Something new I've learnt... honest.'

Arms folded; Ben studied his friend's face.

'Honest,' a wide-eyed Dobs repeated.

Cautious, Ben stepped towards him and pulled his finger, and right on cue Dobs let rip the biggest, loudest fart Ben had ever heard.

Bending forwards, breathless with laugher, Dobs held his stomach with one hand and slapped his knee with the other. 'Every time,' he howled, pointing at Ben. 'Every bloody time.'

A commotion in the far corner of the field forced them to look round. Someone – not anyone they recognised – was riding a bike at full pelt towards the reccy exit, whilst someone else, on foot, was yelling and giving chase.

'What's going on?' Dobs asked.

Ben shrugged. 'Dunno.'

They sped up, trying to get a closer look and quickly realised the person running behind the boy on the bike was Lonny Jackson who had also been playing footie. He was shouting but they were too far away to make out what he was saying. The boy on the bike disappeared over the horizon, Lonny hot on his heels. Trev, another lad from their year, explained that a kid they didn't recognise. 'A gypo, probably,' he added, parroting his older brothers, had quietly crept up when no one was looking and nabbed Lonny's new bike.

'Only it isn't his bike... it's his older cousin Ash's bike... which he's taken without permission.'

Dobs roared with laughter. He'd grown up on the same estate as Lonny and Ash Jackson and although he didn't know the family well, he knew them well enough to know Ash would kill Lonny if he came home to find his bike missing.

'Shouldn't we go and help him?' Ben asked, somewhat concerned.

Everyone agreed Lonny could look after himself.

'Bet you fifty pence he'll get the bike back,' Dobs said.

And sure enough, within a few minutes, Lonny reappeared. However, even from a distance there was no mistaking the buckled front wheel; the clanking sound of the broken chain – not to mention the strange squeaking noise the bike was making.

'Shit. What the hell happened to you?' Ben said, observing Lonny's bloody lip and bruised eye.

'You should see the other boy.' Lonny grinned.

'That's as maybe,' Dobs said, his gaze shifting from Lonny's bruised face to the mangled lump of metal that only minutes ago resembled a gleaming new racer bike. 'But your Ash is gonna kill you when he sees that.'

Holding on to the handlebars, Lonny glanced around as if on some clandestine mission, a trickle of blood escaping the corner of his mouth, which he wiped away with the back of his hand. 'Yeah, well, I've got a plan. Anyone hungry?' A horde of hands shot up, followed by a chorus of *me!* 'Right then, follow me,' he beckoned. 'We're having a barbecue at my house.' Ben began salivating, his thoughts turning to chargrilled burgers and sizzling steaks. 'And we has enough rice and peas to feed dee five towsand,' Lonny continued, in his best Jamaican accent.

A titter of laughter followed, whereas Ben and Dobs just looked at one another.

'Rice and peas?' Ben mouthed.

Dobs shrugged. 'Think I'd prefer a bacon sarnie,' he whispered.

Ben was about to agree when he suddenly remembered Lonny was the brother of Leora – the tall, skinny girl with the mad hair and big eyes that he'd secretly had a crush on for years.

The same girl he had bumped into on his first day at senior school and smiled at, who, when she smiled back at him, had made his head spin; caused a stirring in his groin, but had also, unfortunately, never looked his way again since, despite his many attempts over the years to get her to – which meant she might be at the barbecue too? It was possible. Still, even if she was, it didn't mean she'd talk to him. In fact, she'd probably ignore him, like she did at school. Nevertheless, it was too good an opportunity to miss.

'Actually... I erm... wouldn't mind trying some rice and peas.' Ben kicked a tuft of grass.

'Really?' Dobs wrinkled his nose.

'Really.'

Dobs shoved his hands in his pockets, puffed out his cheeks. 'Oh, go on then, why not! If the food's shit though, we're going back to mine. Capiche?' he said in his best Godfather accent.

'Capiche,' Ben replied, smiling.

# CHAPTER 7

*A*li got up; headed to the window. 'God this is sooooo boring,' she said, puffing her cheeks out.

Jules, eyebrow raised, looked at Leora, who rolled her eyes. She could hear the rise and fall of voices drifting in through the open window; the sporadic sound of laughter; the odd plume of smoke from a dying barbecue; the succulent smell of seared meat.

'C'mon then, losers,' Ali continued. 'Is this *really* all we're gonna do all day?' She was spoiling for a fight. Had been all day; Leora's punishment for not confiding in her about Ben Thompson. Eileen glanced at Leora, mouthed another silent 'sorry' whereas Jules stood up, walked behind Ali and made a strangling motion with his hands. Leora and Eileen laughed loudly. 'What's so bloody funny?' Ali fumed, spinning round, and glaring at them.

Leora felt a flash of annoyance and stood up. So what if she'd confided in Eileen instead of her about Ben Thompson? 'You,' she replied. 'We're laughing at you – for being such a moody cow all day.'

Ali walked towards her. 'Say that again. Go on, I dare you.' She smiled but her eyes challenged.

Leora stepped closer; arms folded defiantly. 'Moo-Dee-Cow.'

Jules immediately jumped up and placed himself between his two friends. 'Right then, children.' He used his hands like stop signs, one for each face. 'Enough.'

'She started it,' Leora said.

'Did bloody not,' Ali replied.

'Will you two just shut the fuck up,' Jules yelled. The room fell quiet. Everyone looked shocked. Jules hardly ever shouted. 'There's people on that stage today,' he continued, pointing to the TV, 'singing their hearts out because other people around the world are starving to death. And then there's you two, arguing like… like… a pair of poodles.'

Leora frowned. 'Like a pair of what?'

Eileen giggled. 'I think he said–'

'Poodles?' Ali interrupted. 'Did you really just call us poodles? Where the hell did that come from?'

Jules shrugged. 'I dunno, I just wanted you to shut up.'

'Oh Jules,' Leora said, stemming the tears of laughter now streaming down her face. 'Please don't ever change.'

Half an hour later they decided it would be a good idea to get some fresh air and agreed to walk to the reccy. That way, Leora wouldn't be too far from home when it was time to change the tape on the video recorder. They trundled into the garden so Leora could tell her parents. To Leora's horror, her father, who was using the fish slice he'd been flipping burgers with as a makeshift microphone, was singing along to Bryan Ferry's 'Slave To Love', now blasting through the living-room window.

'God, he's so embarrassing,' Leora mumbled, holding her head in her hands. Then, as if things couldn't get much worse, Angie picked up a serving spoon and joined him, bumping and grinding her huge hips against her father's much slimmer ones. Behind her, Leora could hear her mother laughing – Leora loved to hear her mother laugh; soulful, it came deep from within, and like sunshine, lit up her whole face. Then, just to add insult to injury,

Leora watched her Granddad George, slightly unsteady on his bowlegs, get up and join them – dancing in that strange, embarrassing way that old people do – quickly followed by her Nanna Ruth.

*Right,* Leora thought, *we need to get away – fast – before we're all dragged up to join them.*

'We're off, then,' she said to her mother, explaining where they were going.

'Aww… stay a bit longer.' Andrea smiled. 'Have a dance.'

Head down, gait low, Leora shook her head. 'Nah, it's okay. We're going to look for Lonny,' she lied.

Andrea smiled, tipped her head to the side. 'Go on then… move frah ya!' Embarrassed, Leora loped towards the back gate, her friends trailing behind her. 'And don't slouch,' Andrea called behind her.

# CHAPTER 8

*B*en watched with amused fascination as Dobs shovelled a second helping of rice and peas into his mouth. 'Your mum makes the best rice and peas ever!' he said, turning to Lonny.

Lonny winced. 'Urgh... watch what you're doing, Dobs!' He folded a protective arm around his large bowl of Arctic Roll to protect it from the shower of rice spilling from Dobs's mouth.

'Didn't anyone ever tell you it's rude to speak with your mouth full,' a voice said behind them. Ben turned to see Lonny's mum, smiling. She shared the same fox-brown eyes as her son and the same rosebud lips as her daughter. 'But I'm glad you like it,' she added. 'It's Mark, isn't it?' She looked at Dobs who, with food-inflated cheeks, reminded Ben of a mutant hamster. Dobs nodded as her gaze shifted to Ben, and the mound of rice and kidney beans still sitting, untouched, on his plate. 'Not your cup of tea?' she asked.

Embarrassed, Ben looked down. 'No... I mean yes... well... the thing is... I've never tried it before. But... I'm sure it's really nice.' He scooped a mouthful onto his fork and tried some. 'Mmm... yeah... sure is tasty.' He rubbed his belly in a circular motion. Dobs looked at him and sniggered, whereas Lonny, eyebrows shooting up, stared at him as if he were some sort of weirdo. Lonny's mum asked him what his name was and when he told her, she glanced at her son. Smirking, Lonny held his mother's gaze for a few seconds before looking away again. Were Lonny and his mother laughing at him? And if so, why? He shrugged it off, convinced he must have imagined it.

'So, you're in the same year as Lonny and Leora then?'

'That's a point,' Lonny interrupted, glancing round. 'Where is Leora?'

'She went out for a bit, with her friends, to get some air, and look for you.'

'Well, I didn't see her,' Lonny replied. 'She must have gone the long way round.'

It was hard to believe Lonny was Leora's brother, never mind her *twin* brother. Ben thought it was a wind-up when he first found out, but it was true, Lonny and Leora *really* were twins. Unidentical twins – or fraternal twins as his mother had corrected him – but nevertheless, twins they were. They were strikingly different; yet, at times, they looked quite similar. Out of the two of them, though, Lonny was more open, more approachable than his sister. However, like his sister he was also uniquely independent. Ben admired that. Admired the fact that both Lonny and Leora were confident enough in their respective skins to do their own thing, be their own people.

Lonny's mum disappeared and came back with a plate of burgers, poured herself a glass of wine and headed outside again. Ben loved how welcoming, how easy-going she was. His mother would never dream of having this number of boys in her kitchen. In fact, she'd probably have a mild heart attack if he trooped back to the house with a handful of friends demanding food.

He glanced at Lonny who, head back, was laughing at Dobs after he'd got him to pull his finger and farted – loudly.

'Ash not about then?' Ben asked.

Lonny shook his head. 'Nuh-uh. No way would I have–' He made quotation marks in the air with his fingers. '"–borrowed" his bike if he had been.'

'Do you think he'll know that it was you... that took his bike?'

Lonny frowned, put his finger to his lips. 'Keep it down, Thompson,' he hissed, his eyes flitting towards the open back door. 'No need to spoil a perfectly good afternoon, eh?'

Ben lowered his voice. 'Sorry.'

'But in answer to your question, yeah... course he'll know it was me. But it was a risk I was willing to take. As Sir Isaac Newton's third law states, "For every action, there is an equal and opposite reaction".'

Confused, Ben and Dobs looked at one another. 'Huh?' they said in unison.

Lonny let out an exaggerated sigh; thrust his hands out like a priest about to deliver a sermon, then to everyone's amusement began talking like Marlon Brando's *The Godfather*. 'Consequences, boys, it's all about consequences. For every action there is a reaction. I knew I was taking a risk by taking the bike, and even though,' more air quotation marks, '"technically" I didn't cause the damage, it is my fault.'

'But... won't Ash get angry?'

'Will he ever!' Lonny laughed. 'He'll wanna kick my arse, I reckon.'

'So... aren't you... frit?' Dobs asked.

Lonny shrugged. 'What's the point? When he finds his bike, he'll know it was me, so then he'll chase me, but I'll outrun him like I always do, then Mum and Dad will intervene. I'll tell 'em all how sorry I am, and Mum and Dad will offer Ash my pocket money to pay for the repairs.'

'Sounds like you've got it all worked out then?' Ben said.

'I have.' Lonny grinned.

Ben asked Lonny, with as much purposeful indifference as he could muster, if he knew when his sister might be back.

Lonny shrugged. 'Dunno. Why?'

'No reason. Just wondered.'

'I can ask my mum if you like?'

Ben hoped his calm exterior hid his nervous interior. 'Nah. It's okay, thanks. It's not like we're friends or anything. Probably never likely to be either if I'm honest.' *What! What the hell did I say that for?*

Lonny stared at him. 'Why's that then?'

Embarrassed, Ben stuck his hands in his pockets, releasing air from his now puffed out cheeks. 'Dunno really.' *Fuck! Think, you idiot. Think!* 'I suppose… we're just… different?'

A flash of something like disappointment flickered across Lonny's eyes. Angry with himself, Ben knew he needed to leave the room, *fast*, so he asked Lonny where the loo was and, following his instructions, headed towards the stairs in the hallway.

The smell of damp towels, Johnson's Baby Powder and Palmolive soap hit him as soon as he stepped into the bathroom. He locked the door, aware of the sound of clinking glasses, general chit-chat and laughter drifting through the open window, from the garden. It was nice, not something, except for Christmases and birthdays – which was the only time Ben's parents had people over – he was used to.

Outside the bathroom he decided to look for Leora's bedroom. *Bingo!* he thought, crossing the landing in pin steps, and pushing on the first slightly open door he came to. He stepped inside; wincing when one of the floorboards beneath the flowery patterned carpet creaked; the smell of roses filling his nose. A rather sad clown poster on the wall opposite stared at him. It was the same Pierrot clown that some of the girls at school had on their pencil cases and stationery. *What is it with girls and clowns?*

Either side of the clown picture there were numerous posters of singers and pop groups, no doubt pulled from magazines like the ones scattered at the foot of her bed; *Just Seventeen, Jackie* and *Smash Hits*. The same ones that Dobs's sisters read, which he and Dobs stole, just to read the problem pages. There were, he realised, a lot of Martin Kemp and George Michael posters. Didn't someone once say he looked like Martin Kemp?

The thud of footsteps on the stairs startled him. Heart pounding, he crept back along the hallway, to the bathroom, just in time to make it look like he'd just stepped out of the door.

It was Lonny. 'What took you so long?' he asked. 'You had a dump!'

'No! Course not.'

Lonny smirked. 'Yeah... I believe yer... thousands wouldn't. See you downstairs then, yeah? We're all heading out again. You coming?'

Ben's heart sank. Wearing his best 'couldn't give a shit' face, he tried to think of a plausible reason to get Lonny to stay a little longer – in case Leora turned up. None was forthcoming. 'Erm... yeah... oh-kay,' he shrugged.

# CHAPTER 9

*O*ut on the street the air was filled with the hum of lawn mowers and the smell of freshly cut grass. Shielding her eyes, Leora looked up, noticed a sparrow hawk wheeling overhead. There were two routes to the reccy: the short way via the lane, or the long way at the end of the street. Leora and Ali both agreed it was safer to take the long way round. This would bring them to the play area entrance, which meant they were less likely to get smacked in the head by a football.

'What does, "move frah ya" mean?' Jules asked, linking arms with Leora.

Leora explained it was a Jamaican term that her Grandma Cedella used. 'It basically means "get out of here!"'

'Cool,' Jules replied.

Leora smiled. Apart from Ali, Jules and Eileen were her only other friends – well, her only other *real* friends. They were an eclectic bunch, she supposed. Eileen, who was short with flaming red hair and a rosy complexion to match the complete opposite to Leora. Whereas Julian – or Jules, as he preferred to be called – whose muse was Steve Strange from Visage, was at least as tall as her. Then there was Ali, of course, her oldest friend, who hid behind her smart mouth and baggy jumpers. Even today, despite the thirty-degree heat, she was wearing jeans and an oversized T-shirt. A quirky quartet who, when they found themselves sitting next to one another during that first nerve-wracking morning of 'big school' quickly became inseparable.

It was hard to believe that was almost four years ago now.

A low thumping sound caught their attention. It grew louder, making Leora's ears twitch like a cat. She could hear music too; the low tinny growl of a car exhaust; the screeching of hot tyres on sizzling tarmac. They turned to see a familiar flash of metallic green, getting closer by the second. The car, a Ford Capri, music pumping from its open windows, screeched to a halt beside them. The passenger, his arm casually resting on the door, wearing a pair of aviator sunglasses, looked at them.

'Watcha, Leora.' It was Neil – Nelly to his friends – Mitchell, one of Ash's friends from the estate; and his older cousin, Des, a car mechanic.

'Hi, Nelly.' Leora strained to hear herself speak above Malcolm McLaren's 'Double Dutch' playing full blast from the thumping car speakers.

He asked her what she was doing, where she was going. Leora pointed to her friends behind her, said they were heading for the park. 'Aww.' His voice was babyish, his tone mocking. 'Are you gonna go and play on the swings and slides?'

'Don't be daft,' Ali, who was now standing next to Leora, replied. 'We're going to look for Lonny.'

'Well, well, well, if it ain't little Alison Evans,' Nelly said, looking her up and down. Ali, uncharacteristically coy, put her hand to her mouth and giggled. She had also, Leora noticed, tied her T-shirt into a knot, exposing her flat brown belly. 'Who are they?' he asked, glancing over Ali's shoulder, his smile vanishing when he spotted Jules's hand going to his face, his nose bleeding.

'Oi you, stand back,' Nelly yelled, thrusting his hand out like a stop sign. 'We've spent all morning cleaning this car. The last thing we need is you dripping blood on the paintwork.'

Ali, whose grin had morphed into a frown, took a step forward. Nostrils flaring; mouth set in a straight line, she looked angry. She opened her mouth to say something but to everyone's surprise, Nelly jumped out of the car and started pulling off his T-shirt, which he gave to Jules to stem the bleeding. Hesitant, Jules looked at Ali; like a child seeking a parent's approval. Ali nodded and Jules took the T-shirt and held it under his nose.

'He's a haemophiliac,' Ali explained, her eyes skimming Nelly's bronzed torso.

Nelly nodded, mumbled something about that not being all he was, before telling them he had an uncle who was a haemophiliac. A loud growling noise made them jump. It was Des, revving the engine. Losing patience, he revved it once, twice, three more times before shouting at Nelly to get his arse back in the car. 'I've got better things to do than sit around talking to a bunch of kids all day.'

'Who's he calling kids?' Ali said, lips pursed, arms folded across her chest so that her cleavage appeared even bigger. Nelly laughed; his eyes lingering just a little too long on Ali's chest before Jules asked Nelly what to do about his T-shirt. How, if he could clean it, he could get it back to him.

Nelly shook his head, told him to forget about it. 'It's old. I only wear it when I'm helping Des. I've got another one in the car. So, keep it.' He glanced at the crimson flower of blood now blossoming on the T-shirt beneath Jules's nose. 'Or bin it,' he added, climbing into the car passenger seat.

'Who the hell were they? Eileen asked, the air thick with the smell of burning rubber as the car sped away.

'Friends of my cousin, Ash,' Leora replied.

Ali smiled. 'Dangerous, is what they are.'

By the time they got to the park it was mostly empty with no sign of Lonny anywhere. Leora's heart sank. She'd secretly hoped she might see Ben Thompson. She knew he played footie at the reccy with Dobs sometimes, so it was possible. But he wasn't... so that was that, she supposed. Seeking refuge from the sun, the four friends perched beneath a large leafy oak tree and talked for a while. The conversation turned to their futures; about how scary and exciting it was that come September, they would all be in their fifth and final year of secondary school. As ever they discussed their plans to go to college, then hopefully on to university; Jules to study art and photography, Ali to study economics, and Leora to study English and drama. Eileen had no plans to go to university. She was, by her own admittance, a home girl, and had her sights on a local clerical youth training scheme, which was at least, Leora thought, a lot more realistic than acting.

Leora knew that acting, as a career, was a bit of a pipe dream. The careers teacher at school had laughed when Leora told him. Still, her parents supported her. And why wouldn't they? She loved acting; had been a member of a local kids' amateur dramatic club for years. What most people didn't know though, her parents included, was *why* she enjoyed acting so much. It was her escape. Acting meant shedding her skin and becoming someone else for a while.

'C'mon,' Jules said, rooting around in the rucksack he always carried with him. 'Bunch up,' he yelled, holding his old Polaroid camera at arm's length as the four of them huddled together. 'Group photo for the album... to mark the end of another school year.'

Jules had been taking Polaroid pics of them since the first year, and it always surprised Leora how much older they always looked at the end of each year compared to the start.

'Say cheese.' Jules tried to steady his arm as he pointed the camera at them.

'How about, "friends forever" instead?' Leora suggested.

Jules looked at her and smiled. 'I do hope so. But yes... I like that. Ready, everyone... after three. One... two... three...'

'Friends forever,' they chorused.

# CHAPTER 10

*U*B40 were pining for red, red wine while Leora, Ali, Eileen, and Jules hovered next to the stage. Lonny, now resident DJ of the school discos, was on the stage donning a pair of headphones, operating the turntables housed behind a couple of huge flashing light boxes. Leora had already spotted Ben Thompson, although she pretended she hadn't. He was wearing jeans, white trainers, and a blue shirt, his hair curtain fringed.

She still couldn't believe he'd been to her house in the summer, and she'd missed him. Still, with Lonny's words rattling round in her head, it was probably a good thing she had. What was it he said, when she'd asked him about it? 'Thompson ain't for you.'

'Really?' she had replied.

'Really,' Lonny said.

'Okay… but why?'

He had shrugged. 'He just isn't.'

Leora had known not to push him, that something must have been said and Lonny was only looking out for her.

'Do you reckon Lonny will play some Visage?' Jules shouted, pointing to the stage.

Leora looked at him and smiled. The old jacket he'd found in the local charity shop looked amazing over his shirt and jeans. She glanced at her brother who, wearing the biggest smile, looked like he was having the time of his life. 'Ask him.' She shrugged.

Jules nodded, headed towards the stairs at the side of the stage where Mr Baxter, their head science teacher – and failed musician – was lingering. As teachers go, he was pretty cool, even though, at thirty-eight, he was quite old. He organised most of the school discos and supplied the vinyl and equipment.

'I need a fag,' Ali said. 'Going to the loos. You two coming?'

Leora looked at her, contemplating the subtle, yet stark changes in her appearance. Contact lenses had replaced her glasses and a peachy metallic eyeshadow emphasised her smoky grey eyes. Her once mousy coloured hair was now streaked with flashes of silver and gold and her crimson surly pout complemented her fuchsia pink ra-ra skirt, all bought with the proceeds of her part-time job cleaning cars at her boyfriend Nelly's cousin's garage, which she'd blagged during the summer.

Leora glanced towards the end of the hall, her eyes briefly flitting towards Ben who, head back, was laughing at something Dobs was saying, completely oblivious to the gaggle of giggling second-year girls circling them, shark-like, waiting, hoping, to be asked to dance by a fifth-former. 'Nuh-uh. Not for me, thanks.'

'Eileen?' But Eileen didn't hear her. She was also staring across the hall, at Dobs, who was watching Sally-Ann Smith, a rather pretty fourth-year student.

Ali made an exaggerated eye roll. 'God, you two do my head in. Stop pining after silly little boys that wouldn't look twice at you,' she called over her shoulder before disappearing into the dimly lit, crowded hall.

'God, she can be a cow sometimes,' Leora said, turning to Eileen.

'Meh… she's okay.' Eileen shrugged. 'She doesn't really mean any harm… it's just… Ali being Ali.'

'Yeah… I suppose.' Leora followed her friend's gaze where Dobs, who now had his arm around Sally-Ann, was whispering in her ear. 'Listen… it's his loss, you know?'

'Clearly not,' she sniffed, the pain in her eyes obvious. She looked, Leora thought, wearing a pale pink dress, which somehow suited her bright red hair, quite lovely tonight.

Free from Ali's critical eye the two friends glanced across the hall again. 'Unrequited love, eh?' Leora rolled her eyes. Like her, Eileen knew what it meant to love someone from afar. Unlike her though, who had barely exchanged a sentence with Ben, Eileen and Dobs talked all the time. Theirs was a friendship that had blossomed when Eileen noticed Dobs was struggling in some of his classes and offered to help. Dobs, somewhat reluctant at first, agreed and gradually, over time, they had become friends. Ali said Dobs was a user. Eileen disagreed, said she knew Dobs would never date a girl like her but they were good friends, and she could live with that.

'I think you'll find that only applies to me,' Eileen said, still looking at Dobs who, spotting her, put his hand up and waved, just before throwing himself forward onto his toes as Michael Jackson's 'Beat It' filled the hall. Eileen smiled, and even under the glare of the disco lights it was obvious she was blushing.

'Sorry?' Leora's cheeks burned when she noticed Dobs nudge Ben, who glanced round and looked at them before quickly looking away again.

Eileen raised her eyebrows and crossed her arms. 'Oh, come off it, Leora, this is me you're talking to. Just admit it why don't you.'

'Admit what?'

'Though you pretend otherwise, you still like Ben.'

Leora looked at her feet, a sea of electric blue coming into view; her new flats, to match her backless jumper.

'The thing is,' Eileen continued. 'I'm pretty sure Ben feels the same about you.'

'What?' Leora cried. 'No way. He won't even speak to me.'

'Only because you've done a good job of ignoring him for the last four years.'

Leora smiled. It was true. She had gone out of her way to avoid him, but only because she knew boys like Ben didn't fancy girls like her... did they?

'He's always looking at you.'

'Really?'

'He's staring at you right now.'

Leora held her breath and looked across the hall again. A strange symphony of emotions started playing in her chest as Ben's eyes locked with hers; a frisson of possibility surged through her body like a jolt of electricity. This time she was determined not to look away. This time she smiled, and to her surprise, Ben smiled back, and for the briefest of moments... it was just the two of them in the room together.

# CHAPTER 11

*D*obs craned his neck to see who his friend was looking at. 'Who have you got eyes on, Thompson?' He squinted into the dangerously darkened assembly hall bedecked with the odd bit of limp tinsel and flashing lights for the annual Christmas disco. He spotted Eileen, grinned, and stuck his thumbs up. Noticeably flustered, Eileen gave a smile that, although hesitant, was painfully full of hope.

*Poor cow*, Ben thought. Even amongst a crowd of students, raging hormones and swirling lights, her face lit up like a Christmas tree whenever Dobs offered her a crumb of acknowledgement. He wondered if Dobs realised just how much Eileen liked him. Surely, he did?

Cocking his head to one side, Dobs shifted his glance to the left of Eileen. 'The rake!' he exclaimed. 'Surely not?'

'Don't know what you're on about, Dobs.' Ben turned his attention to the stage where Lonny was working the decks like a pro. After his impromptu visit to Lonny's house during the summer, he had hoped to get an opportunity to explain himself for the stupid comment he'd made about Leora being different from him. It hadn't happened though and now too much time had passed.

'Oh my God, you were,' Dobs said, as Ben's eyes drifted towards Leora again.

Embarrassed, Ben looked away, noticed Sally-Ann Smith, a fourth-year student, hovering close by, watching them. 'Don't be stupid, Dobs.' He felt a surge of irritability when confronted by Dobs's smug grin. 'I was looking at Lonny, wondered, if I asked him, he'd play "Relax" by Frankie Goes To Hollywood.'

'You'll be lucky,' Dobs snorted, glancing up at the stage where Mr Baxter, donning a bright yellow Christmas cracker hat, was shuffling side to side, dancing in that naff way adults often do.

'Nah… Baxter's okay.' Ben scanned the room, taking note of the adults present. There were two types of members of the parent–teacher association, those that advocated the Mary Whitehouse approach to morals and minors, and those who were slightly more liberal in their thinking. Unfortunately, the more conservative members outnumbered the more liberal ones, most of whom agreed that the outlandish lyrics of 'Relax' were far too risky for the developing minds of their school's pupils. 'It's some of the others that don't like it,' Ben continued. 'And if they're on cloakroom duty, Baxter will turn a blind eye… or should I say, ear.'

Dobs glanced at the stage where Mr Baxter, arms folded, tapping his foot, was now shaking his head like a nodding dog. 'Yeah… go on then, go for it.' The music changed, and Michael Jackson's 'Beat It' started blasting across the PA system. 'Oh… no… hold it. Hold it,' he yelled, grabbing his crotch Michael Jackson style. 'Watch this,' he insisted, thrusting himself forward into a gravity defying lean. Ben had to give it to his friend, life was never dull when he was around.

He turned his attention towards the front of the hall again, looking for *her*. She spotted him looking at her, but this time, instead of glancing away, like she usually did, she smiled at him, tilting her head slightly, so that her hair fell across her face. He smiled back, felt a stirring in his groin, his chest flaring with excited apprehension. Transfixed, he imagined his lips on hers, kissing them. How long they stood there, staring at one another, he couldn't say. Seconds, maybe? Minutes?

A sharp nudge in the ribs made him turn away.

'Come On Eileen' by Dexys Midnight Runners was blasting across the hall and Ben found himself being rounded up like a reluctant bull in a rodeo as a Mexican wave of hands, followed by a furore of demanding whoops, saw him carried along into his circle of friends. Grinning, Ben, like Dobs and the others, clasped his hands behind his back, repeatedly placing one foot across the other, Dexy style, all of them like some badly choreographed Irish dance group. The only person missing was Eileen. During recent years it had become tradition for Dobs to fetch Eileen and playfully thrust her into the middle of their circle, which, leading her by the hand, he was doing right now, as Eileen, laughing, clapped her hands and joined in.

The song finished and as if by magic Sally-Ann Smith, suddenly at Dobs's side again, flung her arms around his neck. Dobs grinned and shoved his tongue down Sally-Ann's throat. Within seconds they were devouring one another. Eileen looked on, and although no one else noticed it, Ben couldn't fail to see the flicker of pain in her eyes. She spotted Ben looking at her, and quickly adjusted her frown to a smile, before wandering back to her friends. Ben followed her, saw how Leora greeted her friend, wrapping her arms around her: holding her, like a mother soothing her distressed child. She glanced at Dobs and Sally-Ann, who were still chewing one another's faces off, and grimaced, which made Ben laugh. Leora spotted him and once again their eyes locked.

He tipped his head to the side, indicating Dobs and Sally-Ann, and shrugged, held his hands up, which made Leora smile... and for a moment he was lost.

*What is it about this girl,* he thought, his breath catching in his throat, *that draws me to her?* This girl who refused to be typecast. This girl who most people, including Dobs, considered quirky, but to him was the most beautiful girl in the world.

Inwardly, Ben cringed. The words in his head made him sound like a lovesick teenager in a bad movie. The sort of movie that would see him and Dobs rolling around the floor in hysterics. Yet here he was, staring at a girl he barely knew, who, for some reason, he felt like he had known all his life.

'Coming for a fag?'

Ben turned to see Dobs, standing beside him, wearing a huge grin. 'What?' he replied, suddenly flustered.

Dobs rolled his eyes. 'A smoke?' He patted the slightly bulging pocket of the jacket he'd thrown over his footie T-shirt. Ben nodded, stealing another glance at Leora. His heart sank. She'd turned away and the heat of disappointment surging through his veins was intense. He glanced at the clock on the wall, the huge one, to the right of the stage. The one with the second hand that ticked oh so quickly during mock exams and way too slowly during assembly. It was 8.40pm – five minutes before the slow songs started and fifteen minutes before another Christmas disco came to an end.

Exasperated, Dobs grabbed Ben by the arms and looked at him, gesturing at the clock. 'Look, Thompson. Just ask her, eh? Just do it.'

Feigning confusion Ben asked Dobs what the hell he was talking about. 'Just do it,' Dobs repeated, wearily. 'For all our sakes. Just ask her to dance... eh... before it's too late.'

# PART III
## 1987

# CHAPTER 12

*L*eora grabbed her bag, called goodbye to her mother, and headed out the door where Ali was waiting for her by the front gate. *You and me... were meant to be* she repeated to herself. The words Ben had said to her, last night, after he'd walked her home and kissed her.

'Someone looks happy.' Ali turned her face upwards. 'Feel that.'

Shielding her eyes with her hand, Leora glanced up, basking in the tepid heat of a glorious spring morning. Every day this week had been noticeably warmer than the previous one bringing welcome relief from what had felt like eternal winter, especially the mornings and the ever-present blanket of ice that lined their path to the bus stop. Leora loved the seasons, even the stark beauty of winter, but this year it had been particularly cold, and frankly she'd had enough. What a relief it was to shed her thick winter coat, not to mention the simple joy of pouring milk on her cornflakes that hadn't frozen on the doorstep.

Spring had made its colourful entrance and everywhere Leora looked she noticed the newly sprung wildflowers in delicious shades of purples, pinks and creams dotted amongst the hedgerows and sprinkled about the parks and playing fields. Even the river; less of a sleek black ribbon and more of a sun-speckled voile, appeared lighter and brighter, while daffodils, strewn along its bank in bright yellow clusters, swayed in perfect unison like flickering flames on a breeze. Granddad too, instead of shovelling snow in his garden was now planting his vegetable patch, which this year, he proudly informed her, included courgettes, runner beans, salad leaves and spring onions.

All around her new life was blooming, and that's exactly how Leora felt, as if she were blooming. Metamorphosing into someone new. Outwardly, of course, she still looked and sounded the same, but inwardly she was transforming, her confidence growing. And the reason? Ben, her boyfriend. She smiled. What a thrill it was to call him that.

She still couldn't believe it at times – even though they'd been together more than two years. Part of her still half expected to wake one morning and find it had all been a dream, or worse still, some cruel practical joke. That's how she'd felt during those first few months when Ben had first asked her out. Especially when she spotted some of the girls in their year staring at her. *You?* their eyes seemed to say during those brief moments Leora caught them stealing a glance at her whenever she and Ben were together. *He's really with... you!*

It didn't help much when Ali said she'd overheard a few of them discussing Leora and Ben, saying how they couldn't believe he was going out with someone so freaky. She wished Ali hadn't told her because, in a way, ignorance was bliss, and what you didn't know couldn't hurt you. They were only words of course, and just the opinion of a few stupid girls, but still, Leora had been mortified. She knew she wasn't pretty, at least not in the traditional sense, and being tall and skinny didn't afford much opportunity to hide. But a *freak* – really?

She had taken forever, that night, in the bathroom, before bed, analysing the girl who stared back at her from the toothpaste splattered mirror. Unlike Lonny who, except for his long skinny legs, was the spit of their beautiful mother, she was a mishmash of both her parents. Her wide nose and her fat crimson lips were so obviously inherited from her mother. Whereas her hair, with its tight spiral curls, as wide as it was long, could have come from either parent. But the colour of it, white, like her pale skin, with a hint of red, like the smattering of freckles either side of her nose, had most definitely come from her father's side of the family. Those girls at school were right she had tearfully concluded. She was a freak.

She cried herself to sleep that night wondering what she could do about it. It hadn't taken her long to figure out that she either needed money or a miracle to change the way she looked, and she had neither. Which was why, although she'd been thrilled beyond belief that Ben had asked her out, she couldn't help feeling suspicious. Yet, two years and four months on, here they were… inseparable. So even if there were those that considered her a freak, Ben obviously wasn't one of them.

Leora glanced at Ali, still jabbering away, relieved that she hadn't noticed Leora wasn't really listening to her. As usual she was moaning about Nelly, and as usual Leora had heard it all before. Nodding here and there where appropriate, Leora drifted off again, replaying the moment, like she'd done so many times before, when Ben had first asked her to dance at the school Christmas disco. How he had tapped her on the shoulder, and how gently he had taken her by the hand. And stomach churning, heart fluttering, she had followed him.

The way he held her, the thrill of his fingers touching hers, and the way her spine tingled. She remembered the surprising stiffness of his hair too, as it brushed her cheek, so at odds with his face that, pressed against hers, felt so very soft. Then, with Yazoo's 'Only You' ringing in her ears, she remembered the soap fresh smell of him when he had kissed her. Her mouth following his, soft and warm; the slight hint of urgency. And how, as a kiss, it had been everything she'd hoped it would be.

'Oi... earth to Leora?' Ali nudged her.

Leora looked up, saw the bus shelter coming into view. 'Sorry, what?'

'I said... you do remember we're seeing Eileen today... after college?'

'We are?'

Ali looked at her, a flicker of disappointment dancing in her eyes. 'You've forgotten... haven't you?'

Leora scratched her head, nodded. 'The thing is... Ben and I have made plans... to go to the cinema tonight.'

Ali frowned. 'Well, you'll just have to unmake them then, won't you. You know how much Eileen looks forward to our visits.'

Leora nodded, pressed her lips together. She had been so looking forward to her night out with Ben, if only because, with exams approaching, her parents were once again, like they had been during the last term of school, much stricter about the time she spent with him. 'Okay,' she said, trying to hide the disappointment in her voice. 'You're right. Ben's meeting me off the bus later, I'll tell him then. I'm sure he won't mind.'

Like her, Ben was studying for his A-levels, but unlike Leora, who had enrolled at college so she could study drama alongside English and history, Ben had stayed on at the school's sixth form to be closer to the army cadets, which he still attended. When he could though, he'd meet her off the college bus and walk her home, just so they could spend time together.

Ali's eyes shot up. 'Tough shit if he does.'

Leora sighed, looked away, pretending not to hear. Why, after all this time, had Ali not warmed to Ben? She was right about Eileen though. She really did look forward to their visits, so Leora couldn't let her down. Becoming a young parent wasn't something Eileen had planned, at least, not so soon after leaving school, anyway. She had genuinely believed, or so she said, that her weight gain during the summer at the end of their fifth year at school was because she'd been overeating. So, when she discovered she was pregnant she was as surprised as everyone else. Leora and the others hadn't even realised she was seeing anyone.

Wayne Roberts, a rather quiet boy, who was a year older than Eileen, lived close by. He and Eileen often passed each other in the street: he on the way to work, she to school. At first, they just smiled at one another, which led to talking, which eventually led to friendship. Then Wayne asked Eileen out and the rest, as they say, is history. Eileen's parents, although somewhat surprised about their impending grandchild, were great, rallying round to help the young couple, which come the winter saw them married, and early the following year, saw Eileen give birth to a gorgeous little boy called Noah.

Eileen loved her baby boy, but she struggled, a lot, especially during the first six months or so after his birth. She had cried almost as much as he had. Andrea suggested she might have post-natal depression and encouraged Leora to support her friend as much as possible.

Lately though, Eileen was doing much better. However, she loved seeing her friends, and as much as Leora wanted to be with Ben, she didn't have the heart to let Eileen down. After all, she and Ben had plans to see each other tomorrow night anyway, so she wouldn't have long to wait.

# CHAPTER 13

*B*en put his hand up, waved goodbye, the taste of her lips still lingering on his. He was gutted he wouldn't be spending the evening with Leora, but he didn't mind. At least, not too much, anyway. Eileen was a lovely girl. She'd struggled a lot after having her baby, and like a true friend Leora had rallied round to support her.

'She'd do the same for me,' Leora had said at the time.

Ben didn't doubt it. So it would be wrong to get annoyed, despite his disappointment. Something about it, though, unsettled him. It wasn't like Leora to double-book herself. She was normally well organised – annoyingly so at times – so it seemed out of character to forget about her plans with Eileen. He wondered if Ali – oh she of the permanent frown whenever she laid eyes on him – had anything to do with it. If, perhaps, she had purposely told Leora the wrong date to sabotage their night out. It wouldn't surprise him.

Then again… He sighed, shoved his hands in his pockets. He wasn't being fair. It was easy to blame Ali because… well… the simple truth was, he didn't like her. He'd tried, but it didn't matter what he did, or how much he attempted to engage with her, he knew, deep down, despite her painted smile, she didn't like him. She'd never openly said so, and when he'd first mentioned it to Leora, Leora had just laughed.

'Don't worry about it.' She waved dismissively. 'That's just Ali. Bit prickly to start with but once you get to know her, she's fine. Give it time, she'll warm to you. When it comes to friends, I honestly don't think I could ask for a more loyal one.'

Leora was wrong though. Ali hadn't warmed to him and for the life of him Ben couldn't work out why. Her dislike of him was subtle though; odd off-hand comments; the way she'd look at him when everyone else was distracted, her eyes, like hot coals, openly hostile, boring into him; totally at odds with the tone of her voice. He didn't want to make a fuss though because he didn't want to make it awkward for Leora. Besides which, if he did, it might look as though he was trying to come between her and her best friend. Which he most definitely wasn't. Maybe, he wondered, he was being oversensitive.

He never felt like that around Eileen or Jules though. He got on well with both. In fact, he was embarrassed he'd never taken the time to get to know Jules – who had a wickedly dry sense of humour, and, like Eileen, didn't have a bad bone in his body – before. He got on well with Lonny too, especially after he'd explained himself; apologised for the stupid comment he'd made about Leora being 'different' to him. What an idiot. He still cringed when he thought about it.

Ali, though, was something else. Ben got the impression she didn't trust him. Maybe that was it – she didn't trust him with her best friend. She was, after all, Leora's oldest friend. So maybe she was simply looking out for her. To be fair to Ali, he had been out with a few girls before Leora, which had, *apparently*, given him a bit of a reputation.

What Ali didn't know though was, most of those girls had asked him out, and although they had had fun for a while, they soon got bored of him because, well, frankly, most of the girls attracted to him were different to him. He often found he had nothing in common with them, and vice versa, so it was hard to have any sort of conversation – at least, any sort of *meaningful* conversation, anyway. Which meant, after a few months or so, they would start drifting apart. He'd been dumped more times than he could remember, but he'd never once been upset. If anything, he usually felt relieved.

Leora, though, was different. Right from the word go they talked, often for hours on end, about *anything* and *everything*. So, he wished Ali would let her guard down, give him a chance. He'd never hurt Leora because... well... he loved her. *Really* loved her... with all his heart and soul. Which, yeah, okay, did scare him at times, if only because he didn't want to end up like his parents, because surely, they must have really loved each other too... once... hadn't they?

Unfortunately, they had split up a couple of years ago, during the summer holidays before Ben started school as a fifth year. His mother had gone on a week's holiday to Wales with some of her church group while Ben and his father went on a fishing trip to the Lake District. Hours spent lazing by the river, laughing and joking most of the time, and catching fish a lot less, had been, for Ben, pure bliss. Two days after their return home though, Ben's father left Ben's mother... for good. Apparently, his affair with Wendy Broadbent – whoever she was – had been going on for some years.

'I'm sorry, son,' his father said. 'I tried; I really did. I had every intention of hanging on until you'd left home but then I realised I'm not getting any younger... and life's too short to be this unhappy.' He then moved into Wendy's house, thirty miles away, at pains to let Ben know he was welcome to stay any time he wanted to.

During his first visit to Wendy's house, Ben tried to be angry, but it was near on impossible. Ben's father was the happiest he had seen him in years, and with Wendy around it was easy to see why. Less well dressed, and slightly plump, she couldn't have been more different to his mother, and although she was loud and brash, she was also warm and welcoming. She and his father were always laughing, so he could see why his father was drawn to her. His mother, on the other hand, remained largely indifferent to her husband's departure. She was slightly concerned about what her church group might think, but other than that, Joyce seemed mostly unaffected. In fact, Ben would go as far as to say she seemed somewhat relieved, which was strange after nearly eighteen years of marriage.

He paused for a minute and looked up. It was dusk. An alabaster moon filled the sky which, alongside the yellow light emanating from the streetlamps, lined his path with silver and gold. *Love*, he thought, shaking his head. Was he *really* in love. It was a rhetorical question because he had been in love with Leora since the first day he'd laid eyes on her. The wonderful part being, of course, or maybe it was the saddest, that until they had got together, he had no idea that she had felt the same way.

Although... he did have an inkling. Remembered odd moments he'd catch her looking at him. But he was so afraid he'd misread her, so afraid of rejection, it was easier, especially as the years passed, not to do anything about it. If Dobs hadn't pushed him that night at the school disco, encouraging him to ask her to dance, he knew, to this day, he probably still wouldn't have. It was hard to believe that was over two years ago. He remembered it like it was yesterday.

The disco was coming to an end, which meant it was time for the slow dances. Wham's 'Wake Me Up Before You Go-Go' slid into the aching saxophone introduction of George Michael's 'Careless Whisper'. Ben, heart racing, took a deep breath and strode over to her. The atmosphere, as he took Leora's hand in his, was electric. Trembling, he led her towards a group of other slow dancers before turning to face her.

With one hand on her shoulder, the other in the small of her back, he pulled her close, remembering how her hair – wild, beautiful, smelling of roses – had brushed his face as head-to-head and nose-to-nose they navigated the dance floor. The song changed again, and it was then, with Yazoo's 'Only You' ringing in his ears, Ben leaned in to kiss her, and she let him, responding with the same warmth he somehow knew she would.

He couldn't explain why, because he barely knew her, but somehow, something deep down inside him told him she was his missing link.

*You and me... were meant to be*, he found himself saying.

He arranged to meet her the following day at the park near her house, the reccy. Nervous, he was worried she might change her mind, not be there. His fears were quickly laid to rest though because when he arrived, she was already waiting for him. They spent the next two glorious hours walking, talking, holding hands and kissing. Being around her was easy because there was something so familiar about her. He felt like he'd known her all his life. Longer, even, which he knew wasn't possible. Nonetheless, being with her made him feel as though... he was home.

# CHAPTER 14

*L*eora kissed Ben then watched him walk away before closing the front door. How, she wondered, was it possible to love someone so much. To feel that love with every fibre of her body, every beat of her heart. Smiling; hand clutching her chest, she turned round, met by Ali's smirking face.

'Jesus,' she said, arms folded, feet crossed, leaning against the kitchen door. 'Don't you ever get fed up with all that lovey-dovey shit.'

'You're just jealous.' Leora smiled, striding towards the phone on the small wooden table in front of the stairs.

'Jealous?' Ali said, eyebrow arched. 'Jealous of *what* exactly?'

'That Nelly doesn't have one romantic bone in his body.'

'No... he doesn't... thank God. I'd hate it if he did. It's pathetic.'

'Leave it out, Ali,' Lonny said, thumping down the stairs. 'Just because you're my sister's best friend, it doesn't give you the right to be fucking rude.'

Ali, eyes wide, looked as surprised as Leora was. Leora

touched his arm, laughed nervously. 'It's okay, Lon, she doesn't mean anything by it.'

'Yeah,' Ali scowled. 'Chill, Lonny... I'm only messing around.' She looked at Leora. 'You do know that... right?'

Leora nodded. 'Of course. Besides,' she shrugged, 'we're all different. Ben and I are a bit lovey-dovey... but I get that not everyone is.'

'Yeah... well... you wanna be careful, Ali. Sometimes your...' he paused; made quotation marks with his fingers, '"messing around" as you put it, doesn't always come across like that.'

Leora and Ali looked at one another and Lonny, unusually sullen, grabbed his keys from the small wooden bowl next to the phone and headed for the door.

'You going out?' Leora asked.

'Got a gig,' he replied, without turning round. 'At the Burghley Club. So, I'll... sees yer later, yeah.'

Concerned, Leora watched her brother's retreating back. She told Ali to wait a sec and followed him out to his car which he'd already started loading with the disco equipment that he kept in the garage. 'Hey, Lon.' She placed a hand on his shoulder, gently squeezing it. 'You okay?'

Lonny shrugged. 'Yeah... I guess so.' He jangled his car keys in his hand.

'Really? Because you... don't seem it?'

He looked at her then, but not before glancing at the front door first. 'I sort of got some bad news today.'

'Really? What kind of bad news?'

Lonny's eyes glanced skittishly towards the front door again. Leora suspected it might be about a friend, a girlfriend, possibly. She didn't know for sure because Lonny's private life was exactly that – private. If he did have a girlfriend, she had no idea who it was because he never talked about her and never brought her home, which, given how welcoming their parents were, she couldn't quite get her head around. Lonny had always done his own thing, gone against the norm, so in that sense his behaviour wasn't that unusual.

'He'll bring the right girl home when he's good and ready,' she'd sometimes overhear her father saying to her mother on the odd occasion they brought it up.

*Maybe he's been dumped?* she thought, aware of the flicker of pain in his eyes. Whatever it was, she knew it had upset him. *Please tell me, Lonny,* she pleaded with her eyes. Unlike her, Lonny rarely, if ever, confided in her, whereas she confided in him all the time. Occasionally though, very occasionally, like now, he would open up.

She squeezed his arm and nodded, gently encouraging him to push the words out. She could tell he had something on his mind, could sense the words hovering on the tip of his tongue. He opened his mouth but a voice behind them interrupted them, which saw him quickly close it again. They both turned and looked towards the door again where Ali, arms folded, stood, tapping her foot.

'Are we going to Eileen's or what?' she called.

Lonny grinned, shook his head and Leora knew, whatever it was her brother had been about to share with her was gone, consigned to his own private reverie.

For the briefest of moments Leora hated Ali. Sighing inwardly, she reminded Lonny that she was always there for him, then asked Ali to go back inside and ring Eileen to see what time she wanted them to go round. Lonny walked to the driver's side of the car, put his hand up, got in and drove off, the gravel beneath his tyres cracking and popping as he pulled away.

Ten minutes later, Eileen, who had recently passed her driving test, pulled up outside the house in Wayne's much loved Ford Escort. Without a second thought, Ali got in the front passenger seat, leaving Leora to climb in the back.

'Bloody hell, Eileen, does Wayne know you're driving his precious car?' Ali asked.

'Of course, he does.' She smiled nervously. 'God help me if I prang it, though.' She giggled.

'So... are we going out... or straight back to yours?' Leora asked, tugging at her seat belt.

Frowning, Eileen glanced at her in the rear-view mirror. 'We're going to see Jules. Didn't you tell her, Ali?'

Ali looked at Leora, sighed and rolled her eyes. 'Yes... of course I did.'

Confused, Leora put her hand to her head. 'Did you? I don't remember. I thought you just said, because she'd passed her test, Eileen had offered to pick us up. Congratulations, by the way.'

Eileen's grin filled the rear-view mirror. 'Thanks.' She blushed.

'Yeah... well done,' Ali added. 'Didn't think you had it in you, if I'm honest.'

'Thanks... I think,' Eileen exclaimed.

'So, erm... how is Jules?' Leora asked, her eye drawn to the discarded pieces of Lego and toy cars scattered on the back seat. 'Sorry, if I wasn't such a crap friend, I wouldn't need to ask.'

Jules hadn't been too well of late. Kept catching a lot of colds; taking forever to get over them. He'd even had to quit his second year at college, but because of upcoming exams and course assignments, both Leora and Ali hadn't seen him for a while.

Eileen shook her head, took her hand off the steering wheel, wiping away, to Leora's surprise, tears running down her pink cheeks. 'Sorry,' she sniffed. 'The thing is... he's had the test results back from the hospital... and it's bad... really bad.'

# CHAPTER 15

*a* car horn made Ben jump as a bright orange Allegro estate pulled up alongside him: the boot full to the brim with disco equipment.

'All right, mate,' the driver said, after reaching across and winding down the passenger window.

'Lonny!' Ben bent down. 'Yes thanks, mate. You?'

'Fine, thanks. Sis says you're not going to the cinema now?'

Ben shook his head. 'No, she forgot she'd made arrangements to see Eileen.'

Lonny grinned. 'Yeah... I heard. So... what you up to now then?'

'Dunno.' Ben shrugged. 'Hadn't given it much thought if I'm honest.'

'Fancy giving me a hand? I'm on my way to the Burghley, been hired to do some old dear's fortieth birthday party.'

Ben hovered for a moment. 'I don't know if I'll be much help but... go on then.' He opened the passenger door, its creaking hinge crying out for some lubrication. 'Why not.'

Ben helped Lonny heave the last of the equipment through

the fire doors behind the stage. 'Bloody hell, Lonny, do you bring this lot to every gig.'

'Pretty much.' Lonny grinned.

'But how... there's too much here for one person to carry.'

'There's usually someone around willing to give me a hand.'

'You need your own roadie, I reckon.'

'Can't afford it.' Lonny smiled. 'At least, not yet anyway.'

You had to admire Lonny, Ben thought. He'd found something he loved doing and through sheer hard graft and determination he now had his own successful business working as a DJ for hire. Unlike Leora, Lonny, although bright, had no desire whatsoever to go to university. To be fair though, not many kids in their school did. In that sense Leora, Ali and Jules were pretty much in the minority. Some kids, like him, stayed on at sixth form, or went to college to study for their A-levels but not many went on to university, including him, because, come the end of the summer, Ben would be heading off to Army Training Centre Pirbright, where, like Dobs before him, he would start training to be a soldier.

He'd wanted to join the army for as long as he could remember and even though it excited him, it also, he had to admit, made him a little uneasy. Not least because, for a while at least, it would take him away from Leora. Pirbright was about thirty miles west of London, where Leora would be studying, so wasn't, strictly speaking that far. Which would be fine while he was training. The problem would be *after* his training, where he might be sent. They'd talked about it, a bit, knew that keeping their relationship going from a distance wasn't going to be easy. However, they'd also agreed, one way or another, they'd manage it.

At the back of his mind though, Ben knew there was a possibility that Leora would get bored of waiting for him, have her head turned by someone else. In an ideal world he'd complete his training and ask Leora to marry him. But even if she said yes, what then? Would she be happy to settle down with him, live in service accommodation, find a job locally? He didn't think so because Leora had her own hopes and dreams. She wanted to be an actor; and who the hell was he to stand in her way?

'Oi! Earth to Thompson.'

Ben looked up to see Lonny grinning, snapping his fingers. 'Sorry, what?'

Lonny threw him a neatly wound electric cable. 'Unwind this and plug it in will you.' He nodded, indicating a socket on a wall behind Ben.

A rather rotund, ruddy-faced man approached the stage and asked Lonny how he was. 'I'm all right, thanks, Arthur, you?' he said.

'Not so bad, not so bad.' He placed two hands on a belly that would make Father Christmas proud. 'I see you've got some help tonight.'

'Indeed, I have. This is Ben... my future brother-in-law.' He winked at Ben. 'Ben, this is Arthur, the club manager.' Ben, who vaguely recognised the older man, put his hand up.

'We've got at least two hundred coming tonight,' Arthur continued. 'So, I was thinking, you should do three sets tonight... two before we put the lights on for the buffet, and one after, finishing around 11.30pm?'

Lonny nodded. 'Sounds good to me.'

Arthur clapped his hands. 'Great,' he said, rubbing them together. 'Now then, what can I get you boys to drink... on the house of course?'

Ben looked at Lonny, who grinned. 'Thanks, Arthur. Ben here will have a pint and I'll have half a shandy.'

'Half a shandy,' Arthur exclaimed, wrinkling his nose in disgust.

Lonny laughed, revealing a row of perfectly white teeth. 'I've got to drive home later, Arthur. And this is my livelihood. Can't risk losing my licence now, can I?'

Arthur lifted two grey, two very bushy eyebrows. 'No... I reckon not. What a sensible young man you are.'

Lonny shrugged. 'I try.'

Arthur walked towards the bar, turned on the lights and busied himself inspecting glasses and checking beer pumps. Ben, who was still looking at Lonny, beamed. *Future brother-in-law*, he said, repeating Lonny's words in his head. But then... there it was again. That sinking feeling in his stomach. That wave of uncertainty that washed over him from time to time making a part of him – a very *small* part of him – feel slightly spooked by Lonny's comment. He and Leora were still so young. Hadn't that been the crux of his parents' problems. Hadn't they, instead of giving themselves time to work out who they were and what they wanted from life, rushed into marriage. That's what his father had said to him recently.

Ben felt a tap on his shoulder. He looked round. 'Yeah,' he said, expecting to see Lonny. But Lonny, who hadn't heard him, was on the other side of the stage concentrating on some other job in hand. Ben shrugged; assumed he must have imagined it and went back to what he was doing. However, when, just a few seconds later, he felt another tap, but this time on the other shoulder, Ben immediately knew it was Lonny.

'Lon-nee.'

Lonny glanced round. 'Yes, mate,' he said, wearing his best poker face.

'I know that was you.'

'Know *what* was me?' Lonny grinned.

Lonny's party trick of tapping someone's shoulder, looking away, then, when he was sure they hadn't worked out who it was and turned away again, would tap the other shoulder, was almost as annoying as Dobs's party trick – *almost*. Unlike Dobs's farting finger though, Lonny's trick did at least require a modicum of skill. When Lonny had first done it to Ben, Ben was convinced, because of Lonny's lightning speed, that he must have used a stick or a prop of some sort, but after watching him do it to others, Ben quicky realised it was simply down to timing and speed.

Ben shook his head, rolled his eyes. 'Righto, Lonny,' he sighed.

By 11.15pm the dance floor was heaving; every square inch filled by many pairs of rhythmically twisting feet. Ben watched from the periphery with amused fascination as women, dancing round handbags, and men, their discarded jackets draped over the backs of various abandoned chairs, ties loose, brows slick with sweat, whooped, hollered, and clapped their hands.

The evening had gone well. It was easy to see why Lonny was so popular. He was good at his job, made DJing look easy. Which, including lugging all the equipment about, to setting up, to knowing what music to play – which could likely make or break an event – it most definitely wasn't. There was far more to being a good DJ than working a turntable and having a good time.

'I'll play for free… for you,' Lonny said, flashing Ben another one of his trademark smiles.

Confused, Ben frowned; pointed to himself. 'Me?' he shouted above the music.

'Yeah… at your wedding… when you marry my sister.'

Ben smiled, took a swig of the pint in his hand, then quickly looked away again towards the bar where a bell was ringing last orders and saw a sudden surge of punters, like bees swarming to a hive, heading towards it before disappearing under a cloud of cigarette smoke. Ben loved Leora but Lonny's comment, especially considering his father's recent admission, made him uneasy. He was worried that if he tried to hold on to Leora too tight, one of them would end up making compromises. He wanted to be a soldier. She wanted to be an actor. She might be required to travel. He'd spend a chunk of his time training or deployed overseas.

There was, he knew, an element of compromise in all relationships. The question being, where did you draw the line? How did you differentiate between what was fair and what was too much? Plus, the thought of him and Leora ending up like his parents, drifting on a sea of resentment for years, scared him.

# CHAPTER 16

*D*espite the merriment and laughter at Jules's house the car drive home was deathly quiet. Nelly had picked Ali up, so it was just Leora and Eileen.

'You drive really well, you know,' Leora said, the first to break the silence. 'Considering you've only just passed your test.'

Eileen wrinkled her nose. 'I'm getting there. Are you going to have lessons?'

Leora shook her head. 'Nuh-uh, I'm saving every spare penny for London.'

'Oh… you're still going then?'

'Yeah… why wouldn't I?'

Eileen shrugged. 'I don't know. I guess… I just thought… considering how serious you and Ben are, you might have changed your mind.'

'Actually… it's funny you should say that. I haven't changed my mind about going to uni, but I am thinking about going to one closer to home and training to be a teacher instead.'

'What… instead of acting?' Eileen asked, glancing at her, her face intermittently lit by the streetlights they passed, before quickly turning away again, maintaining her focus on the road.

85

'Makes more sense. Sort of job you can do anywhere... in any part of the world... should, you know, you find yourself married to a soldier or something.'

Leora laughed.

'Have you told Ali.'

'I did mention it – yes.'

'Oh God... I bet that went down like a tonne of bricks.'

'Actually, she was surprisingly chilled about it.'

'Really?' Eileen sounded as surprised as Leora had been when she'd mentioned it to Ali. She was dreading telling her, knew how much Ali was looking forward to the two of them going to London in the autumn, so she'd fully expected fireworks. But she was fine, her only derogatory comment being she hoped Ben was worth it.

'I take it she's not bothered about leaving Nelly then?'

'Doesn't seem to be. If anything, I'd say it's the other way round, and he's more bothered than she is.'

They pulled up outside Leora's house, and Leora's heart sank. She was hoping Lonny might be home. The news she had received tonight had been heavy; had made her feel low. She needed someone to talk to; someone she could trust. Someone who would understand the gravity of the situation and give her the consolation she needed, and Lonny was that person. He always knew what to say when she was feeling down, how to turn something on its head. Still, on this occasion, that might, even for Lonny, be a struggle.

She had thought about ringing Ben, and if he was home, getting Eileen to drop her off at his house so she could tell him while he walked her home. It was late though, past 10pm. There was no guarantee Ben *was* home, and getting his mother, Joyce, who might well be asleep by now, out of bed just to see if her son was there wasn't an option. Her parents had brought her up better than that.

The flickering lights of the TV screen seeping through the

slight gap in the front room curtains suggested her parents were still awake. Or at least, her mother probably was. Her father; feet up on the sofa, arms folded across his chest, mouth open, would likely be dozing. So, she could talk to her mother, she supposed. But she wasn't sure how her mother would react. How either of her parents would react for that matter. She had a pretty good idea. Her parents were decent, kind people. People who, having been judged themselves over the years, weren't quick to judge others.

Yes, like her, they would be shocked. They might even be a little fearful. It was hard not to be after those God-awful apocalyptic TV ads that had started popping up on the telly last year. The ones where a huge black tombstone with the word AIDS carved into it, toppled backwards, domino-like, to the floor. The backdrop an exploding volcano; clanging noises; a funeral bouquet of lilies – just in case you missed the point – added as a final flourish.

'Awful,' her mother had called them. The type of ads that would, she said, stigmatise those affected and allow the ignorant and bigoted to believe such prejudice was justified.

Still, judging by – she was ashamed to admit – her own slight reluctance to hug Jules when they first arrived at his house, the adverts had been reasonably effective. But the pain etched into the sunken features of his lovely face had made her fear subside. Eileen, however, hadn't given it a second thought. She hugged and kissed Jules like she always did. Ali too, was hesitant at first, but following Eileen's lead, the two girls quickly followed suit and hugged their friend.

'It's okay,' Jules had said, forcing a smile as Leora approached. 'You don't have to hug me. I understand.'

Leora, who had remembered something she'd seen on the news the week before, marched straight up to him, threw her arms around his neck, and kissed his cheek. 'Listen, you,' she said, looking straight at him, doing her best but failing miserably to fight the tears coursing down her cheeks. 'If it's good enough for Princess Di, it's good enough for me, okay?' She was of course referring to the news clip she'd seen of Princess Diana shaking hands with an AIDS patient in a London hospital.

Smiling through his tears, Jules took Leora's hand in his thin, emaciated one and thanked her, which only served to open the floodgates and saw them all crying. They cried. They laughed. Then they cried and laughed some more.

But mostly they had laughed, reminiscing about old times and how, on that first fateful day at senior school the four of them had been drawn together, sticking to one another like glue, best friends ever since.

Eileen turned the engine off, yanked on the handbrake and wobbled the gearstick to make sure it was in neutral. Then the two of them sat in complete silence.

Leora was the first to break it. 'I still can't believe it,' she whispered to the darkness.

Head bowed; Eileen shook her head. 'I know. I feel like we need to protect Jules and his family because... well... you know what they call it, don't you? AIDS, I mean. The gay plague.'

'I know,' Leora groaned, massaging her forehead with her fingers.

'Which is... well... just awful. I mean, we all know Jules probably *is* gay. But that's not the point is it, because he's still a virgin. Not that it matters either way. But he is. But that's not what people will think, is it. They won't care that he's a haemophiliac. That he caught it from contaminated blood. Bent, sick poofter is what they'll call him. I know it and you know it because whenever HIV or AIDS comes up in conversation, that's what people say, isn't it.'

Leora shifted in her seat. She hardly, if ever, got annoyed with Eileen, but right now she wished, with all her heart, she would just shut the hell up. Stop stating the awful, obvious truth so she wouldn't have to think about the added suffering Jules and his parents would no doubt endure once the residents of their small town discovered what was making him sick.

'He looks... awful... doesn't he,' Eileen sniffed.

Blinking back tears, Leora stared out of the window, remembering the skin and bone version of her friend that had greeted her at the door. Tall and skinny, like her, Jules had never been particularly well built, but the skeletal features she had been confronted with, the sunken eyes, the razor-sharp cheekbones, had shocked her to the core. 'Yes,' she whispered, mesmerised by the orange glow that lit up the bonnet of the car, radiating from the streetlight overhead. 'He does. Do you...' She paused, took a deep breath, and turned back to her friend. 'Do you know how long he's got?'

Eileen looked up again, her tremulous eyes mirroring Leora's. 'Twelve,' she said.

'Twelve? What... months?'

Eileen turned away, began picking at a loose thread on her jumper. 'Weeks,' she whispered. 'He's got about twelve weeks.'

# CHAPTER 17

The first emotion to hit Ben when Leora told him about Jules, was, he was ashamed to admit, one of fear. Starting in the pit of his stomach it spread, first to his bowels, then his limbs, quickly followed by an all-encompassing shame. He'd seen the TV ads and all he knew about AIDS was, if you caught it, it was a death sentence. He also knew it was primarily part of the gay scene, spread through unprotected sex, but other than that, he didn't have a clue.

'Shit… I'm sorry.' He reached for Leora's hand, which he brought to his lips and kissed. 'Can't he… his family… do anything?'

Leora sighed, rested her head on Ben's shoulder. 'Eileen said they've done as much as they can. Jules didn't want to talk about it much. He just wanted to talk about old times; catch up with what me and Ali had been up to but it's all just so… sad.'

She paused, and although she was trying to keep it together, Ben knew she was struggling. He squeezed her tight in his arms, kissed the top of her head. She in turn buried her head in his chest; her tears, as her shoulders rose and fell, as silent as the grave. Ben stroked her hair, wished he had some words of comfort, something poignant to say, something profound. Anything, really, that would make sense of the senseless. No words were forthcoming though because, the painful truth was, it didn't make sense and yes… it was sad. *Really* sad. 'Yeah… it is,' his quiet reply.

All cried out, Leora used the sleeves of her oversized jumper to wipe her tearstained cheeks. 'I need a fag.' She swung her legs off the bed, reaching for one of the bright yellow leg warmers lying limp at the end of it.

'Won't your mum and dad smell it?' Ben said.

'Not if we open the window.' Leora balanced on one leg, pulling the leg warmer over her other outstretched one.

Leora's parents were out and Lonny was off DJing, so it hadn't taken much for Leora to convince Ben to sneak upstairs for a quickie before they headed to the pub to meet Dobs.

Leora walked to the window and Ben laughed. 'Is that a new trend? A baggy jumper, nothing underneath, and one bright yellow leg warmer?'

Leora looked down at her one dressed leg, her other naked one and grinned. Shrugging, she turned away again, pushed the window open. Shielding the cigarette in her mouth with one hand, she flicked a lighter underneath it with her other hand. 'Want some?' she asked, holding the fag up, a small cloud of blue smoke billowing above her head.

Ben was desperate for a drag but declined. With just months to go until he started his basic training it was important to keep his fitness levels up. Which, given that soon – he flicked his wrist, checked his watch – very soon, in fact, he'd be down the pub, knocking back pints with Dobs, didn't really make sense. *Oh well,* he reasoned. Dobs was only home for the weekend and a man had to have some vices. There'd be time enough to cut down on the booze when his friend went back to barracks. There was, however, he thought, as Leora flicked the cigarette butt out of the window, which she quickly closed before hop skipping back to him, one vice he'd never give up.

He kissed her then, passionately. His mouth searching hers, caressing her neck, her breasts, his hands tracing her hips, her thighs. Leora in return arched her back; a throaty moan escaping her mouth as Ben, heart racing, felt his cock harden and his heart swell to the point of bursting.

God, he loved this girl.

It was stupid really because his was a logical mind, and yet, despite all his reasoning, despite all his rationale, he also knew, instinctively, right down to the marrow in his bones, he had loved Leora all his life. Longer than that, even. He hadn't so much met her but found her. And soon, very soon, he would have to let her go again... for a while, at least, anyway.

It scared him though, the thought of not seeing her. Of counting the weeks and months before they could be together again.

'You do know how much I'm going to miss you, right?' he mumbled, his hands clamped to her thighs, his head nuzzling her flat stomach.

Leora reached for him; pulled him towards her, so they were face to face. 'I'm going to miss you too,' she whispered, her breath hot, her cheeks damp. 'Which is why...' She paused, drew breath, which suddenly made Ben uneasy.

'Why, what?' he asked, rolling off her and sitting up.

Leora sat up too. 'The thing is – and I've been thinking about this a lot – being with you has made me realise a few things.'

'Really?' Ben replied, a knot of apprehension in his stomach.

Leora nodded. 'And what I've realised is... I don't want to act anymore... I want to teach instead.'

'Teach!' Ben struggled to keep the incredulity out of his voice.

Leora recoiled a little. 'Don't sound so surprised.' She laughed somewhat nervously.

'Yeah but... teaching?' Ben frowned. 'You really want to spend your days teaching kids like… like us… like Dobs… or worse still kids like Cunty Cummings?' he added, referring to Jason Cummings; the bully of their year.

Leora sighed, rolled her eyes. 'He's the exception rather than the rule. Besides which… teaching is a very worthy vocation, you know.'

Ben put his hand to the back of his neck and rubbed it. 'I know it is. I'm not saying otherwise. But you love drama. Look at the hours you've put into all the plays you've organised. What was it you told me when we first started seeing each other – the only time you feel real, feel alive, is when you're on stage.'

Leora smiled, picked at the fluff on the sleeve of her jumper. 'It's true. I did say that, and for the longest time I meant it. But when I met you, I started to change. The real reason I like acting and being someone else is because…well…' She shrugged, embarrassment colouring her neck, flushing her cheeks. 'I don't like being me… or at least… I didn't.'

'What?' Ben frowned.

'It's true. I think you had me down as someone who – what was it you said? – marched to the beat of her own drum, which is a much better description of Lonny than it is of me. But the truth is, as much as I love Ali and Eileen and Jules, there were times at school when I really hated not fitting in. When I just wanted to be someone else. Someone who wasn't tall and skinny, who had smaller lips and bigger boobs. Someone, in fact, that *you* would fancy.

'Then… you asked me out… and gradually… I realised… despite all my flaws… you like me for being *me*. So, I started thinking about what else I might like to do, and teaching came to mind. Which, if I enrol at a university closer to home, also means we'll probably get to see more of each other because when you have leave, you won't have to juggle visits between me and your parents. Then, in a few years' time, when I've qualified, and we're married–'

'Married!' Ben repeated, suddenly sitting bolt upright. He hadn't meant to sound so shocked, so horrified. He loved Leora. He also knew he wanted to marry her – one day. At eighteen though, they were still so young, so what was the rush? There was time enough to discuss marriage – later. Besides, the last thing he wanted to do was to make the same mistake his parents had. After all, hadn't they both said to him recently they wished they'd waited, given themselves more time to work out who they were and what they wanted instead of feeling pressured by family and friends to settle down.

Not that Ben felt pressured, but he did feel slightly alarmed, if only because he was convinced Leora was lying. What was it Ali had said to him when he'd bumped into her a couple of weeks ago? That she knew how much he loved Leora, but she hoped he wouldn't let that get in the way of her plans. 'She's dreamed of being on the stage right from a little girl, you know,' she'd added.

He'd resented her comments at the time, thought she was poking her nose where it wasn't wanted, but despite their angst with one another he knew Ali cared for Leora, and as much as it aggrieved him to admit it, he also knew she only wanted the best for her.

'Oh... okay,' Leora replied, her eyes wide, tremulous. 'That wasn't the response I was expecting.'

Agitated, Ben got up and paced the room; ran a hand through his floppy hair. 'I just think, knowing how important acting is to you, that you shouldn't give up on your dream.'

'But I just told you... I've changed my mind.'

Ben shook his head. 'No,' he said, stroking his chin. 'You're just saying that... because you think it will make it easier on me... on *us*.'

Hugging her knees, confusion etched onto her face, Leora turned towards the door; the phone in the hallway trilling up the stairs. 'I'd... better get that,' she said, clambering out of bed.

Angry with himself, Ben watched her slip out the door.

'That was Ali,' she said, returning a few minutes later.

'Of *course* it was,' Ben's sarcastic reply.

'She's… she's had a really bad argument with Nelly.'

Ben laughed, shook his head. 'What… another one?'

'And she's coming round.'

'When?'

Leora chewed the corner of her mouth. 'Now.'

'Now!' Ben looked at his watch. 'But we're supposed to be meeting Dobs in twenty minutes.'

Leora moved towards him, touched his arm. 'Look, you go, and I'll catch you up… okay?'

Ben looked at her, felt the tendons in his neck tightening. 'You know what? Forget it.'

Leora's eyes flashed with confusion. 'What? What do you mean?'

'I me-an… don't bother. I'd prefer to go on my own.' And with that, he grabbed his jacket and his keys and left.

# CHAPTER 18

The slam of Leora's front door shook the house in a way that, had her father been there, would have seen him opening it again and shouting up the road after the culprit, asking them what the hell they thought they were playing at. Hovering by her bedroom window, shaken by his sudden outburst, Leora watched Ben cross the street and disappear from sight. He didn't even look back. She sniffed and couldn't work out which she felt more – disappointment or anger. She'd never seen him like that before and thought it was childish. Thought *he* was childish.

She looked down at her one bare leg, her one yellow one. She needed to get dressed or at least put some PJs on before Ali turned up. She stood by the window though for a minute, staring into the garden opposite, where Mr Ayres lived. He was a nice old man but seemed lonely since his wife died some five years ago. His son and daughter visited now and again, but they'd moved away, so it was never very often. Leora couldn't imagine only ever seeing her parents a couple of times a year. Even if she did go to London – which, after Ben's outburst she was now reconsidering – she fully intended to come home at *least* once a month.

The light from a streetlamp overhead highlighted an apple tree in the far corner of Mr Ayres' drive, with at the base of its trunk a couple of discarded apples. They looked how she felt – bruised.

Why was Ben *so* angry with her?

She sighed, hot tears stinging her eyes and went back to her bed; flopped down. Was she boring? Is that what this was. Ben was fed up with her and didn't know how to end it? Hoped that, when she went to London and he joined the army, their relationship would just... fizzle out... without any upset... any unnecessary drama? She looked at the dishevelled sheets on her bed and shook her head. No. She didn't believe that. Not for a second.

Hoping with all her heart Ben would come back, she found herself staring at the George Michael poster on her wall. It was a couple of years old now and although George's smile was still dazzling, some of the colour, where the sun had bleached it, had drained from his face. It was curling at the edges too. She should replace it really, but she didn't have the heart. She had confided in George a lot over the years.

'Bet you don't have these problems, eh, George?'

Snuggling under the duvet, she thought about getting dressed; asking Ali, when she turned up, to go with her to the pub. Then again... maybe not. Ben probably needed some breathing space. Time to calm down... and think about what he'd said.

The pub though, would be busy tonight. Heaving. Especially being a Saturday night. Dobs's girlfriend, Sally-Ann, would be there, which also meant her friend Gemma Whitwell would likely be there too. Leora's heart skipped a beat. Gemma liked Ben. She was always flirting with him whenever Leora went to the bar or nipped to the loo. She hadn't really noticed until Ali pointed it out. Now, though, whenever Gemma was around, it was *all* she noticed.

Suddenly hot, she threw her duvet off, stood up and swore loudly.

She felt angry, got dressed. Where the hell was Ali anyway? She'd been in tears – *again* – on the phone. She was the *real* reason Ben had stormed off. Leora slumped back on the bed. It wasn't Ali's fault that she and Ben had argued. Yes, Ali and Ben didn't always get on. Yes, Ali could be needy. And yes, Ali had her faults... but she was always there for Leora. However, as much as that was true, it was also true that Ben loved her. *Really* loved her. So why then, when she said she'd changed her mind about acting, had his reaction been so volatile?

Surely it was all just some stupid misunderstanding.

She would give him time to calm down then she would ask him. In the meantime, she'd let him enjoy his evening with Dobs. She knew how close the boys were, how much Ben missed his friend. Tomorrow was another day and there'd be time enough to talk about it all then. As for Gemma Whitwell... yes, she may fancy Ben, but when all was said and done, Ben loved *her*, Leora. There was no doubt about that. She could feel it in her heart, and she knew, with every fibre of her being, he would *never ever* do anything to jeopardise that.

# CHAPTER 19

*B*en pushed hard on the pub door and strode in. It was a Saturday night so the place was, as he'd suspected, heaving. Brushing rain off his jacket, he headed towards the bar where a heavy layer of cigarette smoke hovered like thick fog from a scary movie. What was really scary, though, was the way he had just walked out on Leora. What the hell was wrong with him? Why had he been so annoyed? A brisk walk in the cold rain had soon put paid to that. He'd been unfair; he knew that. The right thing to do would have been to go back and apologise, but the further he walked the harder it felt to turn round. Not to mention the fact he was soaked. So, in the end, he just kept on walking until he saw the warm glow of the pub lights up ahead.

Squeezing through the throng of bodies surrounding the bar, Ben scanned the room for Dobs, and ordered himself a pint. A slap on the back nearly saw him lose the whole thing before he'd even taken a sip. Spinning round, ready to give whoever it was a mouthful, he was met by Dobs, who, with his barely-there short hair still took Ben by surprise. The mullet, long since gone, now replaced by a rather severe crew cut.

Ben smiled. 'Pint?' he asked.

Dobs grinned. 'Go on then... if you're offering.' He nodded towards a table where some of their friends were sitting. 'Plus, a Malibu and lemonade, ta, while you're at it,' he added, indicating Sally-Ann who, alongside a few of her friends, was also at the table. Ben laughed and rolled his eyes. Dobs may have looked slightly different but he was still the same cheeky git he'd always been.

Carefully weaving themselves between the swarm of bodies hovering by the bar, Ben and Dobs headed over to their friends. Dobs passed Sally-Ann her drink and told her it was from Ben. 'Cheers, Ben.' She raised her glass. 'Leora not with you tonight?' she said, craning her neck to look behind him.

Pint in one hand, Ben put his other hand to the back of his neck; shame crawling up it. 'No. She's got some, erm... coursework she needs to finish,' he lied. He'd been a first-class dick and he needed to make amends. He'd finish this pint, if only to give him a bit of Dutch courage, then he'd sort it out.

Sally-Ann looked at her friend, Gemma, and smirked. 'Come and join us.' She inched along the padded bench to make space for Ben and Dobs.

'Nah, you're all right,' Dobs replied, much to Ben's relief. 'We'll stand for a bit.' He pointed to a wooden pillar. 'We've got a lot of catching up to do.'

Coveting their pints, Ben and Dobs propped themselves against the wooden podium. 'She's got the right hots for you, mate.' Dobs nodded at Gemma. Ben glanced over, caught her staring at him. She smiled, then appeared to drop something, which she slowly bent down to retrieve, which, given how low-cut her top was, was hard not to watch.

Dobs nudged Ben and winked. 'Nice tits, eh?'

Flustered, Ben looked away. 'Don't know what you're on about.'

'Rightio,' Dobs said. 'I believe you, thousands wouldn't. Anyway, never mind all that coursework bollocks, what's really going on with you and Leora? I thought you said she was coming tonight?'

Ben frowned; explained they'd had an argument.

Dobs patted Ben's arm and reassured him they'd sort it out. 'Me and Sally-Ann are always having words. But we soon make up again, which is the best part really, coz make-up sex is the best sex.'

Ben rolled his eyes and shook his head.

'Besides,' Dobs continued, raising his pint and gesturing behind him. 'There's plenty more fish in the sea, eh, if... you know... things don't work out with you and Leora.'

Ben glanced across at Gemma again who, now singing from the top of her lungs with Sally-Ann, was also sort of dancing in her seat; her breasts jiggling along with her. She looked good. Not his type, but attractive, nonetheless. She knew it too, as did most of the other blokes in the pub gawping at her.

Embarrassed, Ben looked away again. 'Nah – there's only one girl for me.'

Dobs raised his eyes, a look of mock surprise creasing his face. 'Bloody hell, Thompson. I do believe you're in love.'

Ben laughed; looked at his feet. 'Maybe,' he replied coyly. 'So what if I am?' he added, glancing up again.

'Fuck! I knew you liked her, like. But... I didn't realise how much. So... that's it then is it... for you? You'll happily never shag another woman again?'

'Yeah, that's exactly what I'm saying. What about you and Sally-Ann?'

Dobs turned to look at his girlfriend. She saw him and blew him a kiss. He laughed; looked at Ben again. 'I dunno,' he said, rocking back and forth on his feet. 'She's perfect really. But it's like... sometimes... it feels like there's something missing; you know?' He shook his head. 'Anyway,' he added, the smile that had morphed into a frown quickly replaced by a smile again. 'No booking the wedding without checking the dates with me first, okay?'

Ben felt his eyebrows shoot up. 'Why's that then?' he asked.

'So I can make sure I've got leave. Especially as you'll be wanting me as your best man and all.'

Ben laughed, half-choked on his pint. 'And what makes you so sure I'd want *you* as my best man,' he asked, using the back of his hand to wipe the beer running down his chin.

'Because,' Dobs grinned, holding a hand out, the beer in his glass sloshing in the other, 'I'm your right-hand man, of course. Always have been and always will be. Not to mention the fact that I am *the* best man for the job.'

The two friends continued talking for a while, and Ben wasn't sure if it was the pure joy of seeing Dobs again, or the fuzzy effects of the alcohol now running through his veins – both probably – but the more he thought about it, the more he realised just how much he *did* want to marry Leora, though he'd been slightly spooked when she'd mentioned it earlier. Yes, like his parents when they married, they were still young. But *unlike* his parents, Ben knew, *really* knew, just how much he loved Leora. He also knew they were best friends and best friends didn't lie to one another. If she'd genuinely changed her mind about acting, then there was no reason for him to doubt it, despite what Ali said to him when he'd bumped into her a couple of weeks ago.

Dobs put his empty pint glass on a table next to them. 'Just going for a slash. Back in a minute.'

Ben, who still had a third of his pint left, glanced round. The pub was even busier, almost full to bursting with cheery, if somewhat drunken punters, but it felt empty without Leora. He should go back and tell her how sorry he is. But she could be out, with Ali, having a good time, and who could blame her? Still, even if she was at home, it was highly likely Ali was with her and the last thing Ben wanted to do was apologise to Leora in front of *her*.

Dobs wandered back just as Ben necked the last dregs of his pint and began rooting around in his pockets for some change. 'Just going to make a phone call,' he said, handing Dobs his empty pint glass. 'I'll have a pint of the same, thanks.' Dobs looked at Ben then looked at the empty glass. 'And don't tell me you haven't got any money – you earn a damn sight more than I do right now.'

Dobs grinned, shrugged his shoulders, and headed for the bar while Ben headed to the payphone at the back of the room. Thankfully no one was using it. He picked up the receiver, listened to the purr on the end of the line and stuck his finger in the dial. He suddenly felt, with the pint he'd just downed fizzing and sloshing in his stomach, surprisingly nervous. Rolling his shoulders, coins jangling in his hand, the dialling tone now a ring tone, he took a few deep breaths and waited for someone to pick up. After a few rings, someone answered, the pips bleeping like a siren as he fumbled to put some change in the slot.

'Hello,' Leora said, a stiffness to her voice.

'Leora... it's me, Ben.'

She didn't reply but he could hear her... quietly breathing down the phone.

'I'm... sorry about earlier,' he stuttered. 'Like... *really* sorry. I...' He glanced round, checking to see if anyone was listening. The men that drank here were men's men; declarations of love only permitted, or forgiven, if you'd had a skinful. Thankfully there was no one around, but still, he lowered his voice all the same. 'I love you. I really do. And... well... I've been thinking about what you said earlier, and there's something I want to ask you. Can I... come round?'

Smiling, Ben went back to the table where Dobs was now sitting with Sally-Ann and the others, a pint waiting for him. He'd had every intention of going back to Leora's and proposing to her. Unfortunately, though, Ali was still there, and the two of them were watching a movie together, which was a good thing really because when he *did* propose, he did also, he now realised, want to do it right… with a ring. He couldn't afford much but he had some savings. Plus, he was sure his dad would lend him some money if he needed it. That would take time though. A couple of weeks at least, anyway, which would give him time to think about where and when he made his proposal.

Leora though, had forgiven him and when he ended the call and told her that he loved her, he felt like the luckiest bloke alive when she said it back. Never again would he walk out on her like that. With love in his heart and relief pumping through his veins he took a glug of his pint; the warm hoppy nectar gliding down his throat. He looked at Dobs, waxing lyrical about some half amusing incident during his army training, and smiled. Soon, he'd be doing a job he loved and married to the girl of his dreams. Life, he thought, taking another swig of beer, really didn't get much better than that.

# PART IV
## 1999

# CHAPTER 20

*L*eora walked to Speakers' Corner and sat on one of the benches. It was November and autumn was morphing into winter. Clouds sculled across a pale watercolour sky and the once green grass was now carpeted in vibrant red and gold, the fallen leaves of skeletal trees, wistfully wary of the chilly arrival of the north wind. Shivering, she pulled her coat a little tighter, then took out the small plastic tub from her bag, prised open the lid, removed one of the rather limp sandwiches she'd made earlier that morning and took a bite.

A tangy explosion of cheese and pickle filled her mouth. Glancing round, she felt the weak warmth of the sallow sun gently graze her neck. She looked up, basking in its tepid heat; relieved to escape the madness of the make-up counter she worked on in Lumley's Department store. She smiled. She loved it here; it was her secret go-to place, full of weird and wonderful people. It was also, notwithstanding the outlandish theatrics of MPs in the House of Commons, or some of the comedians she'd seen in the many comedy clubs dotted around London, one of the only places she knew where bizarre rhetoric was not only tolerated but considered commonplace.

Located on the northeast edge of Hyde Park near Marble Arch and Oxford Street, Speakers' Corner, she learned, during her years as a student, had long been a site for public speaking and debate. Held up to demonstrate freedom of speech, anyone could turn up, get on their soapbox and wax lyrical about any chosen subject so long as it didn't incite violence. Inspired by those that had gone before them, including Karl Marx, Vladimir Lenin, George Orwell, and William Morris, to name just a few, Leora and her fellow classmates had been encouraged to visit Speakers' Corner and practise their public speaking skills.

Leora, who was used to performing on stage in front of a live audience, shouldn't have been fazed by such a task. However, being in such proximity of an audience who had no qualms about heckling, was unnerving to say the least. Ali, who'd come to support her, said her performance seemed wooden, stilted. Sade, one of her classmates thought otherwise. She thought Leora seemed a bit nervous, but other than that, had spoken well. Leora was sure Sade meant well, however – annoying as it was – Ali did tend to tell the truth. So, as grateful as she'd been for Sade's words of encouragement, it was Ali's words she took on board that day.

After all, Ali was one of *the* only people that had stuck with her through thick and thin, especially during that first terrible year when they came to London. Had rubbed her back, dried her tears, and coaxed her to eat. It was a side of Ali that not everyone knew. Outwardly, she could come across as hard, but beneath that tough exterior beat a heart of gold. Ali cared deeply about her friends and if it hadn't been for her love and support over recent years, Leora was sure she would have gone quite mad.

So, if Ali said public speaking wasn't Leora's thing, while others saw her criticism as harsh, Leora saw it as something else. She saw it as advice from a friend who had her back. So, other than doing what she needed to do to appease her tutors, once she'd finished her studies Leora never bothered speaking at

Speakers' Corner again. She did, however, continue visiting. Sometimes to people watch; at others, just to listen. It was a fascinating place, and she couldn't help agreeing with George Orwell's description of it as 'one of the minor wonders of the world'.

Not that there appeared to be any debates taking place today. Often, they were reserved for Sundays. Still, despite the breezy temperatures, there were plenty of people milling about, including breathless joggers, couples taking a leisurely afternoon stroll, and weary parents keeping a beady eye on their young whose animated whoops and hollers were matched only by the excitable yelps and barks of various dogs chasing brightly coloured Frisbees or spit-sodden tennis balls.

Leora spotted a group of students a few benches up. She recognised the uniform: oversized jumpers beneath oversized coats, jeans, and trainers. Heads back, they laughed at something and nothing; their empty polystyrene coffee cups and Coke cans recycled into ashtrays for their stubbed-out fags and roll-ups. She smiled to herself. That had been her – once. Now look at her.

She sighed, looked away again, her eye drawn to the next bench along where a young couple were kissing. He was pale, blond haired; she was darker, had a headful of wiry Afro curls, not unlike her mother's. Nose to nose they kissed, passionately, oblivious to everyone.

They reminded her of her and Ben, which made her feel guilty. Made her wonder why, whenever she saw a couple in a passionate embrace, she always thought of her old boyfriend instead of her husband. It was strange how she still thought of him, how much she still missed him, despite all the hurt he'd caused her. Maybe it was because there was something about their break-up that never felt right, which, given all the evidence, was plain stupid really, and yet, it was a feeling she'd never been able to shake.

Still, every cloud and all that because if Ben hadn't done what he did, she wouldn't have moved to London. Undoubtedly, leaving her parents and Lonny after everything that had happened, first with Ben, then Jules, had been one of *the* most difficult things she had ever done. It would have been much easier to stay and wallow in her grief. A fresh start was the last thing she wanted but, as it turned out, it was also exactly what she needed. Nonetheless, if it hadn't been for the late-night chats with Lonny convincing her to follow her dreams, and Ali, who helped her with her UCAS application, she was confident she wouldn't have bothered.

She was glad she did though. At least, she was for a few months, until her dad phoned and told her the terrible news about Lonny. Which *really* was too much; the icing on the cake for what could be best described as *the* worst time of her life. She went home of course, but all she wanted to do was hibernate, curl up in a ball and sleep... forever. Going back to London after the funeral didn't seem right, but, as Ali pointed out, she *had* to, if only because, consumed by their own grief, it was obvious Leora's parents didn't want her. Especially her mother.

'Maybe it's because you remind her of Lonny,' Ali said. 'After all – and I know you're not going to want to hear this right now – out of the two of you, Lonny was *always* her favourite. So, as much as you love your parents, and I know you do, and as much as you want to be there for them... you can't throw your life away because of some misplaced loyalty on your part.'

Ali's words had seemed harsh at the time, cruel even, like a hot poker through the heart, but the more Leora thought about it, the more she realised her friend was right. It was a hard pill to swallow, and even harder when, two weeks after her arrival, her parents drove her to the train station but didn't bother to wave her off.

Her father got out of the car and lifted the small suitcase she'd brought with her out of the boot, but her mother remained seated. 'Take care of yourself,' her dad said, his voice quivering, his eyes red, grief-stricken, pulling her into a quick, tight hug. When he freed her, she glanced at the car, where her mother remained seated in the front passenger seat.

Her father followed her gaze, squeezed her arm. 'She's... really struggling right now,' he said, his Adam's apple bobbing up and down. Leora had looked at him then, desperate for him to beg her not to go. For her mother to leap out of the car and hold her, tell her how much she loved her. But they didn't. Neither of them said or did anything that gave her any indication they wanted her to stay.

'Aren't we all, Dad?' her whispered reply, and it was then, as her father shook his head, and walked back to the car, she realised, with silent tears coursing down her cheeks, Ali was right. They didn't want her.

Ali, it seemed, was always right.

She glanced at the couple on the bench again, who were still kissing, and realised, although it was years since her split from Ben, the memory of it was still just as raw, just as painful.

She'd been at the breakfast table, eating a bowl of snap, crackle, and pop. The rattle of the letterbox hailed the arrival of the post and among all the usual paraphernalia there was a package addressed to her. She remembered feeling intrigued, wondering what it was and who it was from. She never in a million years dreamed it would contain what it did. Especially as it had been over a week since the 'Gemma and Ben kissing thing' and all was right between her and Ben again.

She had decided, not long after Ben had phoned her to apologise for storming out on her, to go to the pub and surprise him. It was an impulse decision after she'd found herself alone when, after speaking to Nelly on the phone, and making up with him, Ali went back to Nelly's. It was late, cold, and still drizzling outside but Ben had sounded so disappointed when Leora said she'd see him tomorrow, she thought she'd surprise him.

The last thing she expected to see though, as she stepped out

of the cold and into the warm pub was Gemma Whitwell...
locked in a passionate embrace with her boyfriend. Frozen.
Unnoticed. A silent gasp lodged in her throat. She felt an
explosion in her stomach. Shocked, she turned on her heel and
left again, running all the way home, before collapsing into a
heap of tears through the front door.

She felt sick. So, so sick... as if her stomach had closed in on
itself, eventually crying herself to sleep. It had been a fitful sleep
though, two or three hours at the most. When she woke again,
early next morning, she found her mother in the kitchen making
tea. Falling into her arms, crying, she told her mother what she'd
seen, which was also when Ben turned up, tapping on their front
door. She refused to see him at first, but Ben was insistent,
begged Andrea to let him talk to her, and when her mother
suggested that everyone deserved at least one chance to explain
themselves, Leora had relented.

Ben had no idea she'd seen him kissing Gemma but when she
told him and he in turn recounted what happened, explaining
how Gemma had, quite literally, thrown herself at him, he was so
convincing Leora believed him. It was obvious he'd been crying
too. He looked worse than she did, so she could see how
genuinely sorry he was. So much so, in fact, he said he had found
himself wandering the streets during the early hours of the
morning waiting for the sun to rise, so he could call round and
tell her what had happened; explain how very sorry he was,
assuring her it would never, *ever* happen again.

He loved her, he said. Couldn't live without her. Relieved, she
had cried, *again*, although, quite how that was possible after the
river she'd shed, God only knew. Then, later, when her parents
were out, he showed her how much he loved her.

So, when, a week later she opened the package and a handful
of grainy Polaroid photos of Ben and Gemma lying together,
half-naked, fell into her lap, she almost vomited into her Rice
Krispies. They were pictures taken with a Polaroid camera, not

unlike the photos Jules took. However, where Jules's pics were fun; Leora sticking her tongue out, Eileen's sweet smile, Jules's 'peace' sign and Ali's 'fuck off' one, these photos were something else entirely.

Leora, barely able to breathe, sat frozen to her chair as her mother, blissfully unaware of the horror unfolding in front of her daughter, hummed along to a song on the radio. Leora stared at the photos in disbelief, trying to make sense of them. There were some of Ben on his own, naked from the waist up, but most of them were of Ben and Gemma... together.

She closed her eyes. Even now, the memory of it made her feel sick How could he? How could he do that to her? To them? She had trusted him implicitly. Believed in him. Loved him with all her foolish heart and soul. Even to this day though, she found it hard to get her head around. It was so out of character for the boy she thought she knew and loved; went against everything she trusted he was and everything she thought she had been to him.

Opening her eyes again, she looked up, vaguely aware of the head-butting pigeons gathering at her feet, eagerly eyeing up the wilted sandwich in her hand. She ripped what was left of her half-eaten lunch into bite-sized chunks and threw them to the wind. The pigeons chased them, flapping their wings, squawking, the larger ones pushing the smaller ones out of the way, not unlike what the Tube station would look like later after work.

The couple on the bench stood up and Leora watched as the boy kissed the girl again before they headed off, hand in hand; the hazy afternoon sunlight behind them. Tracing her fingers across her lips she wiped away a couple of breadcrumbs. Kissable lips, Ben had called them, she thought, remembering the many times he had kissed her kissable lips. She shook her head. Why, after all these years, could she still remember how *right* they had felt together.

*Because you're delusional, Leora. Because you thought Ben Thompson was someone he wasn't.* That's what Ali would say.

Probably *had* said, over the years. Why she still thought about him though, from time to time, she couldn't say. Maybe it was because her break-up with him had precluded the loss of Jules, followed a short time later by the loss of Lonny. It was impossible to think about one without the other two coming to mind because her memories of that terrible time overlapped one another, and her heartbreak, she supposed, despite the passing of time, was still very real.

It was far more manageable these days though. In the early days her grief had been loud and violent like the sound of a great orchestra; impressive, imposing, and impossible to quieten. She had lost her brother, a best friend, and her boyfriend, who had also not only broken her trust, but had stamped on it until all that was left were millions of tiny pieces that were impossible to put back together again. At that point, the orchestra in her head had risen to such a crescendo she firmly believed she would never think straight again.

These days though, for the most part, the orchestra was resting, only playing when she thought of them. But even then, if it was a good day, like today, it might simply be the faraway sound of a flute, or on a bad day, she might hear a cello playing, albeit the opening to Bach's Toccata and Fugue in D minor, but never the whole orchestra.

Sighing, she flicked her wrist. As usual, time had run away with itself. 'Time to go back to work,' she muttered quietly, putting her lunchbox back in her bag. Married now, with a daughter of her own, it was time she stopped giving any more headspace to Ben Thompson.

After all, she doubted he ever thought about her.

# CHAPTER 21

*L*ying on the bed, naked, Ben put his hands behind his head and listened to his wife singing in the bathroom; Status Quo's 'In The Army Now'. He wished she wouldn't. She did it every time he was home on leave. Thought, for some reason, it was funny. She wandered back into the bedroom wearing nothing more than a smile and a glint in her eye; a cloud of perfume, notes of vanilla and coconut, wafting behind her. It was hard to believe he had ended up marrying the girl who, in part, had been responsible for his break-up with Leora.

It started with a kiss, although not one he'd consented to, and even though it was years ago, he still remembered it like it was yesterday. He and Leora had argued, and he'd stormed off to the pub without her. After calming down, he phoned her and apologised. She, thank God, had forgiven him and they agreed to meet the following day.

Relieved, Ben had knocked back a few beers before Dobs shoved some money in his hand and asked him to get another round. He headed to the bar, the queue at least four people deep by then, and felt a tap on his shoulder. When he turned round, he saw Gemma.

'Hi.' She grinned, sucking on the straw in her glass.

'Hi,' Ben replied, feeling somewhat awkward.

'Oops,' she continued, looking down, wiping away a few drops of moisture that had dripped from the bottom of her glass onto her cleavage.

She was flirting with him, and he was flattered, he supposed, especially as most blokes in the pub would give their right arm to swap places with him. But he wasn't most blokes and as far as he was concerned there was only one girl for him.

'It's really busy in here tonight, isn't it?' Gemma smiled, fingering the thick diamanté necklace – that matched her long diamanté earrings – resting on her bronzed clavicle. 'When you get served,' she held her glass up, shook it, 'can you get me another Malibu and lemonade, please.'

Ben coughed, considered asking her if she had any money but then thought better of it. 'Yeah… okay… I suppose.'

'You have something on your lip.' She stepped towards him, her green eyes meeting his steely blue ones.

He had his back to the door; felt a waft of cold air dance on his neck as it opened; someone coming in or going out. 'Do I?' He frowned, using the back of his hand to wipe his mouth. 'Gone?'

'Nope, missed it,' she said, leaning in.

'Really?' Annoyed, Ben rubbed at his mouth like a six-year-old. 'What is it?'

To his complete surprise, Gemma grabbed his T-shirt and pulled him so close he could feel her breasts pressing against him. 'Me.' She placed her soft wet lips on his.

She tasted and smelled of coconut and for a few seconds Ben was so shocked, so completely taken aback, he didn't exactly return her kiss, but neither did he stop it. At least, not straight away. Eventually though, he came to his senses and pulled away.

'You're a nice girl, Gemma, you really are... but there's only one girl for me.'

Gemma shrugged, raised an eyebrow. 'Okay. Don't forget my Malibu and lemonade.' And with that she wandered back to the others.

Terrified they'd been seen, or worse still, Leora had turned up, Ben scanned the room, sweat pricking his forehead. Thankfully, most people, in their varying cliques of good-humoured inebriation, either hadn't noticed, or, if they had, didn't give a shit, and Leora, of course, was nowhere to be seen. He'd dodged a bullet, he reckoned. Still, even if someone had spotted him and told Leora about it, it wasn't like *he'd* instigated it. Gemma had kissed *him*, not the other way round. So surely, if he did find himself having to explain what had happened, she'd believe him – wouldn't she?

The following day, on a cold Sunday morning, heading to Leora's house, Ben decided honesty was the best policy. Only, he wasn't completely honest, and unfortunately it had come back to haunt him. Yes, he fessed up about the kiss, and luckily, because Leora loved him and trusted him, she had, after he explained what had happened, forgiven him. However, what he failed to mention was, how, when he'd woken up that morning, it was in a stranger's house, which turned out to be Gemma's house. If he'd confessed to that too, then maybe, just *maybe*, they could have salvaged something from the impending bomb that was about to land on Leora's doorstep a week later.

However, it was hard to explain something you had no memory of because, try as he might, he couldn't, even to this day, remember how he had ended up at Gemma's house in the first place, or why he was still there in the morning. All he did know was, when he woke up, half-dressed, disoriented and confused, he wasn't where he should be, at home in bed.

A violent throbbing pain around the back of his skull had forced him to sit up as he tried to remember where he was and how he had got there. Shuffling noises around him suggested he wasn't alone, although he appeared to have a sofa to himself. Holding his head in his hands, he remembered his phone call to Leora. He also remembered Gemma kissing him in the pub, and as his eyes adjusted to his surroundings, he remembered a group of them, in a circle, dancing around Dobs and Sally-Ann after Dobs got down on one knee and proposed to Sally-Ann.

He remembered the fifth pint... and the sixth... and the seventh. Then he vaguely remembered not feeling well; Dobs ribbing him for being a lightweight. He also remembered being led back to Gemma's house, whose parents were away; Dobs and Sally-Ann and a few of the others in tow. He remembered seeing bright lights too, randomly flashing in his eyes. But the rest was a complete blank. With creeping dread, it was then, he realised, if he wasn't home, or at Dobs's house – where he'd been known to crash on the odd occasion – he must still be at Gemma's house?

Unsure, he looked round and spotted a lamp next to the sofa he'd been sleeping on. He was tempted to snap it on but the pain radiating across his head and down through his eyes convinced him otherwise. Instead, he reached for what looked like a small picture frame beside the lamp, which was also when someone close by, on the floor, let out a loud snort. A rustling sound followed, as if someone were shifting position, before the room fell quiet again. Ben squinted at the photo, forcing his eyes to focus. He was, he realised, thanks to a shaft of light radiating through a gap in the curtains, looking at a younger version of Gemma Whitwell. She looked, with her long, limp, rusty coloured hair instead of the short dark way she wore it now, about ten years old. But it was definitely her.

*Fuck*, he thought, putting the photo back just as someone farted, quickly followed by a voice he recognised as Trev's, hoarse from being woken, randomly shouting at whoever it was to keep the bloody noise down. Ben, who didn't say a word, held his head in hands again. Had he been so drunk he'd passed out on

Gemma's sofa? It would be a first for him if he had. Thank God it was just her sofa though and not her bed.

Still, even just being there felt wrong, like a betrayal to Leora.

Racked with guilt he found his discarded shirt, which he screwed into a ball, and headed for the front door, carefully picking his way through the other sleeping bodies strewn across the floor. In the hallway he found his jacket, which he threw over his shoulder, and quietly opened the door.

Outside, he glanced at his watch and shivered. It was bitterly cold and at 5.40am, it was also still dark. He quickly slipped his shirt and jacket on for warmth. It was, he realised, feeling tiny pinpricks of moisture on his face, still raining too, like last night... when he'd left Leora. He stood for a moment, watching the rain intermittently turn to gold dust beneath the orange streetlights, wishing to God he hadn't left her last night. He knew if she caught wind of this, how bad it would look, the damage it might cause, even though, that stupid kiss aside, he was reasonably sure nothing had happened between him and Gemma.

Still, if he hadn't been so bloody stupid and walked out on Leora in the first place, he wouldn't now be walking home in the rain at stupid o' clock in the morning wondering how the hell he'd got himself in such a predicament in the first place. From now on he'd keep his stupid emotions in check. Gathering his bearings, he headed home. He felt antsy though, agitated, found himself, despite the cold and his tiredness, heading for Leora's house instead. It was a little after six by the time he arrived; far too early to be knocking on the door on a Sunday morning, so he headed for the bus shelter up the road, which, like every other bus shelter he had ever sat in, stank of piss. While he waited, he trawled his memories, trying again, to find the missing pieces of last night, but sadly nothing was forthcoming.

A little after seven, he headed back to Leora's house, relieved to see a light on downstairs. Taking a deep breath, he walked up the drive and knocked, quietly, on the front door. Andrea, dressing gown wrapped tight around her slim frame, opened it.

'I know about you and Gemma,' Leora said, when she eventually agreed to talk to him. 'I came to the pub to surprise you but it turns out you surprised me instead.' The anger, the sarcasm in her voice was undeniable, but so too was the hurt in her eyes.

*Shit*, he thought, panicking, following her into the living room, the hissing gas fire welcome relief from the cold that had gnawed at his bones for the last hour or so. *If she knew about that, what else did she know?*

She sat on the sofa, and after some trepidation he sat next to her. Face blotchy, eyes red-rimmed and swollen, it was obvious she'd been crying. His heart sank. He hated seeing her so upset, especially when he was the cause of it.

He reached for her hand, but she snatched it back. Panicking, nausea churning in his gut, he told her how sorry he was. That it wasn't how it had looked. 'She kissed me,' he explained. 'Not the other way round.'

She refused to listen at first. 'You could have pulled away.'

'I know… and I did. I was just so shocked at first… I… I… for whatever reason, couldn't think straight. But I told her… there's only one girl for me.'

It took a while, but eventually, Leora relented, and this time when he reached for her hand, she let him. He told her how much he loved her and how he would never *ever* do anything to jeopardise that again.

He didn't tell her that he'd woken up at Gemma's house. Why? Because it was far too complicated. She'd never understand. Especially when he himself didn't understand how he'd ended up there. Besides, he'd snuck out early, so hopefully, by the time everyone else who had crashed there had woken up, no one would be any the wiser. Never though, after coming so close to losing Leora, would he walk out on her like that again.

So, all was well again, or so it seemed, and life went back to normal – for a week.

Then the photos turned up at Leora's house and Ben's world exploded. There were no second chances this time and when Leora said she *never* wanted to see him again, he thought he would never get over it. Barely able to eat, or sleep, he knew then, for the first time in his life, what it felt like to suffer from a broken heart.

He had gone to see Gemma then. Demanded to know what she thought she was playing at. Bewildered, she said she had neither taken the photos, nor had she sent them.

'Well, who the fuck did then?' he yelled.

'I don't know,' her screamed reply. 'Someone at the party, not someone I know, or recognised, had a camera, and kept wandering round, taking photos of everyone. I thought they were a friend of yours, or Dobs, or one of the others.'

'Male or female?'

'Male. Definitely a boy.' She then explained how, with everyone gathered in the kitchen, Ben, who had been leaning on her, asked her if she wanted to go upstairs. 'We didn't make it that far though. Instead, we ended up in the living room, where you pulled me onto the sofa, took your shirt off and started kissing me.' Confused, his anger dissipating like air from a deflating balloon, Ben put his hand to his head and tapped it, trying to remember. 'The next thing I knew that boy, whoever he was, was leaning over us, taking photos. He left soon after.'

Embarrassed, nauseous, Ben, try as he might, couldn't remember any of it. For the briefest of moments, his anger returned. 'I don't believe you,' he yelled. 'Tell me the truth.'

Angry, Gemma, who burst into tears, said she was telling the truth and told him to piss off.

He didn't give up though. He was determined not to lose Leora, at least not without a fight. He spoke to Dobs, asked him if

121

he could shed any light on Ben's lost hours, but drink-wise he'd been in a pretty bad way himself, and he couldn't.

'I wasn't as bad as you, mind,' Dobs added. 'You were well out of it. Steaming, in fact. I did think about calling you a taxi at one point, or walking you home, but as everyone was piling back to Gemma's house, which was just round the corner, Gemma said it made more sense to take you there, let you sleep it off. It took three of us to prop you up, mind. Me on one side, Gemma and Sally-Ann on the other.' Again, Ben had no recollection. He asked Dobs if he knew what happened next, but he didn't. 'Gemma took you to the living room while everyone else piled into the kitchen, raiding the cupboards for booze. Sally-Ann and I left soon after.'

Again, Ben couldn't remember any of it. *Why?* he wondered. It wasn't like he couldn't hold his drink. And it wasn't like he'd drunk any more than usual. At least, that's what his wallet suggested. So it didn't make sense.

For the next month or so Ben called Leora, daily. She never took his calls, but he kept trying anyway. He also wrote a diatribe of self-loathing letters, marked with the rings of a pint glass, sealed with the tears of a clown. He said he couldn't explain why he'd done what he'd done, but if she would just give him a chance, she'd see how sorry he was. He tried meeting her off the college bus too, but like a guard dog, growling and snarling, Ali wouldn't let him near her.

He even called round to her house, but Marty made it clear that Ben was not to bother his daughter anymore. 'When a woman says no, Ben, she means no.'

'Please let me see her,' Ben pleaded, sick with panic. 'Just for a minute... just to explain?'

Marty folded his arms and shook his head. 'She doesn't want to see you,' he repeated. His delivery was soft but there was no denying the authority in his voice. 'I'm very disappointed in you, son. I thought you were better than that.'

*Son* – Marty had called him son. He'd treated him like one too, which was when the enormity of what he'd done began to sink in. He hadn't just let Leora down; he'd let her whole family down too. And just like that, the fight in him was gone. He headed home then, vowing, from thereon in, he'd respect Leora's wishes and leave her alone. But he did so with a heavy heart. His world had stopped on its axis. He had lost the love of his life and wondered if he'd ever love like that again.

Now, all these years later, he was married to Gemma with a two-year-old son. It wasn't a deliberate act, more fortuitous the way the two of them had ended up together. He had, for a while at least, deliberately gone out of his way to avoid Gemma, blaming her, in part, for his break-up with Leora. He had even, one night at the pub, when she approached him and asked him how he was, drunkenly, and rather shamefully, told her to piss off. So, when, a year or so later he bumped into her again, he apologised and offered to buy her a drink. She accepted, they talked, and when she asked him if he'd like to see her again, he said yes.

Fun, and easy to be around, she worked as a beautician, and whether he was still on the rebound from Leora, or whether it was a case of, if you can't beat 'em, join 'em, somehow, he had ended up marrying the girl. He had no regrets though. Gemma supported his decision to join the Special Forces and even though it was dangerous and meant being away from home for long periods of time without any contact, she never made a fuss. He was grateful to her for that because he loved his job, and he loved her too, in his own way. Leora though, was never far from his thoughts and he often found himself wondering what she was up to.

Whatever it was, he hoped she was happy.

'Do you really have to go?' Gemma pouted, interrupting his thoughts, having spent the last ten minutes bouncing up and down on top of him, making what was hard now gratefully limp and lifeless.

He glanced at his watch, nodded. 'Afraid so. My train leaves in two hours and I promised Dobs I'd nip round and see him before I go.' Gemma, sitting up, her plump breasts on full display, sighed. 'Here,' he said, reaching for his wallet and pulling out a couple of crisp notes. 'It's still early. Go to town and get yourself something nice to wear for the party tonight.'

The corners of her downturned mouth lifted into a smile. 'Okay,' she mumbled. 'Won't be much of a party without you, though.'

'Come on, Gem, don't be like that.' Ben got out of bed. 'At least I got to spend Christmas at home.'

'I know,' she huffed, raking a hand through her hair. 'It's just... this year feels important... and it's a shame you're going to miss it.'

Ben laughed, leaned over, and kissed the top of her head. 'It's New Year's Eve, the same as any other.'

Ben went to the bathroom and showered, listening to Pulp's 'Disco 2000' playing quietly in the background. 1999 was coming to a close and every man and his dog, or so it seemed, had invested in the idea that the start of a new millennium meant the start of something amazing. Either that, or they were going on about the millennium bug, or Y2K as it was referred to, a widespread computer programming shortcut that some were expecting to bring down all the major computer system infrastructures when the year changed from 1999 to 2000. Ben had grave doubts, on both counts.

Creeping into Sam's room, he kissed his sleeping two-year-old son goodbye and felt his heart twinge. He loved his job, but it had been much easier before he had a child. Before his son came along the thought of dying had never really crossed Ben's mind, but when his son arrived, the idea of never seeing him again, or leaving him fatherless, played heavily on him.

*I'll give it a few more years,* he thought, kissing Gemma at the door, *then maybe I'll think about doing something else.*

'Stay safe,' Gemma called, teeth chattering, pulling her dressing gown tighter.

'I will.' Ben smiled, putting his hand up, before climbing into the taxi he'd booked. Dobs and Sally-Ann, who were visiting, were staying with Dobs's parents for a few days. Ben had heard rumours that Sally-Ann had been cheating on Dobs. How true that was Ben couldn't say. If he'd pushed her, he knew Gemma would have told him if she'd heard anything. However, Ben also knew ignorance was bliss. Besides which, the rumour mill in the forces could be brutal, and yes, while some *were* true, others were most definitely not. So, unless Dobs brought it up, Ben wouldn't either.

Wiping the steamed-up window with his cuff, Ben watched the streets of his childhood flash by. After living in married quarters in various locations for several years, Gemma decided, once Ben had joined the Special Forces, she wanted to be closer to her family again, especially once they'd decided to try for a baby, which had pleased his mother no end.

Since her split from his father, Ben's mother, Joyce, had remained single, but happily so, it appeared. As for his mother's relationship with his father, well, it had never been better, which still to this day baffled Ben. Why his parents hadn't split up sooner, or why they had even married in the first place, remained a complete mystery to him. Still, he was pleased his parents had a good relationship. His mother even got on well with Wendy too, which meant there was no awkwardness at family gatherings and was both a blessing and a relief when he and Gemma tied the knot.

They had married on a warm June afternoon at St Michael's church. Gemma's white dress, with plunging neckline, was huge, as were the bridesmaids' dresses – seven of them no less. Dobs was best man and the two of them looked, Ben thought, wearing light grey morning suits and matching crew cuts, quite dapper. A reception for sixty people followed at The George Hotel where tables, heavy with flowers and glassware, complimented the waterfalls of wine and candy-coloured platters of hors d'oeuvres, not to mention the trays of ocean creatures drizzled in various sorts of jus and sauces. For mains, guests had a choice of three dishes and the dessert trolleys with their meringue nests bursting with fruit and profiterole towers dripping in chocolate were enough to make anyone drool. Food fit for an officer's mess, Ben remembered thinking at the time.

It wasn't his cup of tea. He would have happily eloped, preferably to somewhere remote. A small cottage in the Cotswolds, say; a takeaway pizza, a couple of bottles of cheap plonk... and each other. The ostentatious extravaganza that had been their wedding was Gemma's dream, but if she was happy, then Ben was too. All in all, though, it had, despite his initial reservations, been a good day.

Driving by the church, he looked to his left and spotted the Burghley Club. His gasp as he stared at the nondescript building was a silent one, quickly followed by a sinking feeling. *Lonny,* he thought, remembering the gig he'd helped him with on that Friday night before everything with Leora went to rat-shit. That was the other sad reality about his break-up with her, he hadn't just lost her, he'd lost Lonny too, and her parents. Not that, on the odd occasion he bumped into them, they didn't speak. They weren't like that. Even Lonny who, half playfully, half for real, threatened to whoop his arse, had been okay with him. 'You're an idiot, Thompson,' he'd simply said, slapping him on the back, reminding him again how every action had a reaction.

Running a hand across his head, Ben sat back and sighed. He glanced up at the sky, found himself wishing Lonny, who he was sure would be in heaven had he believed in such a place, well. Hoped that, whatever he was up to, he was doing it with gusto and keeping everyone on their toes.

'What d'ya think to this Millennium Dome thing they've built in London then?' the taxi driver asked, interrupting Ben's thoughts. Ben shrugged. He didn't know what to think really. After the sights he'd witnessed over the years, it was hard not to be cynical, to think the money could be put to better use. 'Waste of money if you ask me,' the taxi driver continued, to which Ben smiled, nodded.

'Just pull up here, mate,' Ben said, as the reccy came into view. 'I'll walk the rest of the way.'

Filled with a sudden urge to retrace the footsteps of his youth he headed towards the great oak tree in the park. Rain earlier had replaced the snow, which had in turn brought a rapid and much-needed thaw, although a blanket of delicate lace, crunching under foot, still draped itself across the playing field.

Shoving his hands in his pockets, he paused, watching younger versions of himself and his friends playing footie. He saw Lonny too, disappearing over the horizon, giving chase to the scallywag that had nicked his cousin's bike, and, as he continued walking, he saw Leora, sitting beneath the huge oak tree in the far corner of the field, looking up at him, blinking, shielding her eyes from the sun with one hand, patting the grass with her other. He remembered how, holding hands, they would lie together under the shade of the tree, sharing his headphones, listening to Yazoo's 'Only You' on his Walkman; the same song they had first kissed to at the school disco.

'You and me, were meant to be,' he whispered.

Did Leora ever think about him, he wondered. Married, with a daughter, or so he'd heard, she now lived and worked in London. He hoped she did think about him from time to time. He doubted it though. But if she did, he also hoped she had found it in her heart to forgive him.

# CHAPTER 22

*L*eora watched as father and daughter continued to chase one another in ever decreasing circles around the living room. Arms folded, she pretended to be angry. 'Tim, *please*. I need to give Mia her bath.'

Smiling, Tim glanced at Leora before scooping their young daughter into his arms and throwing her into the air.

Mia squealed with delight. 'More, Daddy, more!'

Leora frowned. 'Tim. We've only got a couple of hours before everyone starts arriving and I haven't even had a shower yet.'

With one arm around his daughter's waist, his cheek pressed firmly to hers, Tim used his other hand to push a strand of dark hair away from her face. 'Uh-oh. I think we're in trouble,' he whispered, loud enough for Leora to hear. Mia looked at her mother, then her father, and started giggling.

Leora rolled her eyes but couldn't help smiling. 'You do remember it's New Year's Eve, right, and we're having a party tonight?'

'I want to go to the party,' Mia shouted. 'Please, Daddy, please.'

'You're too little, Mia,' Leora replied.

Placing two chubby hands on either cheek of her father's face,

Mia ignored her mother and pressed her forehead against Tim's, staring longingly into his eyes. *'Please*, Daddy – I'm a big girl now. *Please* can I go to the party?'

Eyebrows arched; Tim turned to Leora. 'She'll be all right for an hour?'

Leora sighed. There was no use arguing. Father and daughter were as thick as thieves. 'Okay. But you can bath her and get her ready. I have enough to do.'

Mia punched the air with her tiny fist. 'Yay,' she squealed. 'Can I wear my princess dress? The one with the bue fowers?'

'Of course, you can.' Leora laughed. 'But you can only stay up for an hour – okay? That's the deal. Then it's off to bed at nine o' clock.'

'Deal, Mummy,' Mia replied, wriggling to escape her father's arms.

Tim bent down and released her, his eyes following his daughter as she hurriedly clobbered up the stairs. 'C'mon, Daddy,' she demanded. 'I need to get ready.'

'Okay, okay. I'm coming,' Tim replied, laughing; the pitter-patter of her small footsteps echoing in the hallway.

'No rest for the wicked, eh?' Leora said.

'Apparently not.' Tim gently kissed her on the cheek.

'Wilful like her father.'

'Beautiful like her mother.'

'Hardly.' Leora glanced down at her old T-shirt and worn-out tracksuit bottoms. 'Give me thirty minutes though. It's amazing what a bit of make-up can do.'

'You don't need it.'

'Clearly you need your eyes testing.' She laughed.

She turned, caught sight of the two of them in the hallway mirror. She, pasty, eyes rimmed pink, had a bit of a gaunt, slightly haggard look going on, whereas Tim, despite the lines that criss-crossed his brow and the flecks of grey in his five o'clock shadow, looked distinguished. In his mid-thirties he'd aged well. He'd put the effort in. He worked out, ate well, didn't smoke, and only drank at the weekends.

She, on the other hand, ate on the run, hardly ever worked out and loved a glass of wine in the evening. She had quit smoking though, and the baby weight she gained while carrying Mia had gone within a couple of months. Whether that was down to genetics or Ali, she couldn't say. Both probably.

True to form Ali hadn't held back when she noticed a little pouch around Leora's midriff after she'd had Mia.

'Oh my God,' she gasped, one evening when Tim was out gigging. She had popped by to watch Mia for an hour so Leora could have a much-needed soak in the bath.

'What?' Leora said, panicking. Mia was sleeping and Ali had wandered into the bathroom with a glass of fizz for Leora just as she had stepped out of the bath. Following Ali's horrified gaze, she looked down, half expecting to see blood between her legs, but there was none.

'Your stomach,' she said, her hand covering her mouth. 'It's so... well... saggy.'

Leora had been mortified at the time. She'd only been out of hospital a few weeks and was still trying to get her head round the constant demands of a newborn, never mind worrying about how she looked. It was only when Ali pointed out how unsightly her tummy was that she gave it any real thought. Sleep deprived and anxious, she burst into tears.

Ali rushed forward, wrapping her in a bath towel that had been warming on the radiator. 'Oh, Leora, I'm sorry.' She hugged her tight, stroking her wet hair. 'I didn't mean to upset you. I just worry about you. Especially knowing how, in Tim's line of work, there's always going to be younger, fitter women snapping at your heels.'

She wasn't wrong. Tim worked in advertising. Designer suits and power dressing was the norm, including the women who, with their sleek hair, killer heels, and ruthless ambition were as glossy and intimidating as the magazine ads they worked on. Still, it was the kickstart she needed. She started slowly at first, going to a post-natal Pilates class twice a week before investing in a jogging stroller, combining trips to the park with exercise.

She enjoyed it too, getting out in the fresh air, meeting new people. It was just what she needed to help wash away the baby blues. Within weeks the extra baby weight was gone, and within a couple of months she was stronger and fitter than she was before she was pregnant. Tim was thrilled. Even Ali was a little taken aback. Once Mia was walking though, she gave up running, especially after Ali pointed out how gaunt she looked. She had stuck with the Pilates though, until she started working again.

Now she didn't bother with either; with all the rushing around, she didn't need to.

Tim stared at her, gently brushing her cheek with his hand. Her tummy flipped, reminding her of the first night they met.

'It's true,' he continued, tracing the outline of her lips with his finger. 'So, so beautiful,' he whispered, leaning in to kiss her. It was an urgent kiss, full of intent but his lips were soft and warm, a hint of whisky on his breath. She kissed him back; felt him harden as he pulled her towards him, his lips moving to her neck, hot and breathy.

Leora groaned, threw her head back. 'Drinking whisky and feeling frisky?' she heard herself saying, the tone of her voice so very different to her mummy voice or her work voice.

The overwhelming feeling running through her though was one of relief. Relief that her body was responding to his. It had been months since they last made love and she was beginning to think there was something wrong with her. There was nothing wrong with her now though. Every part of her body tingled; wet, yet at the same time on fire. With his back to the stairs, still kissing her neck, Tim stuck his hand inside her T-shirt and slowly caressed her breasts. Lost in the moment, she felt dizzy, until the big voice of a small girl brought her crashing back to earth.

'Daa-dee, are you hurting Mummy?'

Tim snatched his hand from Leora's T-shirt and jumped back, his face as flushed as hers felt. 'Of course he isn't. Mummy and Daddy were just having cuddles.'

'Why were you making ouch noises then?'

Tim laughed and Leora looked to him for help. 'Because that's what adults do sometimes.' He grinned, before turning round and heading up the stairs, scooping Mia into his arms and heading to the bathroom. 'Come on, young lady, bath time. You have a party to get ready for.'

Smiling, Leora watched them disappear. *Oh well*, she thought, heading into the large living room that still contained the huge Christmas tree that days earlier had been surrounded by beautifully gift-wrapped presents, for Mia mostly, *maybe we can play catch up later*. Theirs, a Georgian semi in Tooting, was a beautiful home. A renovation project in an area that was, according to the estate agent when they'd viewed it, with its good bus and Tube links, up and coming.

Deliriously happy when they first moved in, a somewhat rocky patch followed, which was also when Leora discovered she was pregnant. Advice from Ali, and a few others, was to have a termination. She thought about it, initially, but when she broke the news of her pregnancy to Tim, he was so thrilled, she decided to keep it, and despite her initial reservations, Mia proved to be the cement she and Tim needed to bring them back together again. Her only hope now though was, with Tim's offer to work in the States, that it was a strong enough bond to carry them across the water and on to their next adventure.

They hadn't told anyone yet, except Tim's parents, but had planned to make an announcement tonight, which in a way, Leora was dreading, mostly because she still hadn't told the one person who deserved to know – Ali.

She'd meant to tell her, but for some reason she never found the right moment, probably because, knowing Ali, she'd take it one of two ways. Either she'd be royally pissed off – and rightly so – or, she'd be really pleased. Leora hoped it was the latter, especially as not telling her before now felt like a betrayal.

Leora supposed it was in a way. Especially as, during her first two terrible, drink-, drug- and grief-fuelled years in London, Ali was the one person that had stuck by her side. The one person that held her hair back when she was vomiting down the loo, *again*, after a night out. The one person who dried her tears and wiped her mouth. The one person who brought her a glass of water and splashed her face just as gently as her own mother had when she was ill as a child. The one person who had half-carried, half-guided her back to her room, who, afraid she might choke, had laid next to her all night, stroking her hair, and shushing her to sleep. The one person who, after losing Ben, and Jules, and Lonny, and as good as abandoned by her parents, was always there for her, at every single turn.

*Shit*, she thought, scrubbing her face to ease the tension she'd felt bubbling beneath the surface all day. Ali should have been the first person she told. She owed her that much, and yet she'd gone out of her way not to. Why though? She didn't know why. If someone held a gun to her head, told her to explain why in one word, she'd probably say fear. Fear of Ali's reaction. Fear of losing her friendship. Fear of fucking up without her.

Yes, that's what it was. Fear. She was afraid Ali would present her with the whole picture; the great adventure she was embarking on, alongside the huge risk she was taking. Sometimes though, just sometimes, Leora didn't want to see the whole picture. Sometimes, like the snapshots Jules used to take of them when they were kids, she wanted to let the picture develop over time.

She sighed, went to the kitchen to check on the food cooking in the oven; hors d'oeuvres mostly, finger food her guests could eat alongside cold cuts, cheese boards, and fresh bread. Food that was easy to eat but would soak up the alcohol. Glancing up, she heard the faint sound of laughter, the splashing of water. She smiled, pictured Tim singing some bizarre sea shanty, Mia joining in, whipping up a bubble infested storm, the two of them soaked to the skin.

Satisfied that everything was as it should be, Leora went to the window, and looked out. It was pitch-black already. She hated the long, dark nights. In that sense winter always tugged at her Caribbean roots. Even as children she and Lonny preferred summer to winter. That's why LA was so appealing. She wondered what Grandma Cedella, had she still been around, would have thought about her going to America, having not yet told her parents. She would tell her off is what she would do. Shake her head and frown. Tell her she was weak, cowardly, fraidy-fraidy.

She'd be right of course. But her relationship with her parents since Lonny passed away was complicated. Grandma Cedella, when she'd talked to her about it, disagreed. She said, that even though Lonny's death had taken its toll on everyone, if anything, the lesson that should have been learned was how important family was. How it should have brought them all together, not pushed them apart. 'At de end of de day, Lee-ora, family is family and love is love.'

Leora missed her grandmother's wise words and big laugh, but unlike Lonny and Jules, her passing, a little over two years ago now, which, at the age of seventy-two was still not particularly old, had been somewhat easier to process, if only because, she had, Leora reasoned, at least had a life. It was a shame though, she thought, her breath misting up the window, that Mia would never know her feisty great-grandmother.

Pressing her head against the cold glass of the window, her heart suddenly heavy, Leora closed her eyes. She hated not seeing her parents, had found herself wondering so many times how, after growing up in such a happy, loving environment, it had come to this, how the gap between them had become so wide. Grief, she knew, was the biggest culprit. Guns blazing it had blown her family apart and she had no idea how or if she wanted to rebuild it again.

Had her parents really loved Lonny more than her? She remembered her mother's face lighting up whenever he entered a room. Or was it simply that, because, like her, Lonny was, in their small town, seen as a minority, which made her naturally more protective of him?

Leora did remember an incident when she was very little, and she asked her mother what a nigger was.

'Where did you hear that word?' her mother demanded, her rage so swift, Leora was almost rendered speechless. 'You tell me *now*, Leora Jackson,' she fumed. 'Who called your brother that awful word?'

Startled, Leora had been thoroughly taken aback, not least because no one had called Lonny anything. She and her friends had simply been playing French skipping in the school playground.

'We couldn't decide who should stand at the ends, or who should go first. So we did "eenie meenie miney mo",' Leora, lip trembling, explained. 'While we were singing it, we all said we didn't know what a ni...' She paused. 'What one of those words was.' She went on to say that, because it squealed when it was caught by the toe, they all concluded it must be an animal. Something little, maybe, like a cat or a mouse? 'Paula Farrington said her father kept ferrets and they squealed... a *lot*. So maybe it was one of those?'

Her mother had smiled then, the relief on her face palpable, only adding to then teary-eyed Leora's confusion. It was only later, of course, when she was older, and a little wiser, did her mother's outburst make any sense. The irony being, of course, Lonny didn't need protecting. If anything, it was the other way round, and he was always the one looking out for her. Even in their baby photographs, Lonny, who was ten minutes older than Leora, often had his arm around her.

He'd been so good with her too, when she and Ben had split up, encouraging her to eat when she felt too sick, travelling with her to London for her audition. Then, in the autumn, when she finally headed off, he gave her a gift. A CD he had made specially for her; a compilation of all the music they had listened to as kids. 'Whenever you're feeling homesick,' he said, 'play track number one and think of me.'

Track number one, she discovered later that evening, was 'I'll Be There' by the Jackson 5. The same song they had danced to together as two-year-olds, the same song Lonny made her dance to when Ben broke her heart and she thought she would never dance again. When he passed away, she felt like she had been cleaved in two, as if a part of her had become untethered. Ben may have been her soulmate – or at least she thought he was, once – but Lonny, who had shared her mother's womb with her, was, in every sense, her other half.

For the longest time, with her insides feeling hollowed out, her heart a pebble of grief, she couldn't listen to that song because it was just too painful. Lately though, if she heard it in passing, instead of fleeing in floods of tears, she found herself pausing to listen, reminded of happier times. In fact, she would even go as far as to say, when she did hear it, she knew, like she suddenly knew now, Lonny was with her, or at least his spirit was, looking out for her like he'd always done as a child, as a baby, before they were born even.

# CHAPTER 23

*B*en waved goodbye to everyone who had taken it upon themselves to see him off at the door into yet another waiting taxi, this time to the train station. The Dobson family, when he arrived, had welcomed him, like they always did, with open arms; he their adopted son, they his surrogate family. As ever, the house, when he first arrived, despite the early hour, leaked with noise and as usual the hospitality was second to none. Dobs seemed in reasonably good spirits, as did four-year-old Jacob, who, it had to be said, looked more like his father every time Ben saw him. Sally-Ann, however, although courteous, seemed miles away.

'Still enjoying the SF?' Dobs asked.

They were perched on the ends of a pair of sofas and Ben, cradling his second cup of tea, glanced round, his eyes dancing furtively. His profession was not supposed to be common knowledge. As far as the Dobson family knew, he was still serving in the army, like Dobs. Dobs grinned. 'Don't look so worried. No one's listeni–'

'Dad-dee?' A small voice interrupted him. It was Jacob, who jumped onto his father's broad back.'

'Yes, Jacob?' Dobs glanced round at his son.

'What does SF mean?'

Eyebrow arched, Ben looked at Dobs and grinned. 'SF?' Dobs replied, confusion on his face. 'Where did you hear that?'

Jacob climbed onto his father's knee. 'From you,' he replied, pointing to Ben. 'To him... Uncle Ben.'

'Ah, I see. I didn't say SF. I said AF.'

Jacob's small brow creased into a frown. 'AF? Okay... what does AF mean?'

'AF is short for Armed Forces because, like Daddy, Ben is a soldier in the army, remember?'

Jacob nodded, wriggled off his father's knee again and went to join his cousins, engrossed in a game of Operation.

'Too bright for his own good, that one,' Ben said. 'And in answer to your question, yes, I'm still enjoying it. It's a lot harder now though, with Sam, especially now he's older, more aware. Thankfully, he was sleeping when I left.'

'Really?' Dobs's eyebrows shot up. 'Jacob still has us up at the crack of dawn most days.'

Ben laughed, shook his head. 'Sam had me up at four this morning. I should have made him go back to bed, but I decided to sit and play with the little fella for a while instead. By the time Gemma woke up a few hours later, I'd given him his breakfast and he'd gone back to bed for a nap, otherwise they'd have come with me.'

Dobs glanced at his wife, sitting with his sisters. 'Yeah well... I'm sure the girls will catch up with one another before we leave.'

Following his gaze, Ben noticed Sally-Ann, eyes glazed, was not so much talking but staring into space. 'Is... erm... everything all right?' Ben asked.

Dobs shrugged; looked down at his hands. 'Dunno, mate,' he sighed. 'I don't seem to be able to put a foot right these days.' Looking up again, he smiled but his eyes didn't follow suit. 'Nothing we can't figure out, I reckon,' he added nonchalantly.

Ben nodded just as Brenda, Dobs's mother, thrust a plate of food in front of his face.

'It's curry,' she offered. 'Homemade, like. From the leftover turkey. Plus, a couple of mince pies,' she added.

'For God's sake, Mum,' Dobs said, glancing at the clock on the mantlepiece. 'Curry... at 9.30 in the morning.'

Brenda looked at her son like she didn't have the foggiest idea what he was talking about. 'Of course,' she said, very matter of fact. 'Man can't march on an empty stomach now, can he.'

Ben laughed. 'Thanks, Brenda. It's not the first time I've had curry for breakfast.'

'See.' Brenda looked at her son, a smug grin on her face.

Dobs smiled, watched his mother's retreating back, a glint of pride in his eyes. 'Never knowingly underfed in the Dobson household, eh, Thompson.' He winked.

No sooner had he arrived though, Ben, it seemed, was preparing to leave again, and while other family members congregated at the door, Dobs walked him to the chugging taxi, its exhaust smoking like an old steam train. 'Stay safe, Thompson.' He offered Ben his hand. 'Let's try and go for a pint next time though, eh?'

'Course.' Ben smiled, shaking his friend's outstretched hand. 'I'd love to.' He was tempted to lean in, give him a quick manly hug because beneath that cheeky grin, that tough guy exterior, Ben could see Dobs was struggling. 'Write to me if you want?' he said, slapping his arm instead. 'I can't promise a prompt reply... but I'll do my best.'

'Thanks, mate,' Dobs said. 'I might just do that.'

The taxi dropped Ben off at the station where he stood on the platform waiting for his train. Still cold, despite the shift in temperature, he blew on his hands; his breath turning to little puffs of smoke every time he opened his mouth. It wasn't bad though, not compared to some of the arctic temperatures he'd experienced over the years, usually in the unlikeliest places.

Hours from now, he would, he suspected, be back in the searing heat of the desert. What most people didn't know about the desert though, was just how cold it was.

Ben's first real experience of the desert was in 1991 when, on 2nd January he received the phone call he'd both anticipated and dreaded. Operation Granby – Desert Storm to the Yanks – the British name for the build-up to the Gulf War, had been called. Until then Ben had seen very little action, so, for the first time since joining the army, soldiering was no longer an idea but something terrifyingly real. He wasn't afraid to admit that when the call came, and he put the phone down, his legs felt like jelly.

By 30th January, after passing through Jubail, collecting their bergens, weapons and kitbags, Ben, along with the other troops from his platoon were shown their accommodation at Rezayat Camp, Saudi Arabia: a two-man portacabin with bunkbed, toilet, sink and shower, it had all the mod cons, so wasn't half bad. Their duties, they were informed, would include prisoner escort, which Ben knew meant frontline action. Outwardly, he tried to look as excited as everyone else did, inwardly though he wondered if anyone else's stomach was turning somersaults.

Wake-up call the following morning was Sergeant Bridger telling Ben and the rest of the troops to move their fucking arses, followed by kit check and weapons inspection. The troops then went on parade, waiting for transport, followed by a two-and-a-half-hour drive through the desert for training at Devil Dog Dragoon Ranges. Ben bagged himself a window seat and stared out at his surroundings. It was exciting – for a few minutes. However, except for the odd camel lying dead by the roadside, the odd lizard or two taking shelter under the odd rock here and there, the view of the desert remained much the same. Mile after mile of winding road sandwiched between vast expanses of scorched sand as the sun, like a huge ball of yellow wax, rose above the barren land like a malevolent, unblinking eye.

Feeling a sharp nudge in his ribs, Ben looked round to see

Private Andrew Sharp staring at him. His huge grin and bulbous shaped eyes reminding Ben of a wide-mouthed frog.

'All right, Dick. Fuck all going on out there, eh?' He craned his neck, to see out of the dusty window.

Sharpie was bit of an idiot, the class clown. A likeable clown though. He was also the first person to discover Ben's full name – Benedict – a name his mother had supposedly picked because it meant 'blessed'. Whether or not that was true, Ben had no idea. What he did know though was, right from a young age, he didn't like it. His father had always called him Ben, and as soon as he could talk, Ben insisted everyone else do the same. Now though, thanks to Andy, his secret was out.

'Listen up, boys,' Andy said one night in barracks. 'Old Benny boy here likes to eat dick... apparently.'

Ben asked him what the hell he was talking about.

'Well now, Thompson, let's just say that a little birdy tells me that Ben ain't your real name... is it?'

Ben, whose cheeks started burning, warned Andy to keep his trap shut. Which, of course, only added fuel to the fire and made everyone *more* curious. 'Go on then, Sharpie,' another one of the other lads shouted. 'If his name ain't Ben... what is it?'

Grinning, Sharpie drew a breath. 'Benedict,' he guffawed.

Everyone looked at one another, before turning back to Ben.

'Ben-e-what?' someone else said.

'Benedict,' Sharpie repeated, the room thick with amused snorts. 'As in... Ben-Eats-Dicks... get it?' Sharpie continued, now crying with so much laughter, he had to hold his stomach.

'Benedict?' someone else shouted, unable to keep the dismay out of his voice. 'What kind of poncy name is that?'

'Well, lads, as he obviously likes dick so much, I think that's what we'll call him from now on.' Sharpie slapped Ben's back, as all around him Ben found himself the object of the room's good-humoured hilarity.

From that day on, the name stuck. Fortunately, though, the

lads he trained with were a good bunch. They didn't mean anything by it, and besides, if you couldn't stand a bit of ribbing, you had no place in the army.

'You, nervous?' Ben turned to Sharpie and asked.

Sharpie looked at him; grinned. 'What – me?' He shook his head. 'Naaaah. You?'

Ben smiled. 'Course not.' He pushed his foot flat to the floor to stop his leg from jackhammering.

Over the days and months that followed, Ben settled into a routine that included anything from pot washing to the capture of Iraqi soldiers in the desert, the look on their starving, war-torn faces usually one of relief rather than fear, especially as capture meant access to food after days of going without any. It wasn't an easy job though, especially if the POWs needed a shit. Ben's first experience of it had also been the first time since arriving, despite the heat and meagre rations, he had felt like throwing up. Still, he couldn't help feeling sorry for the blokes shouting to get his attention and pointing to their arses.

Where possible, they'd try and find some small bushes for the men to crouch behind, if only because it can't have been easy taking a dump with a weapon in your face. One time though, judging by the sound and smell, Ben was convinced that one poor bloke must have emptied the entirety of his insides, never mind his bowels. How he stopped himself from gagging that day, God only knew!

He also witnessed – thanks to the burning oil wells – the black billowing skyline above Kuwait City. Once thriving and teeming with life it was, when Ben entered it, more akin to a ghost town; nothing more than a pathetic burnt-out shell; its buildings peppered with bullet holes, its streets full of upturned cars and trucks. It was the abandoned books, clothes, and children's toys, however, that made the biggest impression. More so than the first dead bodies he witnessed propped up against sandbanks in the Iraqi desert, or the charred remains of a hand that some sick bastard thought it funny to punch him in the head with when he was letter writing to Gemma.

It was on guard duty though when Ben discovered just how cold the desert was. They had been warned about the temperature drop at night but as with most things in life, no amount of talking about it can prepare you for the experience. During the day the temperature rose to a sticky fifty degrees centigrade, which saw salty, stinging tears of sweat rolling off his nose and forehead and into his eyes. His lips were permanently chapped too, and what was once a tongue became a swollen slab of fur in a dry, barren mouth. He dreamed of crystal cold water and the grey winters of home. Anything to release him from the scorching sun – until, that is, he got his wish. By night the temperature plummeted, sometimes as low as minus seven degrees, equally as merciless and unforgiving as the heat. There were even rumours that one of the SAS guys had died of hypothermia.

Gradually though, over time, Ben adjusted to the harsh weather conditions and the equally harsh sights and sounds that became the norm. It was comforting, yet disturbing, knowing just how quickly human beings could adapt. That said, adaption to your surroundings was also simply about survival. The human and innate desire to go on. The trick being, knowing when to switch off and, more importantly – at least to Ben, anyway – maintaining, wherever possible, a sense of humanity.

It was during this time; Ben was asked to have a one-to-one with his superior. Kit inspection had been called by Sergeant Bridger who, after deliberately slapping Sharpie on the back, waiting to see if he would give away the slightest hint, the smallest indication of the pain he was in, ordered Ben to see him after dixie – pot washing. All credit to Sharpie though, who, poker-faced, didn't so much as flicker an eye or make a single groan.

'Yes, sir, Sergeant Bridger.'

'Fuck meeeee,' Sharpie whispered, his face contorting into frown lines of pain; quiet groaning noises escaping the corner of his mouth when he was sure Sergeant Bridger was well and truly out of sight and earshot as, lifting his T-shirt, he patted his back with a makeshift damp cloth.

Ben laughed. 'Man up, Sharpie.' He took the cloth. 'You're lucky I noticed you were burning when I did.'

'Yep – I know I'm an idiot,' Sharpie replied, the relief on his face palpable as Ben dabbed the areas of his back he was unable to reach.

Army regulations state that anyone who goes off sick or cannot carry out normal duties because of sunburn will be charged with causing a self-inflicted wound. So why Sharpie, whose pale skin would give Casper the ghost a run for his money, had left his top off for so long – in the desert of all places – was a mystery to Ben.

'Cheers, Dick,' Sharpie added. 'I owe you one.'

'Yeah... you do. In fact, I'm starving. So, you can give me your scoff if you like.'

'Fuck off. They call it rations for a reason, you know!' Sharpie wasn't wrong. There was barely enough food in their mess tin to feed a sparrow. Ben found himself dreaming of his mother's Sunday roast. Gemma wasn't a bad cook, and Ben could make a mean lasagne, but nothing beat his mother's roast dinner with thick onion gravy, fluffy roast potatoes and a juicy joint. *What idiot said the army marched on its stomach?*

'What was that all about with you and Bridger?' Sharpie asked.

Ben shrugged. 'Haven't got the foggiest.'

Pot-washing duties complete, Ben went to see Sergeant Bridger as requested.

'There's been talk, Thompson.' His voice sounded remarkably different to the one Ben was used to. This conversation was for

Ben's ears only so the normally booming voice he had become accustomed to, was much quieter, which somehow made Sergeant Bridger's Geordie twang more pronounced. 'You've worked well during this mission, and it hasn't gone unnoticed. We'd like to put you forward for SF.'

'Really?' Ben's eyebrows shot up. He hadn't even considered the Special Forces. He knew he was physically fit and had shown leadership skills, but he also knew, as did everyone else, it took more than that to make SF.

'Really,' Sergeant Bridger replied. 'Don't look so surprised, lad. I don't do this every day. You've got potential and you should give it some serious thought. Obviously, you'll need to have a chat about it at home, then we'll talk again. In the meantime, any questions?'

'No, sir, I don't think so.'

'Good. Dismissed, Private Thompson.'

'Thank you, Sergeant Bridger,' Ben had replied with a curt salute.

Ben smiled at the memory. It was hard to believe that was nearly nine years ago. He had talked it over with Gemma, of course, but he knew, even before he said anything, he was going to go for it. The army had challenged him, and he'd risen to it, well. But he had been ready for more. He wanted to see how far he could push himself, both mentally and physically. The training was brutal, and most of the recruits he trained with didn't make it. He did though. And despite the danger, despite the fear, he loved it.

He wasn't sure why he enjoyed it so much. Maybe it was because, in his own small way, he believed he was making a difference; one of the good guys, righting some of the many wrongs in the world. Or maybe it was because, finding himself in fraught and dangerous situations, he was reminded of his own mortality, which in a perverse way reminded him how precious life was. Maybe though, he just loved soldiering, without all the pomp and ceremony of the regular army. Or maybe, when he was on a mission, he was so focused on what he was doing that, outside of being a soldier, he didn't have much time to focus on who Ben Thompson really was and why, though happily married, he still mourned the loss of Leora Jackson.

# CHAPTER 24

*L*eora looked at Margot and laughed. With her perfectly coiffed hair and manicured nails, Tim's mother was always impeccably turned out. Leora liked her, a lot, mostly because, despite her poise and manners, she didn't suffer fools gladly. In that sense she was, Leora supposed, not unlike Ali. Maybe that's why the two women clashed, because they were so alike.

'More wine, Margot?' Leora offered.

'What kind of foolish question is that, dear?' Margot smiled.

Leora reached for Margot's glass, but Margot stopped her. 'Don't bother refilling it – just bring me a bottle.'

Leora laughed but there was a nervousness behind it. It wasn't even nine o'clock yet. The party had barely begun and the last thing she needed was a drunk Margot with a loose tongue. There were only a few hours of 1999 left and Leora had gone to a lot of effort to make sure this party went with a bang. After all this wasn't just any old New Year's Eve, it was the start of a new millennium *and* a new chapter in her life.

It was also one of the first New Year's Eves that Tim wasn't working. He and his band, Duke N' Blues, could have charged a fortune to play at one of the many establishments that had requested them, but for once Leora had put her foot down. Tim played the saxophone in a jazz band a couple of times a week, and although they only performed at paying gigs, it was nonetheless, a hobby.

Leora filled Margot's glass anyway. 'While you wait,' she suggested. 'Give me ten minutes to see to my other guests and I'll be back.'

Margot nodded. 'I don't see your parents anywhere. Are they coming?' She strained her neck to search the growing number of bodies now filling the room.

Leora pressed her lips together, lowered her eyes. 'No... unfortunately not. They had other plans.' She didn't tell her that she hadn't asked them. They wouldn't have come anyway, so what was the point.

'What a pity,' Margot sniffed, as she surveyed the other guests milling about the room. 'Would have been guaranteed some decent conversation if your parents were here. Oh, good God... not him,' she exclaimed, turning towards the loud voice that had just entered the room. 'Why on earth did you invite him?'

Leora turned to see Ali, whose entrance had been overshadowed by the booming voice of her husband, Hugo, in the hallway.

Leora turned back to Margot, whose stern face was now marked in crumpled lines of disdain. 'I couldn't exactly ask my friend to come without her husband, could I?'

Margot rolled her eyes. 'More's the pity.'

'Grandma!'

Margot turned to see her beautiful granddaughter running towards her. 'There she is.' Margot smiled, pulling her close, filling her fat cheeks with kisses.

Mia giggled then looked at her mother. 'Daddy said you have to help him with Uncle Hugo, Mummy.'

Margot shook her head and sighed. 'Go.' She waved dismissively. 'Mia and I will be absolutely fine together.'

Mia nodded before covering her ears to drown out the one lone voice that could be heard above all the others in the room.

'He's drunk,' Tim whispered, as she approached them.

'Sorry,' Ali mouthed, rolling her eyes.

'...so, I told him. You're a pig. Like that ugly wife of yours,' Hugo was saying, followed by a collective sharp intake of breath as several guests discreetly moved away.

Ali, stony faced, said nothing.

'Leora,' Hugo shouted when he saw her. 'Looking lovely as ever, I see.' He leaned in, kissed her cheek, his lips wet, his breath reeking of whisky.

'That's enough now, Hugo.' Tim grabbed him by the elbow and steered him towards the kitchen. 'You're starting to scare our other guests.'

Frowning, Hugo looked round. 'Really?'

Tim's grip on Hugo was tight and although he smiled, Leora could see he wasn't happy. He ushered Hugo towards the kitchen, pausing briefly to tell Leora to see to their other guests while he took Hugo outside. 'See if I can't have a word with him. Sober him up a bit,' he winked.

Leora and Ali watched from the hallway as Tim guided Hugo into the kitchen towards the back door. Ali, whose eyes flashed with anger, looked at her friend. 'Sorry,' she muttered. 'He's such an arsehole when he's drunk.'

It was true – ish. Hugo was quite charming when he was sober but a bit loud and brash when he was drunk.

Leora smiled, waved her hand. 'Don't worry about it. Tim will sort him out.' She laughed. 'Come on.' She linked arms with Ali. 'Let's go to the kitchen and get you a drink. I was just getting one for Margot anyway.'

Ali rolled her eyes. 'Margot hates me.'

'She does not. It's Hugo… drunk Hugo… she isn't keen on.'

Ali arched one of her perfectly pencilled eyebrows. 'Hmm...' her reply.

'Is everything... all right?' Leora asked, going to the fridge.

Ali sighed. 'Yes... everything's fine. We had a few words before we came out, then Hugo hit the bottle. You know what he's like...'

Taking a bottle of white from the fridge, Leora glanced at her friend, but said nothing. She looked, wearing a simple pewter coloured slip dress with a matching bolero jacket, her hair up, a few delicate curls casually cascading down her cheeks, a simple white-stoned choker – diamonds, probably – gracing her neck, quite beautiful.

'You look lovely tonight, Ali. That dress is stunning.'

Ali smiled, waved her hand airily. 'Thanks. It's a Vera Wang.' She cast her eye over Leora's black floral dress. 'Isn't that the same dress you wore last New Year's Eve?'

Leora blushed. 'It is.' She uncorked the wine, offered Ali a glass. Ali shook her head, picked up a bottle of Rioja from the table, already open, and poured herself a glass; the rich red liquid, as she filled her goblet, making a thick glugging noise. She took a sip, which is when Leora noticed a cluster of brown bruises around Ali's wrist as the sleeve of her jacket lifted slightly. Following Leora's gaze, Ali placed the glass on the table and discreetly tugged at her sleeve.

Leora went to her friend and lightly touched her wrist, asked her again if everything was okay. Taking another mouthful of wine, Ali shrugged, wandering to the other side of the table, casting an eye over a large tray of hors d'oeuvres. 'These look nice,' she said, casually picking one up before just as quickly discarding it.

'Thanks.' Leora found herself stupidly annoyed at the way Ali handled the food, then threw it down again.

'Please stop it, Leora.' Ali glanced at her, her smile tight, a note of impatience in her voice.

'Stop what?' Leora said, her hand going to her neck, her brow creasing in confusion.

'Acting like you actually give a shit about me.'

Leora recoiled. 'What?' she replied, somewhat bewildered. 'I do... I am... I just mea–'

'We don't all live in a perfect little bubble like you, you know.'

Stunned, Leora's hand went to her cheek, which was burning, wondering where this sudden animosity was coming from. Yes, she had a nice life; a good man that loved her, a beautiful daughter, and a wonderful home – but her life was far from perfect.

She was still trying, albeit somewhat half-heartedly these days, to launch her acting career, but it had been years now. She'd had some minor success in the early days, done some TV ads, had a couple of minor roles in a couple of soap operas, but having earned herself a reputation for being late for auditions or turning up on the wrong day – usually because Ali or one of their other housemates had taken a phone message and, for whatever reason, had written it down wrong, or misunderstood what they'd said – the offers had soon dried up. Which was strange really, considering how organised she had always been prior to moving to London.

Ali said it was probably grief affecting her recall, and looking back, she was inclined to agree. Like a lot of students, Leora partied hard during her uni years. But while most of her friends drank to socialise, Leora drank to numb the pain. Then she had met Tim.

Ali had been away at the time, on holiday with Hugo, and Leora was at a loose end, found herself saying yes to another friend who asked her if she wanted to see a jazz band at a club in Soho. The physical attraction between her and Tim was instant and after a whirlwind romance, they eloped to Gretna Green and married. Mia arrived soon afterwards, and Leora loved her new role as a mother. She wanted to be there for Mia's key moments, which also meant less time for auditions. Then, as Mia got older, started going to nursery, and more recently, to school, Leora found herself drawn back to Lumley's – the department store she'd worked at while she was studying. They offered her a job on one of their make-up counters with hours that fitted around school. So, except for the odd commercial here and there, Leora had done very little in the way of acting.

That didn't mean she had given up on her dreams of acting though. That was part of the reason she was keen to move to the States, in the hope that, once she'd got Mia settled in school, she could try and rekindle her acting career. She'd toyed with the idea of teaching again too; a career path she had still considered even *after* her split from Ben. At least that is… until Ali pointed out that teaching was for life's losers.

'You know the old saying,' she'd said, during one of the many nights Ali had sat with Leora after she and Ben had split up; heartbroken and barely able to think straight. 'Those that can, do, while those that can't, teach.'

Straightening up, Leora looked at her friend and took a deep breath. 'I don't live in a bubble, Ali. And while it might look like it is, my life is far from perfect. I haven't even begun to make a dent in my acting career. In fact, right now, I'm nothing more than… how did you put it the other day… a glorified shop assistant?'

Ali smirked. 'I was only teasing… and you know it.'

'Yes, I know you were but you're the one going from strength to strength, breaking several glass ceilings along the way, working in your dream job as a financial analyst.'

Ali: eyes tight, mouth narrowing, frowned. 'Meaning what… you're jealous of me… of my success?'

Leora felt her chest flare, wondering how, even after all these years, Ali was one of the only people capable of pushing her buttons. 'No… of course not. I'm proud of you… like any good friend should be… but I don't appreciate being told I live in a bubble. The thing is…' She paused, glancing at the back door where she thought she heard raised voices, before turning back to Ali again. 'The thing is,' she repeated, thinking now was good a time as any to tell her about the States. 'Come March, I won't be living here anymore.'

Ali put her glass on the table and stared at her. 'I know,' she said quietly.

'You know?' Leora replied, eyes wide. 'Know... what... exactly?'

'About America,' Ali sighed.

*Shit*, Leora thought, her heart racing.

'Is that the thanks I get,' Ali continued, her gaze steadfast, the hurt in her eyes obvious. She didn't shout though. If anything, she lowered her voice, which somehow made Leora feel worse. 'After everything I've done for you... everything we've been through... together... as friends. Sneaking off to America without so much as a by your leave?'

'I meant to tell you... honestly I did but...' Leora paused, her throat constricting, her thoughts turning to liquid.

'But what?'

Leora pulled a chair out, sat down. Like a child she brought her knees up and rested her chin on them, hugging them, tight. She felt like a mouse cornered by a cat. Ali was right, and nothing she did or said from this moment on would make up for her thoughtlessness. Ali was the one constant in her life. The one person who was always there for her. Who had stuck by her when others, including her parents, had fallen by the wayside. She owed Ali so much, yet here she was as good as sneaking off without – how did she put it – so much as a by your leave. Not that she needed Ali's permission to move away. But that wasn't the point, was it? Theirs was a special friendship, one that started when they were very young, and one that, despite their ups and downs, despite their own personal tragedies, had endured.

So why was it then, during some of the key moments in her life, like when she and Tim had eloped, Leora had deliberately *not* told Ali. But it wasn't *just* Ali. She hadn't told anyone. She convinced herself it was because she didn't want any fuss, which was true, she didn't. Tim hadn't even met her parents when he proposed – at a Guns N' Roses concert, of all places – and even though, looking back, it was a little impulsive, it felt right at the time. Tim was the first person, since Ben, who had genuinely made her laugh.

Yes, he was different to Ben, less deep, less philosophical perhaps, but they had a lot in common, including a shared interest in music. Tim's predilection was always towards jazz music, but like her he enjoyed other kinds of music too, including heavy rock.

He was also the first person that she didn't compare to Ben, which was good – meant she was finally over him, didn't it? Either that or she was just kidding herself and was still on the rebound.

But what she did know was, the idea of a big wedding, deciding who to invite and who not to, felt overwhelming; so in the end she suggested they elope.

Eileen, when Leora had phoned and told her, had been really pleased for her, said she completely understood why she'd done it.

Her parents, on the other hand, when she plucked up enough courage to take Tim to meet them, were stunned. She would never forget the look of disappointment on her father's face, the sad realisation that his hope of one day walking his only daughter down the aisle, gone. He, like her mother, had put on a good front though, and welcomed them both.

They had, Leora noticed, softened a little, as had their grief-stricken faces, which meant discussions about Lonny were no longer taboo, either. Old photos came out and old memories resurrected, including the time Lonny got into a punch-up when he'd 'borrowed' their cousin Ash's new bike. By the time they left, Tim said he was hard pushed to understand why Leora didn't get on better with her parents. Privately, she found herself wondering the same, until, of course, Ali reminded her of all the times her parents had let her down, pushed her away.

'The simple truth is,' Ali said, 'and I hate to say this because I hate hurting you, and because, deep down, I think your parents are good people – they were very good to me when I was younger – but they never have, and never will, love you as much as they loved Lonny. But instead of accepting that hard truth, which would have freed you from the guilt of arranging a wedding without them – like I was able to do with my family when Hugo and I married – you chose to elope, chose to, like you always do, run away from the problem.'

Leora smiled. That was the thing about Ali, she always told you the truth, whether you liked it or not. If you wanted honesty, Ali was your woman. Was that why, Leora wondered, she had put off telling her about her move to the States, because subconsciously she was having doubts, and not just about moving to another country, but also about the state of her marriage. Which meant, if Ali had picked up on that too, she would, Leora knew, in no uncertain terms, tell her, which in turn would make that tiny alarm bell that was already ringing in her head, ring just that bit louder.

Pressing her lips against her bony knees, Leora looked at Ali – beautiful, confident, self-assured, and loyal. Leora was lucky to have such a remarkable woman in her life. Not telling her about America before tonight had been a massive faux pas on her part.

Ali took another sip of wine, making her sleeve lift again, which once again revealed the tiny bracelet of bruises on her wrist, which worried Leora. Was she about to leave her friend just when she really needed her? How, she wondered, had the bruises come to be on Ali's wrist in the first place. Her relationship with Hugo could be tumultuous, especially if Hugo had had too much to drink, but Ali had never mentioned him being violent, which didn't mean he wasn't, of course.

The doorbell chimed and Leora stood up, made for the door.

'I'll get it,' she heard Margot shout from the hallway.

'Look, Ali,' she said, turning to her friend again. 'We were... *are*... going to announce our move to the States tonight. I should have told you before, I know that, but...' She paused, pressed her glass to her chest, its icy coldness bringing welcome relief to her flushed neckline.

'But... what?' Ali cocked her head to the side, a half, almost smug smile tugging at the corners of her mouth.

If Leora didn't know better, she would have said Ali was enjoying watching her squirm. She shook her head, held her hands up. 'Oh, I don't know, Ali. I guess... I guess I didn't want to upset you.'

Ali, whose eyebrows shot up, grinned. 'Really. You think you mean that much to me?'

Leora's mouth fell open. She didn't know what she'd expected Ali to say, but it wasn't that. 'I... I...' She tried to think of a suitable reply but when none was forthcoming, she quickly closed her mouth again.

'Look, Leora,' Ali said, walking up to her. 'I'm pleased for you. A fresh start in the States might be just what you need to kickstart your acting career. God knows it can't get any worse than it already is.' She laughed. 'And yes, it would have been nice if you'd told me before, because, well... that's what good friends do, isn't it?'

*Ouch*, Leora thought.

'However, that said, and this may surprise you a little,' she continued, her voice dripping in her trademark sarcasm. 'My life doesn't revolve around you, you know.'

'I wasn't saying it did.' Leora's words were hurried, tripping over one another. 'I just meant that I—'

'Have you told anyone else yet?'

'What?'

'What about your parents? Have you told them?'

Flushed with shame, Leora shook her head, looked down. 'No, not yet,' she mumbled. 'I'm hoping to see them next week... had planned to tell them then.' When she looked up again, Ali was staring straight at her in way that made her uneasy, her mouth dry. 'I am sorry, Ali.'

'For God's sake, Leora,' she replied, her face breaking into a huge smile. 'It's brilliant news.'

'Really? You're not... mad at me then?'

And there it was again, that small smile. The one Ali had carried with her from childhood. The one you were never quite sure *was* a smile, could just as easily be a smirk, or occasionally, depending on the words that fell from her mouth, an assassin's grin. 'I forgive you,' she said, stabbing Leora's chest with her finger with slightly more gusto than necessary. 'Just don't do it again. But otherwise, yeah, it's great news.'

The relief surging through Leora's veins was intense. For some reason she'd expected Ali to be upset, but as usual Ali had surprised her. 'And... you'll visit?' she asked.

'Just you try and stop me,' she said, as the back door flew open and Tim and Hugo stepped inside, bringing a flurry of leaves behind them.

Hugo, eyes down like a chastised schoolboy, shuffled towards the two women. 'Sorry, Leora,' he said, coughing to clear a throat she suspected didn't need clearing. 'Ali,' he added, glancing at his wife, before kissing her on the cheek. 'Think I'll stick to water for the rest of the evening.'

Ali nodded, watching her husband's retreating back as Tim guided him towards the living room. 'Men.' She shook her head. 'Anyway,' she added, raising her glass, indicating Leora should do the same. 'Here's to you.' They clinked glasses. 'And your new life across the pond.'

'Cheers,' Leora replied, clinking glasses again, wondering why on earth she'd been so worried about telling her friend.

They headed into the living room, now ringing with the inebriated good cheer of friends and family.

'By the way,' Leora said, turning to Ali who was looking at Hugo, slumped in a chair in the corner of the room, cradling a glass of water, his bottom lip protruding like a sulky toddler. 'How did you know... about America?'

'Adam,' Ali replied, very matter of fact.

'Adam?' Leora repeated. Adam was one of the five members of Tim's jazz band.

Ali nodded, explaining how she'd taken her friend, Saffy, to watch Duke N' Blues play at a gig in Soho last month.

*Saffy? Who's Saffy?* Leora wondered. *And since when did you start going to Tim's gigs without me?*

'Saffy's a big jazz fan,' Ali continued. 'We were in the area one night after work, saw a poster saying the boys were playing and decided to chance our luck, see if there were any tickets left, which there were. When we left, we bumped into Adam, who told us about Tim's offer to work in the States, and how much the band were going to miss him. To be fair to Adam, I think he thought I already knew.'

Her cheeks blazing, Leora took another swig of wine, the heat from the alcohol burning her throat. 'So... you've known... for a week then?' she asked. 'Why didn't you say something?'

Ali shrugged. 'I guess I was waiting for you to tell me. Anyway, I hope you don't mind, but Saffy was at a bit of a loose end tonight, so I invited her here.' Leora was about to say of course she didn't mind, but Ali didn't give her chance. 'Talk of the devil.' She grinned, waving at someone standing behind Tim. 'Look, she's already here.'

Straining her neck to see, Leora spotted a young woman standing next to her husband. Tall, slim, with long blonde hair, she reminded Leora of herself ten years ago. Tim, who appeared to be talking to both her and his father, Edward, threw his head back and laughed before casting a quick eye behind him at Hugo who, squashed in an armchair, his chubby fingers resting against his plump cheek, looked positively bored.

'At least he's quiet now,' Ali said, following Leora's gaze.

Leora heard her daughter's voice, and turned to see Mia, who had been sitting next to her grandmother, running towards them. 'Ali!' she cried.

'Mia!' Ali passed her glass to Leora, as, arms outstretched, she picked her up and spun her round.

'Ali.' Margot's voice was clipped, her smile a fabrication.

'Margot,' Ali replied, without looking at her, blowing a raspberry on Mia's fat cheek, making her giggle.

'Your husband seems to be behaving himself now,' Margot continued, pouring herself another glass of wine from the bottle Leora passed her.

'Whereas you, it seems, have fallen off the wagon again.' Ali smiled.

'Time for bed now, Mia,' Leora interrupted.

'I'll take her,' Ali offered, much to Mia's delight and Leora's relief.

Mia kissed her grandmother goodnight and Leora promised her she'd be up in a while to check on her. 'Bring Daddy,' Mia called over her shoulder. 'To kiss me goodnight.'

'I will.' Leora smiled, watching them disappear before her gaze turned back to Tim and the young woman standing beside him; the way she touched his arm and laughed whenever he said something.

'Pretty girl,' remarked Margot, who, it seemed, was also watching them. 'Saffy. A friend of your friend, *apparently*. Come along.' She linked arms with Leora. 'I think it's about time you introduced yourself, don't you?' Standing between Tim and Saffy, Margot introduced Leora, emphasising the words *my son's wife*.

Rubbing her back, Tim leaned in and kissed Leora's cheek. 'If she doesn't stop it,' he whispered, glancing at his mother, now completely dominating the conversation. 'We'll have to put her in the naughty chair like poor old Hugo over there.'

Leora looked at Hugo and laughed. When she looked away again, she caught Saffy staring at her. Leora smiled and although Saffy smiled back, her eyes said something else. Something that looked and felt a lot like contempt.

❦

Big Ben struck twelve, fireworks exploded, balloons popped, and everyone cheered. Everyone drunkenly wished one another a happy new year and somewhere in the background Prince's '1999' was replaced by 'Auld Lang Syne'. A small circle of people grew into a large one as everyone jovially linked arms to welcome in the new millennium. Leora looked for Tim among the mass of heaving bodies but couldn't find him. She did notice Ali and Hugo, kissing passionately, in one corner of the room, and Margot and Edward, quietly arguing, in another. Her thoughts turned to Mia. Had the sudden increase in noise woken her. She decided to go and check on her.

In the hallway she stopped when she heard the shrill ring of the phone. *Mum*, she thought. *Ringing to wish us a happy new year.* She lifted the receiver just as the phone rang off. She imagined her mother, standing next to the payphone at the back of the Burghley Club, dressed in her heels and best dress, which in turn made her think of the New Year's Eve parties of her childhood. Of friends and family gathered round, of her and Lonny, as they got older, allowed to stay up and how, on the stroke of midnight, a dark-haired person, usually Lonny or her mother, would exit the house by the back door – after letting the old year out – before entering it again via the front door carrying salt, coal, and bread. First Footing, her grandparents called it, to ensure enough money – salt; enough food – bread; and enough warmth – coal for the new year.

Tearful, heart aching, grief lodged in her throat, she put the phone down, then immediately picked it back up again and dialled her parents' home number, waiting for the recorded message to kick in; her father's voice telling her they couldn't get to the phone right now but to leave a message and they'd get right back to her.

'Hey, Mum, Dad... it's Leora. Sorry I missed your call. I just wanted to say... well... happy new year.' *I love you*, she wanted to add, but try as she might the words wouldn't form on her tongue. 'I hope you've had... a good night... and I'll see you both next week. Okay then... bye.'

She replaced the receiver and wondered if she should buy a mobile phone. Smaller and more affordable, they'd come a long way since the bricks that first came to market in the eighties. Ali had one. Tim too. A lot of people used them to text each other – *apparently*. Although, quite why people preferred to do that than speak to one another she didn't know. Then again, texting her parents rather than speaking to them directly might be a good thing. The only flaw in that plan being, her parents would need a mobile phone too, and she could not imagine that happening.

Her thoughts turned back to Mia. She headed to the oak staircase, resisting the urge to turn the light on, and began, still wearing her strappy heels, her careful ascent. She yawned. It had been a long day. Hopefully their guests would leave soon, although, judging by the noise radiating from the living room, the party was still very much in full swing. Someone brushed passed her, making her jump. She looked round, surprised to see Saffy.

'Hi,' she said, putting her hand up, before disappearing into the hallway at the bottom of the stairs.

*Why is she upstairs?* Leora thought, stepping onto the landing. Puzzled, she realised Mia's bedroom door, normally slightly ajar, was wide open. Concerned, she quickened her pace, relieved to find Tim standing behind the door staring at their sleeping daughter.

'Is she okay?' Leora whispered.

Tim looked at her and smiled. 'She's fine,' was his hushed reply. 'Happy new year, gorgeous,' he added, leaning in to kiss her.

Leora grinned, felt her tummy flip. 'Happy New Year to you too.'

'C'mon.' Tim took her hand and led her to their bedroom. 'Let's celebrate properly.'

'Wait... what?' Leora giggled. 'We can't.'

'Why?' Tim frowned, unbuttoning his shirt and kicking the door shut behind him.

'What about our guests?' Leora protested.

'What about them?' Tim pressed himself against her, his hands at the back of her neck, unfastening her dress.

As usual his want for her was urgent. He kissed her, passionately, before laying her on the bed, the two of them, quite literally, welcoming the new year in with a bang! Afterwards, as they lay in one another's arms, Leora asked Tim if he knew why Saffy had been upstairs.

'No idea. I did tell some of the guests to use the upstairs bathroom if the loo downstairs was busy... so long as they were quiet... didn't wake Mia. So... I guess... she was probably using the bathroom?'

Relieved, Leora turned to look out of the window, where the curtains were still open, and stared at the star-studded sky, surprised to find Ben in her thoughts, remembering how, holding hands, they would often look up at the stars, contemplating how very small and insignificant they were. 'Make a wish,' Ben would say. 'On the stars... but don't tell me what it is, or it won't come true.'

She wished they'd be together forever...

Leora searched for Tim's hand, linking her fingers with his, holding it, tight. She wondered where Ben was tonight, hoped, despite the pain he'd caused her all those years ago, he was happy.

'You and me, were meant to be,' she found herself whispering into the darkness.

'Say again?' Tim replied. 'I didn't catch you.'

'I said the stars are out, we should make a wish.'

Sitting up, resting on his elbow, Tim looked at her. Tucking a loose curl behind her ear, he smiled and kissed her nose. 'You are silly.'

# PART V
## 2009

# CHAPTER 25

*B*en stared at his wife through glassy, bloodshot eyes.

'Well?' Gemma said. 'Say something?'

Unshaven, Ben, who stunk of stale sweat and booze gave her one of his half smiles that said nothing and everything all at the same time. 'What do you want me to say?' he replied, unable to work out if it was the whisky or that he hadn't slept for five days causing his slurred speech. Both, probably.

Gemma shook her head. She would blame the booze regardless. Still slim, her dark hair now shoulder length, she looked good for a mother of two rowdy boys. She had aged though… and it showed… especially on her face. Her marriage to Ben had taken its toll, evident in the worry lines around her eyes and lips, not to mention the deep crevices embedded between her eyebrows. 'So that's it then? You're not even going to fight for us?'

Ben looked at her. He was sick of fighting. The last couple of years had felt like one long fight and there was nothing left worth fighting for. Not even his boys, because the truth was, they were better off without him. How sad was that?

'I know…' Ben held her gaze. 'About you and Felix…'

Gemma folded her arms. 'Know what?' Her tone was curt, dismissive.

'Oh, come on, Gem. Let's not drag this out. You've been fucking him, and he's the reason you're leaving.'

Eyes wide, her face mottled crimson, Gemma looked both surprised and angry at the same time. 'Only because... unlike you.' She stabbed the air with her finger. 'He *wants* to fuck me.' She sighed, put her hand to her head, closed her eyes. 'I've tried, Ben,' she said, opening them again. 'I really have. But I can't do this anymore.'

'So... what you're saying is... in sickness and in health, for richer or poorer... you're giving up and walking away... is that right?'

She shook her head. 'That's not what I'm doing, and you know it. If you really want me, then show me. Fight for me.' She threw her arm out, pointed towards the door. 'And if you can't fight for me, fight for them.'

Ben leaned forward, grabbed the whisky bottle on the coffee table and refilled his empty glass. 'No can do.' He tipped the glass back; the bittersweet nectar coating his tongue and filling his nostrils. He loved the smell of whisky; its promise of oblivion.

A sullen Sam appeared behind the door. 'Can we go now, Mum? We've been sitting in the car for ages.'

Tall for his age, Sam was a quiet, studious boy. He reminded Ben of Kashif, a sweet, curious child who was always asking Ben about his life in England. It went against all the rules, but Ben promised Kashif he'd stay in touch with him and his family. It was the least he could do after they'd bravely taken it upon themselves to help the wounded white men fleeing the Taliban. He meant it too – until the boy and most of his family were massacred.

A lump formed in Ben's throat. He wanted to cry again but he wouldn't. Not in front of his soon to be divorced wife and eldest son. 'Come and give your old man a hug, eh.' Ben slammed his glass down on the table and stretched out his arms. Sam looked warily from his father to his mother and shrugged before looking down at his feet. 'C'mon, mate. Please.'

Robbie, who had also crept in behind his brother, beat him to it. Two years younger than Sam, Robbie was a lot shorter and stockier than his brother. He was also far louder and much less introverted than his slightly serious older sibling and, or so it seemed, more forgiving. With arms outstretched like an aeroplane, Robbie hurtled towards his father and flung his arms around his neck. Ben cradled his small son in his large arms, once again reminded of Kashif. The difference of course being, the last time Ben had held Kashif in his arms he had been limp and lifeless, his short life snuffed out like the flame of a newly lit candle.

Robbie, however, full of life – thank God – squirmed restlessly on Ben's knee. Ben hugged him, using the opportunity to bury his head in his son's small shoulder to mask the tears that fell despite his best efforts not to cry. When he looked up again, he was pleased to see Sam standing beside him. Arms folded, he frowned; reluctantly allowing Ben to pull him into a hug. Ben squeezed both his sons, tight, as Gemma, hovering behind them – like a lioness protecting her cubs – watched on.

He was glad she had Felix. She deserved better than he could give her. She always had. 'Please don't stop me seeing them,' he mouthed, holding on to his boys for dear life.

Gemma shook her head, using the heel of her hand to stem the tears streaming down her face. 'Never,' she mouthed back.

The boys headed outside again, and Ben stood up and looked at his wife. 'Thanks for being such a great mum.' He took her hands in his. 'And wife,' he added. 'Make sure Felix looks after you, treats you better than I did.'

Gemma stared at him, biting the corner of her mouth. Her voice when she spoke, was faint, on the verge of breaking. 'You did treat me well, Ben... for a while. And even when you didn't, even when you struggled, I know you didn't mean it. So, I tried, I really did. But... but... I just can't...'

Ben pulled her to him, holding her in his arms, his chin resting on her head, both crying. He stroked and kissed her head, longing to take her to bed; show her how much he still loved her, how much he still cared. But they had done that countless times before and it always ended the same way – badly. This time it was different. This time, for her sake, Ben had to let her go.

'It's karma, I reckon.' Gemma pulled away, wiping her mascara-stained cheeks with a tissue she pulled from her pocket.

'Karma?'

'Oh, come on, Ben, you and I both know there were three of us in this marriage. You did your best, but you never *really* loved me... at least... not as much as you loved *her.*'

'Who?'

'You know who.'

Ben cupped the back of his aching head with his hand, the tendons in his neck taut, trying, through his drunken inertia, to make sense of his wife's nonsensical ramblings 'What the hell are you talking about, Gemma?'

She looked down, shook her head. 'I'll be in touch... about the boys,' she said, glancing up again. 'But please, Ben.' She reached for his hand, placed it between hers and squeezed it. 'If you want any sort of relationship with them, please, please, *please* get some help.'

And with that, she left.

'Leora,' he said out loud. Was she talking about Leora? He had never talked about her to Gemma, but he had never forgotten her either. How could he? She was his first love and, dare he admit it, if only to himself, his true love. He hated himself for thinking it because he'd loved Gemma, he really had. Still did, but theirs had been a different kind of love and although he had never said as much, had never *ever* brought Leora's name up once during their marriage, clearly Gemma had sensed it.

*Does Leora ever think about me?* he wondered. He laughed. He'd cheated on her, so he doubted it. Guilt gnawed his thoughts. The only people he should be thinking about right now were his boys. He was an arsehole, and a drunken one at that. Gemma was right to take them away because until he got his shit together his sons were better off without him.

Eyes glazed; he stared at the flickering TV screen and reached for the whisky bottle again. Had he really drunk that much already, he thought, holding it up to the light and shaking it. It was New Year's Eve 2008, one of the coldest on record for more than a decade apparently. *Not as cold as the desert*, he thought; neat whisky sliding down his gullet, burning his empty stomach, the sofa creaking beneath his weight.

He woke to the clattering of machine-gun fire, which made him jump. Eyes wide open, he sat bolt upright, his heart pounding in his chest. Gripping the sofa with both hands he searched the darkness for signs of an intruder.

Seconds later the room rattled with yet more ear-popping cracks and bangs as an eruption of colour exploded from the TV screen. Dazed and confused, he watched revellers gathered by the Thames; Big Ben and The Millennium Wheel behind them, their collective whoops, and shouts of 'Happy New Year' competing with various renditions of 'Auld Lang Syne', while fireworks, like starlight, arced across the midnight sky.

*London*, he slurred, his eyes narrowing, his index finger stabbing the air between him and the TV. Wasn't that where Leora lived? He'd heard a rumour a few years back that she'd moved to Los Angeles. Or was that someone else? Was she there now, in the crowd. One of the many happy, smiley people that the cameras kept zooming in on. He stood up... slowly... started shadow boxing. God knows what she'd think of him if she saw him now. That she'd had a lucky escape, probably.

Swaying a little he squinted at the TV where a grinning presenter, microphone in one hand, pointing to the exploding fireworks with his other, was commentating on how incredible they were and how he hoped it signified the start of an amazing new year for everyone. Patting the sofa, Ben searched for the TV remote, which, finding the off button, he aimed at the TV like a gun.

'Amazing,' he muttered, swapping the remote control for the now almost empty bottle of whisky, which he put to his mouth and finished in two easy glugs. He could do without amazing. He'd settle for peace and quiet. For dreams that didn't turn to nightmares every time he closed his eyes. His only goal now, as he staggered towards the kitchen in search of more poison, was oblivion, which alcohol – for a few hours at least – always provided.

# CHAPTER 26

$\mathcal{B}$rushing dirt from the headstone, Leora replaced the wilted forget-me-nots with the carnations she'd bought. This was the second of her thrice yearly pilgrimages, and on each one she liked to bring different flowers, preferably ones that suited the season. Carnations represented love and warmth, their eye-popping pinks contrasting perfectly with the hot yellow sun and cobalt blue sky.

'Hey, Lonny,' she whispered. 'You've been gone more years now than you were here. Doesn't get any easier though,' she sighed, blinking back tears. 'I still miss you…' She asked him then, the same question she always asked. '*Why* didn't you speak to me. Tell me what was wrong?'

She had known when she left for London that he wasn't right. He never said as much and when she asked him if he was okay, he simply offered her one of his incredible smiles, shrugged and said, 'Sure, sis, I'm fine.' He wasn't though. The light in his eyes had dimmed, and no amount of smiling could hide that – at least not from her anyway.

On the day he was knocked down, witnesses said he seemed upset, like he wasn't concentrating. They also said, as he stepped

EVA JORDAN

from the pavement into the road, the driver of the car that hit him didn't stand a chance. 'I... I tried to swerve... to miss him,' he told the police, then later her parents. 'But... but he just stepped right out in front of me.'

The police asked the driver if it looked deliberate, as if Lonny had meant to do it, but the driver, as traumatised as he was, said no, he didn't think he did. 'He just looked like... a man with the world on his shoulders... someone who just wasn't concentrating.'

'I guess we'll never know though, eh, Lonny?' Leora sniffed, plucking at a few weeds that had sprouted since her last visit.

Either way, whether Lonny had intentionally stepped out in front of that car or not, all Leora could think was, she should have paid more attention, should have pushed him to tell her what was wrong, then maybe, *just maybe*, whatever it was that had been bothering him might not have seemed so bad and Lonny would still be here.

She hadn't though. She was so wrapped up in her own grief, in her own suffering, first about Ben, then Jules, that she barely had time for anyone else's problems. Lonny wasn't just anyone, though. He was her brother, and she should have been there for him, but she hadn't been, and she had had to live with that truth ever since.

Clutching her chest, she watched her brother's headstone blur and swim away. The pain of losing someone so close, so young, never lessened over time. It was as real today as it had been all those years ago. The only difference now was, she found her recall of fonder memories with her brother, and the ability to smile about them, happened more frequently. Wiping her eyes with a tissue, she smiled. 'Mia's growing,' she said. 'Fifteen already... and so tall. Not that Tim's particularly small of course. Two inches taller than me if I remember rightly. I saw him the other day, with Saffy, which was... *awkward*. Tim is good with Mia, though. Saffy is too. Which is good because it's not always

174

the case with stepparents and stepchildren. Mia thinks Saffy is cool, whereas I'm just a nag... *apparently.* The one that tells her to get her homework done, what she can and can't wear and what time she needs to get to bed during the week.' Leora smiled, shook her head. 'Fifteen going on twenty-five I reckon.'

Closing her eyes, she looked up, mindful of the sun warming her face; the quiet hum of traffic in one direction, the intermittent stream of birdsong in the another. 'I have news.' She looked down and opened her eyes again. 'I went for an audition the other day. And yes... I know I said I was done with the whole acting thing last time I was here.' She grinned. She imagined him listening to her, rolling his eyes, and shaking his head. 'But it was strange really... how it all happened.

'I bumped into an old uni friend who works in TV production. She told me about a new dating show they're putting together and how they needed two presenters, one male and one female. They had their man, she said, but were struggling to find the right female presenter. Anyway, long story short, she convinced me to go for an audition, which I'm pleased to say went surprisingly well... and basically, well... I only went and got it!' She smiled, rearranging the carnations she'd just placed in the flower holder. 'I wanted you to be the first to know.'

A shadow passed across Lonny's grave. Squinting, Leora glanced round, greeted by Eileen. 'Hey.' She knelt next to Leora. 'Thanks for the carnations. They look beautiful. I decided to go with these today.' She twirled one of two sunflowers she was holding. 'Wayne used to love...' She paused, looked down, her shoulders gently rising and falling. Leora pulled her close, rubbing her friend's back until she was ready to talk again. 'Wayne and the kids... when they were little... used to have competitions, see who could grow the tallest sunflower.' She wiped away the trail of tears from her sun-kissed cheeks.

Leora nodded, watched as Eileen placed one of the sunflowers in the middle of her carefully arranged carnations.

'There.' She sat back, admiring the vibrant display. 'I'm not sure what Lonny would think of carnations and sunflowers. But Jules will love them.'

The two women stood up and hugged one another, united in their grief. Now forty-year-olds, it was fair to say that between them, they had both had their fair share of it over the years. It was over four years now since Wayne passed away from an inoperable brain tumour. Grief-stricken but stoic, Eileen nursed him right to the very end. So now, where they once visited the graveyard twice a year, once on the anniversary of Jules's death, and once on the anniversary of Lonny's, now they visited three times a year, each bringing flowers and laying them at the headstones of the three young men that had all been taken far too soon.

'No Ali again, then?' Eileen asked, linking arms with Leora, twirling the last sunflower in her other hand.

'No,' Leora replied, pea gravel crunching beneath their feet as they slowly made their way toward Jules's grave.

'That's the second year in a row now, isn't it?'

'Yep... it is.' Leora sighed. 'She finds it too sad, apparently. Said she'll meet us at the pub... have a couple of stiff gins waiting for us.'

'Humph...' Eileen, lips pursed, replied.

'Why – what are you thinking?'

Eileen shrugged. 'Oh... I don't know. Maybe I'm just getting grouchy in my old age–'

'Old age! Speak for yourself.'

Eileen giggled, and for the briefest moment Leora found herself looking at the timid schoolgirl she met all those years ago... before adulthood beckoned and, as it had Leora, kicked the shit out of her. 'Well... I feel old,' she added. 'The thing with Ali though is... well... she annoys me sometimes. Coming here *is* sad, but I thought the whole idea of the three of us coming together was to support one another?'

Eileen, although talking in a hushed voice, seemed uncharacteristically angry, which surprised Leora because, in all the years she'd known her, and out of the three of them, Eileen rarely, if ever, had a bad word to say about anyone, especially her friends.

'I know what you mean,' Leora offered. 'But I think it's because of her dad.'

'Her dad?'

Leora nodded. 'She's not really been herself since he passed away.'

Eileen rolled her eyes; *do me a favour* they seemed to say, which again was completely out of character for her. 'What's her dad's death got to do with coming here? It's not like he's buried here is it. He was cremated, wasn't he? And not only that, but she also hated him too, didn't she?'

Leora shrugged. She didn't get it either. However, although Ali could be a pain, she was still one of her best friends. That said, though, Leora had found herself blaming Ali for the break-up of her marriage for a while, which was ridiculous, of course. Yes, Ali may have introduced Saffy to Tim, but it wasn't Ali's fault that her husband had a wandering eye.

Their marriage hadn't been right for a while. Leora knew it and so did Tim but because of Mia, neither of them had been brave enough to say it out loud. It was at their millennium New Year's Eve party, or rather, just after it, when Leora, recalling how Tim had looked at Saffy and she at him, decided she couldn't ignore the obvious anymore and confronted him. Not hysterically, but calmly, resolutely.

Tim confessed that, after Saffy's initial impromptu visit to the jazz club with Ali, she had turned up at several other gigs... on her own. On one occasion, after a quick chat with him, she asked if they could swap phone numbers. Which they did. Tim swore that, other than an exchange of text messages, nothing else had taken place between them. However, he did confess to being attracted to Saffy, and said he'd be lying if he said he hadn't thought about cheating.

Leora had been terribly hurt, but Tim's confession was the catalyst she needed. She didn't want Mia to come from a broken home, but neither did she want to drift along in a loveless marriage for years. Life was, she knew too well, too short for that. Needless to say, Los Angeles never happened, at least, not for Leora it didn't. Tim, on the other hand, who struck a new deal with his employer, agreed to fly over for six months, and help set things up in the new American office before returning to work at the London office again.

Leora and Mia, it was agreed, would stay in the house in Tooting, while Tim moved in with Saffy. Tim said he was in no hurry to sell the house until Mia was older and had left home, which Leora really appreciated, if only because it made things easier for Mia. They agreed not to tell her about their split until Tim's return from the States, which had given Mia time to adjust to her father not living with them. Still, it wasn't a good day when they did tell her. Mia was heartbroken. Tim was good with her though, as was Saffy, and gradually, over time, Mia adjusted.

For a brief period though, given everything else she'd been through, Leora wondered if she had the strength to manage another huge change in her life, but after her anger subsided, and with Ali by her side, she was, she realised, okay. Once the dust settled, she also realised that although she had loved Tim, it had never been with the same passion, the same intensity that she had loved Ben. Yes, Ben had hurt her, deeply, but for some reason – one that made no logical sense whatsoever – there was a part of her that couldn't quite release him.

'Perhaps,' Leora said, realising Eileen was looking at her, waiting for her reply, 'coming here somehow reminds Ali of her dad, and perhaps all she wants to do is forget about him?'

'Really?' The neat arc of Eileen's left eyebrow wrinkled her brow. 'Bit of a stretch, isn't it?'

'Probably.' Leora sighed. 'I don't disagree with you. But maybe, even though she did hate her dad, there's a part of her that *is* grieving him... because... grief is weird... don't you think? Affects people differently.'

Eileen puffed her cheeks out and sighed. 'Yes... and I, of all people, should know that. Oh... just ignore me,' she added, as they came to Jules's grave, where someone else had laid some bright orange poppies. 'I'm just feeling a little emotional today.'

Worried, Leora looked at her. 'There's... nothing wrong... is there?' she said, unable to keep the concern out of her voice.

Eileen smiled, shook her head. 'No. The complete opposite, in fact. Noah's been offered a job. A good one, with a great salary, doing exactly what he wanted to do.'

'But... that's great news.' Leora beamed. 'I'm so pleased for him... and you.'

Eileen, whose eyes were filling up again, smiled. 'It is... except... it's in Leeds... where he was studying... at uni. Which is fine. I understand that's where the work is but... deep down... I think a part of me was hoping he'd come home once he'd finished his studies, find work here. And not only that...' She paused, looked at her feet, before looking at Leora again.

'What? What is it?' Leora asked.

'Well... the thing is,' Eileen replied, sorrow sagging her face. 'I'm scared.'

Leora frowned, felt her eyebrows knitting together. 'Scared? Of what exactly?'

'That I'll lose him.'

'Oh, Eileen.' Leora took her hand in hers. 'Noah loves you... dearly. He's just spreading his wings, but he'll always be a part of your life, visit often.'

'You think so?'

'I know so.' Leora looked straight at her. 'You're both so close. Nothing will ever change that.'

'Yes but...' Sheepish, Eileen took a deep breath. 'Don't take this the wrong way but... you were close to your parents... once. Really close in fact and... well... look how that turned out.'

Leora looked at her and blinked, fighting the overwhelming urge to cry. Eileen beat her to it, though.

'I'm sorry,' she sobbed. 'You do know I don't mean anything by it, don't you? It's just... like I said... I'm scared.'

Leora ran a hand through her hair, felt suddenly exhausted. 'No, it's fine. I understand. But it was different for me. As a family we lost Lonny, and on top of that I was still trying to come to terms with the loss of Ben and Jules... and it was... well... a bit weird really. As much my fault as my parents''

Leora crouched down opposite Jules's headstone, patting the ground, indicating Eileen should join her.

'The thing is,' she continued, weaving the pink carnations in between the orange poppies, leaving a gap in the middle for Eileen's sunflower. 'I don't think any of us meant to become estranged. It just kind of crept up on us. We were all grieving... in our own way, but it was almost as if... having me around... reminding them of Lonny... made it worse for my parents. So we all sort of drifted, until in the end the gap between us was so wide, it seemed impossible to bridge.'

She paused, distracted by a pinging noise coming from her bag. It was her phone; a text from her mother hoping she was okay and was looking forward to seeing her later. 'Sorry,' she said, typing a quick reply before turning to her friend again, holding her phone up. 'I remember when people first started getting these. I thought they were just another fad.'

'What... BlackBerrys?' Eileen frowned.

Leora laughed. 'No... mobile phones... in general. I thought they were just another trend, wouldn't last. I'd be lost without mine now though. I've often wondered, if mobile phones were around when we were younger, if things might have been different... especially with Lonny.'

'In what way?'

'Because... in a way... being able to text your innermost thoughts and feelings without fear of seeing the other person's reaction kind of makes it easier to say the things you want to say. I knew, when I moved to London, something wasn't right with Lonny, and although I asked him countless times if he was okay, he always said yes. But I can't help wondering...' Her voice wavered, cracked. 'If... if I'd been able to text him, if, eventually, he might have opened up, and what happened might... well... not have.'

'You can't blame yourself.' Eileen rubbed Leora's arm affectionately, her voice kind, soothing.

'No... I suppose not.' Leora sniffed, dabbing her tears with the crumpled tissue in her hand. 'I do find texting is helping my relationship with my parents though. Although,' Leora rolled her eyes, shook her head, 'Dad hasn't quite got the hang of it yet. But Mum and I text... quite a lot... and well, let's just say, slowly but surely, we're building bridges.'

Eileen squeezed Leora's shoulder. 'That's great. I'm so pleased for all of you.'

Leora nodded. 'It is... isn't it? I promise you, though, you've got nothing to worry about with Noah. Even if he is a few hundred miles away, he won't forget his mum.'

'Let's hope so.' She sighed, placing her sunflower next to Jules's headstone. And the two friends sat for a moment in quiet contemplation.

# CHAPTER 27

*C*upping his hands above his head, resting his forehead on the window, Ben peered in. The first thing that hit him, despite being outside, was the familiar smell of alcohol; the hoppy notes of beer, the undercurrent of whisky, the flow of wine; red mostly, rich, oaky, competing with popping corks and clinking glasses. He'd love to say that after six months of being sober the smell and sound of booze turned his stomach, but it didn't. It was still as sweet and alluring as it ever was, and would, he realised with terrifying clarity, forever be a temptation he needed to resist.

He wasn't there for the booze, though. He was looking for Leora. Why, he couldn't say, and what he'd do if he did see her, he still didn't know. Yet here he was. He'd overheard Eileen telling Mark – it had taken him a while to get used to calling Dobs by his first name – that she was having lunch there with Leora and Ali. She hadn't said it particularly loudly, but neither had she been especially quiet. So, he couldn't help wondering if she had meant for Ben to hear her, especially when she reiterated, several times, how Leora was *still* divorced and *still* not seeing anyone.

He would have asked her outright, but he didn't want to put

her in an awkward position. He valued her friendship too much. She was an angel who had found him and rescued him just in the nick of time, like she had with Dobs – Mark, even! – and he didn't want to jeopardise that.

At least, that's what he told himself.

He would have been passing the pub anyway because he had things to do; bills to pay, a birthday present to buy for Sam – who still didn't, despite his sobriety, like him very much. But the truth was, he was intrigued. He had an urge to see the girl he'd fallen in love with all those years ago. Did she still look and sound the same, or, after years of living in London, had she changed? What would she think of him? Would she be pleased or disappointed to see him, and would she even recognise him?

The tables were quickly filling up and it was hard to believe this was one of the pubs that he and Mark had frequented in their youth. A place where, even when underage, they had always managed to blag a pint from someone. Now though, The Blue Lion was one of those gastro pubs, which, including a bar and a restaurant with high backed chairs and stylish slate floors, was a far cry from the sticky-floored boozer of its former years.

He moved to a different window for a better view, his eyes searching both the bar and the restaurant, but there was no sign of the three women. They could have, he supposed, as it was such a beautiful day, taken one of the tables in the garden. But as he panned round, he spotted her. Not Leora, or Eileen, but Ali who, wearing shoulder-length sleek blonde hair, a crisp white shirt and dark fitted jeans looked every bit the wealthy city girl Eileen said she was.

He watched her for a moment as, head back, laughing, she talked into the mobile phone pressed to her ear, while the fingers of her other hand caressed a half-empty gin glass. His feelings toward her were mixed. He didn't dislike her per se, but he knew she didn't like him, even though she had pretended otherwise when he and Leora were together. When, however, the photos of him and Gemma came into Leora's possession, she had no problem at all showing her true colours, whereas Eileen, although disappointed in him, had been much more forgiving. Not that she had any problem telling him how much he'd hurt her friend, but she was always polite, always spoke to him on the odd occasion they bumped into one another.

After ten minutes or so, with still no sign of Leora or Eileen, he sat at a table outside the coffee shop opposite the pub and watched the world go by for a while. He ordered himself a latte and a sandwich; picked up a dessert spoon from the cutlery container on the table while he was waiting, turned it over and considered his reflection. He still had a way to go, but his eyes weren't bloodshot anymore and his skin was much clearer too. In part he had his mother – since he'd been staying with her for a while – and her homecooked food to thank for that, not to mention all the fresh air he'd been exposed to during several fishing trips with his father.

If it hadn't been for Eileen though, his parents wouldn't have known the gravity of his situation. Ben had made Gemma promise not to tell his parents how bad things were. She broke that promise, of course, but only because she cared about him. However, despite his parents' concerns, Ben, *somehow*, managed to assure them both it was just a blip, convincing them he had everything under control. Little did they know the depths he had *really* sunk to. On the outside he appeared like any other drunken arsehole, but on the inside, he was slowly dying.

It was karma, he reckoned. Payback for not believing others. He'd heard of post-traumatic stress disorder. He'd even witnessed first-hand how it had affected some of his friends, but he couldn't reconcile it with those who didn't have any accompanying physical conditions, like Mark, who, after having both legs below the knee blown off in an IED explosion, had every right to mentally spiral. It wasn't that he didn't sympathise with those that were mentally struggling; he just found it hard to accept that it was PTSD – until, of course, it happened to him.

He knew what had triggered it. It was during deployment to Afghanistan when he and members of his covert surveillance and reconnaissance team had to abort their counter-insurgency mission. There were only four of them but unfortunately, after being spotted by what, from a distance, looked like a couple of goatherders but turned out to be lookouts for the Taliban, they were quickly hunted down. Two of the patrol were shot dead on sight, whereas Ben and Joe – the other remaining member of the unit – who were both wounded, managed to evade capture, eventually rescued by Mohammed Farid, a kindly villager who, along with his family, took them both in.

Mohammed instructed another villager to get word to the nearest British base to report Ben and Joe's location. Meanwhile, the two soldiers waited to be evacuated while the family tended to their wounds as well as providing food, water, and shelter. Mohammed, a gently spoken man with a kind smile was married to Nazia, who, also softly spoken, seemed both intrigued and in awe of the two British men. Between them they had five children including three sons and two daughters. The girls, and rightly so perhaps, were cautious of the soldiers, the boys less so, especially Kashif – Mohammed and Nazia's eldest son.

Kashif reminded Ben of his own sons. Like Robbie, his youngest, Kashif rarely sat still. Keen to keep his idle hands busy, his languid, youthful, movements were always accompanied by a twinkle in his eye and a cheeky grin. Like Sam though, Ben's eldest son, Kashif was also inquisitive, keen to learn, keen to know more about the world, especially the place the two soldiers called home, which often saw him conversing with them, in limited English, whenever it was his turn to bring food.

'You're getting too close,' Joe warned Ben one evening, after polishing off a bowl of what both men agreed was the best Kabuli palaw they had ever tasted.

Ben ran a hand through his greasy hair and sighed. He knew Joe was right. He was getting too close, not just to Kashif, but the whole family. They were good people who lived simple lives and who, through no fault of their own, sporadically found their existence disrupted by men who waged wars that had nothing whatsoever to do with them.

On the tenth day of their stay, Ben and Joe received word to prepare for evacuation. Only, the gun wielding Taliban beat their liberators to it. From their hiding place in the store cupboard, Ben and Joe got the gist of their demands. They were there for the two British soldiers so they could execute them. The quietly spoken Mohammed, acting as spokesperson for the village, refused to give the two men up. This was followed by much screaming and shouting for several minutes before everything went quiet. Footsteps, which seemed to be retreating, but were merely a ruse, were followed another minute later by gunfire.

Ben and Joe hurried to assist, joined minutes later by their rescue unit. Thankfully most of the villagers were saved, but Mohammed and his family, except for their youngest son Younus, were among the few casualties.

Rushing to each of them in turn, Ben checked for a pulse, but all of them, including Kashif, was deceased. Ben had witnessed scenes like this before but somehow, holding the lifeless body of the small boy who had reminded him so much of his own sons, whose smile, now bloodied and shot to pieces, and whose inquisitive mind lay splattered across the dusty ground, proved too much for Ben, affecting him in ways he never thought possible.

After returning to base, his decline was swift, which eventually led to his medical discharge.

He tried to adapt to civilian life, tried using all the coping mechanisms that had previously served him well, but despite counselling, despite Gemma's support, and despite the booze, nothing stopped the images that played on a continuous loop in his head. Images of a good, kind family who had put the needs of others above their own and in doing so had paid the ultimate price.

Ben couldn't understand it. It wasn't like he hadn't seen such things before and normally, thanks to years of training and experience, he was adept at compartmentalising such experiences. Not to say he didn't think about some of the atrocities he'd witnessed, or that they didn't rear their ugly heads from time to time, but it was a balancing act, and one that, usually, he was very much in control of.

This time though it was different. He couldn't work out if, like Joe said, it was because he'd become too attached to the family, which made their deaths more personal, or if, maybe, after years of living on adrenaline and his nerves, not to mention the fact he was now slightly older and wiser, and thus somewhat jaded about the reasons behind some of his missions, it was his mind's way of saying *enough*. Maybe it was a combination of both, or, in his darker moments, he wondered if it was payback for failing to believe the mental struggles of other men and women he'd served with.

By the time Gemma left him, two years after his discharge, he found it impossible to hold down a job, or to sleep. He'd also hit the bottle, *hard*, because drinking to the point of blackout was the only way he got any rest from his tangled thoughts, which did nothing to help his volatile mood swings. Not that he was violent, or screamed or shouted, but rather he withdrew, became catatonic, so that everything and anything, even engaging with his sons, was too much effort.

Gemma, bless her, tried her best. Begged him to share with her what had happened to him so she could better understand why he would wake from his sweat-drenched nightmares crying. He wouldn't though, so eventually she stopped trying, and instead sought solace in the arms of another. Ben didn't blame her, even though he didn't want her and the boys to leave, he understood why she did.

A week after they left, Ben remembered waking up on the sofa – *again!* Head pounding, mouth parched, he had, he realised, as he stood up and looked down, pissed himself again. He unzipped his jeans, stepped out of them and pulled on a pair of tracksuit bottoms that he'd worn previously which, although whiffy and could do with a wash, were at least dry. Staggering into the kitchen, shielding his eyes from the light streaming through the windows – *what time, or, come to think of it, what day was it anyway?* – he stuck his head under the faucet, turned on the tap, and drank big greedy gulps of water.

Then he went to the cupboards and drawers, flinging and heaving them open, searching for something to numb the pain. Pills, booze, anything would do, but all he found was empty bottles and empty packets on empty shelves. Like Old Mother Hubbard, his cupboards were bare. He wasn't hungry, but he checked the fridge for food anyway, which, except for a bottle of rancid milk and mouldy cheese was, like the rest of his life, also empty.

Stumbling into the hallway he searched for his wallet, which he found in the jacket he'd thrown over the banister. He checked it for cash but there was none, only a bankcard, which would do. Then he threw on his jacket, slipped his stinking feet into an equally stinking pair of trainers, which he'd tossed under the stairs, and headed for the door. Pausing, he stared at himself in the hallway mirror; his bloodshot eyes like two piss-holes in the snow. Stroking his beard with one hand, he used the other to smooth down his greasy hair, which he covered with an old baseball cap that he found tucked in his jacket pocket.

'That'll do,' he said, his fetid, whisky-laced breath invading the air around him.

Head down, he proceeded to the small supermarket up the road. He was doing fine too, until some idiot rattled the trolley rack. His response to the clattering, which sounded like gunfire, was automatic, instantaneous. Heading for the side wall, he immediately crouched down, covering his head with his hands, protecting himself. Like Doctor Who, he had travelled through time and was back in Afghanistan, on that terrible day during that terrible moment when the Taliban opened fire, killing Mohammed and his family. Holding Kashif in his arms, his small brain scattered in large pieces all around him, all Ben could see, smell, and taste was blood, everywhere – in his eyes, on his clothes, and in his mouth.

How long Ben sat there rocking back and forth between that world and his present one, he couldn't say. It could have been a minute, an hour, a day. He didn't know. The only thing he was sure of was, he was trapped, between this world and his past one, and until he was willing to get help, *real* help, he knew, with agonising lucidity, he would never move on from the nightmare his life had now become.

He didn't believe in God but lifting his head from his hands, his body sagging with exhaustion, he looked up into a cloudless grey sky. 'Please, God,' he whimpered. 'Help me. I'm ready now. *Really* ready.'

He looked down again, which is when he saw his cap lying on the floor next to him. He reached for it, realising he must have knocked it off when he took cover. Upside down, it was heavier than he expected it to be, which both confused and surprised him. It jangled too, which is when, as he peered into it, he saw a handful of change, which is also when it dawned on him that some well-meaning passers-by must have mistaken him for a homeless guy, begging. Shame; angry and hot, burned his icy skin. Lowering his head again, he watched the ground swim away. Sobbing like a child, he wondered how it had come to this, how he had let himself fall so far, which is also when he heard his name being called.

Panicking, he immediately stopped crying and listened.

Whoever it was, was standing in front of him. She repeated his name again. It was a woman's voice, one that was vaguely familiar, but not one he could immediately put a face to. When she said his name for a third time, she knelt opposite him.

'Ben?' she asked, her voice warm; thick with kindness 'Are you... okay? It's me, Eileen... Eileen Chambers from school. Leora's friend...?'

Relief coursed through his veins. Thank God it was her, someone kind, someone who wouldn't judge him. Bracing himself, he took a deep breath and slowly looked up. With her head slightly tipped to the side, Eileen stared at him. Her face was slimmer than it had been when they were at school but her smile, like her voice, her eyes, was still just as kind.

She stood up, and offered him her hand, which he took. 'What say you come back to mine, eh, for a nice cup of tea, and tell me all about it?'

Blinking back tears, Ben nodded and followed her to her car.

'Look who I found,' she shouted, throwing her keys on the kitchen table, gently leading Ben by the hand into the living room.

To say he had been surprised to see Dobs was an understatement.

# CHAPTER 28

'*D*o you remember Jules's funeral?' Eileen asked, staring at his headstone.

Leora nodded. 'Surprisingly well. Considering how long ago it was.'

Weather-wise it had been an awful day. Colourless, damp, and windblown, the pavements slick with rain; it looked and felt more like winter than spring. At the entrance to the church mourners huddled, waiting for the hearse to arrive, the smokers cupping their lighters with their hands, intermittently puncturing holes in the rain as tiny puffs of smoke formed an escape route from the gaps in their sombre smiles. When the coffin was carried out Leora let out a silent gasp, grateful for her father's strong arm around her shoulder, Lonny's equally strong one around her waist. Jules wasn't family but it didn't lessen the pain any, especially knowing it was one of her best friends, whose life had barely begun, lying in the polished casket of oak.

During some of her last conversations with him in the weeks leading up to his death, Jules encouraged Leora not to be angry with Ben. 'Try and remember the good times,' he said. He also said he knew, without any doubt whatsoever, that Ben did love her: like her, Jules couldn't make any sense of what he'd done. However, he also pointed out that time was precious and not to waste it on things that couldn't be changed. 'Look at this way,' he added playfully. 'At least you got to shag someone you loved. I only ever managed a kiss.'

He didn't say who it was with, so Leora didn't ask. 'I hope it was good?' she said instead.

Jules had looked at her then, his sunken eyes lighting up in a way she hadn't seen for a while. 'The best.' He grinned.

The pain in Leora's chest, as she followed the coffin, was crushing, her sobs only muted by what felt like a large plum in her throat. The eulogy, brief but poignant, had been jointly written by Jules's parents but delivered by the celebrant, and Leora, whose voice was noticeably shaky, somehow managed to read *Let Me Go*, a short memorial poem by Christina Rossetti:

> *When I come to the end of the road*
> *And the sun has set for me*
> *I want no rites in a gloom filled room*
> *Why cry for a soul set free?*

After the reading, looking out at the congregation, she remembered seeing Ben, alongside Dobs and a few others from school, standing at the back of the church. She was pleased they made the effort to pay their respects, unlike others who, when they heard Jules had died of AIDS, chose to stay away.

Seeing Ben again though, after avoiding him for the last couple of months, had been a shock, and the temptation to run to him; feel his arms around her, holding her, comforting her in her grief, was quite overwhelming, and if Ali hadn't been there, whispering in her ear, reminding her how he'd betrayed her, she might very well have done just that.

When the funeral service came to an end Jules was, at his request, carried out of the church to Visage's 'Fade To Grey', which made her smile. Outside, set against an apt grey sky, Jules was lowered into the ground; his final resting place, which was followed by a small wake at his parents' house. They had tried to book the back rooms of some of the local pubs but sadly, all of them, for one reason or another, seemed to be fully booked.

Linking arms with Eileen and Ali, Leora couldn't help noticing how upset Lonny, who was walking with their mother, was. It was obvious, from his red-rimmed, puffy eyes, he'd been crying, which threw her, if only because, even though she knew Lonny liked Jules, had got on well with him, Jules was *her* friend, not Lonny's, so her brother's grief seemed excessive. But like her, Lonny was sensitive, though most people didn't know because, unlike her, he never usually showed it.

As she followed the river of mourners flowing out of the wrought-iron gates, Leora heard her name being called. It was, she realised when she looked round, Ben. He looked nervous; asked her if he could talk to her. Ali said no, but Leora said it was fine, told her and Eileen to go to the car, with the others, and wait for her.

'What do you want, Ben?' she asked, her voice quiet, curt.

He looked tired, and his tone spoke of grief. He said how sorry he was about Jules, how he had always liked him and that the only reason he had stayed out of the way, at the back of the church, was out of respect to her, so as not to cause her any distress.

Leora had been incensed at first. Who the hell did he think he was to believe she was still so upset about him. She was of course, but that was beside the point. Then, quite out of the blue, he had taken her hands in his. Her first inclination had been to snatch them away, until he said how sorry he was – *again*. How he knew he'd messed up and how he'd always regret it.

'I knew, deep down, you were too good for me,' he added. 'I'm just glad I got to spend the time I did with you.'

He also said that whatever happened, he would always love

her, and that whatever she did in life, whatever lay ahead of her, he wished her well. He then kissed her, gently, on the forehead, before turning on his heel and leaving.

Her heart, as she watched him walk away, melted, and all the anger, all the grief that had consumed her during the last few months dissipated like dandelion seeds on the wind. The temptation to run after him and tell him that it didn't matter, not really, not after seeing one of her best friends die, was almost too much to bear. He said he was sorry, *really* sorry, and she believed him. He also said he still loved her... and deep down she knew she still loved him too. And yet even so, he had cheated on her. So really his words, like Ali said, despite the ache in her heart, despite every other instinct in her body screaming otherwise, meant nothing.

Back at Jules's parents' house, the towers of triangle sandwiches remained largely untouched, as did most of the sausage rolls, cheese and pineapple on sticks, and potato salad. Leora did her best to munch her way through some of it, as did her friends and family, but it wasn't easy to eat when you were grieving.

'I think I overdid it,' someone whispered in Leora's ear.

Leora turned to see Margaret, Jules's mother, whose grief-stricken face, under her forced smile, betrayed how worn out she was. 'I think people tend to eat less at funerals.'

Margaret looked straight at her. 'I think you and I both know that's not true, Leora. But thank you,' she added, taking Leora's hand in hers and squeezing it. 'For your friendship, your support, but most of all, thank you...' She paused, glanced round at Ali and Eileen, huddled close by talking to Lonny and her parents. 'All of you... for treating my son like the normal human being he was.'

Swallowing the morsel of sandwich lodged in her throat, her vision blurring, it was all Leora could do not to burst into tears.

'I thought you might like these,' Margaret continued, passing her an envelope. 'I've kept his albums of course, but most of these are just replicas of what were in the albums, so I thought...' she glanced again at Ali, Eileen, and Lonny '...you might want to share them amongst yourselves... as a sort of keepsake.'

Leora opened the envelope and pulled out a thick wad of Polaroid photos, the first of which showed a picture of the four of them as fresh-faced first years, posing together, and at that moment, as if it wasn't broken enough already, Leora swore she felt her heart break just a little bit more. Biting her lip and nodding her head profusely, Leora hugged Margaret before stepping back, using both hands to stem the flow of hot tears streaming down her face. 'Thank you,' she whispered. 'I...' she glanced at her friends, '...we... will all treasure them... forever.'

Margaret smiled, and this time it wasn't a fabrication. This time her smile, which reached her eyes, was genuine. 'I know you will,' she said, before turning away when someone called her name. 'By the way,' she added, briefly turning round again. 'You don't have Jules's camera, do you?'

Puzzled, Leora shook her head. 'No, why?'

'It seems to have gone missing. He kept saying he couldn't find it. I thought he'd just misplaced it, but I can't find it anywhere. Oh well,' she shrugged. 'If any of your friends have it, or it turns up, let me know.'

Jules loved his camera and would never lend it to anyone, so it was strange that it had gone missing. What was also strange, as Leora sifted through them, was the number of photographs of Jules and Lonny together – five, at least – including a couple which, judging by Lonny's baby-faced smile, had been taken some time ago.

Later when Leora showed Lonny the photos, he shrugged, didn't seem to know much about them, but he did remind her how often Jules had his camera with him. 'I remember him asking me if he could take my pic a few times,' he added. 'Usually,' he grinned, rolled his eyes, 'when he was bored, hanging around waiting for you to get ready, or whatever.' Leora asked him if he wanted the pics of him and Jules. 'I dunno.' He shrugged. 'If you want. I'm not fussed either way.'

In the end, after sharing the photos with Ali and Eileen, Leora had given one to Lonny – as he didn't seem too bothered – and stuck the rest in a photo album, which she bought specially.

She hadn't looked at that photo album for years. It was just too painful. Brought back too many memories, especially as it included photos of Lonny and Ben, as well as Jules. She made a mental note to dig it out again, felt like now might be the right time to take another look.

'His parents are still fighting for justice, you know,' Eileen said, interrupting her thoughts. 'The contaminated blood scandal, they're calling it. I still can't understand how no one has been held accountable. I mean, how, when all those people, like Jules, through no fault of their own, infected with either HIV or hepatitis C, has no one been charged with murder, or, at the very least, wrongful death. Because that's exactly what it was... *is*. And what have the government done about it? Nothing. It's infuriating.' She was trying to keep her voice level, quiet, but her cheeks burned with rage.

'I know,' Leora replied solemnly, staring at her friend's headstone. 'I've heard that the victims and their families are pushing for a public inquiry?'

'They are... and there should be one. It's shocking. An absolute travesty.'

'I wonder what he'd be doing now... if he were still alive.'

'That's easy.' Eileen smiled. 'He would be living in London, or, if not London, then Paris, Rome, or New York, in some fancy apartment. One of those modernist steel and glass box types. His boyfriend would be handsome, although not too good-looking as to take the shine off Jules, and they would have two dogs and three cats. He'd wear expensive designer labels too, which he'd team with charity shop finds.'

Leora laughed. 'And how, may I ask, would he be able to afford this affluent lifestyle?'

'Because he'd be a famous award-winning photographer, of course. Sought after by all the celebrities, portraits of whom would hang on his apartment walls alongside pics of the four of us, which he'd continued taking yearly.'

Leora nodded. 'I like that... and I think Jules would too.'

In the distance they heard a car passing. Windows down, music thumping, they heard a song playing. It wasn't just any old song though; it was a song they knew well. One that made the two friends look at one another in disbelief: Visage's 'Fade to Grey'.

'Well, if that isn't confirmation of his approval, I don't know what is.' Leora laughed. 'Now,' she added, glancing at her watch. 'I have some news. Some good news – I think. So, what say we head to the pub so I can share it with you and Ali.'

Eileen nodded, and the two friends stood up. Then, as they linked arms and headed out of the cemetery, she said, 'Guess what? I have some news too.'

# CHAPTER 29

The look on Dobs's face when he saw Ben wasn't exactly welcoming and Ben's first instinct when he saw his old friend was to turn on his heel and run.

Whether or not Eileen sensed that, Ben couldn't say, but standing in front of the door, as if to block his hasty retreat, she gestured towards the sofa, telling Ben to take a seat. When she was sure he had, she walked over to Dobs and gave him a quick peck on the lips. 'I'll make us all a nice cup of tea. I'm sure you two have got a lot of catching up to do.'

'Seems you've got a bit of a habit of collecting waifs and strays.' Dobs smiled, pulling her towards him and kissing her again, so softly, so tenderly it almost made Ben cry. Eileen laughed and wandered into the kitchen. 'Well, mate,' Dobs turned to Ben, 'I have to be honest; you look like shit.'

Head bowed, hands resting on his knees, locked in prayer, Ben slowly looked up again and faced the friend he'd abandoned – just when he'd needed him most.

It was about year or so before the incident in Afghanistan when Ben got wind that Dobs – Mark, even! – had been involved in an IED explosion, and just prior to that, Sally-Ann, who had been having an affair, had left him. Ben rushed to see him as soon as he was able to, but it was a shock to see how, both physically and mentally, bad he was.

Coming from a large, tight-knit family helped because there was always someone on hand, so that, even on his darkest days, there were plenty of people lending their support; reminding Mark how loved he was. Ben did what he could; writing to him when time allowed, calling him when he could, visiting between assignments, and even though Ben knew Mark appreciated his efforts, whenever Ben left him, or rang off, or posted his letters, he always did so with a heavy heart, convinced that nothing he did or said ever really helped his friend.

Mark, a man normally so active, so physical, whose trademark smile rarely left his face, metamorphized from someone who was mostly happy all the time to someone continuously sad. It was easy to see why of course. The day Mark lost his legs was also the day the light went out of his eyes, and try as he might, there didn't seem to be a damn thing Ben could do to help him.

Then of course the incident in Afghanistan happened, which saw Ben spiral into his own nervous breakdown, which was also when Ben broke off all contact with Mark. He hadn't done it deliberately. He just couldn't face his friend, not when physically, there was nothing wrong with him. Mark had every right to be depressed. Ben didn't. So how could he stand in front of his best friend, when his best friend would never be able to stand again, and admit he had his own struggles, was fighting his own demons?

He couldn't. So, in the end, it was easier to stay away.

Mark's aloofness was therefore both justified and understandable. However, after copious cups of tea and some gentle coaxing from Eileen, Ben found himself opening up. He explained what had happened during his last mission, and how it had affected him.

'So how could I help you, when I couldn't even help myself. And it's not just you,' he added. 'I've pushed everyone away, even my kids, which is the worst bit... because... they hate me. But not as much as I hate myself.'

Something had shifted in Mark then, his eyes, his demeanour, so that when Ben finished talking, Mark wheeled himself over to his friend and hugged him, while Ben sobbed in his arms – his *very* strong arms – like a baby.

Making up a bed for him in her son's room, who, she said, was studying at university in Leeds, Eileen invited Ben to stay, which he did. They talked long into the night about everything and anything, including school, which was when Ben asked Mark and Eileen how they had got together, how they'd ended up as a couple.

Eileen explained that, still recovering from the loss of her husband Wayne, after a gruelling couple of years nursing him with a malignant brain tumour, she bumped into Dobs at the Burghley Club. It was a charity event, which she'd helped organise, raising awareness of brain tumours. Mark, who was still very depressed at the time, had been persuaded by his older sister, Cathy, to go with her and her brood.

'Reluctantly,' Mark said, 'but thankfully, I agreed.'

'I was shocked when I saw him,' Eileen said. 'Not about his legs. I'd heard about his accident, but what upset me the most was what he'd done to himself. Dishevelled, emaciated, ruined by drink, he was a mere shadow of the boy I'd falle– of the boy I knew at school.'

'I, on the other hand,' Mark continued, 'couldn't believe how beautiful she still was. Thinner, yes, slightly fatigued, yes, which, after what she'd been through was hardly surprising. But that smile, I knew it was her the minute I laid eyes on her, which, if I could have stood up, I swear to God would have made my knees go weak.' Mark looked at Eileen and winked. 'Mind you,' he continued, 'once I realised it *was* her, if I could have, I would have made a run for it.'

'Why?' Ben frowned.

'Because... I was ashamed, I guess. Not just because I'd lost my legs, but because of what I'd let that do to me. I was a mess. A self-pitying fucking mess. Yes, my life was... is... never going to be the same again, but instead of appreciating what I could still do, I was concentrating on everything I couldn't. And for some reason, seeing Eileen again, hearing what she'd gone through, the way she'd handled it, the way she was getting on with her life, made me realise what a loser I was. Which wasn't necessarily a bad thing, because at least then I knew I was still capable of feeling *something*.

'Anyway, Eileen came over, said hello, and we ended up talking for most of the night, much to our Cathy's delight. Then she started visiting me. Once a week to start with, like, which became once a day, which, well...' Mark, face flushed, turned to Eileen and grabbed her hand, squeezing it between both of his, '...turned into this... into us. She saved me, Ben,' he said, choking back tears. 'This incredible, beautiful woman showed me that life really was worth living, even without legs.'

By the time Mark had finished talking, all three of them were crying. Ben slept surprisingly well that night too, even though he hadn't touched a drop of alcohol in over twenty-four hours. This also meant he woke without a pounding headache for a change. Mark and Eileen insisted Ben stay with them a few more weeks while they helped him put together a recovery plan. He was reticent at first, didn't want to put on his friends, but they were adamant.

'Don't be a twat, Thompson,' Mark said. 'After all, no man's an island.'

At the end of a month Ben was much more mentally, physically, and emotionally stronger than he'd been in a long time, and thanks to counselling sessions with one of Eileen's colleagues, plus the support of his parents, who, again, thanks to Eileen, were now fully on board with his plight, Ben was slowly but surely recovering. It wasn't easy giving up the booze but the best thing about being sober was being a dad again. However, he still had a long way to go. Both boys were still very wary of him, especially Sam, but they were getting there, slowly.

Laughter, across the street, made him look up, brought him crashing back to the present. Two women, one tall, one small, arms linked, were heading towards the pub. Heart pounding, Ben immediately squared his shoulders. He recognised the smaller woman instantly. It was Eileen, which meant the other, taller woman was Leora. Clutching a small handbag, sunglasses on her head, she looked, in her floaty summer dress, flat strappy sandals, and long blonde hair – slightly shorter, slightly tamer than it once was – every bit the sophisticated woman he'd expected her to be. He could still see the quirky, funny, skinny girl he'd fallen in love with all those years ago, except now she was a woman... and my oh my, didn't she wear it well.

Putting his hand to his throat, mouth dry, he had an overwhelming urge to stand up and call out to her. At least he did, until he caught sight of his reflection again in the sunglasses he'd placed on the table. Besides, even if he did talk to her, ask her how she was, what then? She'd probably ask him the same, and what could he tell her? That he was a divorced father of two, currently unemployed, and a recovering alcoholic? He shook his head. She'd try not to show it, but he would see the shock, the disappointment even, in her eyes, which meant at best it would be awkward, and at worst, painful. And the one thing he didn't need right now was any more unnecessary pain.

He casually slipped his glasses on and continued watching her. It was years since he'd last seen her, but she was still beautiful. More so, in fact. Nudging Eileen, she appeared to glance in his direction.

Panicking, he pulled his cap down, and sunk into his seat.

Heart hammering, he folded his arms and waited to see if she had seen him. He hoped not. Which was ironic given that, less than two minutes ago, that was exactly what he wanted.

Squinting, Eileen's eyes followed Leora's before they both looked away again, disappearing into the pub. Relieved, Ben grabbed his phone and keys and made a hasty exit. He didn't know if Leora had seen him, or, for that matter, if Eileen had, but what he did know, without any doubt whatsoever, was what an idiot he was.

# CHAPTER 30

*L*eora and Eileen turned into the high street and headed towards the pub. The Blue Lion, once a rundown watering hole of their youth, had, like several shops and businesses in the area, recently had a make-over. Gone were the sticky wooden floors and the garish patterned carpets; gone was the glass-panelled room divider and the nicotine-stained walls; gone were the leaky loos and the noisy one-armed bandit; and gone was the dartboard and the jukebox. Now, it was unrecognisable.

Like the pubs and bars Leora frequented in London, the Blue Lion boasted sleek walls, a high, partially glass centred ceiling and a slate-tiled floor. The restaurant, with its crisp linen tablecloths and straight-backed chairs, extended out to a paved seating area, including a children's play area to the left, and a smoker's garden to the right. Cleaner, smarter, and functional, catering to families and adults alike, it was just what the town needed – yet Leora couldn't help feeling something was missing. Yes, the smoke-filled pubs of her youth, where the beer was cheap, the hair big, and the fashion questionable, weren't ideal, but there was always a buzz about them, a sense of belonging, which, with its sumptuous interior and pricey drinks menu was, perhaps, what the Blue Lion lacked.

It was lunch time, so the high street was humming with activity. 'Is that new?' Leora asked, pointing to a coffee shop across the street. 'I don't remember seeing it last time I was here.'

Eileen followed her gaze; nodded. 'Uh-huh. Opened a couple of weeks ago, I think. I haven't tried it yet, but it looks nice.'

Leora's eye was drawn to a table outside the coffee shop where a boy, no more than six or seven years old, made her smile. His mocha skin and big brown eyes reminded her of Lonny, as did the dreamy way he was tucking into a huge slice of cake; eyes closed, licking the icing, he looked as if he was savouring every sensuous mouthful. Her eyes drifted to the next table along to a man, sitting alone. Stubbled, in an artfully dishevelled sort of way, his eyes, which briefly collided with hers, seemed vaguely familiar.

Heart racing, for the briefest moment she thought it was Ben, but as she squinted, trying to get a better look, the man, whoever he was, had already looked away. Of course it wasn't Ben. He did, however, wearing aviator sunglasses, a cap pulled over his head, blue jeans and a white T-shirt, have a bit of a *Top Gun* look going on, which again reminded her of Lonny. He and Ben had loved that film. She lost count of the times the three of them watched it together, the tag lines repeated verbatim, always followed by a high-five.

A fat sob escaped the corner of her mouth, taking her completely by surprise.

Concerned, Eileen looked at her, touched her arm. 'You okay?' she asked.

'Just having a moment.'

Eileen nodded, squeezing her arm affectionately. There was no need for further explanation. Like Leora, she understood how odd moments of grief could creep up on you, usually when you least expected them.

After a brief pause, they headed into the pub.

'Do you ever hear much about Ben Thompson?' Leora asked casually, stepping into the welcome cool of the air-conditioned pub.

'Funny you should ask.' Eileen grinned. 'Let's get settled and I'll tell you.'

Intrigued, Leora felt her scalp prick.

Ali didn't get up. 'Ladies.' She smirked when they sat opposite her. 'Fuck me, Eileen,' she exclaimed – much to the disapproving eye of a mother and her two small children sitting at a table behind them. 'You've lost *more* weight.'

Embarrassed, Eileen looked at the young mother, her expression one of an apology, firm disapproval for Ali. 'Do you have to swear?' she hissed.

Ali glanced round and put her hand up. 'Sorry.' Her tone was bored, indifferent. She appeared drunk, which also meant, if she was in a bad mood, telling her to stop it would only make her more provocative. Diversionary tactics, Leora had learned over the years, usually worked best in this sort of situation. 'New bag?' she asked, glancing at the black and green rectangle on the table.

Ali looked at the bag, placing her hand on it, gently stroking it with her thumb. 'Hmm.' Her fingers slowly traced the metal letters that spelled the word PRADA. 'It's from their *cahier* collection,' she added. 'French for notebook, apparently.'

Leora nodded. It was, with its two-tone leather and bronze clasp, quite beautiful. God knows how much it had cost her though. That was Ali for you, always flaunting the by-products of a successful city career, not to mention marrying a man who was loaded. Secretly, Leora wasn't that impressed. She appreciated the craftmanship that had gone into making it. But even if she could afford such an exquisite handbag, which she couldn't, she wouldn't invest in one. *Still, each to their own,* she thought. *It's Ali's business what she spends her money on.*

'Let's have a look, then,' Leora said.

'*Careful*,' Ali warned, passing it over with the same trepidation of a mother handing over her newborn. 'I don't want to get anything on it.'

'It's beautiful,' Leora cooed, showing it to Eileen who, although probably not that impressed either, nodded anyway.

A waiter came over with three gin and tonics, which Ali had got for them, and asked them if they were ready to order food. Leora and Ali chose their usual chicken piccata, whereas Eileen opted for a salad.

Ali wrinkled her nose as if she'd just sniffed something noxious. 'Salad,' she exclaimed. 'Why? You're not exactly overweight. Granted your arms,' she waved her hand in Eileen's general direction, 'are a bit saggy. Nothing a few sessions at the gym won't rectify. But you're hardly the lard arse you were at school.' She laughed but her eyes, firmly fixed on Eileen's, challenged her.

Ignoring her comments, Eileen smiled. Like Leora, she'd learned, over the years, that when Ali was in one of her moods it was best not to give her any ammunition. 'I ordered the salad,' she said. 'Because... well, actually... I *am* watching my weight.'

Leora and Ali exchanged glances. 'But... why?' Leora asked.

Eileen's smile lit up her whole face. 'Because,' she gushed, 'I need to make sure I can fit into my dress.'

'Dress? What dress?' Leora said, confusion creasing her brow.

Grinning like a schoolgirl, Eileen placed both hands, palms down, on the table and took a deep breath. This time when she spoke, her voice was softer, quieter, a whisper almost. 'My wedding dress.'

'What!' Leora placed a fist either side of her head, the disbelief in her voice palpable. 'But... but... I didn't even know you were seeing anyone?' It was stupid, but just for a moment Leora felt a tremor of disappointment. Whoever the lucky guy was, it must be serious, so why hadn't Eileen told them before now, or at least, told her, anyway? She shrugged it off. She must have her reasons, and regardless of what they were, it was easy to see how happy she was. 'Well... c'mon,' she asked, her voice filled with giddy enthusiasm. 'Are you going to tell us who the lucky man is or what?'

Eileen, pink faced, looked at her. 'It's... someone you know.' Her gaze switched to Ali. 'Someone you both know.'

A smile tugged at the corner of Ali's mouth who, up until now, unlike Leora, had mostly kept quiet. 'Don't tell me it's that knob from school. The one you had a crush on.'

Eileen looked away, adjusting the angle of her head, as if trying to free a trapped nerve. A flicker of something – hurt maybe, anger? – flashing in her eyes.

Leora gasped. 'Is it... Dobs? Mark Dobson... from school?'

Eileen, eyes wide, cheeks burning, smiled. 'It is.'

'Blimey,' Ali replied. 'You kept that quiet. Why?' Her eyes narrowed. 'What's the catch?'

Eileen looked at her; smiled sweetly. 'No catch,' her simple reply.

Ali opened her mouth to respond but Leora beat her to it. She suspected Ali and Hugo were having problems again, which would account for Ali's foul mood today. However, she also knew how in love Eileen had once been with Dobs – as much as she'd been with Ben – so knowing that, and knowing how much sharing this news with them, her two oldest friends, meant to Eileen, she wasn't about to let Ali spoil it for Eileen.

'Oh Eileen,' she gushed, taking both her hands in hers. 'I'm thrilled for you... for both of you. Really, I am.' And she was. Truly. So why then, did she also feel that she might burst into tears?

The waiter arrived with their food, which was also when Ali decided to nip to the loo. 'Well,' she said, throwing her napkin down. 'Not another word about this until I get back.' She smirked. 'Something tells me this is going to be *very* interesting.'

When they were sure she'd gone, Leora and Eileen looked at

one another and burst out laughing. 'She's her usual happy self then,' Eileen said, drolly.

Leora shrugged. 'I think she's drunk... and if I was to hazard a guess why, I'd probably say it was because she was having problems with Hugo.'

Eileen rolled her eyes. 'What, again? Doesn't mean she has to take it out on us does it. She didn't even ask us how we got on at the cemetery.'

'I know.' Leora sighed, unfolding her napkin which she laid in her lap. 'The thing is,' she continued, spearing her pasta with her fork, 'I think things get... physical with Hugo.'

Eileen's eyebrows shot up. 'What do you mean?'

Leora glanced over her shoulder, making sure Ali wasn't behind them. 'I think they drink, then they fight, then I think Hugo hits her. Not very often. But that's not the point is it because, no matter how difficult things get between them, he shouldn't hit her... ever.'

Eileen asked Leora why she thought Hugo was being physical, and Leora reminded her about the bracelet of bruises Ali sometimes wore around her wrists.

'Yeah... but that was ages ago, wasn't it? I don't recall seeing any such bruises recently.'

'They did make an appearance again a few months ago, plus, I did spot some really nasty bruises on her back a couple of weeks ago, when her T-shirt slipped.'

Eileen's jaw clenched; a flicker of surprise in her eyes. 'Really? Did you ask her about them?'

'I did, but she just shrugged it off, said she'd fallen off her chair or something.'

They discussed confronting Ali about it, but decided, given her current mood, it was probably best not to. 'I'll keep an eye on her,' Leora said. 'And if anything else happens, I'll keep you posted.'

'Okay.' Eileen toyed with her salad. 'By the way... sorry I

didn't tell you earlier... about Mark... I just thought, considering how long we've all known each other, that I should tell you both together... but... well... I kind of wish I'd told you first now.'

Resting her fork on her plate, Leora placed her hand on top of Eileen's and squeezed it. 'It's fine,' she said. 'It's wonderful news and I can't wait for Ali to come back so you can tell us more.'

Back from the restroom, Ali seemed calmer, less agitated. Leora wondered if she'd given herself a stern talking to, or, if drugs – legal or otherwise – were responsible for her slightly more relaxed demeanour. If she were to hazard a guess, she'd say it was the latter.

Eileen told them about Mark. That how, divorced, and a bit down on his luck, they met at a local charity function she was speaking at. How their weekly meet-ups turned into daily ones, until eventually, after falling in love, Mark moved in with her.

'Why did he leave the army?' Ali asked.

'Because,' Eileen replied, staring at her with priestly calm, 'he had an accident.'

Ali's smile was slow; conspiratorial. 'What kind of accident?'

Leora watched her friends with bewildered fascination. Like a dog with a bone Ali had clearly sensed, or picked up on something she hadn't, and to say the atmosphere between them was uneasy would be an understatement. It was obvious Eileen was reluctant to reveal why Mark had been discharged, so she wished Ali would just leave it for now. Eileen would tell them when she was ready to. It didn't help either, that both women seemed slightly volatile today. Leora needed to do something to ease the tension. Once again, she opted for diversionary tactics.

'Is Mark still friends with Ben? Do they... still see each other?'

Eileen drew her shoulders down, the relief in her eyes, at Leora's attempt to change the subject, tangible. 'Yes.' She smiled. 'He does. Like us, they're still very good friends. Plus...' Eileen, eyebrow arched, looked at Leora and grinned. 'I don't know if you've heard, but he and Gemma have separated.'

Leora's tummy flipped.

'They're still friends, which is good for the boys but–'

'Boys? Ben has sons?' Leora could see Ben as a father. Imagined that, like Tim with Mia, he was probably a good dad.

'Yes, two. Sam and Robbie. Lovely lads.'

'You've met them then?' Leora was unable to keep the surprise out of her voice.

'A couple of times, yes.'

'Does he... has he, that is... ever mentioned me?'

Eileen's smile was filled with warmth. 'Yes.' She nodded. Leora felt her heart flutter. 'He has. And I was thinking...' She picked up her glass, took a swig of gin. 'I know he regrets what he did to you, but it's obvious, at least to me it is, anyway, that he still has feelings for you. So, I thought... as you're single and he's single... how about the two of you join Mark and me for a meal one night. I know–'

'No,' Ali roared, banging her fist on the table. 'No. No. No.'

Stunned, Leora and Eileen looked at her.

'Have you forgotten what a complete shit he was to her.' She looked at Eileen but pointed to Leora. 'What a complete mess she was. Christ, I spent most of my early years in London making sure she was okay, that she didn't do anything... stupid.'

*Did you?* Leora thought.

Ali turned to Leora. 'If I wasn't watching out for you, usually because you were drunk or high, making sure you weren't tripping over yourself, or that some bloke wasn't taking advantage of you, then I was either holding your hair back while you puked, or hugging you while you cried yourself to sleep.'

Leora frowned. 'To be fair, I remember holding your hair back a few times too. I did cry at lot yes, but it wasn't just for Ben, it was for Lonny too, and Jules. All of them! And although my behaviour was a bit erratic, some of that was just because we were young, and enjoying ourselves... sort of.'

'Yes, but who was there mopping up your tears and picking

up the pieces. I'll tell you who,' Ali said, pointing to herself. 'Me. And *she*,' she added, picking up an unused knife and pointing it at Eileen, 'hasn't got a bloody clue what that was like, otherwise, she wouldn't make such a stupid suggestion.'

*Was it... I... really that bad?* Leora wondered. She thought back to that day, sitting at the breakfast table, staring at the photos of Ben and Gemma that had just arrived, the two of them together, and in that moment, all the hurt, all the grief, and all the pain she felt then, she felt now.

'Ben Thompson caused you nothing but pain and misery,' Ali added. 'You know it, and I know it. End of.'

Eyes cast downwards; Leora looked at Eileen. 'Thank you... but...' her gaze switched to Ali, then back to Eileen again, '...she's right,' she shrugged. 'It's probably not a good idea. Besides, don't they, whoever *they* are, say you should never go back. He's my ex for a reason.'

'Of course,' Eileen replied, sombrely. 'I understand.'

The conversation lulled, the waiter adiosed their plates of half-eaten food and Ali ordered another round of drinks.

Holding her gin glass up, Leora tapped it with a knife. 'Right.' She coughed to clear her throat, deciding now was as good a time as any to share her news, and hopefully lighten the mood a little while she was at it. 'I have some news. Some good news... I think.'

When she had finished telling them, Eileen's jaw dropped. 'So... you'll be on TV?'

Leora smiled; lifted her shoulders. 'Looks that way.'

'What... like proper *proper* TV?'

'Proper, proper TV.' Leora laughed. 'And not only that, but I also get my own stylist plus a whole wardrobe of clothes... plus... and this is the real kicker... depending on the success of the show, they might film some of the episodes in the Caribbean.'

'No way,' Eileen gasped. 'Really?'

'Really.' Leora beamed. 'And what with having family there

that I've still never met, having never had the chance to visit, I'm kind of keeping my fingers crossed they might choose Jamaica.'

'Wow... that would be like... amazing,' Eileen said. 'I've never been to the Caribbean.'

'Me neither.'

'It's not that special,' Ali said, dryly. 'Hugo and I much preferred Mauritius.'

Eileen, mouth twitching, eyes steely, turned to look at Ali and this time she was the one that looked like she'd smelled something nasty. She opened her mouth, as if to reply, then seemed to think better of it, and instead turned her attention back to Leora. 'I'm so pleased for you,' she said. 'And so, *so* proud of you. If that's not proof that you should never give up on your dreams, I don't know what is.'

'Don't be ridiculous, Eileen,' Ali snorted. 'It's TV presenting. Hardly bloody Hollywood.'

Fighting the urge to get up and walk out, Leora folded her hands into fists under the table, and pressed her nails into her palms, trying her best to ignore Ali's barb. She was clearly unhappy about something, hence her provocative bad mood. Leora, however, was determined not to rise to it.

Eileen, meanwhile, turned to Ali, her head movements slow, stilted. 'No...' She took a deep breath. 'It's not Hollywood, but it's a start, and not only that, it's primetime TV, so who knows where it could lead to.'

Ignoring her, Ali looked at Leora. 'I thought you said you weren't doing any more auditions.'

'I wasn't. Had made up my mind not to, in fact. It was purely by chance I bumped into Sade, and if we hadn't got talking and she hadn't told me about the show, suggesting I audition for it, I wouldn't have even known about it. I asked her later, once the offer was confirmed, why she thought I was a good candidate. She said it was because she remembered how well I spoke at Speaker's Corner during one of our assignments at uni, which is bizarre really, because all I can remember about that time is thinking how crap I was.'

'Yes, but aren't you, at forty, a little old?' Ali asked.

'Two years younger than Cilla Black was when she started hosting *Blind Date*,' Eileen quipped, nudging Leora with her knee. 'So... when do you start filming?' she continued.

Leora explained that they'd already started rehearsals, but other than that, all she knew for now was, come September, there'd be one episode a week, filmed live, and aired on Saturday nights. Eileen clapped her hands. 'It's so exciting,' she squealed. 'I might have to re-think the date Mark and I get married now.'

'Do you have an actual date then?' Leora asked.

'We've got a couple in mind. Nothing set in stone as such because we're still waiting to hear back from a couple of venues. Not that it's going to be anything big or fancy. We can't afford it.' She laughed. 'Plus, what with Mark being in a....' She paused, stared at the table, her finger circling a small stain. 'The thing is,' she continued, looking up again. 'The reason Mark was medically discharged from the army is because he lost both legs below the knee in an explosion. So, he's in a wheelchair.'

Ali, much to Leora and Eileen's complete surprise, and horror, started laughing. 'I knew it. Some people never change.'

Eileen looked at her in utter disbelief; clearly defined *what the fuck?* lines furrowing her brow. 'And what the hell is that supposed to mean?'

'He's a user,' Ali said, her eyes glinting. 'He used you at school and he's using you now.'

Eileen pressed her lips together, took a deep breath. 'How so?' She cocked her head to one side, eyes tightening, mouth narrowing.

'Isn't it obvious. He knew you liked him at school, yet the only time he took any real interest in you was when he needed your help.'

Eileen's pink face turned positively puce. 'That's not true,' she snapped.

'Oh, come off it, Eileen, of course it is. You adored him, any idiot could see that, but despite everything you did for him, it was never enough, because you were never thin enough or pretty enough to be his girlfriend. And now... now he's disabled... and nobody wants him, he's decided to lower his standards.'

Leora gasped. 'What the fuck, Ali?'

'What?' she replied, her expression quizzical. 'I'm not saying that's what *I* think of Eileen – she's my friend, and like you I love her, think she's beautiful, inside and out – I'm simply pointing out what everyone else around this table is thinking but is too afraid to say.'

'Which is?' Leora asked.

Ali sighed. 'Which is,' she repeated, her eyes flitting back to Eileen, 'if Dobs–'

'*Mark*,' Eileen corrected her, her words curt, dismissive. 'His name is *Mark*.'

Ali rolled her eyes. 'Okay... if *Mark* was still able-bodied, he wouldn't look twice at you.'

Head down, gait low, Eileen pushed her chair back and stood up. 'No,' she said quietly. 'You're wrong.' She reached for her bag, began fumbling for her purse. 'Here.' she placed a couple of purple notes on the table. 'Money for my share. It's been... lovely... as usual... but I'm– I have to go.'

'Oh, don't be silly, Eileen.' Ali tutted. 'Stay. I only say what I say because I'm your friend and I worry about you.'

'I know.' Eileen slipped her bag on her shoulder, and smoothed down her dress. 'I'm not leaving because of what you said. I'm leaving because it's late, and I have things to do.' She smiled, but it was a fabrication, until she turned to Leora. It was subtle but this time when she smiled it was genuine, reached her eyes. 'I'm so proud of you, Leora.'

Leora blushed. 'Thank you, that really means a lot to me.'

Eileen nodded, put her thumb to her ear, her little finger to her mouth. 'Call me in the week... yeah?'

'I will,' Leora promised, and with that Eileen turned on her heel and left, but not without pausing to look at Ali first. 'Thanks for your concern, I do appreciate it. But you're wrong about Mark.' And with that she was gone.

'Jesus.' Ali took a large swig of gin. 'Some people can't handle the truth.'

Eyebrow arched, chewing her thumb, Leora looked at her. 'Back in a minute,' she said, getting up and heading for the door. It was still gloriously sunny outside, which meant, for a few seconds, Leora had to squint to see. Looking left to right, she searched the busy high street for her friend. She spotted her a few feet away on the opposite side of the road. She called out to her and on her third attempt, Eileen stopped, turned round.

Putting her hand to her chest, Leora sprinted towards her. 'Are you... okay?' she puffed.

Eileen forced a smile. 'Yes, of course, why wouldn't I be?'

'I just wondered... if what Ali said had upset you?'

Eileen shrugged. 'She's allowed her opinion.'

'True... but she doesn't always have to share it with us, does she.'

'It's just...' Leora knew what she was going to say, 'Ali being Ali,' they said in unison.

They both laughed, before Eileen added, 'I guess... if you say it often enough you start to believe it... don't you.'

Leora asked her what she meant.

'I just think, that sometimes, when we dismiss what Ali says as just...' she made quotation marks with her fingers, '...Ali being Ali, it excuses her from some pretty shitty comments.' She shook her head, told Leora to forget it. 'Ignore me,' she added, waving her hand in the air. 'I told you I was having an off-day.'

'If it's any consolation,' Leora said, putting her hand to her collarbone, 'I think she's wrong about Mark.'

Eileen grinned. 'Me too. Are you...' she paused, looked thoughtful, 'sure about *not* seeing Ben?'

*Ben,* Leora thought, feeling her heart thud. *Yes, I would love to see him again... but... then again...* 'I'm sure,' she said. 'Ali's wrong about Mark, but right about Ben.'

When she went back to the pub, Ali was getting ready to leave. 'Got to go. I'm meeting someone. Listen, I've taken Eileen's cash, because I don't have any on me. Are you okay to settle the bill, then I'll write you a cheque for our share when we're back in London.'

Leora sighed. Ali had done this to her a couple of times just recently, and she never did pay her back, but before she could say anything, Ali was already walking away.

'You owe Eileen an apology,' she called.

Ali put her hand up. 'I'll send her some flowers,' she said dismissively. 'That usually works. See you later, at the station...'

Leora shook her head. 'No. Sorry, but you won't. I'm staying with my parents for a few days.'

Ali stopped walking, turned round. 'Really? That's not like you.'

Leora shrugged. 'We've been getting on a lot better just recently... so when they invited me to stay, I said yes.'

Ali's smile was crisp. 'How *very* cosy. Say hello from me.' And with that she was gone.

# CHAPTER 31

*A*fter their session at the gym, Ben drove Mark home. Mark and Eileen were right. Getting physically fit again was doing wonders, both for his mental and physical health, alongside a healthy diet and counselling of course. He knew it would. His training in the forces had taught him that, but his drink-fuddled brain had quite forgotten for a while. As a drunk, he'd forgotten everything and everyone. Now though, since hitting rock bottom, he was, slowly but surely, making his way up again. Swimming for air. Back in the land of the living, which is exactly where he wanted to be, despite the pain it caused him, the demons he had to slay.

He was taking charge of his life again and for the first time in a long time it felt good.

Seeing Leora today though had been difficult. She reminded him of all the shoulda-woulda-couldas he had long ago buried. He missed her, even after all these years; confirming what he'd always known, which was, he never had, and never would, stop loving her.

This time though, instead of adding it to his pint pot and drowning it in whisky, he faced it head on. She was the love of his life, but like his marriage, he had fucked up. Instead of beating himself up about it, he accepted it, owned it and was learning to move on. He wished Leora well and above all else, he wished her happiness. Then, instead of hitting the bottle, he hit the gym.

'Coming in for a cuppa?' Mark asked, easing himself into the wheelchair Ben had just pulled from the boot of his car. Mark struggled for a minute, and it was all Ben could do not to help him. Mark was fiercely independent, and even when people meant well, he hated being treated like an invalid.

'I'd love one,' Ben replied, walking behind him as Mark navigated his chair towards the front door, his neck muscles taut, his powerfully built arms propelling him forward at alarming speed.

'Do you know what I really miss?' Mark continued, unlocking the door, bumping his chair across the entrance.

Ben followed him into kitchen, which smelt of freshly cut flowers and a hint of last night's curry. It was a nice house; three-bedroom semi in a quiet cul-de-sac with a gravelled drive at the front and neatly manicured garden and small patio area at the back.

Everywhere you looked though the house echoed with reminders of Wayne, Eileen's deceased husband, including photos of the four of them; Wayne, Eileen and their two sons. Ben had once asked Mark if it bothered him. He had replied, 'Course not. I'd be a bit of a twat if it did, wouldn't I?'

'Go on then,' Ben said. 'What do you miss the most?'

Mark nodded at the back door. 'Open it will you. Get some fresh air in the place, eh.' Ben went to the door, unlocked it, and pushed it open. Mark busied himself at the tap, filling the kettle. Ben had learnt the hard way not to offer to do it for him.

'Take a seat,' Mark said, head tilted, gesturing to the table. Ben pulled a chair out, sat down.

'Running,' Mark continued, wheeling his chair to the fridge, fetching the milk. 'That's what I miss the most. And playing footie, of course,' he added.

Ben asked him, as he was a below the knee amputee, if he'd tried prosthetic legs. 'Yeah… didn't really get on with them though.'

Carefully placing one steaming mug of tea on the table at a time, Mark grabbed a packet of fig rolls from another cupboard and joined Ben at the table. He brought one of the mugs to his mouth and took a mouthful, let out a breath. 'Not a bad cuppa if I say so myself.' He placed it down again, opening the fig rolls. Taking two out, he stuffed one in his mouth and pushed the packet towards Ben. 'Course, what I could really do with,' he mumbled, 'is a pair of blades, like that Pistorius bloke.'

'Can't you buy some?' Ben asked, glancing out the window at the small patio area, his eye drawn to a row of colourful pots containing herbs for cooking that Eileen had shown him last time he was there.

Mark laughed. 'I could… if I could afford them.'

'They're expensive then, are they?'

Mark looked at Ben askance, although not unkindly. 'About six grand.'

Ben almost choked on his tea. 'Six grand,' he repeated.

'Each.'

'Really?' Ben used the back of his hand to wipe his mouth. 'I had no idea.'

Mark shrugged, took another glug of tea, patted his wheelchair. 'I get about just fine with this… now I've got used to it.' A key rattled in the front door. 'That must be Eileen. Just a word of warning,' he whispered. 'She's not always herself when she's been to the cemetery. Can be a bit… quiet. It's nothing personal though.'

'I can leave… if you want?' Ben pointed to the door.

Mark shook his head. 'Nah, it's fine. Stay.'

A scrape and a hiss as the door opened was followed by the rattling of the letterbox as it banged shut again.

'That you, love?' Mark called out. No reply. 'I've just boiled the kettle... if you fancy a cuppa.' Still no reply. Thirty seconds or so later footsteps: slower than usual, trudged towards the kitchen.

Eileen wandered in; her eyes red-rimmed, puffy. 'Hi,' she sighed, looking at Mark. 'Oh, hey Ben,' she added, offering him a Mona Lisa smile.

Mark reversed his chair and pushed himself towards her. Taking her hand in his, he arched his neck, as if expecting her to kiss him, but she didn't. She discreetly shrugged him off, made her way to the sink, took a glass from the draining board, turned on the tap, and filled it, drinking without pause.

Mark, who had turned slightly pink, put his hand to the back of his neck; looked at Ben.

*Shall I go?* Ben mouthed.

Mark frowned, shook his head. 'How erm... did it go today then?' He asked, angling his chair to face the sink. 'How's Ali... and Leora?'

Using her hand to wipe the bead of water from her mouth, Eileen spun round. 'Yeah, they're good thanks,' she said, slamming the glass down, her voice uncharacteristically curt, dismissive. 'Leora's been offered a job as a TV presenter for a new dating show.'

*Wow. Good for you, Leora*, Ben thought.

'Wow, that's brilliant news. And Ali?' Mark asked, his eyes, like Ben's, flitting to Eileen's hands, gripping the worktop behind her: her knuckles noticeably white against her otherwise pink skin. 'How's... she doing?'

Quiet for a moment, Eileen looked at Mark. 'Why are you with me?' she asked.

*Oh fuck*, Ben thought.

Mark wrinkled his nose. 'What?'

Unflinching, she asked again. 'I *said*, why are you with me?'

'Eileen... what are you talking about, love?' Mark replied, eyebrow arched, powerful arms folded across his broad chest. 'You know why I'm with you. The same reason you're with me... I hope.'

Ben coughed, pushed his chair back and stood up. 'I erm...' he pointed to the door, '...think I'll get going.'

Eileen glared at him. 'You're not going anywhere, Ben Thompson. Sit down.'

Lowering his head like a chastised schoolboy, Ben immediately sat down again. 'Okay,' he gulped.

Scratching his head, Mark looked from Eileen to Ben, then back to Eileen again. 'Come on, love, what's wrong? You can't talk to Ben like that.'

'I'm not talking to Ben like anything,' she snapped. 'I just want the truth... and Ben to bear witness to it.'

Mark put his hands up. 'Bear witness? Witness to what, exactly?'

'The truth,' Eileen barked. 'That's all I want. Nothing more, nothing less.' She took a deep breath. 'So... I'll ask you again. Why are you with me? Why have you asked me to marry you?'

'Because...' Mark replied, face flushed, '...I love you. But you know that.'

Folding one arm across her chest, which she tucked in the crook of her armpit, Eileen brought her other hand up to her face: kneading her cheek. 'Really? Or are you just with me because no one else wants you?'

Mark, wounded, sat back in his chair. 'Wow,' he finally managed to say. 'Is that what you think? That I'm with *you*... because no one else wants to be with me?' He sounded choked, the pain in his eyes flickering like two blazing flames.

Eileen, now chewing her thumb, turned her back, began pacing the kitchen. When she looked round again, her eyes had softened. 'No,' she said, her voice barely a whisper. 'It's not what I think; it's what someone else thinks. They say you're using me, like you did at school. That you knew how I felt about you, but the only time you bothered with me was when I helped you with your homework, but I was never thin enough or pretty enough to be your girlfriend. The same person also said, if you weren't disabled, you wouldn't look twice at me.'

Mark banged his fist on the table, sloshing tea from his mug. 'Who?' he demanded. 'Who said that? Surely not Ali... or Leora?'

Eileen shook her head, looked away. 'No... of course not.' She pressed her fingers to her lips.

*She's lying*, Ben thought, watching a murky river of tea creep across the table.

Mark closed his eyes. Tapped the space between his brows with his fingers, his elbow resting on the arm of his chair. 'Eileen... please sit down,' he said when he opened his eyes again.

'I need to clean this up first.' She made a dash for the worktop, her eyes flitting nervously between the kitchen roll that sat on the side and the table where the tea spillage was now more of a sea than a river.

Ben, however, beat her to it, and within seconds there wasn't a spot of tea left. Stuffing the wet sheets of kitchen towel in the bin, he remained standing, while Eileen, somewhat reluctant, pulled out a chair opposite Mark and sat down.

Mark placed his arms behind his head, muscles bulging, and looked up at the ceiling. Whatever he was about to say was going to be difficult. 'The truth is,' he said, looking directly at Eileen. 'I love you... and I always have. The only difference now being, unlike when I was younger, and afraid, I'm happy to tell the world! I did treat you badly though.' His gaze shifted to Ben, then back to Eileen again. 'Why? Because I was an idiot. To me, you were... *are*... beautiful, but because I was a shallow "Jack the lad" type at school, who thought he had to act a certain way and have a certain type of girl on his arm, I was afraid no one else could see what I saw.'

'What you mean is, I wasn't pretty enough,' Eileen replied, her voice wavering.

Mark shook his head. 'No.' He scrubbed his face with his hands. 'That's not what I'm saying. Not what I'm saying at all. The thing is, I thought I had an image I needed to keep up.' He rolled his eyes, as if mocking the absurdity of his younger self. 'Ben and I hung out with a group of lads who thought they were the bees' knees, but really, we were just a bunch of dickheads. But we were popular, and it followed that your girlfriend had to be too, which, let's face it, you lot weren't.' He looked at Ben again. 'Which is ironic really because... we were talking about school the other day, and both of us agreed how cool we thought you four were.'

Eileen's eyebrows shot up, a small smile on her lips. 'Really?'

Mark smiled. 'Really. We never said as much at school, but later, when we were older, we often talked about you lot.' He glanced at Ben again, who nodded. 'About how, unlike us, you weren't afraid to be different. And... well, the truth is...' his hand went to his neck, which was red and blotchy. 'You and I both know there was more to *us* than you helping me with my homework, and by the time I'd worked that out, by the time I'd got the balls to do something about it, you were marrying someone else.'

Eileen's gasp was barely audible. 'You... you know then?' Her eyes were wide, incredulous.

*Know? Know what?* Ben thought.

Mark nodded, placing his hands, palms down, on the table. 'I came to see you, you know. Rode my bike to your parents' house. Shitting myself, I was. Terrified what your dad might do to me if he saw me.'

Still none the wiser, although he was starting to have his suspicions, Ben, silent, watched his two friends.

'I had it all worked out, though,' Mark continued. 'Kind of. I even went to see Sally-Ann first, to finish things. Then, hiding from view, trying to summon the courage to knock on your door, I saw it open and there you were, walking down the drive. To this day, I can still remember...' he paused, put a fist to his chest, '...how much my heart was pounding. Then I saw Wayne... behind you... and my heart sank. I know he was only a couple of years older than us, but he seemed so grown up, whereas I just felt like a stupid kid.

'I watched you both for a minute, noticed how your hand went to your tummy, the gentle way Wayne guided you to his car. I mean...' Mark held his hands up, '...that said it all, for God's sake. There I was on me pushbike and there *he* was with his car. Then I saw the way he looked at you...' Mark shook his head. 'With so much love in his eyes. It was obvious how much you meant to him. Worse than that, though, was the way *you* looked at him; the same way you had looked at me... once. I knew then, that I'd blown it, lost my chance. But more importantly than that, I knew I didn't deserve you. So, with my tail between my legs, I went back to Sally-Ann and tried my best not to think about you...'

Eileen, who was opening and closing her mouth like a goldfish, looked stunned.

'Wasn't easy though,' Mark continued. 'Sometimes, when I was on leave, visiting my parents, I'd sneak by your house, watch you pushing Noah in his pram, taking him to the park.'

Ben looked at Mark. *All those drunk conversations*, he thought. *And you never told me any of this!*

'In the end though, it was just too painful, so I stopped, and before long, me and Sally-Ann were married, followed a few years later by the arrival of Jacob.'

Ben decided he needed another drink, strong coffee instead of weak tea. 'Okay if I put the kettle on?' he asked.

Eileen, who was staring at Mark, didn't hear him, whereas Mark, who was rubbing his hand across his chin – sandpaper chafing wood – looked at Ben and nodded.

'So... you've known then, all these years, that Noah is yours?'

Mark lifted his shoulders. 'I wasn't a hundred per cent... but I was reasonably sure. But since living with you and getting to know the boys... well... it's obvious, isn't it?'

'Is it?' Eileen frowned, forming two deep grooves in the space between her eyebrows. 'How?'

Mark pointed to his chin. 'Same dimple. Same widow's peak,' he continued, his hand moving to his hairline. 'Not to mention the same eyes,' he added, fluttering his lashes for effect. 'He even rubs his chin like me when he's nervous.'

Ben had only met Noah a couple of times, but Mark was right, the likeness between the two of them was uncanny.

Thoughtful, Eileen smiled. 'He does, doesn't he. But... if I'd known,' she stammered. 'If you'd come to me... sooner... that time you saw me with Wayne... things might have been different.'

Knuckling his eye, exhaustion glazing his face, Mark sighed heavily. 'I know... The thing is,' he said, wheeling to the other end of the table. 'I've thought about it, us, Noah, a lot. And in the end, I keep coming back to the same conclusion.' He placed his hand on hers.

'Which is?' Eileen asked.

'Which is, to quote something, Jeff, Ben's dad said to him just recently.'

Ben, who was spooning coffee into mugs glanced round.

'Regrets,' said Mark, 'are a waste of time. If I hadn't met Sally-Ann there'd be no Jacob. If you hadn't met Wayne, there'd be no Oliver. In an ideal world we would have married, I wouldn't have lost my legs, and my son wouldn't come from a broken home. On the upside though, I've been reunited with the woman I love... *really* love... who is not only beautiful inside and out, and a wonderful mum and step-mum, but is also – he winked – a good shag.'

Eileen, who now had tears running down her cheeks, gasped.

Red-faced, she punched Mark's shoulder. 'Don't be so bloody crude,' she laughed.

'Ouch.' He rubbed his arm with exaggerated concern. 'That hurt.'

'I doubt it.' She grinned.

'Come here, you.' Mark reached for her other hand, threading both with his. 'I haven't finished yet.' Suddenly serious, resting his forehead on hers he looked straight at her. 'You taught me how to live again, you know. And if you think, for one minute, I won't fight for you, for us, then you really don't know me very well at all. I let you go once... but I won't be making the same mistake again. I love you, Eileen... with all my heart. Always have and always will.'

Any doubts Eileen had up till then, Ben thought, surely must have gone. It was obvious how much his friend loved her, and if he could see it, she must be able to see it too. Envious, he watched his friend, now cradling Eileen in his arms, kiss the top of her head. Ben smiled. Mark's younger self would never have dared to be so open, so honest about his feelings.

*Good for you, mate,* Ben thought. *Good for you.*

Resting his cheek on her head, Mark stroked Eileen's hair. When he looked up, he spotted Ben smiling at them and grinned. Giving him the thumbs up, Ben pointed to the door. 'I'm going,' he mouthed. Mark blinked, giving him a diminutive nod of the head. Stealthily, his former SAS training coming to the fore, Ben quietly slipped out the front door.

Out in the fresh air, he paused and looked up. It was just after five, the sky was still cloudless, and the sun, still a bright orange orb floating in a cerulean sea, still hot. Taking a few deep breaths, the air thick with the smell of freshly cut grass, he listened and realised as, dogs barked, kids laughed, and people talked, it could have been any street, in any town, in any part of the world, but the place he was reminded of was one of his formative years. One of never-ending summers, of kick-abouts at the reccy with Dobs, of long, drawn-out evenings with Leora, blanket on the ground, lying together, holding hands, kissing, watching the sun go down until the stars came out.

Shoving his hands in his pockets, he gave a final glance back at the house. He was proud of Mark because he knew, if he had a second chance with Leora, he would fight tooth and nail for her, and this time, he would never, *ever*, let her go.

# CHAPTER 32

*L*eora listened to the constant clanking of metal trolleys echoing along disinfected corridors, her eye drawn to various doctors and nurses, some relaxed, others wearing a look of hurried urgency, that every now and again thrust open or pulled closed curtains to various cubicles.

'I hate hospitals,' a voice said, interrupting her thoughts. Leora turned to her friend. She looked, with one eye so swollen, so bruised, she was unable to open it, like she had been in a car crash. Dried blood formed a crust around her split lip, and she winced as she tried to reposition herself without moving the arm that the X-ray confirmed was, thankfully, sprained but not broken.

Leora braced herself to speak. This was serious. The outcome could have been so much worse. She needed to tread carefully though. She did her level best to keep her voice gentle, quiet, but she couldn't hide the urgency in it. 'Do you think I honestly believe... that they believe,' she nodded at a passing doctor, 'that you fell... down the stairs?'

Ali turned her head, the less bruised side, and buried it into the plump, white pillow she was resting on. Leora knew from the slight rise and fall of her friend's shoulders, she was crying. She felt bad. She hadn't meant to make her cry, but she also didn't want a dead friend. Stroking Ali's matted hair with one hand she took the hand that wasn't sprained and gently held it in hers.

'What happened, Ali? Please tell me.'

Ali turned her sodden cheek to look at her. 'He's here, you know,' she whispered. 'Hugo, I mean. He's the one who brought me here, in a taxi.'

Alarmed, Leora swung round. 'Where? Where is he?'

'He went for coffee. When I said I was going to call you. Which was a while ago now. He's probably wandering around outside, collecting his thoughts. Feeling bad. Like he always does.'

'So it was him? Hugo? You're admitting it this time?'

Ali shook her head. 'You don't understand.' Her eyes darted towards the half-closed curtains. Shaking, she put a finger to her bloodied lip. 'Shhhh. See if he's there, will you?'

Leora poked her head through the curtains, looked left to right, watching the constant flow of hospital staff and patients. There was no sign of Hugo though. Although she did check and double check – just to make sure.

'Can't see him.' She took a seat at her friend's side again, listening as Ali attempted to explain what had happened.

'We had a table booked at a little bistro, for lunch. Hugo wasn't working today, and I'd booked the afternoon off. But I was running late. So, I left him a voicemail and a text message, saying I'd rebooked it for an hour later. By the time I got home, he said he hadn't got my messages and was steaming drunk, which really pissed me off. We started arguing. He then accused me of cheating on him. I told him he was being ridiculous, but like a dog with a bone he wouldn't drop it. So, I went to the bedroom and started packing; told him I thought it best if I stay with you for a few days. You wouldn't have minded, would you?'

Leora shook her head. 'Of course not.'

'However, that seemed to make him worse. He hates you,' she whispered.

Leora was stunned. 'Me? But... why?'

'He thinks you don't like him. Thinks you want to take me away from him.'

Leora frowned. 'Really?' She had always got on well with Hugo, or at least, she thought she had. The only time she struggled with him was when he was drunk. Not because he was aggressive; she had never ever seen him drunk and angry; it was more how excitable, how incredibly loud he got; his inability to filter whatever came out of his mouth, which, sometimes, came across as offensive. That said, he had never been particularly derogatory to her over the years. So, to hear that he hated her, even if he was drunk, was shocking to say the least.

'Anyway,' Ali continued. 'He grabbed me... and the next thing I knew... I was at the bottom of the stairs... and Hugo was telling me how sorry he was.'

Both women jumped as the partially closed curtain to Ali's cubicle swished open. A nurse popped her head round and asked her if she needed any more painkillers.

Ali shook her head. 'No. Thank you. I'm fine.'

'You don't look fine.' The nurse smiled kindly. She asked who Leora was and Ali introduced her as her best friend. 'Might be an idea to keep an eye on your friend,' she said to Leora. 'It could be very bad if she were to have another *fall* down the stairs. Not everyone survives a fall.'

Leora assured the nurse she had everything in hand and the nurse with the kind smile and knowing eyes said she would be back shortly to sort out Ali's discharge papers.

'Well,' Leora said, squaring her shoulders. 'I don't give a shit what Hugo thinks of me, you're coming home with me. At least for a few days anyway, until you decide what you want to do.'

Ali nodded: silent tears rolling down her cheeks. 'He won't object,' she sniffed.

'Really?'

'Really. He never does when... when...' She paused. 'It's... difficult to explain but it's like there's a power shift... for a few weeks, anyway.'

'Power shift?'

Ali nodded. 'At home, Hugo is the boss.'

Looking at her friend's battered face, Leora didn't doubt it, but had she not seen the cuts and bruises for herself, she would have struggled to believe it, if only because, out of the two of them, Ali always seemed the more assertive, the more dominant. *Which just goes to show how appearances can be deceiving*, she thought.

'And I suppose, just for an easy life,' Ali continued, 'I've learned to go along with it. But when...when he does something...' Ali looked down, her pallid face suddenly flushed, '...when he hurts me. It's strange, but afterwards there's a power shift. Which is when I see the *real* Hugo again: charming, funny, attentive, the man I fell in love with.'

Leora stared at her friend and prayed to God her face didn't give away her disbelief. Why couldn't she see it? This man, who claimed to love her, didn't know the meaning of the word. This wasn't about love; this was about control.

They were quiet for a minute, each absorbed in their own thoughts. A woman in the cubicle next door tried to comfort her crying child while on the other side an elderly gentleman, clearly confused, kept asking when the next bus was due. Leora stared at the grey floors that matched the grey walls that every now and again were cast in shadow when the bright light from fluorescent tubes above them flickered on and off. Guilt ridden, she looked up again and stared at her friend, wondered why she hadn't done more, in the past, to help her.

Wincing, Ali smiled at her. 'Thanks for being here. You do know how much I appreciate it, right?'

Leora reached for her hand. 'Of course I do. I'm always here for you, Ali, just like you are for me.'

'He's… not like this very often you know.'

Leora nodded, and in that moment, she realised. The reason she hadn't done more for Ali was simple; how could you help someone that didn't believe there was a problem?

'Mia won't mind me being at yours, will she?'

'Of course not.' Leora smiled. 'She loves her Aunt Ali, you know that. Although, to be fair, she won't be at home much.'

'Oh…?'

'Well… what with rehearsals and the promo stuff for the show, I've arranged for her to stay with her dad.'

'Doesn't she… miss you?'

Leora laughed. 'I doubt it. Out of the two of us, Tim's the fun one whereas I'm just the fun sucker, apparently.'

'Oh… Oh well, you and I can have a bit of fun, eh; stay up late drinking cheap wine, eating toast and Marmite, talking shit, like the old days.'

Leora smiled. 'That would be nice, wouldn't it. Not really possible at the mo though, I'm afraid. Like I said, things are manic right now.'

Ali's smile faded and Leora suddenly felt hot; her chest flaring with guilt and anxiety. Her friend needed her, *really* needed her… but she couldn't just drop everything. That's not how TV worked.

'It's just over a month until the first episode airs, you see.' She talked quickly, as if embarrassed, as if obliged to explain herself. 'A car picks me up most mornings at six and by the time I get home in the evening, I'm knackered. The only thing I'm fit for is a bath and bed before the madness starts again the following day.'

'Yes but… surely you can ask for a couple of days off? I took time off work for you… when you and Tim split up.'

'I know you did, Ali, but… I didn't ask you to and–'

'That's because you didn't *have* to ask me, Leora. Good friends don't *need* to be asked.' Mulish, she looked away, and for the briefest of moments they were teenagers again; Leora having had, albeit unintentionally, or unwittingly, committed some misdemeanour or other that Ali deemed fit to call her out on.

Bracing herself, Leora took a deep breath. 'I was, and always have been very grateful for your support, Ali. I didn't always expect it, but I've always appreciated it. However, to insinuate, because I don't take a couple of days off work, that I'm not doing the same for you is unfair. I'm here now, aren't I? I should be at the studio filming another trailer. But when you phoned, and I realised the potential seriousness of the situation, the production team kindly gave me a couple of hours off. However, they made no bones about letting me know that time is money and whatever happens, I'll need to make it up later, because that's just how TV is, how it works.'

'So... what you're saying is,' Ali said, turning to face her again. 'If I stay with you at your house... I'll be on my own?' She seemed annoyed, angry even, and Leora couldn't work out which she felt more, guilt or irritation; both probably.

'Well... yes... but you'll be safe. Besides, what about work?'

Ali pointed to her face. 'I can't go in looking like this.'

'No.' Leora chewed the corner of her lip. 'I don't suppose you can. Do you have any leave you can take?' Ali nodded. 'Even better, then. The peace and quiet will give you time to think about what you're going to do. Because...' Leora stood up, gently touched her friend's face. 'It doesn't matter if this happens once in a blue moon or once a day. He shouldn't do this to you, Ali. It's not right. Surely you can see that?'

'You look beautiful, you know,' Ali replied, completely ignoring her question. 'In the trailers, I mean, for the show. Almost doesn't look like you.'

Leora smiled, let her hand fall to her side and sat down again. 'Thanks... I think.'

'You know what I mean,' Ali said. 'All the clothes, the hair, the make-up, you look... different.' She sighed. 'I suppose I'd better make the most of you while I still can.'

Bemused, Leora tipped her head to the side. 'Meaning what... exactly?'

'It's obvious, isn't it?'

'Is it?' Leora replied, her smile quizzical.

Ali looked up, pointed. 'You'll be up there soon with the gods; too rich, too famous for mere mortals like me.'

Leora laughed. 'You are joking, right? Firstly, if the public don't like the show, or me, my presenting career could be over before it's even started. Secondly, and far more importantly, even if it is a success, it changes nothing. We have been, and always will be, friends forever. Nothing will *ever* change that.'

Ali glanced down, her fingers tracing the outline of a flower-shaped blood droplet on her blouse. 'Hmm... we'll see,' she mumbled.

Leora sighed... quietly. Why didn't Ali believe her? And why, as she had for as many years as she could remember, did Leora feel the need to prove herself? 'I've got an idea,' she said, standing up. 'I'll go and find the nurse that was here a minute ago, see if we can get you out of here, then I'll take you back to the studio with me.'

Ali's head shot up. 'Really?' She smiled.

'Sure. We'll have lunch together, then I'll introduce you to Greg, my co-presenter, then I'll book a car to take you back to mine. I don't know what time I'll be home tonight, but I'll make sure it's not too late. At least... I'll try, anyway. Now, don't move,' she said, swishing open the curtains, 'I'll be back in a minute.'

It was good to see Ali smiling again, however the overwhelming emotion Leora felt right now was one of relief. Guilt too. Relief that her friend was okay, but guilt because, no matter how much she wanted to be there for Ali – especially given her predicament – their relationship always felt more difficult than it should.

Hadn't their friendship always been slightly tumultuous? Why then, of late, when she thought about Ali, when they arranged to meet up, did she not so much *want* to see her, but rather she felt obliged to see her. She never felt like that about Eileen. But Ali and Eileen were like chalk and cheese, so it was unfair, wrong even, to compare them.

Dodging the traffic of people roaming the hospital corridors, she paused, leant against a wall, and took a minute; guilt and shame washing over her in equal measure. Ali was a friend, not an obligation. One who, no matter what, had always been there for her. She sighed, scrubbed at her tired face with her hands. Maybe Ali was right. Maybe this new job *was* going to her head, pulling her away.

She heard her name being called and, startled, looked up. Horrified, she saw Hugo, at the opposite side of the corridor... looking straight at her.

# CHAPTER 33

*S*am opened the door. 'Oh... it's you,' he said, sullen, unsmiling. 'It's not your turn to have us today, is it?'

'No.' Ben smiled. 'Mum has offered to help me with a few things on the computer.'

It was a lie, of course. Ben knew how to navigate a computer. All special force operatives did, and things hadn't advanced that much since his discharge. However, after recently meeting with his soon to be ex-wife to discuss their sons, both he and Gemma had agreed, now Ben was getting back on his feet, how keen they were for the boys to see them together because, whether it was amicable or acrimonious, and whether you admitted it or not, divorce affected kids.

Even now, despite the obvious improvement, the obvious effort Ben was making with his sons, Sam was still very wary of him. And who could blame him. Ben certainly didn't. But neither was he prepared to give up on him. He had, for a short time, let them down. It wasn't intentional, and one day, perhaps, when they were old enough to fully understand the implications of PTSD, he hoped they would find it in their hearts to forgive him. However, he loved his sons, and he wanted them to know, despite his recent blip, he would, from now on, always, whenever possible, be there for them.

He was also keen for them to see, as was Gemma, that just because they had separated, it didn't mean he and Gemma couldn't get along. His own parents had showed him that, and after witnessing the devasting fallout of some divorces, he couldn't thank them enough. Plus, Gemma was genuinely interested in Ben's current project and more than keen to help.

'Oh, right.' Sam couldn't have sounded more disappointed if he tried. 'You'd better come in then.' He stepped aside to let Ben into the large, light, and airy hallway. 'Mum,' he yelled. 'Dad's here.'

'Hello, Ben,' a voice said.

Ben looked up, saw Felix coming down the stairs.

'How are you?' He offered Ben his hand when he reached the bottom step. In his late forties, tall, with short, swept-back hair and bright eyes, his grip, like Ben's, was firm, confident. Recently widowed, with two older children at university, Felix was also ex-forces, now specialising in contract work for the MOD, which also meant, unlike some of his civvy friends, Felix had every sympathy for Ben.

In fact, unbeknownst to Ben at the time, when Ben was at his lowest, Felix, who seemed genuinely very fond of the boys, had sat them both down and explained to Sam and Robbie, in the very simplest way, why Ben was behaving like he was. He compared PTSD to a physical injury but explained that instead of a broken arm or leg, it was Ben's thoughts and memories that had temporarily broken. He also said that he was sure, with time, and the right treatment, Ben would get better again.

He could have bad-mouthed Ben. He could have taken the opportunity to put Ben down, and in doing so make himself look better; a knight in shining armour come to their rescue, but he didn't. Instead, he helped give two very worried little boys the tools to understand what was going on with their father, and for that, Ben was extremely grateful.

'I'm good thanks, Felix. You?'

'Yeah, yeah. I'm fine thanks.'

'There you are.' Gemma wandered into the hallway. 'Sam said he'd let you in, but I thought he'd left you here, waiting.' She turned to Felix. 'You off to the gym then?'

'I certainly am.' Felix opened the door to the cupboard under the stairs.

Ben put his hands up. 'Don't feel you have leave on my account.'

Felix, sitting on the bottom stair, pulling on a pair of trainers, said he wasn't. He stood up again; breathed out, made a show of pointing to his stomach. 'Too many takeaways.' He grinned. 'Either that or it's middle-age spread. Either way, it has to go.' Patting his pockets, he kissed Gemma on the cheek and headed for the door. 'Gemma told me what you're doing, by the way,' he added. 'Well done you. It's a brilliant idea. I'll reach out to a few of my old cronies, see if I can't get some of them on board.'

Ben thanked him and with that he left.

'Come in.' Gemma ushered him into the living room where Robbie, head slightly tilted, mouth slightly ajar, was watching TV.

'Hey, Robbie,' Ben called out.

Robbie looked up, his features morphing into a look of complete surprise. 'Dad,' he yelled, jumping up and running to him. 'I didn't know you was here.'

Sam, ensconced in an armchair, legs dangling over one arm, elbow resting on the other, looked at his brother with bored indifference. 'I told you he was here, *ages* ago.'

Robbie spun round; glared at his brother. 'Did not.'

'Did too.'

'Did not.'

'Did. Did. Did.'

Ben threw his hands up and clapped them, hard. 'Now, now, boys, behave.'

'Or what?' he thought he heard Sam mutter under his breath.

Ben looked at him, but Sam, whose face had turned crimson, arms folded across his chest, refused to make eye contact.

Gemma gave Ben a minuscule shake of her head. 'I'll go and fire up the computer.' She pointed to the dining room. 'Fancy coming to help me?' She ruffled Sam's hair.

Sam looked up and smiled. 'Nah... I'm still watching this.' He nodded at the TV. 'If these two noisy bones will shut up,' he added, glancing at Ben and his brother in disgust.

Ben couldn't help himself. 'Who wants some Munchies,' he yelled, pulling a couple of packets from his jacket pocket.

'Me, me, me!' Robbie shouted, hands up, fingers spreadeagled, balancing on his tiptoes.

Laughing, Ben gave one packet to Robbie before offering the other packet to Sam. Arms still folded, Sam eyed the chocolate with caution, as if weighing up his options. To accept it would mean having to acknowledge the gift, albeit small, from his father, which in turn would mean having to thank him; whereas declining it meant he could continue his campaign of punishment. Which was fine by Ben. He got it. But what Sam didn't know was, Ben was in it for the long haul.

'Don't like Munchies,' Sam said, after a few seconds.

'Really?' Ben replied. 'You said they were your favourite, last week.'

Sam shrugged. 'Yeah... well, they're not anymore.'

'I'll have them,' Robbie; cheeks stuffed like a hamster, shouted.

'No, it's fine.' Ben placed them on a nearby bookshelf. 'I'll leave them here, and if you want them, then just help yourse–'

'I don't,' Sam interrupted.

'Okay... but if you do change your mind' – Ben tapped the bookcase – 'help yourself. If not, I'll take them home with me when I leave.'

He wandered into the dining room where a large oak table sat centre stage. Like the rest of the house, with its duck egg blue walls, and large patio doors that opened onto a huge sprawling garden, the dining room was a light, bright and airy space.

'You okay?' Gemma asked, her brow wrinkled in slight concern.

'Of course.' Ben removed his jacket, which he placed over the back of the chair next to Gemma. 'He's still angry with me, I get it. But we'll get there.'

Gemma squeezed his arm. 'You will.' She pointed to the computer screen, whirring, waiting for their attention. 'Thank God we don't have to use dial-up anymore, eh? I used to be able to clean the whole house in the time it took me to get a connection.'

'I dunno.' Ben grinned. 'That was half the fun, wasn't it. The anticipation, the build-up, waiting for the modem to connect.'

Gemma raised an eyebrow. 'Hmm... you... patiently waiting... isn't quite how I remember it. I do, however, remember the odd swear word.'

Ben threw his head back, laughed, then pointed to the patio doors, asked if he could open them.

'Sure.' Gemma fanned her face with her hand. 'It is a bit warm in here, isn't it?'

Ben unlocked the doors, and pushed them open; a gentle breeze brought welcome relief to a room that had spent the best part of the morning being cooked by the sun.

'Go out,' Gemma said. 'And look to the right.'

Stepping onto the patio Ben spotted two shiny new kids' goalposts at either end of a cordoned off section of lush lawn. Felix had mentioned creating a space for Ben and the boys to have a kick-about, but at the time he hadn't paid much credence to it.

'He's a good man,' Ben said, sitting down again.

Gemma grinned. 'He is, isn't he.' She leaned in, sweet-smelling, citrusy, and nudged him. 'As are you,' she added.

'I'm getting there.' He stroked his chin. 'Look...' He drew a breath. 'I know I've said it before... but... I'm sorry.'

'For what?'

He pulled on his Adam's apple. 'For... for not loving you enough.'

Half-smiling, she tipped her head to the side. 'It's fine, Ben. Honestly, I'm really happy with Felix.' Ben nodded, looked away. 'Not that I wasn't with–'

'I'm glad,' Ben interrupted, looking at her again. 'I can see how happy you are and I'm glad... for both of you. And the boys. This is a great house.'

Blinking back tears, Gemma smiled, pointed to the computer screen. 'Do you want to get up what you've done so far while I make us some coffee?'

Ben nodded, took out the USB stick he'd brought with him from his jacket pocket.

Robbie wandered in. 'What's that?' he asked, pointing to the piece of plastic Ben was holding.

'This,' Ben replied, holding it up, 'is called a USB flash drive, or thumb drive.'

Robbie frowned; looked at his thumb and wiggled it. 'A flashing thumb drive? What's one of them?'

Ben laughed and pulled him onto his knee. 'It's a device that allows me to transfer information from my computer onto other computers and it's called a flash drive because it uses something called flash memory to store the information on it, or thumb drive because look,' Ben placed it next to his thumb, 'it's roughly the size of a thumb, see?'

Gemma came back from the kitchen carrying two mugs on a tray which she placed on the table next to the computer desk. 'Help yourself.'

'Can we play football in a minute, outside?' Robbie asked.

'Sure,' Ben replied. 'Let me just show your mum something on the computer first, then we'll have a kick-about.'

'O-kay,' he sighed. 'Guess what, Mum?' he said, jumping, much to Ben's relief, off his knee. Ben had quite forgotten how restless his youngest son was. 'Dad's got a flashing thumb.'

Gemma almost choked on her coffee. 'Has he now,' she said, trying but failing to keep a straight face. 'I suppose it's better than a farting finger.' She glanced at Ben, whose face was creased with laughter.

Confused, Robbie stared at his parents. '*Hey!*' He folded both arms across his chest. 'What's so funny?'

'You are.' Ben tickled him under the arms before wrestling him to the ground. After several minutes of rolling around on the floor, including lots of good-humoured whoops and hollers, father and son stood up; composed themselves.

Gemma shook her head, rolled her eyes. 'You two.' She grinned.

Ben asked Robbie to help him insert the USB stick into the computer, which brought up what he'd been working on, including the spreadsheets detailing all the money he'd raised so far.

'Wow,' Gemma said, peering over Ben's shoulder. 'That much already?'

'I know. I'm honestly bowled over by the generosity of people.'

'Does Mark know yet?' Ben shook his head. 'Eileen?'

'Yeah, she knows. The thing is… we're both a bit… worried… that Mark will take offence. He can't stand folk feeling sorry for him.'

'What are you talking about, Dad? And why will Uncle Mark be upset?' Robbie asked.

Ben explained about his plan to run from John O'Groats to Land's End in the hope of breaking the current world record. However, just to make it extra hard, being a former soldier he planned to complete it with a sixty-pound bergen on his back.

'Who's Johnny Groats and why will you run with a burger on your back?' Robbie asked.

Ben and Gemma looked at one another and smiled.

'Don't be silly, Robbie,' a voice said behind them. They turned to see Sam. How long he'd been standing there, listening, Ben couldn't say. He was just pleased his son was taking an interest.

Sam confidently informed his younger brother that John O'Groats was right at the top of the country, while Land's End was at the bottom. He also explained what a bergen was, reminding Robbie of the photos of Ben carrying one on his back, on the desks in their bedrooms.

'Oh… yeah. I remember,' Robbie replied. 'Like the rucksack I take to school.'

'Hardly,' Sam said, rolling his eyes. He turned to Ben. 'So, what's this got to do with Uncle Mark?' he asked.

Ben explained that he was doing it to raise some money to buy Mark some running blades. 'Because they're very expensive,' he added.

'But… how does you running get the money?'

'People sponsor me,' Ben replied. 'A bit like you when you do your sponsored walk at school.'

'But you don't think Uncle Mark will like it?'

'He might not, no. Not if he thinks it's charity.'

Thoughtful, Sam tipped his head to the side, chewed his bottom lip. 'Uncle Mark is strong, isn't he?'

Confused, Ben nodded. 'Ye-es… he's very strong. Got much bigger arms than me. Why?'

'Well… I was thinking. Instead of you doing the run, why don't you ask him if he wants to do it instead… in his wheelchair. Or maybe you could both do it… together?'

Grinning, Ben and Gemma looked at one another.

'That's a great idea, Sam,' Ben said.

'It really is,' Gemma agreed, clapping her hands enthusiastically.

'Why the hell didn't I think of it?' Ben continued.

'Well done, Sam.' Robbie patted his brother's back. 'But can we pleeeeease play football now?'

'Course we can. You coming, Sam?'

Sam shrugged. 'I'm not very good at football.'

'So... you don't have to be good at things to have fun.'

By the time Ben was getting ready to leave, he wasn't sure who was more worn out, him or the boys. Saying goodbye to his sons at the door; he noted that the Munchies on the bookcase had gone.

Gemma ordered the boys upstairs for a shower before tea.

'Bye, Dad,' they shouted, thundering up the stairs.

'Bye, boys. Be good for your mum.'

'We will,' they shouted.

'Thanks again,' he said, turning to Gemma, 'for letting me come round and spend time with them.'

'My pleasure.'

'Right then.' He gave her the thumbs up, as he stepped onto the driveway. 'I'd better go.'

'I've seen the trailers,' Gemma called after him.

'Trailers?'

'Of Leora. For that new dating show starting soon.'

'Ah... right... yeah. Me too.'

'She looks... good... doesn't she?'

Ben stuffed his hands in his jean's pockets. 'Yeah... she does.'

'Do you... ever... see her?'

Ben shook his head. 'Haven't seen her to speak to in years. Why?'

'Just wondered.' Gemma hovered by the door. She looked, Ben thought, chewing her thumbnail, like a woman with something on her mind. 'Okay then, bye. I'll text you in the week about seeing the boys.'

And with that she closed the door.

# CHAPTER 34

'So... how long did she actually stay at yours... in the end?' Leora was on the phone to Eileen.

'Five days in total.' Leora looked up, the sky a brilliant blue, its clouds like white carriages.

'Then she went back to him?'

'She did.'

'And they've been all right since?'

'Apparently so. It was weird though, you know, when I bumped into him... Hugo, I mean... at the hospital. He looked...' She paused.

'Looked... what?'

'I don't know if I can explain it. I was so angry when I saw him, a little scared too, if I'm honest. Especially after what Ali said... about him not liking me. Still, I took a deep breath and asked him what was going on... what the hell he thought he was playing at.'

'And... what was his response?'

'Not what I was expecting, I suppose.' She stood up, clutching a pile of crumpled, papers. Her notes for the show, which she'd been reading in the garden. 'At worst I thought he'd be angry, at best, defensive. If anything, though, he was the complete opposite. Stooped shoulders, glazed eyes, he looked exhausted... more like a man beaten down by life than a man that had just knocked his wife down the stairs.' She wandered into the kitchen, stared at the crumb-infested worktop, and shook her head. 'He said he loved Ali,' she continued. 'But didn't know how to make her happy anymore, said whatever he did was never good enough.'

'Ah right, I see... So instead of walking away, or trying to work things out, he decided to knock some sense into his wife instead, is that it?' Eileen sounded angry, and rightly so, Leora thought.

'I know,' she sighed, heading into the hallway, and calling up the stairs, reminding Mia what time it was. 'But that's another thing,' she said, her eye drawn to the pile of clean washing still on the bottom stair, which, like the crumb-infested worktop, she chose to ignore... for now. 'He said he has no memory of pushing her down the stairs.'

'Of course he doesn't,' Eileen snapped.

'He said they were at the top of the stairs arguing and he was trying to stay calm, talk reason, but Ali was having none of it. In the end he lost his temper; started shouting back, but he swore the only thing he raised was his voice.'

Leora headed back to the kitchen, picked up the kettle and went to the sink. 'It didn't make any difference, though. If anything, he said it made Ali worse, and she was the one that started pushing *him*.'

'Fuck's sake,' Eileen muttered.

Spotting Mia's breakfast bowl, still in the sink, Leora sighed, filled the kettle. 'So, in the end, in a bid to defuse the situation, he said he went to another room to calm down. He half expected Ali to follow him, but when she didn't, he said he remembered feeling relieved. After ten minutes or so he said he realised how quiet the house was, assumed Ali must have gone out. So, he went to check, which was when he said he found her, at the bottom of the stairs, crying. He could see she was injured, and when he asked her what happened, he said she just kept asking him, over and over, why he'd pushed her down the stairs.'

'Unbelievable,' Eileen exclaimed. 'So... what he's saying is... she threw herself down the stairs?'

'I know... ridiculous, isn't it.' Flicking the kettle on, Leora took the bowl from the sink and scraped remnants of soggy cornflakes into the bin before loading it into the dishwasher. 'He did seem genuinely remorseful though. Mind you, he stunk of whisky. Which I did mention, and he did admit to having a problem. He also said, although he asked me not to mention it to Ali, that he's made a doctor's appointment to have some tests done because he keeps forgetting things. Is afraid he may have a brain tumour, or early onset dementia.'

'Which would of course,' Eileen replied, her voice filled with sarcasm, 'rather conveniently explain his behaviour, I assume? Jesus... did he honestly think you'd fall for that?'

Leora didn't reply.

'Leora...? You don't believe him, right?'

'No... I don't... but–'

'But what?' Eileen cried.

'Oh... I don't know. I guess I just found myself feeling sorry for him. He looked... broken, crushed, even.'

'That's because, like a lot of abusers, he knows how to manipulate people, how to spin a good yarn.'

The two friends were quiet for a minute, before Leora, the first to break it, asked Eileen if she was okay.

'Yeah... I guess so. I just feel like... like... I've been a bit of a shitty friend lately. Ali really pissed me off the other week, at the pub; her mood, the sarcastic comments, but it all kind of makes sense now. She's obviously confused, so she got drunk and took it out on us... which, in a way, is sort of like a cry for help, isn't it?

Which makes me feel crap because... well, if I'm honest, I had no idea how bad things had got.'

'I know. If it's any consolation, I feel the same. I did try and talk to Hugo, though, told him he's got to quit the booze and get some counselling.'

'And... is he?'

'I don't know. I'm seeing Ali today, so I'll ask her, let you know.'

'Yeah, do, and if she says he isn't, tell her she has to insist he does.'

'I'll try.' Leora glanced out of the window, watching a pair of blue tits in the garden; smudges of blue, dashes of yellow, flitting around the birdfeeder. 'But you know what she's like.'

'I do,' she sighed. They were quiet again. Leora knew that, like her, Eileen was worried about Ali. But for now, there wasn't much they could do. Their hands were tied.

'Anyway,' Eileen's voice was noticeably chirpier. 'How's things with you? Five more days to go,' she squealed.

Leora suddenly felt jittery, her stomach a cold knot of jumbled nerves. 'I know.' She took small sips of air. 'Rehearsals are more or less done, which is great, meant I got to spend some time with Mia yesterday. But I've never been more nervous in my whole life.'

'Hey, Mum...'

'Hang on a minute.' Leora turned round.

'Smile!' Mia yelled, as Leora, momentarily blinded by a flash and a whir of what, after a few seconds, she realised was the flash of a camera. It wasn't a regular camera though, it was an old Polaroid, not unlike the one Jules used to have. She was about to ask Mia where she'd got it from when she noticed what she was wearing. 'Mia,' she said, her voice calm and collected. 'Can you go back upstairs and get changed, please.'

Mia, eyes flashing, fanning her face with the photo she'd just pulled from the camera, threw her hand up. 'Why?' she demanded. 'What's wrong with what I'm wearing?'

Leora asked Eileen if she could call her back. 'Of course,' came Eileen's amused reply. 'I've got a few things on today anyway, so no rush. Call me in a couple of days if it's easier. Oh... and by the way, don't be nervous about the show, you'll be amazing.'

'Thanks.' Leora ended the call and turned her attention back to her daughter. 'There's nothing wrong with what you're wearing, Mia. You look lovely.'

'So...' She held her hands out, the look on her face one of disbelief. 'Why do I have to get changed then?' she asked, one Doc Marten booted foot crossed over the other.

'Because you look like a twenty-year-old.'

'Do I?' Mia beamed.

'Yes... you do. But you're not twenty, Mia, you're fifteen. I know it's only five years, but that five years makes a huge difference.' She could hear her father's voice in her head, telling her she was too young to go to the Live Aid concert, which made her smile. 'I just don't think a miniskirt and fishnets is a good choice for a jazz festival.' She paused. 'But... you know what... you're right. You're old enough to make up your own mind. I just... worry about you.'

Arms crossed, pouting, impossibly pretty, Mia finally acquiesced, but not without making a spectacular show of it by stomping upstairs, before quickly racing down again just as Tim pulled up at the front of the house honking his car horn.

Leora hated it when he did that. It always set Milo off, who she knew, even before she got to the door, would now be at the window, barking. Milo: a large German shepherd, belonged to Joan, her next-door neighbour. Joan was a retired headmistress in her late seventies and Leora wasn't sure, when she and Tim first moved into Brixwell Road all those years ago, who she found scarier, Joan or her dog. She soon realised though, as she got to know them, it was all a façade, that they were both a pair of softies at heart. Joan had a different dog then. Jasper, who, also a German shepherd, was, like his successor, just as big, just as fierce but also just as soft. Like Milo, he adored Mia and saw her as a playmate, and someone, like Joan, to be loved and guarded.

Joan too, doted on Mia, and there had been many a time, over the years, she had offered to sit with her for Leora and many a time Leora had taken her up on her offer. However, Joan could also, on occasion, be quite cranky. She couldn't abide bad manners, 'and honking one's horn,' she once informed Leora, 'is the height of bad manners.'

Leora smiled to herself, knew Joan would have something to say about it when she next saw her. Most of the time though, to be fair to Tim, he would park the car and come to the door. Today though, revving his engine, Saffy at his side, he was clearly in a hurry to leave.

Mia, who was now wearing ripped jeans in place of the belt she'd called a skirt, swept past her, smelling of apple blossom and cherries. She paused at the door, grabbed her rucksack and stuffed the camera on top of the clothes she'd packed for the week.

'Have fun.' Leora smiled, trying to keep her voice upbeat, perky.

'Fun sucker.' Mia threw her rucksack over her shoulder before yanking the door so hard the letterbox rattled.

'I love you, sweetheart. You do know that, right?'

Mia, who had her back to her, paused, turned round, and looked at her. 'Say hi to Ali for me.' She turned on her heel and slammed the door shut in one final act of teenage angst.

Leora sighed; wandered back into the kitchen, loading the dishwasher with the cups and plates Mia had brought down from her bedroom, before wiping down the crumb-infested worktops. A familiar buzzing sound caught her attention. She saw her phone dancing on the island. Too late she picked it up and saw a missed call from Ali. She was about to call her back when a text flashed up.

> Hey hun, sorry, but I'm running late. Will try and be there in the next hour or so. You ok to do brunch instead of breakfast? xxx

Leora tapped out her reply; said brunch was fine. She could do with some fresh air: wondered if she should go for a walk. She glanced at the oversized clock on the wall, the one she and Tim had chosen from the high-end antique shop they'd visited in Wales a year or so before their split. A trip she'd arranged to resurrect the ruins of what, albeit subconsciously perhaps, she knew was a crumbling relationship, to a place called 'before' when Tim, like Ben, had found her fascinating and exciting and couldn't get enough of her.

Looking back, theirs had been such a whirlwind romance, she couldn't help but wonder if she had still been on the rebound from Ben. She had loved Tim, though. Maybe not in the same way she'd loved Ben, but nonetheless, she had.

She also knew, with hindsight, their separation wasn't a bad thing. However, even though she'd been the one to initiate the split, all she could remember feeling at the time was an overwhelming sense of loss and rejection, and all she could think was, *why?* What was it she did that kept driving the men in her life away? Even Lonny had left her, although, arguably, not intentionally. And now, as she stood there in her quiet kitchen, she couldn't help but wonder, again, as she did from time to time, why she was so unlovable.

Annoyed with herself for wallowing in such self-indulgent moroseness, she blinked back her tears and watched the patinaed browns and blues of the clock's worn copper frame swim back into view. Half past nine, it read. Time enough for a quick walk around the block, she thought. But what if Ali turned up sooner rather than later? She looked at the kettle, which had not long boiled, went to the fridge instead, poured herself a glass of orange juice, and went out to the garden again.

After ten minutes or so, the morning sun deliciously warming her face, she heard the doorbell ring. *Ali?* She wondered. *Already?* She wasn't expecting anyone else, so it must be her. Placing her glass on top of her notes on the coffee table, she got up and headed to the door.

When she opened it, she was met by a figure whose face was concealed, by a hood, or a hat or a scarf. But before she had time to ask them who they were and what they wanted, she felt a swift, searing pain behind her eyes followed by a burning sensation at the back of her throat. A strew of words that made little to no sense quickly followed, but the tone of the said person's voice left Leora in little doubt about their sinister intent.

Terrified, trembling with pain, unable to see, unable to hear, Leora tried to call for help, but the words, despite her training as an actress, including throwing her voice in a theatre, wouldn't come. Blindly, she stepped forwards, trying to feel her way to Joan's house, desperate for help. Heard the pitiful sound of someone screaming, followed by a dog barking, the whirring of a siren, blurred flashing lights, and eventually, more voices.

Unlike the stranger at the door, though, these voices were kind. They were asking her to listen to them, to stay with them, and if she could, to tell them what had happened. She couldn't though, because she had no idea. The only thing she was certain of was the intense heat surging through her body, which, like a forest fire gaining momentum, was filling her veins, boiling her blood, and sealing off her windpipe, making it impossible to breathe, never mind talk.

She had never felt pain like it. It was unbearable, and all she wanted was for it to stop. For the strangers with the kind voices to make it stop. If they didn't make it stop soon, she knew, felt it right down to the middle of her burning core, she would either pass out, or pass away, and right now she didn't care which it was, just so long as the pain STOPPED.

Suddenly, the pain dissipated, and like a balloon she felt herself drifting, up, up above herself, staring at the commotion below. She, or at least her body, was outside an ambulance and the kindly strangers, who she could now see were paramedics, were leant over her, monitoring her vitals, as various tubes and wires, connected to a machine, criss-crossed her body like the train lines on an underground Tube map.

She saw her body convulsing. Nothing more than a twitching torso at first, it quickly spread to her arms and legs, which in turn began thrashing this way and that, so that, eventually, each limb took on a life of its own. The paramedics' response was both swift and professional; the epitome of urgent calmness as, still hovering above herself, Leora continued to watch in confused fascination. One of the medics sat back and wiped his forehead with his hand, which is when she saw herself.

Only it wasn't her... it was a monster.

Alarmed, she started screaming, and once she started, she couldn't stop.

The pain returned. Only this time it was worse, by a thousand-fold. She was in agony and all she wanted was for someone to make it go away. No longer floating, she was, she now realised, inside the ambulance; lights flashing, siren blasting, weaving in and out of the busy London traffic, before being wheeled into a corridor, intermittent bright lights flashing overhead, as someone yelled for a doctor.

A warm, soothing sensation followed, dousing the flames of her pyretic body, until eventually, everything around her began to fade. All the voices, and all the versions of herself, including Leora on the gurney and Leora watching from above, grew smaller and smaller. This was her final broadcast. Someone had switched her off. She was a shrinking white dot fading... fading... to nothing...

# CHAPTER 35

*T*he doors hissed open, and Ben stepped aside to let Eileen off the train first.

'Should we get a taxi... like Mark said... or do you think the Tube would be quicker?' She looked fitfully round.

'It's much of a muchness in London.' Ben glanced round. King's Cross was humming with commuters, most of whom seemed to be heading for the Underground. 'A taxi would be less stressful; fewer people to navigate.'

Eileen nodded and they headed for the taxi rank. Unlike the fifty-minute train journey where they'd chatted most of the way, laughing about old times, the taxi ride was relatively quiet, relatively subdued. The information they'd received about Leora was limited. All they knew was, she'd been attacked and was seriously ill in hospital.

It was pure luck Ben had been visiting when Leora's mother, Andrea, had phoned.

'Attacked? Oh my God,' Eileen gasped down the phone. 'Yes. No. Of course not. I want to come. I'll catch the next train to London and meet you there.'

'What? What is it?' Mark asked when she'd hung up. 'It's not any of the kids, is it?'

Putting her hand to her mouth, Eileen stared at Mark and shook her head. 'No… not the kids. That was Andrea. Apparently, Leora has been attacked… and she's in hospital.'

Ben and Mark looked at one another. 'Attacked?' Mark replied. 'Attacked… how?'

'Andrea doesn't know yet, but it sounds serious. I… I… have to go to her.'

'Course you do, love,' Mark soothed. 'You get yourself off straight away. Ben here will give you a lift to the train station.'

Ben nodded, stood up. 'Yeah… yeah… of course I will. No problem.'

'And here…' Mark manoeuvred himself from the sofa to his wheelchair and pushed himself towards the sideboard where he pulled out a rusty old tobacco tin. Removing the lid, he retrieved a small wad of cash. 'Take this. I've been saving it… for a ring… but this is much more important. Use it to get a taxi from the station to the hospital if you need to. Or a room for the night if needs be. Whatever you need to get you there quickly and safely. It's yours.' He thrust the money into Eileen's hands.

Dumbfounded, Eileen stared at Mark's outstretched hand. 'A ring?'

Mark nodded. 'Yes… an engagement ring.'

'But… I don't understand. I thought we'd agreed not to bother with a ring, said it was an expense we could do without?'

'I know. But…' Mark, suddenly coy, his face crimson, looked at Ben, who in turn, pretended to read something on his phone. 'The thing is,' he continued, 'I just want you to know how much I love you.'

Eileen sat down next to him. 'As lovely as that is, and as much as I appreciate it, I don't need some fancy ring to know you love me. What I do want to know though,' she laughed, holding up the thick wad of notes in her hand, 'is where the hell you got all this money from?'

'I've given up smoking,' Mark replied. 'I know I told you I hadn't; that it was my only vice, but I haven't smoked for a while now. Saving what I would have spent on fags for a ring.'

Tearful, Eileen threw her arms around Mark's broad neck and hugged him. 'You are a daft bugger, you know. But you're my daft bugger.'

Ben hadn't intended to go to the hospital. He'd toyed with the idea while driving Eileen to the station when, as if reading his thoughts, she asked him if he would go with her.

'I don't think so. It's not really any of my business.' He still loved Leora, but like him, she had moved on with her life: his connection to her now, nothing more than a distant memory.

'Please,' Eileen pleaded. 'I'll tell Andrea and Marty that I asked you to come... in case you can help.'

'Help?' Ben looked at her, confused. 'Help how?'

'Andrea said something about Leora's attack being chemical?'

'Chemical?'

Eileen nodded. 'I didn't say in front of Mark because I didn't want to worry him.'

'Fair enough. But what do you mean... chemical? What else did Andrea say?'

'Nothing. She wasn't told any more than that. She was just told it was serious and to get there as quickly as possible. It's sad really... because Leora and her parents have sort of been estranged.'

'Really?' Ben said, surprised.

'Hmm... it was after Lonny died. They all just seemed to... drift apart. From the outside looking in, I'd have said it was Leora that didn't want to see her parents, but when I've talked to her about it, she said, after losing Lonny, her parents simply pushed her away. Which is strange really, because I often see Andrea and Marty out and about, have the occasional chat, and as far as I can see they both still love her dearly. Not that they say much – Andrea's quite a private person – but you can see it in her eyes, hear it in her voice, just how much she misses Leora. Recently though, from what I understand, they've been getting along much better again. But Andrea knows how close I am to Leora, which is why she called me, I think. Which reminds me.' She pulled out her phone. 'She asked me to let Ali know too... but I haven't been able to get hold of her.'

She put her phone to her ear and excused herself for a minute while Ben, still driving, stared out of the windscreen, brake lights flashing on and off like sirens as the traffic, due to roadworks, temporarily slowed. *Chemical attack?* he thought, leaning on the steering wheel, glancing up to where the fringes of the sky were darkening with a gathering storm. *What the hell is that supposed to mean?* In his experience that could be any number of things, none of them pleasant, all of them potentially fatal. 'Fuck,' he muttered under his breath, sitting back again, as large raindrops splashed the windscreen. Why had it taken him until now to realise the gravity of the situation.

'Strange.' Eileen stared at her phone. 'I've tried her mobile, her landline and I've texted her... twice... but she's still not answering? Oh well.' She put her phone in her bag. 'I'm sure she'll get back to me as soon as she can. So...' she turned to Ben again. 'What do think? Will you come with me... to the hospital? I just thought... with your experience, your background, you might be able to–'

'I'll come,' Ben said.

'You will?' Eileen breathed out a large sigh of relief.

Ben nodded. 'But only if the family don't mind. If they don't want me there, then, as much as I'd like to, I'm not hanging around.'

'No... of course not. I understand. But I'm sure they'll be fine about it.'

Ben wasn't so sure. He wanted to make sure Leora was okay,

but now, in the taxi, he was starting to wonder again what the hell he was doing, what her parents would think when he rolled up with Eileen. He'd be the last person they'd expect to see.

No. The more he thought about it, the more ludicrous he realised it was. He had no right being there. His mind was made up. He'd drop Eileen at the hospital, then he'd ask the taxi driver to turn round and take him straight back to King's Cross.

Once again, though, Eileen, persuaded him otherwise. However, as soon as they stepped out of the taxi; the huge hospital building looming over them, Ben felt his arse fall to the floor; his only inclination to turn and run.

# CHAPTER 36

*B*en hated hospitals. Whether it was a flagship, glossy, state of the art building like this one; or a field hospital in a battle zone; or a hospital where, due to corruption, civil war and looting, lack of clean water, medication, and equipment, patients lay for hours on bloodied beds in operating rooms, more the stuff of nightmares than healthcare. All of them, he thought, whether bright and airy, or dingy and squalid, reverberated with sickness and death. However, Ben also knew that beneath this hospital's fluorescent strip lighting and among its bleeping machines, with its masked physicians and their brutal way of doing things, Leora was in the best place possible right now.

Following Andrea's instructions, they headed for the intensive care unit.

'ICU.' Eileen looked at Ben, the linoleum floor squeaking beneath his feet, his heart, like a tight hammer, striking against his ribcage. 'That means... it's bad... doesn't it?'

Hitting another set of swing doors, which Ben held open for Eileen, he nodded. 'It doesn't sound good,' he admitted.

'Can we stop for a minute?' Eileen sniffed, using the heel of her hand to stem the tears Ben hadn't noticed her crying. 'Sorry.' She rummaged in her bag, dabbing her tearstained cheeks with a crumpled tissue. 'I promised myself I wouldn't do this. But... but... well... if anything bad... you know... happens... I don't think...' Her grief spilled over into short, sharp sobs and the only thing Ben could do was hold her, tight, in his arms.

'Look.' He held her at arm's length when her sobbing subsided. 'We don't know anything yet, so for now, let's try and stay positive, eh, because, if there's one thing I've learned, it's that human beings are remarkable creatures with an innate ability to survive... often some of the worst things imaginable.'

Eileen shook her head. 'Not always,' she whispered, her eyes shadowed with grief.

Ben sighed. He knew she meant Wayne. Lonny and Jules too, possibly. 'No... you're right. Not always. But...' He took a deep breath, squeezed both her arms reassuringly. 'Let's not go there right now, eh? It won't help anyone, least of all Leora. For now, whatever it is that's happened to her, she's alive. Which means there's still hope.'

Eileen nodded, straightened her shoulders. 'Of course. Good advice. Good advice.'

When they got to the intensive care unit, they noticed several uniformed police officers lingering in the corridor. Again, as instructed by Andrea, they headed straight for the family room where they were greeted by Andrea and Marty; any fears Ben had about being there were quickly alleviated.

'Ben gave me a lift to the station,' Eileen explained, hugging Andrea. 'And I asked him to come with me. I hope you don't mind.'

'No, of course not.' Andrea took Ben's hand in hers. 'Good to see you, Ben.' Her voice was wavering, her eyes tremulous, blinking back tears.

'Ben,' Marty said, approaching him, shaking hands. 'How are you, son?'

'I'm good, thanks, Marty. But... how's Leora? What do you know?'

Andrea and Marty looked at one another. 'It's... not good,' Andrea replied. 'She's not in a coma but because the pain is so bad, they're having to pump her full of pain relief, so she's more or less unconscious, plus her breathing is being assisted by a ventilator.'

'Can we see her?' Eileen asked.

'Of course,' Andrea replied. 'Mia and Tim are with her at the moment. Leora's daughter and ex-husband,' she explained to Ben. 'But they could do with a break, so I'll take you through.'

Voice calm, eyes frantic she told them what little they knew. Leora, she said, had been the victim of an acid attack at her front door. Her neighbour, Joan, had found her and called the emergency services. 'They acted fast,' she added, turning right out of the door, and up a small corridor. 'Neutralised as much of the acid as they could... dressed the burns... but then...' She paused, put her hand to her chest, as if struggling to breathe. The grief in her voice when she spoke again was heart-wrenching. 'Apparently the next few days are... are crucial... and they can't promise anything. Can't...' her voice trailed off to a whisper. '... guarantee she'll make it.'

'The police have been,' Marty added, squeezing his wife's shoulder, the look on his face willing her to keep it together. 'Interviewing us. Taking statements from witnesses, including Joan, and anyone else they think might be relevant, but for now they don't have any leads.'

'Who, though?' Andrea's voice was choked. 'Who would do such a wicked, wicked thing?'

When they entered the room, Ben could see one person in a bed and only one solitary figure sitting beside it.

'Where's your dad?' Marty asked.

Ben thought he heard the girl – Mia, he assumed – say he'd gone outside to make some phone calls. Eileen went straight to the girl and hugged her, whereas Ben, more out of respect to the family, lingered on the periphery. His eyes, however, went straight to the body lying in the bed. Swathed in bandages, it could have been anyone. Motionless, like a mummified shop mannequin, Leora was unrecognisable, her breathing helped by the steam engine clunk of a ventilator.

Andrea, who was still standing next to him, her voice hushed, wobbling, explained what the doctors had said. How likely it was they would need to put Leora into an induced coma while they tried to rebuild her. 'What the hell is that supposed to mean?' she added, her face wracked with grief, her fists covering her mouth. 'I can't do this,' she said, her hands moving to her chest. 'Not again. This isn't how it's supposed to be. Your children are meant to go after you, not before you.'

Gasping for air, she looked like she was struggling to breathe. She called out to Marty, asked him for help. For all intents and purposes, it looked like she was having a heart attack, but Ben knew otherwise. Marty rushed to his wife's side, but by then Ben was already holding her hand, telling her not to worry.

'Just… go… with it,' he said. 'I know it feels like your lungs are being crushed but believe me, they're not. Now…' Holding her at arm's length he gently tilted her face towards his and told her to follow his lead. 'I need you to breathe in through your nose as slowly, deeply, and gently as you can… that's it. Now… breathe out again… slowly, slowly… through your mouth. Brilliant. And again… in through your nose… and… out through your mouth. That's… it. You're doing really well.'

Andrea did as Ben instructed and before long her breathing was back to normal. Marty patted Ben's shoulder and thanked him, and Ben suggested they take a break. 'A proper break,' he added. 'Get yourselves something to eat or–'

'I can't eat,' Andrea interrupted.

'A cup of tea then.' Ben led them to the door.

'But… but what about Leora?' she protested. 'What if she–'

'If anything happens, I'll ring you,' Eileen interrupted, holding her phone up.

'C'mon, love, you know they're right,' Marty joined in.

Andrea's eyes flitted towards the bed. 'Oh-kay. Mia... you want to come with us?'

The girl, head down, her hand gently resting on Leora's arm, shook her head.

'She'll be fine with us.' Eileen guided Andrea out of the door. 'Now go. Get a cup of tea, and some fresh air. You know it makes sense.'

'You promise you'll ring me... if anything happens.'

'I promise,' Eileen assured her.

'Okay. But I'm not going for long,' Andrea added, turning to her husband.

'No, love. Not for long,' he said, as they shuffled out of sight.

'Now then, young lady,' Eileen said, her voice warm, soothing. 'What say I give your dad a call, find out where he is, and get him to take you for something to eat too? Then you can come back, batteries charged, ready for when Mum wakes up.'

The girl looked up and Ben was stunned. She was, except for the colour of her hair, which was dark, like Andrea's and Lonny's, the image of her mother. 'Who's he?' she asked, eyeing Ben suspiciously.

'This is Ben, a good friend of Mark's, went to school with us, including your mum.'

She wrinkled her nose. 'But... why's he here? Mum's never mentioned him before.'

'No... well. He was at my house when your nan phoned, and Mark asked Ben if he'd give me a lift to the train station. But because I was... well, because I didn't want to travel on my own, and because Ben is a former soldier and has a lot of knowledge about things that might be helpful, I asked him to come with me.'

'Okay.' Mia frowned, her pouty lips a carbon copy of Leora's. She turned her gaze back to the bed. 'What do you think she looks like,' she asked, eyes glazed, lips quivering, 'under those bandages?'

Eileen shook her head, placed a reassuring hand on her shoulder and squeezed it. 'C'mon...You mustn't worry about things like that for now.'

Shoulders heaving, Mia's head dropped. 'What... if... you know... she doesn't...' She burst into tears. 'I was horrible to her earlier. Horrible.'

Eileen knelt beside her and gently rubbed her arm. 'Now, now. I'm sure that's not true.'

Mia looked up, her eyes huge, her face crumpled. 'It is,' she sobbed. 'Mum asked me to get changed, said I couldn't go out wearing a miniskirt and fishnets. I called her a fun sucker and when I left, because I was in a mood, I didn't even hug her... or... or say goodbye.'

Eileen tucked a damp strand of hair behind Mia's ear and gave her a clean tissue from her bag. 'She'll know you didn't mean it. All girls argue with their mums when they're growing up. It's normal. In fact, it's the law.'

'Yes... but... what if she... doesn't make it. That will be the last thing I ever said to her.' Mia's sobbing was now uncontrollable.

'She will make it,' Eileen soothed.

'But... how do you know?' Mia protested: her face red, tearstained.

'I don't. But what I do know is, your mum is one of the strongest people I know. And as long she's still breathing, there's still hope.' She glanced at Ben, who nodded. 'So, you take that hope.' She folded Mia's hands in hers and squeezed them. 'And you hold on to it real tight. Okay?'

Mia nodded, dragging the tissue Eileen had given her up, down, and across her face. A gurgling noise from her tummy made her glance down, laugh.

'I think someone's hungry,' Eileen said, playfully poking her midriff.

'I don't feel it,' Mia replied.

'No, I know. But it's your body's way of reminding you to eat.' She stood up, offered Mia her hand, suggesting they go and find her dad. 'Let's get you something nice to eat, eh? Even if it's just something small,' she added. 'You need to keep your strength up.'

'But... what about Mum?' Mia's eyes flitted back to the figure in the bed. 'I can't leave her on her own.'

'She won't be on her own; Ben will stay with her. You don't mind, do you, Ben?'

'No... not at all,' Ben replied. 'You go and I'll keep watch until you get back. Plus...' He held up his phone. 'I've got my phone if I need to get hold of you.'

Mia seemed reluctant to leave her mother at first, but Eileen could, as Ben had discovered, be quite persuasive, and eventually Mia agreed. Eileen thanked Ben and promised she wouldn't be long.

Alone, Ben went to the foot of the bed and stared at Leora. Her head, beneath the dressings that covered her face, was swollen, football shaped, and what skin he could see, was both black and orange. She could have been, with breathing tubes jutting from her mouth and drips connected to her arms, anyone.

Mesmerised, he watched the rise and fall of her chest as the mechanical clunk of the ventilator, which, strangely soothing, was helping her to breathe. He knew from his years in the forces she was in a bad way. Her chances of making it largely dependent on how much, if any, of the acid she had swallowed. And even then, even if she did make it, it would be a life forever changed. One plagued by health issues, not to mention years of gruelling operations.

He moved round to the side of the bed, pulled out a chair and sat down next to her, gently taking her hand in his. 'You and me, were meant to be,' he whispered. Nervous, he glanced round, making sure no one had heard him. He hadn't meant to say it, shouldn't have said it, really. Unbidden, the words, spoken like a talisman, had simply slipped from his mouth. He stroked the back of her hand with his thumb, found himself shaking his head. To this day, he still couldn't believe he'd let her go. The spectacular way he had fucked things up. And all over some stupid, reckless, drunken moment that he couldn't even remember.

He should have fought for her. *Really* fought for her. Made her see what a stupid mistake it was. But he didn't. Or at least, he did... but only for a couple of weeks. It was pathetic. He'd gone on to become a soldier; part of an elite fighting force whose motto was 'Who dares wins'. So why then, when it came to her, to this woman, a woman he had never stopped loving, had he given up at the first hurdle?

What if he hadn't? What if he could go back in time and change everything? Make her see how much he loved her. What then? Would she have forgiven him, taken him back, eventually, and more importantly, would she, all these years later, be lying here now, in a hospital bed clinging to life? He inched forward, rested his elbows on his thighs, brought his hands to his mouth in prayer. He knew such thoughts were a waste of time. And besides, even if he could go back and change things, that would mean no Sam and no Robbie. And he loved his boys dearly.

No. His time now would be better spent focusing on who had done this to Leora, and why.

He pushed his chair back and stood up, began pacing the room. *Who?* he wondered, the fist of one hand pounding the palm of his other; pent-up frustration fuelling his fury. *Who would do this?* He knew, only too well, what human beings were capable of doing to one another. The question here though was why Leora? It had to be someone she knew because this was up close and personal. Whoever did it, or whoever was behind it, had deliberately meant to maim Leora. But why?

He felt a tap on his shoulder, and turned round, but no one was there. Confused, he did a full 360-degree turn. He even went to the door, pushed it open, and peered left to right along the corridor, but again, couldn't see anyone. Scratching his head, he went back to Leora's bedside and sat down again. Resting his elbows on the bed, he brought his hands together, closed his eyes, and lowered his head in benediction. Aside from the continual clunk of the ventilator, his ears picked up the sound of something else, something like music playing... in the distance. He opened his eyes again, and looked up, cocking his head to the side to better listen. It wasn't just music. It was a song. A familiar song. From his youth, maybe? His childhood, even?

He tried to hum along to it, to work out what it was, but it was too far away. Another tap, this time on his other shoulder, saw him leap up, sending his chair flying across the room behind him. Glancing from left to right, he swiped at his shoulders, brushing off anything that might be there, like a spider perhaps. A spider would tickle, though. This had been a definite tapping sensation. He searched the room, but other than Leora, there was nothing and no one else present.

He sat down again and waited to see if it happened again. But it didn't. He could have imagined it, he supposed. After all, he was still recovering from PTSD. However, he had also spent most of his adult life working as a trained soldier, often on many covert missions, and part of his training, part of the skillset he had developed over the years, was to use and trust his senses. His senses told him someone, or something, had tapped him on both shoulders. Why? He couldn't say. He was sure it would come to light though... eventually.

# CHAPTER 37

*W*as she awake or asleep? Dead or alive? It was impossible to tell.

Perhaps she was somewhere in between? Partly awake, yet half asleep. Half alive, yet partly dead. Hovering between this life and whatever followed next. That would at least explain the voices she kept hearing. Familiar voices like Mia's, her parents, and Eileen. But it might also explain why she could hear Lonny, Jules, and Grandma Cedella. She could have sworn she heard Ben's voice too, talking in low hushed tones to her mother.

Why though, whether real or simply part of her confused dreams, had he made an appearance now? Had he come to rescue her? Bring her back to life with a single kiss like a prince from the fairy tales of her childhood. Or had he simply come to pay his respects and say goodbye?

She tried again to remember what happened before she ended up here, in this strange limbo. A place that, with its bleeping and hissing, whooshing and clanking, smelt and sounded a lot like a hospital but in her dream-like state looked anything but.

She spent her hours wandering places she didn't recognise. Sometimes they were dark and menacing; dank alleyways filled with faceless black shapes. At others, like now, she roamed flower-strewn meadowland filled with light and warmth, and felt instinctively safe, able to rest for a while and try to work out what had happened to her.

She remembered having words with Mia about what she was wearing, and how Mia had sulked, slamming the door on her way out. She remembered a text from Ali, too, saying she was running late. Then she heard the doorbell, and, going to answer it, remembered how, greeted by a figure whose face she couldn't see, she wondered who it was. She remembered being about to ask, but then there was a searing heat behind her eyes, followed by a burning sensation at the back of her throat.

Her face was on fire, or at least, that's what it had felt like. She could hear her skin sizzling, taste blood in her mouth, and strangely enough she remembered the smell of bleach. She remembered too, putting her hand to her face to kill the flames, only to find there weren't any. Which made no sense. No sense at all. From there, the fire that wasn't there, spread down her neck, onto her chest and across her arm. She remembered a voice too, low, looming, sinister, and the hum of whisky, the grassy whiff of tobacco.

Then came the screaming, pitiful, followed by a dog barking, the whirring sound of a siren, the blurred kaleidoscope of lights, and voices. This time, though, the voices, although laced with kindness, were threaded with urgency. She remembered too, looking down at herself on a gurney then, back in her body again, she remembered the overhead strip lighting of a hospital corridor, swing doors opening and closing... and rain. Cold, cold rain. To wash away the pain, she thought she heard someone say. Only it didn't, it made it worse. Much worse. Then she remembered running from the pain, glancing over her shoulder as it gave chase, eventually succumbing to sleep.

When she woke again, she was curled up under a tree. A big tree, not unlike the oak tree at the reccy. The one she and Lonny used to climb as kids, the same one she and Ben had kissed beneath. Hearing voices, she sat up. She couldn't see them, but she realised it was her parents, only it was crackly; their voices fading in and out like a radio being tuned. Her mother seemed to be crying. Then she heard Mia, also crying. But why?

The next voice she heard was Grandma Cedella's. Leora could see her too, in her flat, cooking. She was shaking her head and clucking her tongue. 'Get back home tuh yuh mada, girl,' she said. 'Yuh cya visit mi anotha day.'

Then she saw Jules. Not the sickly, pasty person before he passed away, but a younger, fuller, fresh-faced version of himself. He was in his bedroom, dancing to Visage's 'Fade to Grey'.

'Not your time yet,' he called, his outline, like a candle whose light had been snuffed out, fading to a plume of smoke, rushing skywards.

Up on the horizon she could see Lonny, earphones on, working his decks. He spotted her, giving her one of his incredible smiles. She smiled back and felt her heart both soar and break at the same time. She waved to him, watching how, tension fixing his face, his smile faded. 'The next song is for you, sis,' he said, into his microphone. Music, tinny and distant, began playing across the meadow. It sounded familiar, a song from her childhood maybe. She smiled. It was the Jackson 5 singing 'I'll Be There'. She ran to him, so she might better hear it, but the closer she got, the further away he became.

Overcome with exhaustion, she sat down, found herself under the same tree again. Weary, she lay down and closed her eyes. When she opened them again, she was in bed. She tried to speak but found she couldn't: her mouth was stuffed with what felt like a ball of plastic. She glanced round, her vision blurred, out of focus, and spotted a white desk in front of some blue slatted curtains. Large ring binders were propped up on the desk, with soap dispensers at one end and a stand, containing sheets of paper, at the other. Separate to the desk she noticed what, at first, looked like a TV screen, but was, she realised, a monitor. At her bedside she noticed the figure of a man.

*Dad?* she wondered. *Is that you?* She blinked once, twice, three more times, realising, as the face of an older Ben Thompson swam into view, she was still dreaming.

# CHAPTER 38

$O$ ver the next half an hour or so, a nurse, bright, plucky, who introduced herself as Jane, wandered in and out, making random checks on Leora, scribbling down notes, and filling out charts.

'Everything all right?' She smiled, brushing past Ben.

Ben nodded, unsure whether to tell her that, not two minutes ago, he thought he saw Leora's eyes flicker open. In the end, he decided against it.

'Don't mind me,' Jane said.

'Sorry?'

'If you were talking to her.' She nodded, gesturing to Leora.

'Oh right...'

'I know, she seems out of it, but I think talking helps.'

'Yeah... I don't disagree.'

'Some people find it a bit awkward, don't always know what to say. I always say keep it simple. Tell them what you've been up to recently.'

Ben laughed, albeit half-heartedly. 'The thing is... I... *we...* haven't seen each other in years. So, I'm not sure where to begin.'

'Well,' Jane said, 'why don't you start at the beginning.' She headed to the door again, saying she'd be back in a minute.

Ben put his hand to the back of his neck and tilted his head from side to side, as if limbering up for a race. 'Start at the beginning, she says.' He laughed. 'She makes it sound easy.'

He tried to think where the beginning was. When, other than seeing her with Eileen a couple of weeks ago, was the last time he had properly seen Leora? Was it Lonny's funeral? Surely not. What a terrible day that was. February, grey sky, damp air, the ground so hard, the grass in the churchyard so frozen it snapped beneath his feet. He wasn't sure whether to go to the funeral at first; didn't want his presence to cause Leora any more unnecessary pain. He was glad he did though, especially as most of their school year turned up to pay their respects, which didn't surprise Ben in the least, because Lonny was extremely well liked.

Like Jules before him, months earlier, there was no denying, given how young Lonny was, how very tragic it was. The only difference being, where there had been a small window of opportunity to plan for Jules's death, Lonny's had been completely unexpected.

He remembered talking at the wake to Leora – Eileen on one side, her smile warm, eyes kind; Ali, on the other, scowling – telling her how sorry he was. And although she had thanked him for coming, it was as if she wasn't there, as if she had been replaced by a robot, her words, on repeat, programmed. The anguish behind Leora's eyes, however, had left him in little doubt about her suffering, and all he wanted to do was take her in his arms and hold her, tell her how much he loved her. But he couldn't... and it had killed him.

The door burst open, breaking him from his reverie. Startled, Ben looked up. A man, wearing jeans and a shirt with a white medical jacket over the top, approached the bed. He was carrying a camera: a stethoscope hanging casually around his neck.

He pointed to the bed. 'Leora Jackson?' he asked, snapping pictures of her before Ben had had time to reply.

Ben stood up, immediately on edge. 'Er... who are you?' he asked, squaring his shoulders, puffing his chest out. 'And why the hell are you taking photos?' He tried to stay calm, keep his voice cogent, controlled, but something about this bloke made him uneasy.

The camera-happy doctor pointed to the door and mumbled something about the department needing photos for a research paper they were working on. It didn't take Ben many seconds to work out that the ratty-faced man with small ratty eyes, his greasy skin – the legacy of fast food, fags, plus countless early mornings, and late nights – had nothing whatsoever to do with the medical profession and everything to do with the paparazzi. Ben was surprised, given the TV coverage of the dating show Leora was supposed to be hosting, they hadn't got here earlier.

*I'll rip his fucking head off*, Ben thought, about to lunge at the bloke when a commotion, outside, in the corridor, saw the weaselly rodent scuttling away at speed. Ben sprinted after him but by the time he reached the corridor, the vermin was already weaving his way among the throng of people filling the area. The rage in his chest as he imagined the lurid headlines that would follow once the said photos had been sold to the highest bidder, was barely containable. He wanted to run after the scumbag and smash his fucking camera to bits.

He couldn't though because, despite the arrival of hospital security and a couple of uniformed coppers who were doing their best to work out who should be there and who shouldn't, he couldn't leave Leora alone; prey to the next piece of shit that wanted his or her pound of flesh. So, arms folded, legs apart, Ben guarded the entrance to Leora's room with his life. Anyone, other than friends or family, who hoped to see her, would have to get past him first.

When Eileen, and Andrea and Marty returned, Ben told them

what had happened. How sorry he was for not realising sooner who the bloke was and what he was up to. They were kind, told him not to beat himself up about it, that it could so easily have been one of them instead.

'We should have expected it,' Andrea said, 'given all the media coverage she's had just recently. But we didn't; and I suppose that's not how we think of her. To me, she's simply Leora... my little girl.' Her fist flew to her mouth, her face shadowed with grief, and something else... regret, maybe. She looked at Marty. 'We should have done more,' she whispered. 'Should have made more of an effort, should have tried harder. We were so close but... after Lonny...' She buried her head in Marty's chest, started sobbing.

Marty, whose grief spilled into the grooves of exhaustion that stretched out from his eyes to each side of his mouth, pulled her close, resting his chin on her head. 'Come on, love, you can't keep beating yourself up. We did our best.'

She looked at him. 'Did we though, Marty, really?' She shook her head. 'To this day I still don't know how we became so... so distant.' Eileen squeezed Andrea's shoulder, reminded her how well they'd all been getting on just recently. 'But... but... all that wasted time.' Tears were running down her cheeks, her tone speaking of grief and incredulity.

'I don't know if this well help much,' Ben offered. 'But when I was at my lowest, my father told me that regrets are a waste of time, that they keep you locked in the past instead of living in the present. And yes... while that's easier said than done... it's also true. Leora needs you... now more than ever... and you're here. That's what's important.'

'He's right,' Eileen said, her face full of kindness.

Andrea sniffed, nodded. Something had shifted in her. There was a softer element in her eyes. Lead instead of steel. Absolution instead of guilt. Or at least, some, anyway.

Eileen said she had some news and invited Ben to the family

room to share it with him while Andrea and Marty stayed with Leora.

Parched, Ben went straight to the coffee machine, pulled some change from his pocket, and selected a black coffee. It looked... positively archaeological. He took a mouthful, winced: it tasted as shitty as it looked.

'There's a café downstairs... if you'd rather get a coffee there? Or a Costa over the road?' Eileen offered.

Ben shook his head, sat down. 'I'm fine. What's this news then?'

Eileen pulled a chair out next to him. 'After I found Tim, and left Mia with him, I tried to get hold of Ali again, and this time when I rang her, she replied. She said she knew about Leora, plus the police have arrested someone.'

Ben frowned. 'Okay... that's good news... I guess. But how, or why, does she know?'

'Because...' Eileen took a deep breath. 'It was Ali who alerted the police in the first place... and the person they've arrested is... Hugo... Ali's husband.'

'What?' Ben stood. 'But... why?'

Eileen shook her head. 'Honestly, Ben, I don't know. I mean, I've got my suspicions.'

She told Ben about Ali and Hugo's recent problems, how Ali had ended up in hospital after *supposedly* falling down the stairs. Ben hadn't seen Ali to speak to for years, nor had he met her husband, Hugo. However, it was hard to imagine Ali – remembering how forthright, ambitious, and unafraid to speak her mind she'd been, even if it caused offence – putting up with anyone's crap. Then again, most abusive relationships didn't start out like that, did they. They developed over time, wearing the recipient down.

'Hugo took her to the hospital to get her checked out and while she was there Ali phoned Leora, who went to the hospital and picked her up. There's been a couple of incidents over the years when Leora and I have spotted bruises on Ali's wrists, or her back, but this was the first time it was bad enough for Ali to go to hospital. Leora managed to speak to Hugo, at the hospital, told him to quit the booze and get some counselling, which he seemed to take on board, then Ali went back to Leora's. She only stayed with Leora for a few days though, then she and Hugo talked things through, and Ali went home again. We assumed, for now at least, all was well again. Clearly it wasn't though... was it.'

Ben paced the room like a caged wild animal. 'But... why Leora? It doesn't make sense. Surely... if this Hugo was going to hurt anyone... it would have been Ali? Not that,' he added, putting his hand up, 'I'm saying it should have been Ali. I wouldn't wish this on anyone. But why Leora?'

'I agree. It doesn't make sense but when Leora went to collect Ali from the hospital, Ali told Leora that Hugo hates her.'

Ben looked at her, felt the tendons in his neck flex. 'Hates Leora? Why?'

'Ali said it was because Hugo had got it into his head that Leora was trying to take Ali away from him. Which she wasn't... of course. She was just looking out for Ali; wanted to give them both some breathing space, time apart to think things through. It's weird though...' Eileen paused, looked thoughtful.

'What is?' Ben walked to the window and peered out. It was dusk and the last of the sun's rays had turned the sky into a watercolour of amber and purple brushstrokes while the city itself, ever lit, ever awake, ever pulsating, began its nightly light show.

'Well... it's just... I've only ever met Hugo a handful of times, but I never got the impression he disliked Leora. In fact, I'd have said the opposite was true, that he really liked her. Then again, I haven't really met anyone who didn't like her.'

Ben turned to look at her again. 'That's because some people are good at hiding who they really are. Clearly, if this Hugo's been knocking Ali about, he's got issues. Throw in some booze, add some drugs maybe – illegal or prescription – and who knows what the hell he was thinking. Besides, the police wouldn't be questioning him without good reason.'

Eileen sighed, ran a hand through her hair. 'No, I know. It's all just... so shocking... so awful.'

'So... where's Ali now?' Ben asked, arms folded, head down, staring at his dingy trainers.

'At another hospital, also being treated for acid burns.'

Ben's head shot up again. 'What?'

'Nothing like Leora's. Quite minor, in fact; one hand and the lower half of one arm apparently.'

'What?' Ben repeated, frowning.

Eileen held her hands up. 'I know... I know... I don't get it either. She said she'd explain when she gets here. She's waiting for the hospital to discharge her, then she's planning to get a taxi straight over.'

The door burst open, making them both look round. It was Mia, who, eyes wide, seemed somewhat alarmed. Concerned, Eileen stood up and went to her, asked her if everything was okay.

'It's Mum!' And Mia burst into tears.

Without a second thought, Eileen took her into her arms and hugged her, tight. Her voice, when she spoke, was kindness itself but her eyes, when she glanced at Ben, told a different story. Like Ben, whose stomach had dropped out of his arse, he could read both the fear and panic in them. 'What is it, love?' Eileen stroked Mia's hair. 'What about Mum?'

Sniffing, Mia took a step back and looked at them both. To Ben's surprise, Eileen's too, judging by the look on her face, Mia smiled. 'She opened her eyes.' Her smile metamorphosed into a huge grin. 'She opened her eyes, they took her off the ventilator, and she looked at me, then, after a few seconds, she said my name.'

Eileen's eyebrows shot up. 'She did?' Mia nodded; started

crying again. 'See now.' Eileen held her at arm's length. 'Didn't I tell you she was strong?'

The relief in the room was profound. This was good news, but Ben wasn't under any illusions. He knew, depending on what was going on internally, Leora could, at any moment, take a turn for the worse again.

# CHAPTER 39

The next two days passed by in anxious fits and starts because, unlike the movies, most people when coming round from such trauma do so gradually. Leora slept a lot, and when she did open her eyes, she was often quite confused, quite agitated, which didn't surprise Ben in the least. However, it was still distressing to witness, especially for Leora's parents, and Mia – poor kid.

The medical staff were very good, going out of their way to describe what was happening and why, explaining how – partly because of her injuries and partly because of the morphine she was being fed to deal with the pain – she might say things that seemed strange, didn't make sense. Things that everyone else knew weren't real, but felt very real to Leora.

Ali didn't turn up until the following morning, and because during that first terrible night Leora was, for the most part, comatose, Ben managed to convince the others to get some sleep while he watched over her. It took some persuasion, but with Eileen's help, Ben made them see how much Leora was going to need them once she was fully conscious, and how they wouldn't be fit for anything and anyone unless they got a few hours' kip.

Reluctantly, they agreed, but only because they were staying in the patients' hotel, an on-site facility for families of patients.

'If anything happens,' Marty insisted. 'Anything at all, you ring us *straight* away.'

Ben promised he would. Eileen booked herself into a room at a Travelodge she'd spotted up the road earlier, while Tim, a tall, slim man, with a square jaw, pale blue eyes, and whose grip, when Ben offered his hand, was firm but reverent, suggested Mia go home with him, promising to bring her back in the morning. He seemed genuinely concerned about his ex-wife, and he clearly cared for his daughter, but with his second wife expecting their first child any day now, he had his hands full.

Mia refused. Said she wouldn't leave her mother's side until she knew, for sure, she was okay. She was clearly distraught; yet there was a steeliness in her eyes, an understated grit and determination that reminded Ben of Leora. In the end it was agreed that Mia would stay with her grandparents and Tim would come back in the morning anyway. All Ben could think was, *Poor kid.*

Between 12pm and 4.30am, Ben kept vigil over Leora. The hospital, although active, was noticeably quieter, the room, all dimmed lights, and eerie shadows. Jane, the nurse, who had finished her shift, was replaced by Carl who, equally vigilant, equally as sanguine as his predecessor, carried out regular checks on Leora, telling her, as was common practice, what he was doing and why, even though for the most part, she neither heard nor saw him. Ben held her hand, sometimes quiet, sometimes talking to her. He kept it light, told her about Sam and Robbie, how pleased he was that Mark and Eileen were getting married.

He talked about school too. Asked her if she remembered the time Lonny borrowed his cousin's bike. 'I couldn't believe how laid back he was about it. Mark and I would have been shitting ourselves. But not your Lonny.'

He talked about their first dance too, at the school Christmas disco, how nervous he was and how, when he'd kissed her, with Yazoo's 'Only You' playing in the background, it had felt like the most natural thing in the world.

'I know it sounds daft,' he said, nervously glancing round, making sure no one else was there listening, 'but when we kissed, it was like… there was a connection between us. I felt like I'd known you all my life… longer even. Which… I know isn't possible… but that's how it felt… Still does… if I'm honest.'

Twice she opened her eyes and looked at him, and once she whispered his name. Most of the time though, she slept.

A little after 4.30am, Andrea was back. 'Can't sleep,' she said, her eyes red with exhaustion. 'How's she been?'

'Quiet,' Ben replied. 'Sleeping, mostly. Although she did open her eyes a couple of times.'

Scrubbing her face with her hands, Andrea went to her daughter, the fear and the heartbreak painfully evident in her eyes. It was a look Ben had seen many times before. It suddenly proved too much for him, and he had to look away. PTSD wasn't something you just found yourself cured of. It took time, and even though he'd been managing it much better just recently, it was surprising how sometimes, just the smallest thing could threaten to trigger him again.

Andrea suggested he go back to their room for a rest, said there was a sofa he could use, or a kitchen if he wanted to make himself a tea or coffee. Ben was about to decline her kind offer when he realised, she wasn't asking him; she was telling him.

By 9am everyone was up and about, taking it in turns to sit with Leora, or converge in the family room. Around this time Ali, arm bandaged, wearing huge sunglasses, turned up. Dressed in designer jeans and T-shirt, her hair piled on top of her head in a messy bun, wearing brown strappy sandals that matched the large leather handbag slung over her shoulder, she screamed of money and sophistication. Mia went straight to her and hugged her, followed by Andrea and Eileen.

'Oh...' She peered over her sunglasses when she saw him. 'Ben? Ben Thompson? What are you doing here?' She smiled, but there was a haughtiness about her, a look of friendly disgust, if there was such a thing.

'He came with me,' Eileen said, before Ben had time to reply. 'He was visiting, when Andrea rang, and he kindly offered me a lift to the station. But because we weren't sure what had happened to Leora, only that she'd been involved in a chemical attack, I asked Ben, with his military background, if he'd come with me, I thought his expertise might prove useful. I'm so glad I did too.' She turned to look at Ben, her smile, as usual, full of warmth and affection. 'He's been such a great support.'

Ali's eyebrows rose above her sunglasses, before she reached into her oversized handbag and pulled out a stack of newspapers. 'Ugh... I take it you've seen these,' she said, tossing them on the coffee table.

Most of them were tabloid papers and most of them had photos of Leora splashed across the front page; one as she had previously looked, and one as she looked now, each with its own lurid headline. It was sickening, and for the life of him, Ben couldn't work out what Ali was playing at, what she thought the family would gain from seeing such images, reading such salacious, speculative crap.

A temporary silence fell about the room as each one of them, except Ben, picked up a paper and read it. Mia, whose index finger quickly traced each line of black print, burst into tears before bolting from the room. Tim, who threw his paper down in disgust, chased after her.

Ali hung her head. 'Oh God,' she whispered. 'I'm so sorry... I just thought... you'd want to know.'

Andrea patted her arm, told her not to worry about it. 'I suppose, with her face all over the TV for the last month or so, we were going to have to face this kind of attention at some point. There was mention of it, briefly, on the news this morning... but seeing it... like this...' she stared at the newspaper in her hand, '...in black and white... Well, it's all rather shocking.'

Marty, whose face was thunderous, scooped up the papers, went to one of the windows, opened it, and threw the whole lot out. 'No more,' he said to no one in particular, slamming the window shut again, although Ben got the distinct impression he was talking to Ali, and Ali alone. 'I don't want to see any more shit like that again. Not in here.' He took a deep breath; squared his shoulders, then, pulling a chair out opposite Ali, sat down. 'Now, are you going to tell us what your bastard husband did to my daughter or what?'

'Marty,' Andrea exclaimed. 'What the hell's got into you? Ali's not the enemy here.'

Marty put a hand to the back of his neck, adjusted the angle of his head, tipping it first to one side, then the other. 'I know. It's just–'

'It's fine.' Ali placed her hand on top of Andrea's. 'You're upset and need to know what happened. I understand.' She closed her eyes then opened them again. 'Right,' she said, her bandaged hand going to her throat. 'Let me tell you.'

For the next twenty minutes or so Ali explained how she had made plans to spend the day with Leora, how they hoped to have brunch together, do a bit of retail therapy followed by a light dinner and an early night, as a car was collecting Leora at 6am the following morning to take her to the studio for a final dress rehearsal.

'Only, Hugo and I got into another fight,' she continued. 'I threatened to leave him this time... for good. Said I'd go and live with Leora until I got on my feet, but this time I wanted a divorce, which...' She looked at them then, her eyes dancing fitfully back and forth between them all. 'Which made him *really* angry. Then... then...' She shook her head, looked down. 'Hugo hit me,' she whispered, glancing up again, removing her sunglasses to reveal a very swollen, very bruised eye. 'Actually...

that's not technically true. He didn't hit me as such, he smashed my face against a wall.'

'Oh Alison, love,' I'm so sorry.' Andrea rubbed her shoulder.

'I swear to God I saw stars.'

Andrea and Eileen were on the verge of crying whereas Marty, his breathing heavy, his brow furrowed, stood up, started pacing the room. 'And? What happened next?'

'Hugo was raging,' Ali continued. 'Said how that, once and for all, he'd make that interfering bitch pay. Then he took all the keys to the house and locked me in. I tried to get to my phone to call Leora and warn her, but I must have passed out, because the next thing I knew, I was waking up with Hugo standing over me, pouring something on my arm, which started to burn. He was laughing, but he had this strange look on his face, and I knew, right there and then, if I didn't get away from him, he'd kill me.' Covering her face with her hands, she started sobbing. 'And... and somehow...' she said, rocking back and forth. 'Although, God only knows how... I managed to get out the door and run. And I just kept on running... for my life.

'I didn't know if anything had happened to Leora, but because my arm was burning, I couldn't think straight. I knew I needed medical attention, so I waved down a taxi, which took me to the nearest hospital, where I was treated for burns and kept in overnight for observation. It wasn't until later in the day I found the courage to call the police, which is when they arrested Hugo. Apparently, he'd gone into work as usual – as if nothing had happened.'

'I'll kill him,' Marty said quietly, still pacing back and forth. 'I swear to God,' his voice grew louder, his face puce with anger. 'If I get my hands on him...' He pounded the palm of his hand with his fist. 'I will... I'll kill him...'

*He's not the only one*, Ben thought, a rage swelling inside him. It was all he could do to hide it.

Frantic, Andrea stood up and went to her husband; grabbed

his arms and implored him to look at her. When he didn't, she reached for his chin; tilted it in such a way that he had to look at her. 'Listen to me, Martin Jackson,' she said, her voice firm but wavering. 'I want to kill him too... but what good will that do? Leora needs us now... more than ever. That's where our focus should be. Let the police deal with *him*, and we'll look after Leora.'

Marty nodded, the fury in his eyes gradually dissipating. 'Okay,' he sighed, pulling his wife into his arms and holding her. 'Okay, okay, okay,' he repeated. *But he wants to pray to God he never comes face to face with me,* were the unspoken words Ben guessed Marty was thinking.

Once the dust had settled, Ben excused himself for a few hours and booked himself into the same Travelodge as Eileen. He needed a couple of hours' kip, which wouldn't be easy because he was wired. However, as he was still navigating his own path to recovery, he also knew how important it was to rest, how quickly he could fall by the wayside again if he didn't take care of himself.

By the time he got back to the hospital, most of Leora's dressings had been removed so they could be changed, finally revealing the devasting extent of her injuries. The family were shellshocked.

Ben too, though he had prepared himself and knew what lay beneath those oozing, blackened bandages, was horrified. He had – foolishly, perhaps – hoped it wasn't as bad as he suspected. Unfortunately, though, it was worse. Far worse.

Andrea and Marty looked sick with worry. Their disbelief and despair, profound. Ben wished there was something he could do to ease their suffering, but there wasn't, only time could do that. Mia, however, was so distraught, it was decided, in the end, both for her sake and Leora's, that she would go home with Tim for a couple of days and take some time to process what had happened to her mother. It changed nothing for Ben, though. He always had, and always would, love Leora.

The police visited again, confirming that Hugo, who they were reasonably sure was their man, was in custody and was being interviewed. They still, however, needed to interview Leora before they could move forward with the investigation. It was agreed, now Leora was more compos mentis, they would come back tomorrow. Marty and Andrea then busied themselves, working out the practicalities of how Leora would manage and how best they could help their daughter when she was eventually discharged, while Eileen popped to an internet café, researching other treatments that could help Leora's recovery once she'd had her skin grafts.

It would be weeks, months, possibly, before they would need to confront these issues, but keeping busy, doing something productive, helped.

Ali, on the other hand, seemed dumbstruck, positively prostrate with grief, especially when Leora's dressings came off. She kept crying, repeatedly blaming herself, saying, almost to the point of annoyance – thankfully out of earshot of Leora – how terrible Leora looked and how she hadn't been expecting it.

Ben was struck how personally she seemed to take it. Then again, it was *her* husband who had done this to her friend, so it was understandable, he supposed, that she felt so responsible.

Ali suggested she sit with Leora that night, but Andrea told her that Ben had already offered. 'Sorry… I know you didn't,' Andrea whispered, taking him to one side. 'But I feel like she's safe with you. And even though I didn't get much sleep last night, the little I did get, helped.'

Ben said he was honoured she'd asked him, and for a second night kept vigil at Leora's bedside. Her face was dressed again, but having glimpsed her injuries earlier that day, he now knew she looked every bit as bad as he'd imagined she would… but it changed nothing… his love for her, still strong. If it was okay with her, he hoped he might stick around. He had no agenda, no expectations. He simply wanted to be there for her. Her sleep that night was troubled, full of yelling and screaming, fuelled, he suspected, by a mixture of pain and drugs.

The following morning, Eileen talked to him about various treatment centres she'd found, including a specialist rehabilitation clinic in Germany. 'They're using cutting-edge rehabilitation methods that aren't available in the UK,' she explained. 'And I think, after speaking to her consultant, Mrs Catherine Shields, that something like that, alongside the skin grafts and physio, could really benefit her. The only problem is the price. It's not cheap, and although she could apply to the NHS for funding, God only knows if she'll get it.'

Later that day Ben had an idea that might help with the funding issues for treatment for Leora. He went to Leora's room to look for Eileen, hoped to have a quick word with her about it. Only, when he arrived, the door was slightly ajar and he overheard the three of them, Ali, Eileen and Leora, talking. Ali was asking Eileen what the hell she thought she was playing at bringing Ben here.

'Can't you see she's got enough to think about without the added confusion of having *him* around?'

Eileen fought his corner; said he was simply being a friend. 'A very good friend,' she added.

Ali responded by saying that although Ben was Eileen's friend, he was most definitely *not* Leora's. 'Don't you think it would be best if he left?' she added.

Ben couldn't see their faces, but he could hear Leora's croaky response. 'I... I suppose so.'

Ben's heart sank. He put his hand to his forehead, shook his head. He didn't like to admit it, but Ali was right, his presence wasn't helping, not really. He took a deep breath and, knocking loudly, stuck his head round the door and asked to speak to Eileen.

He told her he was getting ready to leave. 'I just want to run an idea by you first.'

She loved his idea; swore to keep it a secret but was disappointed that he was leaving.

'I need to get back to the boys. Tell Leora I said goodbye, will you.'

Her eyebrows shot up. 'You're not going to say goodbye... yourself?'

Ben shook his head. 'I think it's best if I just slip away.'

Eileen opened her mouth to protest, then seemed to think better of it, hugged him instead, and asked him to check in on Mark and Oliver for her, which he promised to do. Then he went to find and say goodbye to Andrea and Marty, who also seemed a little surprised at his departure, but thanked him, nonetheless. Andrea said his support, during those first terrible hours, that first terrible night, had been invaluable. 'Don't be a stranger,' she added, holding his hand in hers. 'You know where we live. Next time you're about, pop by for a cuppa?'

Stepping into the bright sunshine, swapping the stagnant air of the hospital for the polluted air of the city, Ben headed for the Underground. He was feeling, he realised, as his feet pounded pavements that moved like a great river of humanity, both heartbroken and lifted. Heartbroken because, after Ali's comments, he realised, yet again, he had no place with Leora, but lifted because he had a plan to help her. She would never know it was his idea either, which meant she would never feel the need to thank him. But he would know, and that's all that mattered.

He felt a tap on his shoulder and turned round, but just like at the hospital, no one was there. He continued walking. *Someone must have bumped into me,* he thought. At least that is, until he felt a second tap on his other shoulder and heard the same tinny sound of a song playing in the distance. He stood for a moment and listened, trying to locate the source of the music, but try as he might, he couldn't. Just like at the hospital, the song seemed familiar, but even when he concentrated on drowning out the noise of the city, he couldn't work out what it was.

Unlike his mother, Ben wasn't religious, but he had become, over the years, thanks to several unexplained phenomena, more spiritual. During his youth he would have dismissed what had happened to him at the hospital as coincidental, would have looked for, and no doubt found a logical explanation. Now though, now he was older, and more experienced about life, he was quite prepared to accept that it might be something else entirely.

Someone was trying to tell him something. What it was and why, he still hadn't worked out yet. He would though, he was convinced of that.

# CHAPTER 40

*P*ain. That was the place Leora inhabited now. A world of pain. She'd already had three surgeries. The first was on the third day of her admission to remove all the burned and dead skin from her face, neck, some of her chest, hands, arm, and leg. Then on the following day, the fourth day, she had the same procedure again, only this time she had a face mask fitted, which, made up of donor skin from corpses, was stapled to her face and worn for eleven days to aid recovery and prevent infection.

Following that, her surgeon, a very nice lady called Mrs Catherine Shields, who had a stern face but an angelic voice, explained that Leora would be given a pioneering new treatment called Matriderm: something she described as a skin substitute or filler made of collagen and elastin that, because of the way it helped skin accept skin grafts, she compared to the foundations and scaffolding used in the building industry.

'Then… once we've applied that,' she continued. 'We'll take skin from your buttocks and back, and graft it onto your face, neck, and chest.'

She also went on to explain that a team of five doctors, led by her, would perform the six-hour surgery, after which, Leora would be put into a coma.

'The pain will be too great for you to manage otherwise; too traumatic,' she said. 'Plus, I need you to lie perfectly still for the skin graft to heal properly. The sulphuric acid thrown at you has stripped away four layers of skin, which means you've suffered third degree burns and I'll be honest; it's one of the worst cases of acid burns I, or any of my colleagues, have ever seen. Trust me though, Leora, even though you've got a long road ahead of you, I promise you, me and my team will be with you every step of the way.'

Unlike the movies, the ten-day induced coma was not a deep peaceful sleep, instead – mostly due to the morphine used to manage the pain – it was a drug-induced nightmare. Most of her time was spent wandering a red barren landscape that was devoid of life, save the odd blackened tree and a few scorched buildings. The air was thick with smoke and the smell of burning, and rain fell that, like her tears and her blood, was as thick and as black as treacle.

When she did happen upon a group of people she was always met with the same gasps of horror, the same look of repulsed disdain that, during her lucid moments before being placed in a coma, she'd seen on the faces of her friends and family. All of them, every single one of them, had cried when they'd seen her. Even her dad.

When she begged the people in her strange, imagined land for help, pleaded with them for a few drops of water to quell her singed throat, the grim-faced individuals would always shake their heads, turn away, and shun her.

It wasn't real though, this place. The stuff of nightmares maybe. But it was also a figment of her comatose, morphine-doped imagination where she and her muddled thoughts drifted, as her damaged body tried to heal itself and her traumatised mind tried to make sense of it all. She knew, somewhere beyond her forced sleep, beyond her wild imaginings, she was not wandering the landscape of some dystopian nightmare but was instead laid up in a hospital bed, in the burns unit, the victim of an acid attack.

The memory of it, of that fateful morning when the doorbell rang and she went to answer it, played constantly in her mind. She remembered a face shrouded in a hood and two eyes, like cracks in the snow, dark and foreboding, peeping out. She also remembered the glint of a smile, and the smell of burning flesh – *her* flesh. And yet, despite the toxic fumes that gnawed at her skin there was no mistaking the familiar smell of stale sweat, strong whisky, and expensive cologne. It was Hugo. No doubt about it.

She remembered the swirl of beige; his trench coat, the designer one – she couldn't remember the name – the one he wore all the time, his Ralph Lauren polo shirts beneath it during the summer, his tweed jacket or Barbour during the winter months. Dapper, he said it made him look. But it always reminded Leora of the dancing men in trench coat sketches on *The Benny Hill Show*, which she and Lonny had watched and laughed at as kids. Instead of wearing his favoured green baseball cap, though, which would have been a dead giveaway, Hugo had worn a hoodie beneath his coat. He might have even worn a scarf over his mouth, but it was definitely *his* smell, *his* coat.

Which is what she told the two police officers that came to interview her. The relief she felt, when they told her he'd been arrested, was like nothing else she had ever known. He was locked up, which meant he couldn't hurt her anymore.

'He's denying it,' they said. 'Adamant it wasn't him, but what with the trench coat you mentioned, and the hoody, which we found stuffed in his neighbour's bin, plus some, albeit very grainy, CCTV footage, the evidence is pretty conclusive. We're conducting a search of his computer too, to see if there's anything incriminating in his search history. But it's not looking good for him.'

*Why me though?* she wondered. *Why not Ali?* Not that she wished this on Ali. She didn't wish this on anyone. But he'd gone back for Ali afterwards. Poured acid on her arm, after he'd finished with her. Perhaps that was his plan all along, first Leora, then Ali. Only, by the time he'd finished with Leora and got back to Ali, he'd used more of the acid than he'd intended to, so Ali had got what was left. And perhaps, if Ali hadn't got away, he'd have killed her.

Then again... why did he go to work that afternoon? Act like nothing had happened. Surely, he must have known the police would catch up with him eventually. Maybe he thought Leora hadn't recognised him; hoped Ali would be too afraid to say anything.

In truth, Leora didn't care. The important thing was, he was off the streets. No longer a danger to her or anyone else.

# CHAPTER 41

*L*eora looked at her mother. 'What time is it now?' she asked.

Andrea smiled, looked at her watch. 'Five minutes later than when you last asked me.'

'So... she's late? She's not coming, is she?'

Andrea put her head on one side, gently patted her daughter's hand. 'It's only five minutes, love. I'm sure she'll be here in a minute.'

Today was a big day. Today, her psychiatrist, Alex, agreed that Leora could see herself for the first time since the attack. There had been no mirrors in the single room she had first been placed in, and none in the room she had since been moved to, which she now shared with three other burns patients. Leora had asked on several occasions if she could see herself but there had been a concerted effort by all, including staff and family, to ensure she didn't, not until Alex was sure she was ready. 'We have to give her time,' she'd overheard her saying to her parents.

'Talk of the devil.' Marty stood up just as Alex entered the room pushing an empty wheelchair.

'Leora, Marty, Andrea,' she said, glancing at them all in turn. With short, auburn hair and persuasive mahogany eyes, her profile was what Grandma Cedella would have described as handsome. 'So,' she turned to Leora, 'are we ready?'

Leora took a deep breath. 'Yes... I think so.'

'Great.' Alex turned to Marty for help getting Leora into the wheelchair. 'I've booked one of the consultation rooms for half an hour, so we can have some privacy.'

Marty pushed Leora along the corridor, while up ahead her mother and Alex made small talk, about the weather, mostly. Leora looked straight ahead, but from her periphery, though she was on the burns unit, she was aware of people staring at her. Even some of the nurses did a double take. She tried to ignore them, brush it off because, really, how bad could it be?

She was keen to know what she looked like because it felt like the next stage in her recovery. She also believed, once she had seen her injuries for herself, she'd be better equipped to start making plans. Her parents had offered to take her home to live with them for a while, which was sweet. Ali too, had kindly offered to take six months off work and care for her.

'It'll be like old times, and, when my divorce comes through, perhaps I can help you set up an online business, something you can do from home. Especially as... you're not likely to want to go out much.'

Blink and you'd have missed it, but Leora remembered the way her parents had looked at one another then, the briefest exchange of glances between them; the flicker of annoyance in their eyes. If Leora could have, she would have frowned. *Why am I not likely to want to go out much?* she remembered thinking. But when no one contradicted Ali, she was too afraid to ask. Leora thanked Ali, said it was very thoughtful of her, but she needed time to think about it.

'Take your time,' Alex warned, clutching a small mirror in her hand. Leora, somewhat bemused, despite the pounding of her heart against her ribs, almost smiled. Alex was really drawing this out. 'I mean it,' Alex said, as if reading her mind. 'Take your time. Start at your chest, then work your way up... slowly.'

Leora didn't want to take it slowly though. She wanted to see what everyone else saw. Sure, she expected some damage; patches of red, scarred skin, like she'd seen on her chest, arm and leg, but the person staring back at her would still be her, wouldn't it? Hand trembling, she reached for the mirror. She gasped, then choked, almost, as if she were drowning in the air she swallowed. The image that met her was monstrous. She opened her mouth, tried to scream, tried to fathom who... or what... was looking back at her. Her face looked as if it had melted like wax. Confused, she recoiled. *This is a joke*, she told herself. *Some sick, macabre joke. Or... or Alex has made a mistake, given me the wrong mirror?*

The air in the room, deathly quiet, seemed to disappear into a vacuum.

Clinging to the mirror; her hands rigid, her fingers frozen, Leora scrutinised every square inch of the stranger staring back at her. Her skin *was* red. But it wasn't just the odd patch here and there. It was *all* red. All red, and all raw; like the slabs of meat that hung from large silver hooks in the window of Brown's Butchers when she was a child. Gone were her eyelashes, gone were her eyebrows, and gone too, was her nose, replaced instead by a small hillock of skin. She observed all this from bulbous, bulging eyes protruding above sunken cheekbones. Her lips too, were swollen beyond belief; a parody of what they were before, like the cheap plastic ones found in Christmas crackers, or some ghoulish set made by the special effects department for a horror movie.

She felt a wail rise inside her. She was a monster. Frankenstein's monster.

'No,' she whispered, her chest heaving. 'No. No. No!' She

wanted to cry but the damage to her eyes was such, she couldn't even do that.

Shame, hot and angry, oozed from every part of her. From the tip of her partially shaven head down to her toes. No wonder Mia was on the verge of tears every time she visited, wore the same look of incredulity, the same rabbit-in-the-headlights expression. No wonder her mother cried, quietly, when she was alone with Leora and thought Leora was asleep. No wonder her father, whose knowing eyes, despite his big smile and broad shoulders that always made her feel so safe, so protected, betrayed something else. Something base. Something primal. A pent-up fury so deep, yet so visceral, it radiated off him in waves. No wonder Eileen's voice, her beautiful smile, wavered from time to time, and no wonder Ali, whose eyes looked sore and gritty, blinked all the time; hay fever, she'd said the other day, even though she'd never suffered with it before.

And, of course, no wonder Ben had left.

She wasn't even sure he was real at first. Thought, during those first terrible days, he was a figment of her drug-induced imagination... like Lonny, and Jules, and Grandma Cedella. Eileen assured her he wasn't. 'He *wanted* to be here,' she said. 'Sat with you... for two nights in a row... so the rest of us could get some sleep.' She remembered then, feeling the back of his thumb delicately strumming her hand, how he had talked to her about school. Reminding her of the first time they danced together, the first time they kissed.

She had found his presence strangely soothing, strangely reassuring, and strangely protective. He'd always had that effect on her. When she first saw him, at school, all those years ago, before they even started dating, she knew their paths had crossed before. When, where, and how, she couldn't say, but intuitively, she had felt it... in her bones... and in her heart. Sensed it that night they danced together. Felt, not so much a connection between them, but rather a reconnection. Knew that, somehow, she knew him, and he knew her.

At least, that's how it had felt at the time. She thought they would be together forever, but then he'd cheated on her, which had been so unexpected, so painful, and yet, at the same time, so alien to everything she had come to believe about him. If she hadn't seen those God-awful photos of him with someone else for herself, she never would have believed it. But try as she might, over the years, she often found herself thinking of him. It was insane. Their time together had been so brief, and yet their love had been quite unlike anything she'd experienced before or since.

Maybe it wasn't that though. Maybe it was simply that, when she thought of Ben, she was in fact thinking of a time in her life when, despite her teenage angst, she was happiest. To a more carefree place when life somehow felt simpler and more predictable, surrounded by people that loved her. Whatever it was, she was glad Ben had come. She had felt safe with him by her side, knew, should the need arise, he would protect her. And yes, in her drug-addled confused mind, she hoped he might stay a while longer. But he hadn't. He had slipped away, and now, as she stared at the monster in the mirror, she realised why.

He didn't want her. No man would. Those days were over. Her life as she knew it, was now well and truly over. Ali was right. Except for hospital appointments, she would probably never set foot into the outside world again.

Putting a fist to her mouth, the mirror still glued to her hand, she tried to stifle the strangled noise climbing, unbidden, up her throat. Still, try as she might, she couldn't stop it, and the sound that left her mouth, partly because of the injuries to her throat was, like a low foreboding pharyngeal growl, not unlike the sound of a woman in the last stages of labour.

'Give it time, love,' she heard her mother's soothing voice say. 'It's early days yet.'

Alex nodded. 'Your mother's right. You're under the care of

one of *the* best plastic surgeons in the world. Like the Bionic Woman, Mrs Shields will rebuild you, and before you know it, your face will be as good as new.'

Leora's heart hammered thick and fast against the wall of her damaged chest. She didn't care about Mrs Shields, or how good she was. She didn't want a new face, she wanted *her* face, her old one. Letting the mirror slip from her hands – she didn't care if it smashed, what difference would another seven years bad luck make now? – she glanced out of the window. Alex, with the reflexes of a ninja, caught the mirror. Rain tapped the window, sliding down the glass; tears Leora wanted to cry but couldn't. 'Take me back to my room,' she whispered, her head down.

Covering her head with her hands, Leora refused to look up as her father wheeled her back to her room; the whispered mumblings of her mother and Alex behind them. They were greeted by two police officers, the same ones that had previously interviewed her, hovering by her bed. Their faces were grim, and she knew, as panic swelled in the pit of her stomach, straight away that something was wrong. *Very* wrong. They asked her if they could talk to her; pulled the curtains round for privacy, her parents and Alex still in attendance.

'I'm afraid,' the shorter one of the two started to say. 'We've had to release Mr Hugo Stevens without charge.'

'Why?' Leora yelled, her throat constricting, her thoughts dissolving. 'Why would you do that. Why?'

*Oh my God. Oh my God. Oh my God. What are they doing? Can't they see what he's done to me... what he's capable of. He'll come back... in the night... when no one's around... and finish me off.*

'Evidence would suggest...'

*Evidence would suggest what? You said... promised in fact... that you'd keep me safe... protect me from my perpetrator. And yet here you are telling me you've had to let him go. Why?*

Leora didn't hear any more. She felt sick, started screaming, only, unlike in the consultation room, when she'd been staring at the thing in the mirror, this time the sound that left her mouth was shrill, like a vixen; a cry that sensed death. When she tried to stand, she was dizzy, felt her head spin, as if she were standing on the edge of a cliff looking down.

*I'll kill myself*, she thought. *I'm a burden now, anyway. So I'll kill myself. Then he can never hurt me again.*

# PART VI

## 2011

# CHAPTER 42

*B*en looked at Mark and Eileen and smiled. Holding hands, Eileen leaned in and said something that made Mark laugh. They looked like a couple of lovesick teenagers.

'Leave it out you two,' Ben said playfully. 'We're going away for a couple of months, not years.'

Mark looked at Ben and grinned. 'You're just jealous,' he quipped.

Ben shrugged, felt his eyebrows shoot up. 'Maybe.'

'You all set then, Dad?' Ben turned round to see Sam, smiling at him. At fourteen, he was now slightly taller than Ben but hadn't filled out yet; long-limbed and skinny, he was all arms and legs.

'Yep,' Ben replied, checking, and rechecking the equipment.

In the last two years, Ben, Mark and Eileen had successfully put together a non-profit organisation called 'Where There's A Will There's A Way', whose sole purpose was to support veterans who found themselves struggling with life after leaving the forces.

The foundation achieved this through education by giving public and private talks. It also helped applicants access specialist counselling and therapy. And it offered physical help, too, like the courses Ben and Mark were leading over the next couple of months in a remote part of Wales. These took people back to basics, helping them challenge both their mental and physical capabilities and were perhaps best described as immersive survival courses.

It wasn't something they had set out to do, but rather something that had evolved after Ben and Mark had completed their LEJOG – Land's End to John O'Groats – run, to raise money to help Leora with some of the specialist treatment she needed for her recovery.

Overwhelmed by the support and donations they received, both men had, in their separate ways, found the experience deeply cathartic. There was something innately healing about helping others when you yourself were, or had been, struggling. Hence the Winston Churchill quote used as the foundation's motto: 'We make a living by what we get, but we make a life by what we give.'

It had been Ben's idea originally, borne out of a desire to help someone who had helped him, because to help others was a step toward helping yourself, in his humble opinion. The original plan, of course, was to raise enough money to buy Mark some running blades.

Then had come the incident with Leora, and so, taking on Sam's idea about getting Mark involved in the run, Ben explained the plan to Mark and asked him how he felt about donating the money raised to help Leora, instead of buying blades for him. Mark, as Ben expected, loved the idea of taking part in the LEJOG run. As for giving the money to Leora, it was, he said, a no-brainer.

'What do I need a poncy pair of running blades for anyway,' he added, giving Ben one of his trademark smiles.

So, with meticulous planning, and plenty of back-up, both men set off – Ben with his bergen, Mark with his wheelchair –

together. Ben completed the run in just under ten days. He then swapped his bergen for a bike, and cycled alongside his friend who, exhausted; hands red, and blistered, completed the route in a record-breaking twenty-two days.

Eileen, in the meantime, wrote a daily blog about their progress, drumming up TV and newspaper coverage along the way, which in turn saw a massive increase in donations. Ben took a back seat when it came to the publicity though, insisted that Eileen and Mark take credit for the idea. This was for two reasons. The first was, he liked his privacy, and secondly, and more importantly, he didn't want Leora to feel she owed him anything. She had enough to deal with, without carrying that burden.

'Wish I was coming with you,' Sam continued.

'I know. I wish you were too. But right now, you need to focus on school. Besides, we've got our week away in the summer to look forward to.'

'Yeah... I know.' Sam sighed, his eyes drawn to the ground, one foot kicking the other. 'But we won't be doing all the fun stuff that you lot will be doing.'

'It won't *all* be fun.' Ben laughed. 'In fact, some days, it's going to be bloody hard work. But, if you want... if Robbie's up for it too... there's nothing stopping the three of us doing some of the stuff I'll be doing now, during our week away in the summer. We are going camping after all, so at the very least I think we should build our own shelter, make our own fire.'

Sam looked up again. 'Really?' He beamed.

'Sure. Why not.'

They heard a whistle, turned to see Mark; his son, Jacob, standing beside him, beckoning Sam over. 'I've got something to show you,' he said, face straight, mouth twitching.

Jacob rolled his eyes, told Sam not to bother. 'It's a trick.'

'Yeah.' Mark wore a look of mock offence. 'A neat trick.'

'Do you think,' Eileen said, now standing beside Ben as they watched Sam become Mark's next willing victim, 'if I'd known how childish he still is, I'd still have agreed to marry him?'

Ben looked at her and grinned just as Sam pulled Mark's finger, and Mark let rip. 'Every time,' he said, slapping his thigh, his face wracked with laughter. '*Every* bloody time.'

Ben couldn't resist it. 'Don't be a twat, Dobs,' he called out, much to the amusement of Jacob and a rather red-faced Sam. He turned back to Eileen. 'Someone's got to love him, I guess. Talking of which, have you set a date for the wedding yet?'

Eileen shook her head. 'No... that's all down to Leora I'm afraid. I only want one bridesmaid, and it's her. So... until she's ready, it's just not happening.'

'How... is she?' Ben asked.

Eileen smiled, but it was the same smile she had worn for months, one that rarely, if ever, lit her features. 'She's getting there... I think. She still won't go out much though, and if she does, she insists on having someone with her. Point blank refuses to go out alone. Still, it's an improvement, especially when I think back to what she was like when she first moved in with her parents. Those first few months were just...' she closed her eyes, looked down, '...awful,' she said, glancing up again. 'You could literally feel her despair the minute you walked into the room. I hate to admit it, but sometimes, I didn't want to be there because I always felt so low, so guilty when I left. Not to mention the fact we were all still so afraid she might... you know...'

Ben nodded. It wasn't a sentence that needing finishing.

'She didn't though... thank God... and her mood since has been classic grieving if you ask me: shock, denial, anger, and now, I'd say she's hovering somewhere between depression and acceptance.'

'Makes sense,' Ben replied. 'She's not only grieving the loss of the person she was but, added to that, she's got the burden of trying to get her head around who her perpetrator was.'

'I know.' Eileen sighed. 'I still can't believe it. Find myself waking in the middle of the night wondering how I was so easily taken in. I blame myself you know, because there were lots of times I questioned things, knew something was off, but then I'd shrug it off, convince myself I was being unfair, overreacting. Clearly, I wasn't though, was I? And I can't help thinking... if I had spoken up, would what happened have still happened?'

Eyes glazed; Ben rubbed his forehead. 'I'd tell you not to blame yourself, but I think we all feel like we could have done more.'

They were quiet for a minute, watched Mark thrashing Sam and Jacob, now shooting hoops into the basketball stand in front of Ben's garage. 'And he scores again,' Mark shouted, as the basketball teetered, then slipped through the net for the umpteenth time.

'C'mon, boys,' Ben yelled. 'He's putting you to shame.'

'Yeah,' Mark grinned. 'I am. And I'm a spaz, too.'

'Mark,' Eileen gasped, rolling her eyes.

'What?' He grinned. 'I am.'

'Yes, but that word...'

'Spaz? What about it?'

Eileen sighed. 'Well... it's just not very PC... can... cause offence.'

Now it was Mark's turn to roll his eyes. 'Sorry, boys.' He glanced at Jacob and Sam. 'It seems my language is offensive. So... I'm not a spaz... I'm a cripple.' He looked at Eileen and grinned. 'Better?'

Eileen rolled her eyes again, held her hands up. 'Whatever,' she sighed.

Ben shook his head, laughed. 'That's Dobs for you.' He glanced at his watch. They had a few minutes before they needed to be on the road, so he was happy to let the boys play a bit longer.

'You know... I've been meaning to ask you,' Eileen said. 'But for whatever reason, I've just never got round to it.'

'What's that?'

'Do you still believe, when you rang me that night... it was Lonny... trying to warn you.'

Ben folded his arms, took a deep breath. 'I do,' he replied. 'I really do.'

He remembered it like it was yesterday. After leaving Eileen at the hospital in London, Ben had caught the first train home and went straight to see Mark, to run the LEJOG idea by him and bring him up to speed about Leora. Eileen had kept him up to date anyway, with daily phone calls, but over a cup of tea, Ben confirmed the sheer horror of it all.

'I've seen some things in my time, but...' he lowered his head, felt his heart spasm; visions of Leora's face, that wasn't her face – wasn't anyone's face in fact – swimming into view. Inflated lips, bulging eyes, skin; red raw and weeping, its blackened edges lifting, curling, crumbling... falling away... like the embers of a dying bonfire.

'It's... bad.' He struggled to get the words out. '*Really* bad,' he finally managed. 'I mean, I've never met the bloke before... but that *thing* that did that to her...' He looked up again, felt the veins in his neck throbbing, his chest swelling with rage. Like the comics of his childhood, Ben was metamorphosising from the mild-mannered Bruce Banner into *The Incredible Hulk.* 'Let's just say... he wants to thank God the police have him in custody.'

Mark shook his head. 'Fucking animal,' he growled, placing a firm hand on Ben's shoulder. 'What say you, me, and a few of your,' he winked, '*mates*, break him out of prison and kill him.'

Ben put his hand to his head and laughed. It was just the tonic he needed. 'Don't be a twat, Dobs.'

'Think about it,' Mark replied playfully. 'In the meantime, how's about another cuppa?'

Ben stretched his legs out in front of him, leant back on his hands and looked up. 'I'd rather have a beer. Better yet... a whisky.'

'Don't be a knob, Thompson.' Although said in jest, there was just a hint of concern in Mark's voice. 'So,' he remarked, the kettle rumbling in the background. 'You erm... didn't want to stick around then... at the hospital, like, with Leora?'

Ben sighed, sat up again, brought his hands to his mouth and shook his head. 'I did... but... well, let's just say, after overhearing something, I decided Leora had enough on her plate... without me being there... complicating things.'

Mark frowned, opened his mouth to say something then seemed to change his mind again and closed it.

'I'll tell you what though,' Ben continued. 'I had the weirdest experience.'

'Oh yeah?' Mark raised an eyebrow. 'What was that then?'

Ben explained about the tap on his shoulder... both shoulders... in and outside the hospital.

'And you thought you heard music, you say... a song... both times?' Mark asked.

'I don't *think* I heard it, I *know* I heard it, and it was the same song both times.'

'But you don't know what the song was?'

Ben stroked his chin, shook his head. 'It was familiar... but I couldn't quite make it out. It sounded distorted... like it was playing on the wrong frequency.'

'Weird,' Mark said, twisting his mouth thoughtfully. 'Although... you know who used to do that, don't you? Tap one shoulder, look away, then, when he was sure you hadn't worked out who it was and turned away again, would tap the other shoulder?'

'Fuck,' Ben whispered, suddenly sitting bolt upright, the proverbial penny not only dropping but clanging, loudly, like an alarm bell. 'Lonny... Lonny used to do that all the time. To the point of, like you and your farting finger, being bloody annoying.'

Mark grinned. Folded his arms across his broad chest, the veins in his biceps bulging like thick electrical cables. 'See,' he winked, 'I'm not just a pretty face.'

Ben stared straight at him. 'You don't think that I'm...' he paused, felt his cheeks burn. 'You know... that I'm imagining it then? That it's part of the PTSD?'

'Fuck, no,' Mark replied, without a second's hesitation. 'Well, that's to say, it could be, but it doesn't sound like it to me, especially as I've had similar experiences over the years.'

Ben's eyebrows shot up. 'Really? You never said.'

Mark coughed; drummed his fingers on the table. 'Yeah, well, it's not the sort of thing you shout about is it, because if you do, most people call you a nutter. Which I am, of course.' He grinned. 'But... if there's one thing I'm certain of, it's that there's more to us, to life, to death, than we know.'

Ben felt the corners of his mouth lifting into a grin.

'What?' Mark's expression was earnest.

'You never cease to surprise me.'

Mark smiled, glanced out of the window, which was open. The smell of rain; fresh, green, invigorating, after a recent shower, filling the room, as raindrops, like diamonds, dotted the windowsill, glistening in the September sun. 'Personal growth, Eileen calls it. I, however, think of it as life, kicking the shit out of us, until we learn.'

Over the next two weeks Ben tormented himself trying to work out what it was Lonny wanted him to hear. Every now and again, he'd feel more taps on his shoulders and just like before he'd hear a song playing, which again would sound crackly, playing on a frequency he couldn't quite tune into. Then it came to him, one night in his dreams, hitting him like the sonic boom of a fighter plane. He was so sure he knew what it was, he leapt from his bed, rushed downstairs, and began rifling through his vinyl collection until he found his *My Aim Is True* album by Elvis Costello. Thankfully, unlike a lot of his friends, who had got rid of their record players in favour of CD players, Ben had kept his.

Hands shaking, he placed the black disc on the turntable and counted the grooves until he got to song number five – 'Alison'.

And as he stood there in his boxer shorts, his toes kneading the carpet beneath his bare feet; Elvis Costello's dulcet tones resonating across his living room, Ben felt something visceral, something fearful trickle down his spine. He knew instinctively, felt it in his gut, in each individual hair that stood on end at the back of his neck, Hugo hadn't thrown acid at Leora; Ali – Alison had.

Frantic, taking three steps at a time, he rushed upstairs, grabbed his phone, and called Eileen. She had left London by then because of work commitments, so Ben knew, like him, she couldn't do anything to warn Leora. However, Eileen *did* have a number for Andrea and Marty, who were still in London, and still staying in the hospital's family accommodation. After several rings, Eileen picked up, her voice, husky, sleep filled.

Time, Ben felt, was of the essence so, without going into too much detail, he explained that he thought Leora was still in danger; that Ali was her attacker, not Hugo. Eileen, thank God, believed him. She could have dismissed his ramblings. Said it was just a nightmare, trauma triggered by recent events. However, whether it was the urgency in his voice, or simply that she trusted him, she chose to believe him and dutifully rang Leora's parents. Again, without going into too much detail, Eileen implored them, even though it was 3am, to go to Leora immediately, which they did, where they found Ali sitting at the end of Leora's bed, watching her sleep.

Spooked by what Eileen had told them, and unnerved by Ali's presence, Andrea and Marty, without saying why, eventually persuaded Ali to leave, and stood guard over their daughter for the rest of the night. Several hours later, Ali was arrested, and later that afternoon Leora and her parents were informed.

'Do you think she was going to do something else to Leora?' Eileen asked, interrupting Ben's thoughts.

Ben looked at her. 'God knows. But I don't think Lonny was taking any chances.'

'Have you ever wondered, since everything came to light about Ali, if she was the cause of your break-up with Leora?'

'I have,' Ben replied. 'I've thought about it a lot. And, since I can't remember much of what happened that evening, it would make sense. However, as much as that would make me feel better about myself, at the end of the day the camera doesn't lie, does it?'

Eileen smiled and nodded placidly; yet her face, Ben thought, didn't follow suit.

# CHAPTER 43

*C*autious, Leora opened the front door, the rattle of the letterbox making her jump. Heart thumping, she stepped outside. *Come on, Leora, you can do this*, she thought, taking a deep breath. The sun, as she walked to the front gate, although not particularly strong, warmed her face and was, given her dislike of most things hot, strangely comforting.

At the end of the drive, she took a right, but not before vigilantly looking left to right, then left to right again. When she was sure it was safe; sure that no one was following her, she pulled her hat down and made her way towards town. It was a beautiful spring day, a carnival of scents to the nose and colour to the eye.

By the time she reached the small café in town, having summoned the confidence to smile at a few passers-by – people she knew, mostly, or people she recognised – she felt remarkably okay. It was a fragile strength though, especially if anyone approached her or got too close. Then she would flinch; find herself backing away like a stray dog, beaten and abandoned. Which was okay, because the important thing was, she'd done it.

She'd walked all the way from her parents' house, alone and unaided.

*Small steps*, she told herself; the counsellor's words ringing in her ears. *It's all about the small steps.*

Tugging her hat down, she went to the door and peered in. Café-au-Lait, a quaint little coffee shop with friendly staff, which she'd recently visited with Eileen and her mother, was busy. *Very busy.* Still, there were a couple of empty tables. *Oh well*, she thought, gripping the handle, *it's now or never.*

Heart in her mouth, she took a deep breath, pushed on the door, and stepped inside; hit by the nutty aroma of coffee. It was pleasantly warm, pleasantly relaxed inside... or at least... it would have been... had half the customers not turned to look at her. Suddenly hot; her legs wobbling beneath her like a new-born calf, she scanned the room for a table; such a simple task, now so intolerably difficult.

Rosie, the café owner, who was clearing away one of the tables, spotted her and smiled. 'Hello, love,' she said, walking towards her, wiping her hands on her apron. 'Lovely day out today, isn't it? This table is free.' She gently guided Leora towards it. 'Or... there's one over there,' she added, gesturing to a table in the corner. 'If you prefer?'

Leora looked at Rosie. Tried to swallow the lump lodged in her throat, blinking back the tears pricking her eyes. Her first thought was a defensive one; Rosie had suggested the table in the corner because she didn't want her other customers to see Leora and feel uncomfortable. But as Leora stared into Rosie's twinkling eyes, she saw nothing but kindness. Leora shifted her gaze to the table in front of her then to the one in the corner.

'I think... I'll sit here, please.'

Rosie beamed and squeezed her arm reassuringly. 'Good choice. Coffee?'

Leora nodded. She was about to ask for something cold, like an orange juice, but decided to be brave. 'Cappuccino, please.'

'Coming right up,' she replied. 'You take a seat and I'll bring it over in a sec.'

Stirring her coffee, Leora glanced round, drinking in the atmosphere. Every now and again the odd person would look her way. Some, with pity in their eyes, would quickly look away again when she spotted them staring at her, whereas others merely nodded and smiled. However, as her shoulders relaxed, she was, she realised, surprisingly okay. She even found herself wondering why she hadn't ventured out on her own sooner. She loved being around the general chit-chat of people. It was reassuringly human, and reminded her, though she felt otherwise, she wasn't alone.

Still, she thought, catching a small child, a boy, no more than two or three years old, staring at her, the incredulity on his face making her insides knot, she still had a long way to go. She watched him for a moment as he leaned across and tugged at the sleeve of the woman sitting opposite him – his mother Leora assumed – and pointed at her. The woman, in turn, glanced round to see who or what he was pointing at. When she spotted Leora, her face fell. Mouthing an apology, her smile awkward, she grabbed the child and sat him on her knee so that he had his back to Leora. A mild admonishment followed, which Leora caught the odd word, including, 'poor lady' and 'rude to stare'.

Forcing back tears again, Leora looked down and stared at her half-drunk cup of coffee. She was doing okay until then, but like it often did, the orchestra in her head started playing again, and although not particularly loud, did give rise to all her usual fears and anxieties. She was a freak. Belonged in an old Victorian freak show, like poor Joseph Merrick – aka the Elephant Man – where people paid money to marvel at his deformities. Didn't someone call her a freak once, at school? She'd taken it to heart too. The irony being, of course, she'd give anything now to look like she did then.

Discreetly dabbing her tears with a paper napkin, she smiled, remembering Mia as a three-year-old. How inquisitive she'd been about anything and everything. It wasn't the boy's fault that he stared at her. He was an innocent, and like most small children, merely curious. Was this it though? she wondered. Was this what the rest of her life was going to be, a walking sideshow for people to point at and either laugh at or feel sorry for?

She still wasn't sure which was worse, the fact that she was now a sad postscript of her former self or knowing that the person who had done this to her was her best friend. Even now, she would wake in the night, remembering all the good times she had shared with Ali, convinced, for the umpteenth time, that the police had got it wrong. 'Ali is my best friend,' she had told them. 'She's like a sister to me. She would *never*, not in a million years, do something so terrible, something so abhorrent.'

Only... she had... hadn't she.

Disbelief though, was the place she inhabited when she first moved in with her parents after it was agreed it was the best place for her recovery, while Mia, in her final year at school, moved in full-time with Tim and Saffy and her new half-sister.

In one fell swoop, Leora had lost everything, her face, her livelihood, her daughter, and her best friend. Ali had stripped her of it all, which was so unbearable, it threatened to rob her of her sanity too. For the longest time Leora refused to see or talk to anyone except Mia, Eileen, and her parents. And even then, it was with the curtains drawn, in the shadows; no mirrors or photographs allowed – at least, not in the rooms she frequented.

She was a monster, and not just on the outside, but on the inside too. Slovenly, lazy, miserable, if she wasn't shouting or crying, she was curled up in the foetal position, stupefied. Poor Mia had looked positively petrified when, visiting one day, Leora heard a whir, saw a flash, and immediately leapt up to see Mia taking a photo of her using the same Polaroid camera she had used on that fateful morning.

'No,' Leora screamed hysterically. 'No photos. You know that... where the hell did you get that stupid camera anyway?'

Mortified, lip trembling, Mia looked at her mother, then the camera, then back to her mother. 'Al... Ali,' she mumbled. A detail that, judging by the look of sheer horror on her face, she had quite forgotten. Leora's anger then was so powerful, she couldn't have controlled it if she tried.

'I... I didn't... mean...' Mia stuttered, holding the camera in such a way, she looked like she might drop it. But before she did, Leora snatched it out of her daughter's hands and threw it against the wall. It fell to the floor, skittering everywhere. Shocked, Mia gasped and ran from the room crying. Andrea ran after her while Eileen gathered all the broken pieces and put them in a bag.

'You need help,' Eileen said, a flicker of disappointment in her eyes. 'You can't let this define you. You can't let her win, Leora.'

'Hah... you are joking, right?' Leora replied, sarcastically; sarcasm being her default setting these days. 'She's already won.'

'Only if you let her. But...' Eileen nodded, indicating the door where Mia had just fled, '...if you don't sort yourself out. You'll lose her.'

Leora stared at the door, put her hand to her chest; felt her heart spasm, a stone settling in her gut. *History repeating itself*, she thought, thinking of her own mother, of their once fractured relationship, again the handiwork of one Alison Evans.

'I don't know if you're aware,' Eileen continued. 'But there's some suggestion Ali and her sisters were sexually abused by their father when they were younger. If it's true, then it's terrible, absolutely appalling, and it may, in time, help you, *us* even, better understand what shaped her as a person. However, being hurt and abused doesn't give people the right to do it to others, especially to people that love and care for them.

'Likewise, what she's done to you is horrific. I can't even begin to understand how it feels to be in your shoes, and nor do I wish to. Nevertheless, it's also not an excuse to hurt the people that love you, Leora. There was a reason Mia was taking your photo, and when you've calmed down, apologised, perhaps, I'm sure she'll explain it to you.' Her words were clipped, but there was an underlying note of concern in her voice. Eileen had hugged her then, her full breasts flattening against Leora's slight chest. 'In the meantime,' she added. 'You need to get back to counselling, which I know you've been skipping.'

Eileen's words winded Leora like a kick in the stomach. They were also the kick up the backside she needed. She agreed to go back to counselling where she learned about narcissistic abuse, which, in between the love bombing and the highs, typically involves emotional abuse, often in the form of put-downs, accusations, and threats, all of which Ali had been guilty of doing to her over the years, but all which Leora had dismissed as 'Ali just being Ali'. She also learned that narcissists have an arsenal of tactics to destroy a friend or a partner's reality, including gaslighting, as well as emotional, mental, and physical forms of abuse. Which meant, like her, Hugo had also been a victim of Ali's mistreatment.

Cognitive dissonance though, is a shit, and for the longest time Leora struggled with the truth. 'But... but what about the bruises... on her wrists?'

Eileen, who had also felt duped and betrayed by Ali, albeit on a much lesser scale than Leora, arranged a meet-up with Hugo to help try and make sense of what happened, for her own, as much as Leora's sake. 'The bruises on Ali's wrists,' she said, '*were* caused by Hugo, but only on the odd occasion and only as a last resort when he was trying to restrain her from hitting him, usually with an object of some sort.'

'Oh-kay... so what about the bruises on her back?' Leora protested. 'They were awful. Black and blue, she was. How do you explain them?'

'Cupping.'

'What?'

'I must admit, I'd never heard of it before either. It's an alternative therapy, like acupuncture, used to treat conditions like skin problems, high blood pressure, migraines, and anxiety, to name a few. A therapist uses glass cups on the skin to create a suction, which can sometimes result in large angry bruises. And... if you remember, when you spotted them, and asked Ali what they were, how she'd got them, she said she'd had a fall, which is also what she told several other people apparently, because she knew it would create suspicion and doubt.'

'But... what about her *real* fall... down the stairs?' Leora was trying to keep the hysteria out of her voice.

Eileen pressed her lips together, shook her head. 'The police found evidence on her laptop of deleted searches for things like,' – she made air quotation marks with her fingers – '"how to fall down the stairs safely".'

'But... she had cuts and bruises?' Leora replied, slack jawed, incredulous.

'Again, more deleted searches suggesting they were more than likely self-inflicted. Bearing in mind she had poor old Hugo so gaslighted, so drugged up, he didn't know if he was coming or going most of the time.'

'But... on the day of the attack... I saw his coat... smelled the whisky on his breath.'

'You saw *his* coat, yes, and smelled whisky on it, but Ali was wearing the coat with a hoodie underneath.'

Leora knew this though. The police had already explained it to her. Ali and Hugo had argued. Hugo said he had had enough and wanted a divorce. Ali hit him over the head with an ornament and knocked him unconscious – had spiked his coffee too. Ali then left the house wearing his coat, taking the acid – which she'd ordered on Hugo's computer and paid for using his bank card – with her, and set off to Leora's house.

'What the plan was after she'd left you,' the police said, 'we don't know. Whether or not it was to go back and finish Hugo off, then call it self-defence... thankfully... we'll never know.'

What the police did know though was, that while Ali was out, Hugo, head bleeding profusely, had come round and staggered to his next-door neighbour's house.

The neighbour, who had had his suspicions about Ali for some time, offered to take Hugo to the hospital. Hugo, whether out of guilt or shame, or fear – or all three, maybe – refused. Instead, he asked if he could just clean himself up and maybe get a lift to work – he'd already had too much time off to warrant taking any more. The neighbour, who was going to New York for a few weeks, agreed, and dropped Hugo off on his way to the airport.

The neighbour said Hugo was welcome to stay at his house if he wanted, while he was away, but Hugo had made his mind up. He had a friend at work that he had recently been confiding in. She offered him a place to stay.

Ali didn't know about her, or where she lived, so he knew he could hide there for a while and start putting the wheels in motion for a divorce. The tests and scans he had arranged with his doctor had come back clear, and in a moment of clarity, Hugo realised Ali was the problem, not him, and finally, after all these years, he had decided enough was enough.

Hugo and the neighbour heard Ali return. Ten minutes later, they heard the front door slam and spotted her leaving again, seeking, although they didn't know it at the time, medical attention for the acid burns to her arm, caused by the splashback when she threw acid at Leora. An hour after that Hugo was at work, and several hours after that he was arrested. Unfortunately, for Hugo, the police couldn't contact the neighbour to corroborate Hugo's version of events until he returned from New York. And as the only thing that stood out on the rather grainy CCTV footage was Hugo's coat, Hugo, for all intents and purposes, looked to be, as Ali told the police, Leora's perpetrator.

*Poor Hugo,* Leora thought, her handbag vibrating on the table. He'd clearly been through the wringer too, the difference being of course, that although they were both damaged goods on the inside, Hugo's outer shell, unlike hers, was still very much intact.

Leora took her phone from her bag, saw a text from Mia:

> Woo-hoo! Way to go Mum! I'm so proud of you
> xxxxx

Leora felt her throat constrict. Mia's text was in reply to one she'd sent her, telling her she had ventured out for the first time on her own. *I mustn't cry, I mustn't cry,* she told herself, watching her phone swim away. In that moment, it felt as though she and Mia had traded places, Mia now the proud mother, and Leora the timorous child.

She still cringed when she thought about the camera incident, hated herself for behaving so badly in front of Mia. She had, of course, apologised, profusely. When the dust settled, she bought Mia a new camera. She deliberately hadn't bought one straight away because that was something Ali used to do, which, looking back, had all the connotations of buying someone's forgiveness, and this in turn had left a bad taste in Leora's mouth.

The reason Mia was taking her photo, she learned, was to show Leora how far she'd come, how, every month, they could all see, even if Leora couldn't, noticeable changes to her damaged body and face.

Mia wasn't wrong either. When Leora looked at the photos of herself now, compared to then, almost two years ago, the improvements were vast. Still, it didn't feel enough. However, it did make her appreciate the people in her life who had helped her, like Mrs Catherine Shields, her surgeon, Eileen and Mark, who had raised all that money to help her with some much-needed complementary therapies, and of course family, and friends – *real* friends, who, during some of her darkest days, unlike Ali, had no other agenda than to support her and lift her spirits.

When she looked up again, Leora caught a woman on another table glancing at her and it was all she could do to force herself not to leave. What had, less than an hour ago, seemed like a good idea, was now starting to feel like a bad one. Reaching for the book in her bag Leora saw the woman, from her periphery, push her chair back and walk towards her. Shifting uncomfortably, Leora lowered her head and randomly flipped open her book, pretending to read.

'Um… excuse me,' the woman said.

Leora closed her eyes; took a quiet intake of breath. *Please fuck off.*

'It's Leora, isn't it?' the woman continued. 'Leora Jackson?'

Bracing herself, Leora put her book on the table and looked up. The woman, who had kindly green eyes and dark hair, seemed vaguely familiar.

'Do I know you?' Leora hadn't meant to sound so curt, so flippant.

'Yes, well… sort of,' she replied, her smile unwavering. 'It's me.' She nodded, indicating the empty chair opposite Leora. 'Do you mind… if I… sit for a minute?'

*Yes… I do,* Leora thought, wondering if she was one of those awful tabloid journalists that kept ringing her. 'Actually, I'm leaving in a minute.' Leora's voice was brusque, her tone dismissive.

'Me too,' the woman said, sitting down anyway. 'But I thought it was you and I just wanted to say hi. It's me… Cathy…'

'Cathy?' Leora repeated. She frowned, but her face, leathery, tight, didn't follow suit.

'From school,' she added. Leora felt her cheeks flush with embarrassment, although, with all her scarring, it was doubtful Cathy could tell. 'We used to play–'

'Netball,' Leora interrupted, suddenly remembering. 'Yes... I remember.' *At least we did... until you got weird and stopped talking to me.*

'That's right.' She shifted in her chair, her hand going to her collarbone. 'Listen,' she continued, 'I heard about what happened to you and...' She paused. Leora's chest flared with anxiety. 'Well, I just wanted to say how sorry I am. It's awful. Truly awful that someone could do something... so cruel.' Instead of pity in her voice though, which is what Leora had become accustomed to, Cathy sounded genuinely angry, outraged even. 'She fucked up though, didn't she.' Cathy's smile was triumphant.

If it had been possible, Leora's drawn on eyebrows, with little sprouting hairs beneath, would have shot up. 'Sorry... I don't quite follow.'

'Well... look at you. Most people would, after what happened to you, be too afraid to go out on their own. It takes real strength, real courage to do that, you know. Mark my words, there won't be one single person in this room that doesn't think that. And not only that, yes, your face is scarred, and I can't imagine how painful it is, and what you've endured, *but*, and I'm not blowing smoke up your arse here either, you're still you.'

Leora, who at this point was unsure whether to feel annoyed or amused, folded her arms, and stared at her. 'Sorry... I'm still not with you.'

Cathy sighed. 'Look... the simple truth is, beauty... *real* beauty that is... is rare, and it isn't just skin deep, it goes much further than that.' She put one hand to her chest, then crossed it with the other. 'It comes from here, from the heart, and it shines through. I noticed that about you at school. You had that inner something, and you still have it now. Even after everything you've gone through, you're still you. That inner light, albeit slightly dimmer perhaps, for now, is still there.'

*What? What the bloody hell are you talking about?*

'And no,' Cathy replied, as if reading her mind. 'I'm not talking shit because, well, if I can see it then I'm pretty sure others can see it too.' She slumped back then, as if exhausted, as if a great weight had been lifted from her shoulders. 'Have you got time for another coffee?' she added.

Leora was reluctant at first, yet at the same time she felt oddly at ease with this woman she hadn't seen in nearly thirty years and, quite surprisingly, found herself saying yes. Cathy smiled, went to the counter, and ordered two more cappuccinos.

'I still can't believe it was Alison, that... you know... did it.' She placed two cups of frothy coffee on the table.

Leora's stomach flipped. 'No... well... neither can I.'

'Do you know... *why* she did it?'

Leora looked away, glanced out of the window. 'Look...' She returned her gaze to Cathy. 'I know you mean well and what you said... just now was... well... very sweet. But honestly, you have no idea what I've gone... what I'm *still* going through, and if it's all the same to you, I'd rather not talk about it anymore.'

Cathy pressed her teeth into her bottom lip, nodded. 'No, I'm sure you don't. Sorry. That's totally understandable. But what I will just add is, if Alison's intention was to break you... well... she failed. Remember that.'

Leora was stunned. She'd never been close to Cathy Palmer at school, except for a brief period during their first year when they played in the school netball team together. They hadn't been best friends or anything, but they had got on well, for a while, then, out of the blue, Cathy stopped talking to her. She wasn't unkind to Leora, but it was obvious Leora had been sent to Coventry and because Cathy was quite popular, and captain of the netball team, everyone else on the team followed suit. Perhaps that's what this was about. Perhaps, after all these years, Cathy felt guilty, wanted to make amends.

'Also,' Cathy said, again, as if reading her mind. 'While I'm here, I just want to say how sorry I am that I stopped talking to you at school. I... I didn't want to...'

Leora tipped her head slightly. 'So… why did you then?'

'Firstly,' she said, putting her hands up in surrender. 'I'm not blaming Alison–'

'Ali? What the hell has Ali got to do with this?'

Cathy shook her head. 'Hear me out… please. Like I said, I'm not blaming Ali, I take full responsibility for my decision to stop talking to you. However, I was also young and afraid. The thing is… I'm not straight. I was– *am* a lesbian.' She paused then, as if expecting a reaction from Leora but when none was forthcoming, she continued.

'When we were at school, it wasn't like it is today, where – she rolled her eyes – it's almost fashionable to say you're gay, or lesbian, or bi or whatever. I always knew I preferred girls. However, even though attitudes in the eighties were changing, not being straight was still frowned upon, which is why I respected the way you and Ali and Eileen rallied round Jules – Julian. Unlike Jules though, who didn't exactly shout about what he was, but nor did he hide it either, I wasn't brave enough to stand out. So, I kept who I really was a secret. Which is where Ali came in. I got the impression she didn't like our – mine and yours – friendship, which I think was blossoming – purely in a platonic sense. One day, she took me aside, and told me, confidentially, that you were a lesbian and that you–'

'What?' Leora sat back in her chair. 'Why… why would she do that?'

'Well,' Cathy said, two neatly plucked eyebrows shooting up. 'I've had a lot of time to think about this and I've concluded that not only was Alison very manipulative, but she was also very good at reading people, too. Working out their strengths and weaknesses and using them to her advantage. I think she knew I wasn't straight, and how fearful I was about people finding out, so by telling me it was you, I think she was working on the premise that I wouldn't want to be tainted by association. I also believe that she knew I had a bit of a crush on you… Still do, a bit, if I'm honest.' She grinned, glancing down, her cheeks turning slightly pink.

Again, Leora was stunned, and all she could think was, *Really? You're attracted to me? To this face.*

'It's sad though, because I think we could have been great friends, but unfortunately, I let my own worries, my own fears and insecurities fuck it up. Alison knew I wanted to keep my sexuality a secret, and it wasn't just the fear of being teased about it at school, it was the fear of my family finding out. To this day, my mum has struggled with who I am. That's why I'm here actually. I live up north, but my mother passed away just recently and I'm staying at her house for a few weeks, sorting out all her stuff and getting the house ready to sell.'

Leora offered her condolences, and a slightly tearful Cathy thanked her, any barriers between the two women now well and truly swept away. Then, over carrot cake and copious cups of coffee, they reminisced about life in general, and about school. While they were talking, the woman with the young son who had pointed at her earlier, wandered over.

'Excuse me,' the woman said, her face slightly flushed. 'Sorry to disturb you, but my son, Albie, asked me if I'd ask you if he could touch your hair.' She laughed, nervously. 'He's got this thing about hair and...' She looked down at her chubby cheeked son and realised he was already, very gently, stroking Leora's hair, which had, rather remarkably, though chunks had been shaved off for her many operations, grown back quite well again.

He stared at Leora and smiled. His big eyes boring into hers. His little hand moving from her hair to her face, which, unbelievably, Leora found herself allowing. She could feel his tiny fingers tracing her mouth, her cheeks, her forehead. 'Beautiful,' he whispered, before leaning in to hug her with so much tenderness, Leora was moved to tears.

'Thanks,' the boy's mother smiled. 'My nan thinks, like her grandmother, which would have been my great-great-grandmother, that he can read people's auras. I'm not sure I believe that, but Albie's right about one thing, you are beautiful. You have a beautiful soul as my nan would say, and it shows.'

Leora; choked, unable to speak, smiled and nodded.

The woman and her son left and as she wiped her tears with her napkin Leora was surprised to see Cathy was crying too.

'Seems I'm not the only one that has a bit of a crush on you.' She laughed.

When they parted ways the two women hugged one another and mourned a friendship that could have been, but because of one person's lies had been thwarted. They made a promise to stay in touch and Leora didn't doubt they would. By the time she got home, she felt brave enough to tackle the oven – the heat, and the idea of burning herself normally terrified her – and cooked dinner, which both pleased and surprised her parents no end. It felt good too, to do something for them for a change.

Bumping into Cathy had been a godsend and had confirmed what everyone had been saying all along, which was, despite the horror of what had happened to her, underneath the pain, the scars, and the trauma, she was still there. The woman she once was... and would be again... in time.

She was furious that Ali's lies and deceit stretched so far back, though. Ali had been manipulating and controlling her life for more years than she dared to admit, which although disturbing, and made her question her own sanity, her own self-worth, more than anything made her feel foolish, ashamed even, that she had been so easily taken in by someone whose intentions were only ever about what best served her.

Leora had, over the months, thought a lot about what Ali had done to her, what her thinking was behind it. She'd discussed it at length with friends and family, and like her they all concluded that Ali believed Leora belonged to her. That she controlled Leora, and for whatever sick and twisted reason in her head, also believed that control was slipping away.

As far as Ali was concerned, Leora was, first and foremost, *her* friend, and as long as Leora didn't threaten that, didn't step out of whatever invisible parameters Ali had put around that relationship, then all was okay. However, the minute Leora jeopardised that control, like moving to America say, or a job that might limit what time they could spend together, or worse still, pull her away from her altogether, then Ali would, Leora realised, always put a stop to it.

It was never done in an overt, obvious way, but rather a covert, underhand way. In that sense, Cathy was right, Ali was good at reading people, good at figuring them out, using their strengths and weaknesses to best achieve the outcome she wanted. Ali knew, when Lonny died, that both Leora and her parents were grieving and vulnerable, which made them easy prey. She convinced Leora that her parents didn't want her around, while all the time telling her parents that Leora felt stifled by them, smothered in fact; convinced they were using Lonny's death to guilt trip her into staying with them.

This of course isolated Leora from her parents and kept her in London. Likewise, Ali also knew that Leora and Tim were having marital problems because, being her best friend, Leora had confided in her. Ali also knew that Tim had almost strayed once before, so, using Saffy as bait, she set a honey trap, which, as Ali no doubt hoped, meant Leora abandoned her move to the States.

Ali had, Leora realised with terrifying clarity, steered the outcome of her life so many times. Now she couldn't help wondering if Ali had caused her break-up with Ben. Ben always said he never remembered anything about that night with Gemma. Nevertheless, it would be too easy, too convenient to blame Ali for everything, especially when the said photos told their own story.

However, though she felt as though she were starting from ground zero, including how to trust her intuition, Leora had, she felt, turned a corner, albeit a very small one. The road ahead wasn't going to be an easy one, but something inside her had shifted. She was sick of being a victim and from here on in she vowed not to be. From here on in she was in control. From here on in she was a survivor.

She wasn't naïve enough to believe that when she climbed into bed, the orchestra in her head, which would frequently wake her in the small hours of the night, wouldn't play on all her fears and anxieties and convince her otherwise. Or that, come tomorrow morning, she wouldn't wake with the same sinking horror that, for a few minutes at least, made her feel entombed. She knew that, both mentally and physically, there were mountains to climb, but today was proof that people could and did, despite her scars, see her for the person she was. She was also, she realised, far stronger and far more capable than she'd given herself credit for.

# PART VII
## 2016

# CHAPTER 44

*L*eora paced the bedroom nervously, her doubts percolating the room. Less than an hour ago, she had just finished speaking to a room of 500 people, and she was fine, not a single nerve in sight. Well, maybe one or two, initially. She was always slightly nervous to start with, but once she got talking, she was fine.

She'd been publicly speaking now for more than four years, so she had, to a certain extent, got used to it. It was easy though, when you were passionate about your subject matter, which, whether recounting her life story, discussing the warning signs to look for in abusive relationships, or campaigning for funding for acid attack victims, Leora most definitely was.

She had set up a charity too, to help burn victims, thanks to the help of her mother, Mia, Eileen, plus a host of other amazing people; an idea suggested to her after she bravely agreed to make a documentary about her experience. She'd originally been approached, by Sade – the production assistant of the dating show she should have been hosting before her whole world combusted – a year after her attack. Leora, who was not in a good place at the time, refused, so Sade told her to think about it, and if she ever changed her mind, to contact her.

A year later, after bumping into Cathy Palmer at the coffee shop, Leora did have a change of heart; contacted Sade, and said she was ready to tell her story.

She was terrified at first because after hiding for two years, she was suddenly thrust into the public eye. As expected, there were some awful responses to the documentary; some of the comments on social media cruel beyond belief. Overall, though, it was very well received. It was also very cathartic; restored Leora's faith in human nature because there were, she realised, a lot of very good people out there, and the milk of human kindness did, in fact, run deep.

Laughter interrupted her thoughts. She went to the door, listened, heard Ben's baritone voice, her mother's jubilant laugh. God how she loved to hear her mother laugh. She hadn't realised how much she had missed it over the years. Like Grandma Cedella, it was a loud, soulful laugh; infectious. Now and again, she would think about all the wasted time, all the lost years with her parents and feel a deep sadness, a deep sense of regret. Regrets, however, she had come to realise, were a waste of time. Second by second, minute by minute, hour by hour, and day by day, regrets ate into time, and time, she knew only too well, was precious.

Still, it was hard sometimes, not to feel angry, not to feel bitter. Gradually though, she was learning to replace bad memories of Ali with nicer ones; the all-night parties in their student days, the two of them drunk on cheap wine or cider – sometimes both mixed together – swigged from chipped mugs, or plastic tumblers; binge-smoking roll-ups. Illegal raves: crammed into their friend Jay's battered Allegro, music pumping, dropping E, synapses jumping, in old warehouses, wall to wall with people, dancing till dawn. Late-night trips on the

Underground; scaring themselves witless after a trip to the cinema, convinced that every shadow, every noise was *An American Werewolf in London*.

These were the memories she focused on when, occasionally, on a bad day, she would catch her reflection in the mirror and self-loathing rose like nausea. When a passer-by, wearing a hoodie, would set her nerves jangling like loose change. When the simple act of a waiter pouring her a glass of wine, or a friend offering her a bottle of water would see her recoiling, her mind racing; the contents of the glass, the bottle, a possible hazard, a potential threat; panic rising precipitously as ridiculous scenarios, worthy of soap operas clean out of ideas, played across her mind.

'It's understandable,' Eileen said, one evening when, over a glass of wine, the two of them were discussing it.

'I wonder, though,' Leora said, 'if there will ever come a time that I won't be looking over my shoulder?'

'Maybe. It's just going to take time.'

'But it's been years.' Leora took another sip of wine, the bubbles frothing in her mouth like popping candy.

'Stop beating yourself up. It's not just the trauma of the attack; it's the years of abuse, the years of gaslighting you've endured too. That shit takes time to recover from. Just remember how far you've come and how amazing you are.'

Leora smiled. 'I couldn't have done it without you. And Mark,' she added, nodding towards the living room where Mark was watching football.

'That's what friends... *real* friends, are for, isn't it? Actually, I wasn't going to mention this...' Eileen's head was fractionally tilted, considering, '...but if it's any consolation, you're not the only one looking over their shoulder.'

Quizzical, Leora, frowned. 'Meaning... what... exactly?'

'You do know Ben is ex-SAS, right?'

EVA JORDAN

'Ye-es?'

'Well... let's just say, that both behind bars, and once she's out, Ali, like you, now knows, and will continue to know, what it's like to live on her nerves... and doubt herself... constantly.'

'Wait... what?' Leora was confused. 'Did... Ben... go and see her then?'

Eileen shook her head. 'No...' Coy, she looked down, a slight grin tugging the corner of her lips. 'But some of his friends might have,' she added, glancing up again.

Leora shifted in her seat. As stupid as it was, she felt conflicted. Couldn't work out if she was pleased or shocked. She never wanted to see or speak to Ali *ever* again. Never wanted her to come within a hundred miles of her or her family. However, she had also moved on with her life, and while she didn't necessarily wish her well, she didn't wish her any harm either because, surely, to do that would make her as bad as Ali – wouldn't it?

'Don't worry,' Eileen said, as if reading her thoughts. 'They didn't lay a finger on her... but it's amazing the effect a few words, the element of surprise can have on someone. So... next time you're having a bad day... remember that.'

Leora couldn't help herself, found her lips turning up too. 'How is he?' she asked. 'Ben, I mean. How's he doing?'

'Yeah... he's good. Actually... I'm glad you've asked, because he's asked me to ask you, *again*, if you'll meet him... just for one hour, no more no less.'

Leora shook her head, glanced out of the window. A monochrome moon, huge tonight, sat centre stage in a star-studded sky. 'No, I can't. What could he possibly want to talk to me about? Don't get me wrong, I know, during those first terrible days after the attack, he was there at the hospital, holding my hand, encouraging me, willing me to pull through, and I can't thank him enough for that. Mum and Dad have nothing but praise for him and how supportive he was, but after a couple of days he was gone again. Not a phone call, not a message, nothing. I know that, after seeing me, when the bandages came off, he probably didn't want to stick around, and I don't blame him for that, but–'

'Right,' a voice yelled behind her, making her jump. Leora turned to see Mark, who had quietly wheeled himself into the kitchen. 'I've had enough of this bollocks. I wasn't supposed to say anything, but sod it. Ben didn't *want* to leave. He was happy to stick around. It was that bitch's idea. He overheard her saying to you that you had enough to deal with, without having him hanging around, complicating things.'

Stunned, Leora looked from Mark to Eileen.

'It's true,' Eileen said. 'You probably don't remember, not with everything going on.'

'Course, none of us knew at the time that *she* was the cause of your injuries,' Mark continued. 'And unfortunately, Ben happened to agree with her.' He looked at Eileen then, his hand covering his mouth, going to his neck, the look on his face as much to say *God knows why*. 'It didn't mean he stopped caring for you though, or that he didn't check in with us, asking us how you were. It was his idea to raise all that money for you, you know.'

'What?' Leora frowned, her hand going to her mottled chest, her heart racing.

'Again, true,' Eileen said. 'Mark wasn't aware of it at the time, but initially Ben was trying to raise some money to buy him some running blades. Then, after what happened to you, Ben told Mark what he'd been up to and asked him if he minded if they gave the money to you instead, and if he wanted to get involved.

'Oh...' Leora replied. 'I... I had no idea. So... why didn't he tell me?'

Eileen sighed, sounding as exasperated as Mark looked. 'He said, as I'd helped to organise it, he wanted Mark and me to take the credit for it because he didn't want you to feel you owed him anything.'

'Which, again,' Mark said, 'as I told Ben at the time, I thought was a load of bloody bollocks. Why he just couldn't tell you is beyond me.' He turned to Eileen. 'Tell her about that other thing.'

'You think?'

'Fuck, yeah.'

Eileen briefly disappeared then came back with a carrier bag. 'Do you remember this?' She emptied what looked like pieces of a broken camera onto the table.

Leora frowned, picked up some of the parts and looked at them. 'It... looks... like... Mia's camera. The one I threw... against the wall,' she said; cheeks flushed, shame crawling up her scarred neck.

'It is,' Eileen replied. 'Only, if you remember rightly, Mia said it was Ali's, and that Ali had given it to her.'

Embarrassed, Leora nodded. 'Of course... that's why I threw it at the wall.'

'The thing is...' Eileen picked out a piece and handed it to her. 'See that there?' She pointed to what looked like a bright pink flaky painted letter J. 'Jules painted that, using my nail varnish. It wasn't Ali's camera, it was Jules's, and even though it's taken me–'

'*Us*,' Mark interrupted.

Eileen looked at him, rolled her eyes. 'Okay *us*,' she grinned, 'a couple of years of asking around, we've finally figured something out.'

Leora went back to her parents' house that night and told them what Eileen and Mark had discovered. None of them were surprised.

'So... are you going to see Ben now?' her mother asked.

Leora said she didn't know. 'So much has happened, and so much time has passed between us, I don't really see the point.'

'But, if I'm not mistaken, you still love him, don't you?' Leora shrugged, which is when her mother told her about Lonny.

She explained that Jules's mother, Margaret, had contacted her and asked to see her. 'She gave me some of Jules's diaries, which she'd found hidden behind a board at the back of his cupboard, told me to read them, then give them back to her.' Bewildered, Leora asked her mother why. 'She thought it might help us understand Lonny's state of mind at the time of his accident. Go and get that bottle of wine in the fridge,' she said, turning to Marty. 'I think we're going to need it.'

Marty came back with a bottle of white and three glasses, while her parents explained that Jules and Lonny weren't just friends, they were in love with one another. Leora was shocked. Why hadn't she known that? And yet, when she thought about it, there were *some* signs, not least Lonny's uncharacteristic outpouring of grief at Jules's funeral. The saddest part being, of course, that for whatever reason, Lonny didn't feel he could tell her, or their parents. Why, they couldn't say, and for a while it felt like they were mourning him all over again.

'Maybe if it had happened ten years later, when attitudes had moved on a bit, and all that terrible stigma about AIDS and HIV had died down, things might have been different,' her mother said. 'I had my suspicions. My only regret is, I didn't say something. Which is why I won't make the same mistake again and is also why I'm saying something now. You love Ben and he loves you, and even if you don't end up together, can't you at least give him an hour of your time to hear him out? After all,' she said, quoting C. S. Lewis: '"You can't go back and change the beginning, but you can start where you are and change the ending".'

So, taking her mother's advice, here she was, waiting to have an audience with Ben Thompson.

The sound of laughter interrupted her thoughts again, Ben's this time, as well as her mother's. She stepped away from the door, felt the beating of her panicked heart. *It's just Ben*, she reminded herself, shaking her hands out at her sides. *Just Ben Thompson.*

This time when she placed her hand on the doorknob, she was determined to open it, and with a swift flick of her wrist, she turned the handle and pushed the door open.

Shoulders back, she strode in. 'Hello, Ben.'

# CHAPTER 45

*B*en looked towards the door where he knew Leora was. Wondered how much longer she was going to be, or worse still, if she was going to change her mind, decide she didn't want to see him after all. Over the last few years, he had watched in awe as, like the proverbial phoenix rising from the ashes, she had completely turned her life around and was not only an inspirational public speaker and campaigner, but also, like him and Mark, had set up her own charity.

'Oh… I'm sorry, Ben,' Andrea said, interrupting his thoughts. 'I haven't even offered you a drink. Would you like something?'

Nervous, mouth parched. 'Thanks, I'd love a glass of water,' he said.

Andrea got up, went to a table laid out with various bottles of water and soft drinks. 'Still, sparkling, or flavoured?' she asked.

'Still is fine, thanks.' Ben got up and went to the window again. The hotel room, although big, felt boxy, clammy with the heat of summer, or maybe it was just him, just nerves. For the first time in years, he was going to talk to Leora face to face, and he still didn't have a clue what he was going to say. He would tell

343

her he loved her, he supposed. Whether she felt the same about him, he didn't know, but he had to tell her, regardless.

When everything had come to light about Ali, he suspected, as they all had, that she may have had a hand in his and Leora's break-up, but at the same time, and without any real evidence, it was mere speculation. Had he fucked up though? As ridiculous as it was, especially after all these years, he wanted to know. Then Gemma had asked to see him, confessed that, on the night he went back to her house, she hadn't exactly lied to him about what had happened, but nor had she been entirely honest either.

'You were out of your head, and knowing what we know now, I can't help but wonder if your drink had been spiked.' She went on to explain that Ben hadn't asked her if she wanted to go upstairs, but he did say he needed to lie down. 'I took you into the living room, and you started taking your shirt off, said you were hot, couldn't breathe. Then you collapsed on the sofa, taking me with you. It was all very innocent, but then that boy, whoever he was, that had been wandering around with a camera, started taking pics of us, kept getting me to pose with you. I was pretty drunk myself at the time and just thought of it as a bit of fun, but when you came knocking on my door a week later, asking about the photos, I let you think there was more to it than that because...' She hung her head then. When she looked up again, she was crying, tremulous eyes; guilt sodden, spilling down her cheeks. 'I liked you... a lot... and I guess I saw an opportunity. I'm so sorry, Ben.'

'So... nothing... whatsoever... happened between us that night?'

She shook her head. 'No... nothing,' she whispered. 'I tried to tell you over the years, but... there never seemed to be the right moment.'

Her confession pierced his heart like ice. He felt his face harden, a rush of anger, so powerful he wanted to shout out loud. But within seconds it was gone again, like the twisted threads of smoke from a snuffed-out candle his anger rushed up, up, up, disappearing into the ether. What was the point in being angry? It was strange though, being caught in the juxtaposition of wishing things had been different yet at the same time, not.

If he hadn't gone back to Gemma's house that night, if those photos hadn't been taken, there is every probability that he and Leora would have stayed together, which means it was less likely that Ali's tentacles, Ali's grasp on Leora could have taken root in the way it did, which in turn meant Leora may never have been the victim of such a horrific attack.

The flip side of that though was, he and Gemma would never have married, which means there would be no Sam and no Robbie, and Ben loved his sons dearly, and couldn't, quite frankly, imagine his life without them.

His mother, who had softened over the years, and was now a lot more tactile, a lot more physically demonstrative, understood his suffering only too well. Still single after her divorce from Ben's father, her heart, she confessed, always had been, and always would be, with another. 'Don't get me wrong,' she said. 'I loved your father, in my own way, and if we had never met and married, I wouldn't have you… or Sam and Robbie, and I love you all… so very much.'

'So… what's your story then?' Ben asked. 'What was his name?'

Coy, his mother looked away. 'Donald,' she said, when she looked up again, her eyes dancing skittishly. 'I was nineteen, he was thirty-four. We both came from strict, church-going backgrounds and not only that, but he was also married with children. Nothing happened between us… well, we kissed… once. But he was never going to leave his wife and family for me, and I never expected him to. However, that was it for me. He was the love of my life, and in another lifetime maybe, things would have been different, could have worked out, but there never was, and never will be another man for me. He was my soulmate, and I was his. We just met at the wrong time and place.'

His mother's confession gave Ben a lot to think about, especially when he spoke to Mark and Eileen, and told them what Gemma had said.

'Makes sense,' Eileen said.

'In what way?' Ben asked.

'Well... we didn't discover this overnight. It's taken a couple of years and a lot of poking around, but long story short, we now know for sure, Ali *was* behind those photos. She stole Jules's camera, which, if you remember how ill he was at the time, was a pretty sick thing to do. Then she paid someone – money and a blowjob, we've been told – after admitting she'd put a sedative in your drink, to get some pics of you and Gemma, or *any* girl for that matter, in what might be construed as compromising positions.'

Ben was stunned, but he wasn't surprised. Ali's obsession with Leora was the stuff of nightmares. However, it was, along with Gemma's confession, the confirmation he needed. He had never cheated on Leora, and he wanted to... no, *needed* to... let her know that. So, here he was, in her hotel room waiting to talk to her. They agreed to meet here, at this time and place because like him, Leora, who was residing in London again, was constantly on the move, often involved in charity events, or speaking engagements, which meant arranging to meet up wasn't easy. He himself had a flight to catch to Afghanistan in three hours, so he didn't have long.

'There you go.' Andrea passed him a glass of water, which he downed in two nervous gulps. 'Beautiful room, isn't it?' she said, following his eyes now flitting about fitfully, restless energy radiating from him like static.

'It is.' He ran his hand across a section of wood panelling. 'Lifestyles of the rich and famous, eh.'

'I should say.' Andrea grinned. 'Not that we could afford a

room like this. The hotel kindly upgraded our standard room to a suite, which was nice of them. I think it's because Leora's spoken here before, and the staff really like her. But then... we've found that over the years... discovered just how lovely people can be, surprisingly so at times. Don't get me wrong, there's no shortage of idiots out there.

'In fact, we were out for a walk just recently when a couple of men, probably in their thirties, so old enough to know better, looked at Leora, then muttered under their breaths something along the lines of, if that wasn't a walking advert for too much cosmetic surgery gone wrong, they didn't know what was.'

Ben felt his nostrils flare, his eyebrows shoot up.

'Don't worry,' Andrea said, reading the fury in his furrowed brow. 'Leora's very adept at handling herself, and she bravely, calmly but loudly explained what had happened to her and suggested that if they didn't have anything nice to say, not to bother saying anything at all.'

Ben grinned. *Good for her*, he thought.

'Overall, though, I still think there's more good people out there than bad.'

'Yeah... I've found that too.' He nodded towards an arch in the far corner of the room, where man mountain, who had earlier answered the door to Ben, sat with his head in a newspaper. 'I see you're not taking any chances though.'

Andrea followed his gaze. 'Oh... Mattia, you mean. Yes, we hire him as a bodyguard from time to time. Not for every event, but sometimes, just having him around makes Leora feel safe. She's achieved so much over the last four years, done so well, but she still has her moments. Still has nightmares... although, nowhere near as many as she used to.'

Ben shook his head. 'No... well, it's completely understandable, especially–'

The bedroom door flew open before Ben could finish his sentence. A tall woman stepped into the room. She looked, wearing a pale blue fitted dress with navy heels, her curly hair gathered in a neat chignon, wispy strands skimming her cheeks, striking. 'Hello, Ben,' she said.

'There she is.' Andrea smiled, the pride in her eyes obvious. 'Right.' She turned back to Ben. 'Mattia and I are going out for lunch, so... we'll leave you two to it.'

Mattia, who had wandered in, offered Andrea his arm, then, smiling at Leora, gave Ben a curt nod before he and Andrea left the room.

'Not a man of many words, is he?' Ben said.

Leora threw her head back, laughed. 'To be fair, I don't hire him for his stimulating conversation.'

'Ah... I see.' Ben grinned. 'He's the silent but deadly type, is he?'

Leora, still smiling, looked thoughtful. 'Something like that, yes.'

She looked... amazing. Scarred, of course. But it was still her. Leora was still there. Still the girl he'd fallen in love with all those years ago. They stood for a moment, staring at one another, memories oozing, merging, unfolding across time.

'So,' he said, his heart racing, his breathing shallow, his hand covering his mouth, moving to his neck.

'So,' she repeated, eyebrows shooting up, her brown eyes meeting his.

He wanted to go to her, but his legs felt shaky, as if they might give way. He paused, his breath tight in his chest, willing them to move. Seconds later, he walked towards her. 'So,' he repeated, threading his fingers with hers, the scent of her making him dizzy. 'They told you, then, Eileen and Mark, about the photos?'

'They did.' The look on her face was pained, her eyes swelling with something he knew well, something that looked a lot like regret. 'The thing is,' she said, 'I knew.' She brought his hand to her chest and held it there. He could feel her heart beating; the skin beneath her dress, ridged and rippled, had a smoothness to it too, like a shell on the beach weathered by the tide. 'Right here, in my heart,' she continued. 'I knew you didn't cheat on me.'

He leant forwards then, squeezing her shoulder, kissing the top of her head, the air between them quivering with emotion. 'I love you, Leora,' he whispered. 'Always have and always will.'

She lifted her head and looked at him, and suddenly they were sixteen again, dancing to Yazoo's 'Only You' at the school Christmas disco, all the hurt, all the pain, all the lost time, melting away. 'I love you too, Ben,' she said. 'Always have and always will.'

Feeling the rise and fall of her breath, he lowered his mouth on hers and kissed her, his thoughts jumbled with longing and relief, his desire swift, as if lit by a fuse. Then, taking his hand in hers, she led him to the bedroom.

# CHAPTER 46

Startled, having drifted off on a sea of bliss, Leora opened her eyes, felt the warmth of Ben's breath on her neck, his head resting against the dip of her collarbone, his muscular body moulded to hers.

'You and me, were meant to be,' he whispered, bringing her hand to his mouth, kissing her wrist.

She smiled, felt his words travelling through her body, all the way to her heart. 'Do you have to go?' she asked.

Propping himself up on his elbow, Ben, who had his arm wrapped around her waist, pulled her round to face him, the light streaming through the window, soft, diffused. 'I'd rather not.' He kissed her forehead, the tip of her nose. 'But I must. I've got a flight booked to Afghanistan. It's something I do once a year.'

He explained to her then about the family that, all bar one, had been killed while helping to save his life many years ago during a covert mission that went wrong when he was in the SAS. 'Only the youngest son, Younus, survived. So, once a year, I fly out there to visit him, which I've been doing for the last seven years or so, helping him and the other villagers in whatever way I can. It's the least I can do.'

Leora nodded, felt her heart ache. Like her, Ben had had his struggles over the years. 'Yes, of course, *absolutely* you must go. Can I ask you something though… before you go?'

'Of course,' Ben replied, his blue eyes boring into hers; burrowing into her heart and reaching into her soul. 'Ask me anything you want.'

'Okay,' Leora said, taking a deep breath. 'Will you… marry me?'

Ben smiled and Leora held her breath.

'Yes,' he said without a second's hesitation, and in his eyes, she could see there was no doubt.

None whatsoever.

# EPILOGUE

CLIPPED FROM 'THE EVENING NEWS', 25
NOVEMBER 2017

*L*eora Jackson and Ben Thompson, after briefly dating over thirty years ago and reuniting last year, were married on 12th November 2017 – also the bride's birthday – at a small ceremony on a beach in Jamaica. In attendance were the couple's respective friends and family, including family members of the bride who reside in Jamaica.

The bride had two bridesmaids, her daughter Mia Hamilton, and best friend Eileen Dobson. The groom's best man was Mark Dobson. The bride was given away by her father Martin Jackson, and the song that played as he walked her down the aisle was 'I'll Be There' by the Jackson 5 in honour of the bride's deceased brother, Lonny Jackson.

A wedding breakfast of traditional Jamaican food, including rice and peas – a favourite of both the bride and groom, and based on the bride's late grandmother's recipe – followed.

Back in England, the happy couple threw an eighties-themed party to celebrate their nuptials with friends and family that couldn't attend the wedding in Jamaica, including the bride's 89-year-old grandmother and 94-year-old grandfather.

The bride and groom danced to Yazoo's 'Only You'.

Afterwards, the DJ was asked to play 'Come On Eileen' by Dexys Midnight Runners, and 'Fade to Grey' by Visage. A good time was had by all.

When asked how she overcame the horrific acid attack she suffered at the hands of her supposed best friend, Alison Evans, back in 2009, the bride quoted Martin Luther King: 'I have decided to stick with love. Hate is too great a burden to bear.'

## THE END

# ACKNOWLEDGEMENTS

If you've got this far, thank you. I hope you enjoyed reading Leora and Ben's love story as much as I enjoyed writing it. I started writing this story many years ago. But it's a story I struggled with, and often found myself abandoning and coming back to until, eventually, I was sure I'd got it right. Like my previous novels, *Only You* does not shy away from difficult subject matters. However, I always try and make it my goal to leave you, the reader, feeling uplifted and hopeful because, despite the hardships of life, we can never, in my humble opinion, have enough love or hope.

Leora's character was inspired by the very bold, the very brave, and the very beautiful Katie Piper, seen here in a photo with me, which Katie has kindly given me permission to use.

This shot was taken in 2017 when I had the privilege of meeting Katie who, warm and welcoming, proved to be every bit as lovely in person as she is on TV. Like Leora, and the proverbial phoenix rising from the ashes, Katie has, despite her terrible ordeal, completely turned her life around. If you'd like to know more about Katie Piper and her backstory, and the work her foundation does, please check out the following link: https://katiepiperfoundation.org.uk

As well as Katie's story, I have, over the years, also followed and been moved to tears by the contaminated blood scandal, which is part of Jules's story. If you'd like to know more about this, and The Infected Blood Inquiry, follow this link: https://haemophilia.org.uk/public-inquiry/the-infected-blood-inquiry/the-contaminated-blood-scandal/

Moving on, I'd like to thank everyone at Bloodhound, including Betsy, Fred, Abbie, Vicky, Katia, and Clare Law, my editor, who once again made my manuscript shine!

I'd also like to thank my family, including Steve, Jade, Callum, and my parents for their continued support, especially my mum who is always the first person to read my stories and never shies away from offering an honest opinion. Big thanks also to all my friends and writing buddies, whose support and guidance never ceases to amaze me.

Thank you too, to every single blogger, reviewer, reader or online book group member (several of whom I now call friends) who champion my books. Also, big thanks to the lovely Catherine Shields, who kindly lent me her name after winning a competition to have a character named after her.

Last, but not least, I would like to thank you – the fantastic reading public. Thank you so much for buying my novels, reading them, then taking the time to post such heart-warming reviews. Book reviews are extremely helpful to authors, and I appreciate every one of them, no matter how short.

I love to hear from readers, so if you'd like to get in touch, my website and social media details are as follows:

Website: EvaJordanWriter.com

Twitter: @evajordanwriter

Facebook: https://www.facebook.com/EvaJordanWriter/

Instagram: evajordanwriter

# ALSO BY EVA JORDAN

## THE TREE OF FAMILY LIFE TRILOGY

183 Times A Year

All The Colours In Between

Time Will Tell

❧

A Gift Called Hope

# A NOTE FROM THE PUBLISHER

**Thank you for reading this book.** If you enjoyed it please do consider leaving a review on Amazon to help others find it too.

**We hate typos.** All of our books have been rigorously edited and proofread, but sometimes mistakes do slip through. If you have spotted a typo, please do let us know and we can get it amended within hours.

**info@bloodhoundbooks.com**

Printed in Great Britain
by Amazon

39727839R00209